BETWEEN HOPE & THE HIGHWAY

CHARISSA STASTNY

Tangled Willow
Press

Cover Design: Christina K. Perry

Cover Photo: Tiffany Skelton Photography

ISBN: 978-1-948861-00-7

TITLES BY CHARISSA STASTNY

Ruled Out Romances

Game Changer

Package Deal

Collateral Hearts

Bending Willow Trilogy

Finding Light

Guarding Secrets

Embracing Mercy

Stand-Alone Novels

Between Hope & the Highway

A Wrinkle in Forever

Of Stone and Sky

For Christina,
my little cowgirl

Between
HOPE & the
HIGHWAY

SHATTERED HOPE

Happiness in the present is only shattered by comparison with the past.

~ Douglas Horton ~

1

LIZ

SOMETIMES LIFE GETS so messed up there's no other option but to grab your boots and get the heck out of Dodge. I'd reached that point. I slammed the picture of the smiling couple onto my desk. Faces down. I wouldn't think of him again.

I swiveled, knocking my white chair onto the hot-pink rug Mom adored. Grr. She'd designed my room to look like Cupid had barfed Pepto Bismol all over the floor, bed, and adjacent walls. I rubbed my knee and picked the chair up, scanning my room one last time to make sure I hadn't forgotten anything.

The velvet box on the nightstand made my eyes twitch.

Dang it. No tears.

"Liz, honey," Dad called from the hallway. "You need help?"

I leaped over my bed to hide the box behind my back. Dad would go all mushy on me if he saw it still out.

He peered around the edge of my door. "You finished packing, baby doll? I can take those down for you if you are."

"That'd be great." I slipped around the foot of the bed to unzip my pink luggage—another dreaded gift from Mom—and wedged the ring box inside.

"Honey, are you sure about this?" he asked, fiddling with the handle of my prissy pink abominations. "It's not too late to change your mind. Montana's so far away."

I pasted on a smile. "Nothing's far anymore, Daddy." I'm way too old to still call him that, but he considered *Dad* too stiff and formal for his baby girl to use. "I can call and talk to you every night. We can even FaceTime."

His brow furrowed. "You think they have reliable internet there? It sounded awfully remote from how you described it."

"So maybe we won't FaceTime." One could hope. Talking on the phone would be bad enough.

He trapped my face between his work-calloused hands. "Are you sure you're not running away, baby doll?"

I squirmed, wanting to be gone already. Without a doubt, I was running. Sprinting for my life, more like it. Memories could be weapons, and mine had become incoming missiles.

Where was Viktorya?

For the past five months, I'd gone through the motions of living. My heart pumped blood, my lungs brought in oxygen, my stomach digested food I forced down my throat. During the week, I answered phones at Ruthersford Construction for Dad. But my heart had shriveled up and died, and without a heart, I might as well be one of those gross zombies shuffling around in movies, with listless eyes and creepy outstretched arms, moaning for someone with a brain to put me out of my misery.

"Honey?"

I blinked. "I'm sure, Daddy."

The doorbell rang.

Hallelujah. I rubbed my hands together. "That's her."

Dad grabbed a suitcase in each hand. "If you want to come home, all you have to do is call. Even if you've only been there a day, I'll drive up and get you if you hate it."

"Thanks for the vote of confidence." Geesh.

"You're my baby girl. I can't help but worry about you."

"I'll be fine."

He carried my luggage out. I grabbed my leather satchel and followed.

Mom waited at the bottom of the stairs. She'd presented many arguments against my leaving. I wouldn't know anyone. School would be put on hold. Worst of all, I'd get older without any dating opportunities. She couldn't bear to think of me as an old maid, but since I approached the ancient age of twenty, she obsessed about my love life. Or lack of it.

"I can't believe you're going through with this ridiculous scheme. You don't love me at all." Her bright-pink lips quivered.

I crossed my arms beneath my smallish chest—a deficit she'd bemoaned for years and had hoped maturity would fix. It hadn't. "I love you, Mom." Those words were the path to least resistance.

"You're not acting like it, leaving me like this to hide away with a bunch of stinky animals in a place that doesn't even garner a blip on a map."

Ugh. Why couldn't she ever be happy for me?

"You're throwing your life away." She flicked one of my unruly curls. "You should've taken time to straighten your hair, Elizabeth."

Nails dug into my palms. Mom had always said my untamed curls resembled Merida's from Disney's *Brave*, though my hair was blond, not red. And I did take a pick to it at least once a day. But whatever. I kind of took pride in being compared to the girl who broke the Disney princess mold.

"And you're not wearing a speck of makeup. How many times have I stressed how important first impressions are? Why don't you ever listen to me?"

Dad cleared his throat. "Ilene, she looks fine."

Mom dabbed at her eyes. "She's behaving so irrationally."

She had never believed in my dreams, except with Justin. And he was gone. Moistness made me blink and swallow.

No tears. Not now. That'd just prove I was too emotional to leave. I needed to boot Justin out of my head. He was Stage IV cancer to my soul, embedding himself in my heart and popping out in the faces of strangers. His breathy chuckle taunted me in the rustling of olive branches, and his Nordstrom cologne mocked me during rare rainstorms. I needed geographic chemotherapy to keep memories of him from destroying me.

"Are you ready, Liz?" Viktorya's thick accent from the entry shattered the awkward stand-off between Mom and me.

"Yep. Let's hit the road." I couldn't get out of here fast enough.

I followed Dad out to Vikky's truck. The smell of hay and horses perked me up. As a child, Mom had pushed me onto the path of popularity by enrolling me in gymnastics and cheer camps. Dad, bless his heart, had sensed my misery and had let me hang out at his construction sites a couple afternoons a week, where he'd taught me how to wield a hammer, run a belt sander, and be confident with a power drill. We never told Mom. But she'd found out about my secret tomboy identity when Dad had taken a job building a fancy stable for Viktorya Lohman during my seventh-grade year. When Vikky had seen how the horses had taken to me, she'd offered to let me clean stables in exchange for riding lessons. Best deal ever.

Mom had freaked when I'd traded my pink tutus in for riding apparel. She'd thought I should be attending dances, not scraping manure off the bottom of my boots. Since that day I'd defied her, she'd nitpicked and had used my most hated word—TOO—excessively. I was too skinny, my chin too pointy, my forehead too wide, my laughter too obnoxious, my hands too calloused, my expression too stern, my complexion too freckly, my hair too curly. She'd mastered in Lizzieology, the science of picking me apart.

Dad threw my luggage into the bed of the truck while I hugged Mom.

Deep down, I believed she loved me. I also knew we could stand some distance between us. A lot of it.

"I wish you wouldn't go. That Robinson boy watched you quite intently at church last week. I bet he'd ask you out this Sunday if you were here."

No doubt. Mom would likely corner him after the sermon and throw me on the poor, unsuspecting man. She'd done it before in her quest to see me married.

Dad swept me into his arms. "I'm going to miss you, baby doll."

"I'll miss you, too, Daddy." I blinked back tears. "Be excited for me."

"I'm trying."

I climbed into the passenger seat and mouthed *Go* to Viktorya.

She didn't need to be told twice. We pulled away from the curb, and I blew kisses out the window. When we turned the corner and my parents disappeared, I relaxed into the vinyl seat.

When I'd first approached Dad about working in Montana, he'd frowned and asked if I'd prayed about my decision. Grr. Of course, I had. So what if I hadn't received a heavenly sign letting me know it was the right thing to do. I wanted out of Vegas anyway.

Mom had immediately campaigned to stop me. She'd claimed I wouldn't have any friends in Montana, but I didn't have any here. Not really. I'd never been able to stomach the mindless chatter of girls my age, and guys just irritated me.

Until Justin.

I don't know what it was about that man, but he'd pushed horses from my mind when we'd met in the library elevator my second week of college. I'd been caught hook, line, and sinker. Love at first sight, and all those types of stupid clichés.

But I no longer believed in happily-ever-afters.

Viktorya reached over to squeeze my hand. "You're excited, no?" My expat-Russian friend said her sentences backward.

"Yeah. I can't wait to see the place in person. The pictures on their website looked amazing."

"The Bar-M-Law Ranch is more than amazing. It's spectacular."

I dug into my satchel for my employment contract. The packet of papers had resurrected hope after I'd skimmed the stipulations sent by the ranch owner, Mr. Law.

"Are you worried about the workload?" Vikky asked.

"Not really." Thanks to her and Dad, I knew how to get my hands dirty.

"Don't worry," she chewed the words in her thick accent. "The work may be grueling at first, but once Bart sees you in action, he'll give you a raise and a promotion, I'm thinking. Life will get easier, no?"

I hoped not. The blunt paragraph specifying the required twelve- to sixteen-hour workdays and stating that I'd receive no special privileges due to my gender actually had lured me into accepting the offer. That chauvinistic, no molly-coddling attitude had sounded like the ideal medicine for my broken heart. If I was beat-up and exhausted each day, I wouldn't have time to think about my pain. I'd forget my loss. Forget him.

BENTLEY

*T*HE LATE-SPRING sun warmed me as I hobbled to the aspen grove. Right step. Left leg-lift, swing-out, step-down. Right step. Left leg-lift, swing-out, step-down and wince. I focused on moving my left leg smoothly, but my boot hit the ground with an awkward thud and pain shot up my hip. I grimaced but kept moving. *No pain, no gain.* That was Dr. Bowler's motto.

At my sanctuary of sand and water, I nestled between the white-barked trees behind Dad's office. The white building with green metal roof matched the nearby stable and indoor arena. Dad's office, as well as those of the foreman and trainers, took up the upper story, where five dormer windows looked out onto fenced pasture. The lower level stabled our champion breeding stallions.

As a kid, Dad's office and stables had seemed like a castle. The cupola had served as the ramparts. I'd climbed, jumped, and ran as well as any other kid back then as I'd pretended to fight dragons. Now, five years later, at the ripe old age of thirteen, I had to content myself with forming castles out of mud. No exploring the kingdom for me. One had to be able to get up and down from his horse to do that, and unfortunately, that simple feat was beyond me.

I grabbed a stick to mix the goop inside my bucket. Dad and Mom had flown out to attend my older brother's graduation from Stanford, but Rawson wouldn't return with them. I glared at the gray-tinged clouds, still angry that he'd taken a dumb modeling job in Europe instead of coming home to see me. My brother wasn't a girly man. He was a cowboy, like me.

I added handfuls of dirt to thicken my slop. Rawson had ruined my whole summer. Instead of feeling whole, I now felt holed in at home with my little sister. My only escape was hiding in these trees and fretting over the correct amount of dirt and water to make concrete blocks for an imaginary kingdom.

"Addie! Where are you? Adeline Francesca Law! Get back to the house this instant!"

Susa's hollering interrupted my pity party. I sympathized with our poor housekeeper who had to tend my hellion sister in my parents' absence. I raised my stiff neck and hobbled out of the trees just as someone wearing a red jacket disappeared inside the stable. I stopped to text Susa.

:She's under Dad's office.

Susa: Keep her there for me.

Yeah, right. I should've been able to accomplish such a simple task. I was twelve years old, for crud's sake; my sister only ten…and she had Down syndrome. But Susa might as well have asked me to climb Mount Everest in my half-crippled state.

Right step. Left leg-lift, swing-out, step-down. Right step. Left leg-lift, swing-out, step-down. I didn't try to keep my torso straight or my movements fluid as I shuffled into the stable.

Addie was reaching through a stall to pet Restless Shadow. The steel-gray stallion nickered and pawed sawdust.

"Hey, sis." I came at her nice-like, so as not to spook her. Horses and sisters were similar.

"Horsie!" Her deep booming voice made Shadow rear back and neigh. Addie's thick tongue slipped out as she smiled.

Mom had worked with her as a baby to keep her tongue in her mouth. She hadn't wanted Addie to be treated different than other kids. Lots of my friends back then hadn't know anything was wrong with my sister as she'd followed us around, playing games of the kingdom. She'd parroted what they said and had grunted a lot, but what five-year-old didn't? Occasionally, her tongue had trailed out, but I'd flick it and she'd pull it right back in her mouth. Amazing the difference that'd made in her appearance.

But the accident ruined everything.

After we'd buried my brother, Mom had spent her days driving me to and from town for physical therapy. Addie had been shoved to the back burner. None of us had had time to watch her tongue or insist she behave as we'd struggled to survive. That's how she'd transformed into a holy terror and now looked like all other Down's kids. If Mom hadn't been worn out caring for me, she would've had time to raise my sister right.

Addie gave me an open-mouthed smile. "Horsie!"

"Keep that thing in your mouth." I flicked her lazy tongue.

She wailed, as if I'd hit her with a two-by-four. "Benny mean!"

"Hush." I didn't want Susa to hear.

"Benny mean!" she screamed.

"Bentley Howard Law," Susa said as she entered the stable. "Stop torturing your sister."

Addie ran to our housekeeper and tapped her tongue. "Benny mean!"

I snarled and made a fist. I'd show her mean.

"Young man, apologize to your sister." She pronounced it *seester*.

"I was just trying to keep her here for you." She should be grateful.

"Benny mean," Addie said again.

"All I did was tap her tongue."

Susa raised dark brows. She was old enough to be my grandma, and I had her by a foot, but her stern expression cowed me.

"Fine." I kicked at the sawdust. "I'm sorry, okay?" I might as well have said "You suck," but my words appeased our housekeeper.

She tousled my hair and gave me a wrinkly smile, before gripping Addie's hand and heading back to the house.

I hit the weathered wood. Everyone let Addie get away with murder. Being handicapped myself, I realized how important it was that my sister look normal so she wouldn't get singled out by bullies. Just last week, that idiot Rich Sweeney had pointed at Addie on the bus and had called her a retard when she'd let her tongue hang out and had signed EAT to me. I'd wanted to punch his ugly face, but all I could do was change places so Addie would be by the window and I could take the brunt of his bullying.

Before the accident, I'd been the cool kid at school…at least as cool as you can be in second grade. I'd had friends and had received invites to birthday parties. Girls had written me love letters and chased me during recess. But after being held back a year for surgeries and intense physical therapy, my friends were a grade older when I'd returned. My new classmates had found me odd with the way my neck didn't stand up straight and how my left leg jerked out with each step. I'd started hearing whispered taunts in line: "Bentley's bent." *Bent-head* became my new nickname when the teacher turned her back, that and *Spaz-Legs* or *Pretzel Boy*.

The accident had taught me that people do judge you by your appearance. That's why I wanted Addie to look normal.

I returned to the house and wrangled my way upstairs to change for supper. Mom hadn't been too keen on me moving to the upper bedroom, but I'd begged her to allow me the challenge. Even Dr. Bowler had felt it'd be good for me. My leg muscles hurt like the dickens going up and down the steps, but pain was my friend when it came to healing. Or so he said.

I changed out of muddy clothes and hobbled to the window to watch the sunset. With Rawson not coming home, I couldn't help think about all

I'd miss out on this summer. No horse rides. No skinny dipping in the water hole. Nobody to watch *Star Wars* with at night. I kicked the wall. What was my brother's problem? I mean, he hadn't come home for Christmas because he'd taken some chick to Maui. And now he wanted to tour Europe?

A shadow outside snagged my attention. My jaw dropped when I spotted a girl crossing the circular driveway to the garage.

"Hubba bubba." She must be the new hand Dad had told the foreman to watch for this week. I'd overheard him tell Abe to put her in the room above the detached garage, but to have her take meals in the bunkhouse with the other hands. Made me wish I was a hired hand so I could eat with her. Milt could serve me his slop, and I'd even like it, if I could stare at her across the table.

Susa's scratchy voice belted through the intercom. "Dinner's in five minutes." She pronounced it *deener*, like wiener.

I buckled my belt and stared at the mirror. *Normal, normal, normal.* I channeled positive thoughts as I straightened my neck and counted. Picturing the new girl motivated me to endure the pain. If I ever ran into her, I wanted to appear normal. I wagged my eyebrows, like Rawson. Girls went crazy for my older brother. I had darker hair and plain-blue eyes rather than his greenish-blue ones, but some people said we looked alike. Maybe they were just being nice.

My face turned red when I reached sixty-seven. Damn. Neck muscles burned. I ceased making sexy faces and concentrated on holding my neck steady. *Normal, normal.*

At eighty, I shook and counted faster. When I said one hundred, I let my neck droop onto my shoulder. Ten seconds longer than yesterday. If I ever met that long-legged beauty, I'd make sure to talk less than a minute, standing still, so she wouldn't notice my crooked neck.

"Benny," Susa asked through the intercom, "are you coming?"

"Be down in a minute." I pronounced it *meen-it* to tease her.

I headed downstairs, picturing the new girl smiling at me, the same way girls always smiled at my brother.

Imagination was so much cooler than reality.

3

RAWSON

*C*LINKING ICE AND scraping metal wheels against the airplane aisle grated against my nerves. What kind of cheap modeling company had I contracted with that couldn't even fly me first class to Paris? I'd definitely be having words with someone when I reached my destination.

I threw my head back and stared at the ceiling knobs. Though I'd just graduated from Stanford with honors and was heading to Europe, I had zero enthusiasm. Honestly, I'd jumped on this modeling gig to avoid going home. But sitting in coach—middle seat no less—had me regretting my rash decision. I missed the quiet nights on the ranch, where millions of stars lit up the sky and where the chirping of crickets and the occasional bellow of cows put one to sleep. I longed to gallop over the hills on my faithful stallion. I even missed the intense physical labor that'd made me feel like a man.

I didn't miss Dad.

Why had he even bothered to attend my commencement exercises?

I pulled an airline blanket up to my shoulders and stewed over our last exchange outside my apartment this morning. Guilt stung me as I recalled Mom's pained expression while she'd stood by the rental car, listening to us shout at each other. But no way would I let Dad run my life. I wasn't one of his cows he could yank around by a rope.

The blanket's scratchy texture made my skin crawl. I shoved the material off and adjusted the knob above me.

An airline attendant stepped up to my row. "What can I get for you, sir?"

I craned my neck to read her name tag. "I'd love a seat in first class,

Alexa. You could even join me." I winked, though I doubted she could help. But over the years I'd learned that flirting harvested surprising rewards.

"Tempting." She giggled.

"I'd even settle for an aisle seat."

"I wish I could switch you but we have a full flight." She blushed. "What beverage would you like?"

"A Coke." I knew they didn't have Pepsi.

She poured soda into a plastic cup, and once more, I berated myself for not checking my ticket. If I sat beyond the almighty curtain a few rows ahead, I'd be drinking from a glass.

Alexa handed me my beverage and our fingers touched.

"Thanks, darling. You think you could round me up some headphones?"

"Of course." Her cheeks turned brighter. "I'll be back after I finish my rounds."

I smirked as she moved on up the aisle. Women were so easy.

Coach seats hadn't been formed with my 6'3" frame in mind. My legs ached. My arms itched from the blanket. I needed a shower and a change of clothes, but the plane was somewhere over the Atlantic, with hours between me and my destination.

My attendant returned when she finished watering us circus elephants in coach. "Here are the headphones you asked for, Mr...?"

"Call me Rawson."

Alexa acted as though I'd gifted her with a diamond ring. Fake eyelashes fluttered and her voice turned breathy. "Okay, Rawson." She licked her lips. "Since I can't switch you to first class, consider these a gift."

I hadn't expected to pay. Women always gave me what I wanted if I showed them a little attention. "Thanks, sweetheart."

Her hazel eyes told me she wanted more—maybe an invitation to meet after our flight or my number, at least—but that wasn't in the cards. I still nursed a broken heart. She'd have to be a whole lot hotter to get me to jump into the game again.

"Let me know if you need anything else, Rawson." Hope laced her words. Hope that'd come crashing down when I walked off the plane and out of her life forever.

I plugged her gift into my iPhone, adjusted the headphones, and leaned back to zone out. But Randy Travis's *Storms of Life* started playing. I grimaced. It'd been months since I'd thought of Damon Hollis, and now, because of a stupid song we'd probably played pool to in a bar ages ago, he took center stage in my mind and refused to leave.

Damon and I had been best buds since junior high. He'd been cool and had been scared of nothing except his alcoholic old man. The accident had added insult to injury. When I'd awakened in the hospital to my parents crying over me, I'd learned that Detrick, my twelve-year-old brother, had been thrown from the Explorer and killed instantly; Benny, my baby brother, was struggling for his life in intensive care; and Damon, my right hand man, had been carted off to the juvenile detention center in Billings for negligent homicide.

The itching sensation in my chest and around my collar made me want to scrape off my skin. Stupid OCD. I yanked off my headphones and snatched my backpack from under the seat. I bumped knees and woke my seatmate getting out of my row. I headed down the aisle to stand behind a woman to wait for a chance to use the casket in the sky.

When she exited, I crammed my body into the restroom and dug inside my pack for a new shirt. My fingers shook as I ripped off my offending garment and stuffed it into another pocket. I patted my chest, arms, and neck with water to relieve the compulsion to peel off my dermal layer. Avoiding the sandpaper towels on the wall, I hand-fanned my body dry before donning a white, silky shirt. *Please, don't itch.* I only had one more wardrobe change with me and planned to use that when I exited the plane.

I stepped out of the restroom, catching several dirty looks from people in a much longer line. Someone muttered a *pretty boy* comment that made my blood boil. But fighting on a plane was tantamount to messing with a bull when one of his cows was in heat. More trouble than it was worth.

The elderly lady by the window snored. I wedged into my seat beside her, experiencing serious envy. I'd pay good money to copy her. Instead, I fidgeted and occasionally winced as the overweight man across the aisle kept coughing. That's all I needed was to catch an airborne virus on this flight.

I returned the headphones to my ears, knowing memories would return with the music, but at least I wouldn't hear Mr. Infectious Disease hacking up a lung.

Damon's life had spiraled out of control after the accident. I'd wanted to help him, but with my inheritance off-limits until I proved myself, my hands had been tied by Dad.

A hand on my shoulder snapped me from my reverie. I looked up into the hazel eyes of the desperate attendant.

"You need to fasten your seatbelt, Rawson. We'll be landing soon." She squeezed my shoulder and dropped a business card onto my lap.

I tugged at my collar. She'd probably be a lot of fun tonight, but I slipped her number into my pocket. I wouldn't be calling her. I wouldn't be calling anyone. All I wanted was to strip off my clothes and take a long, hot shower to cleanse me of the itching sensation and germs I'd picked up on this torturous journey. After having my soul sapped dry by my blood-sucking ex, I didn't have energy to entertain a giggly stranger.

4

LIZ

THE TIDY BUILDINGS of the Bar-M-Law Ranch appeared over the rise. I slowed my mare and inhaled the fragrant spring air. If any place could be heaven on earth, this was it. The smell of barn and beast laced the breeze. Lush foothills climbed up to rugged, snow-capped peaks. The buildings' white siding and green metal roofs gave everything a clean, orderly appearance, while cupolas, pillars, arches, and Dutch doors added stylish elegance.

I guided Friday Night Gin past the arena, pulling the black mare's head up when she tried to stop to eat the long grass. "No, girl. I'll feed you after we cool you down."

She neighed her displeasure. I patted her neck, knowing I'd be moody too, if my name reeked of alcohol. Easing back on the reins, I led her to the washing bay.

I ran the hose over Ginny's sleek coat as she nuzzled me. "And Mom said I wouldn't have any friends up here. Guess we proved her wrong." I patted her flank and moved the stream of water over her hindquarters.

I dried her off and led Ginny to a stall off the arena. My domain.

Mr. Law had partnered me with an older fellow named Larry Andersen to work with the yearlings that needed ground and saddle training. He'd also placed me in charge of mucking stalls in the indoor arena and main stable. My days started before dawn and ended long after supper, but I loved every minute with my equine friends.

I closed the tack room door and headed to the bunkhouse, my stomach growling as I wondered what Milt, the cowboy version of Betty Crocker, had whipped up for supper. Before I entered, I threw back my shoulders and put on my poker face. Though the other hands were nice, I had to prove myself, since I was not only new, but female as well. That seemed to be a sin to some around here.

Rusty and Mike played war games on the X-box. "Hey, Liz," Mike said.

"Hey." I nodded to the lanky teenager as I crossed the room to wash up. The aroma of beef made my salivary glands squeal.

"Howdy, Liz," the trainer said from the doorway.

"Hey, Seth." He'd helped me learn the ins and outs this week, and I didn't get the impression he found my gender sinful.

"I saw you out on Friday Night Gin. Did she give you any trouble?"

I shrugged. "She balked a few times, but mostly followed my lead."

He smiled. "You have a gift with horses."

I shook my head.

"I'm dead serious. You might be better than Rawson Law, and that's saying something, yes, it is."

I tucked that detail away. Since arriving, I'd discovered that my boss had two sons. One in his early teens and an older one in college. Rawson. I remembered his unique name because it kept surfacing like an apple in a bobbing contest. Each time he'd been mentioned, his name had evoked different emotions from the speaker. Mr. Law had railed about his irresponsible nature to the foreman one day. Larry, on the other hand, had bragged like a grandparent when he'd told me about him as we'd worked. According to him, Rawson had graduated *magna cum laude* from Stanford and had been vice-president of his fraternity. He was a real go-getter. Tony, one of the cow hands, had made a snide remark about Rawson's masculinity, saying Rawson was in Europe, modeling for some trendy magazine. Of course, since Tony also wolf-whistled and held my gender against me, I hadn't given much credence to his words. Though if Rawson liked guys, I wouldn't hold that against him.

"I miss that son of a—"

"Watch your mouth, Baker," Bill barked. "There's a lady present."

I smiled at the ranch veterinarian.

Chance, a hand about my age, blushed. "Sorry, Liz."

"You were just saying you missed that son of a biscuit, right?"

The others snickered as Chance gave me a toothy grin. "That's right. I wasn't gonna swear."

Bill scoffed.

I ladled out stew. "So why do you miss Rawson Law?" My curiosity was piqued. The information I'd gleaned hadn't painted a picture of a man who'd be missed by these rugged cowboys.

Chance gulped down a spoonful of stew. "He livened things up."

The table erupted in guffaws, making me feel as if I was missing out on something.

14

"Remember the time he rewired Abe's truck so the brake lights activated the horn?" Mike said.

Rusty hit his leg. "Abe was madder than a wolverine. Couldn't figure out what was wrong for half a day."

Chance snickered. "Abe knew Roz did it but couldn't prove nothing."

"He never could pin anything on that kid," Seth said. "Remember when Bart found a load of manure blocking his truck?"

Mike snorted. "Mr. Law almost lost a lung telling Rawson to get out there and clean up his sh—" He yelped as Bill whacked him. "I mean *mess*. But Rawson had an alibi. He'd been grounded for hanging out with Damon. Still, everyone knew he did it."

Milt took a break from the cooking to join us. "That whippersnapper's too smart for his britches."

"I'd wager he's smarter than his old man," Chance said.

Milt huffed. "No shame in that. Bart would be the first to admit it. But smarts and wisdom ain't the same, and wise is something Rawson's not. That boy's reckless as the day is long. Never gave jack sh—" He winced when Bill elbowed him. The older gentleman was fast becoming my hero for how he reined in the language for me. Milt gave me a sheepish grin. "What I mean is, Rawson ain't never cared much about the future. He only lives for the moment, drinking and carrying on with that worthless SOB friend of his."

When Bill glared, I laughed. "I can handle acronyms."

Milt headed back to the kitchen. "That's the nicest thing I can think to call the loser."

The others agreed with his assessment of the friend, but by how the younger hands kept discussing other pranks Rawson had pulled, I sensed something akin to hero-worship from them.

I'd never understand guys.

After supper, I worked the new gelding in the round pen until well after dark, before calling it a night and heading to my cramped room above the garage. I twirled as I crossed the pasture, feeling free and happy. The enigmatic Rawson Law was plain loco for leaving this place. But I wouldn't hold that against him. If he'd returned, I wouldn't have been hired. And that would've been tragic, because after playing the part of a zombie for the last six months, I felt alive again, like those green hills Julie Andrews had sung about in *The Sound of Music*.

The work exhausted me, but the hours spent with high-pedigreed horses were a dream come true. As soon as I hit my pillow each night, I zonked before I had a chance to recall the nightmare that'd altered my life.

I considered that success.

5

BENTLEY

ODAY I GOT caught, but getting busted never felt so good. I'd been spying on the new girl, sketching in my notebook and trying to capture her fluid beauty on vellum. I'd overheard Seth call her Liz, and thought that name was prettier than a Montana sunset. Liz had performed miracles with the horses that'd given Larry grief for months, especially Kodiak Kisses.

When I'd discovered Liz working that devil horse in the arena, I'd hidden under the bleachers to watch through the slats. Every evening, she'd brought him out and talked quietly as she led him around on a long rope. He snorted and pawed the ground, but her sweet voice kept him from bolting. By the end of the week, he even ate from her hand.

Earlier, she'd let the wild cuss loose. I'd worried she'd never catch him again as the stud had galloped around the arena, bucking like a Tasmanian devil on Red Bull. Yet, when she'd whistled, he'd trotted over calm as can be to eat from her hand. I'd almost hit my head on the metal bleacher, that's how surprised I'd been. And relieved.

But Liz was either nuts or full-blown Horse Whisperer because she'd grabbed his mane and had mounted the psycho horse bareback. I'd been sure I would witness her grisly death. We'd nicknamed the feisty three-year-old chestnut Kisser because everyone who'd tried to mount him had ended up on theirs.

But strangest thing, he only nickered and pawed the ground.

That's when Liz had met my gaze and grinned.

In my fear that I'd see her thrown, I'd crawled out from my hiding spot into plain view. Thankfully, she hadn't stared, but had rested her head on

Kisser's neck and urged him around the arena. When she'd returned, she'd slid off his back and had given him a sugar cube.

"What's your name, squirt?"

I'd kneaded my neck, feeling hotter than an ant under a magnifying glass in the summer. She'd been even prettier up close. Her curly blond hair had been pulled back in a poofy ponytail that'd framed her angelic face.

"Ben...Bentley." I'd held my neck as straight as possible, wanting to look normal.

"Ben Bentley. Hmm? I thought you might be a Law boy. My mistake."

"I-I-I am a Law boy. Bentley Law."

Her chocolate eyes had crinkled at the corners. So pretty. "Glad to meet you, Bentley." She'd held out a hand. "I'm Lizzie."

When I'd clasped her fingers, my body had gotten all weird and tingly. Never had I held a girl's hand before, but I'd liked it. A lot.

"I've watched you with Kisser. You're amazing," I said.

"Kisser was a challenge. I still wonder if he might throw me. He's not broken yet." She patted his flank, making me wonder if she admired the mean stallion.

I hobbled a few steps over to the horse. "You're the first to sit him without being thrown." Realizing I'd displayed my handicap, I sank onto the nearest bleacher.

"Can you ride?" she asked.

I nodded. "Han's mine. The palomino in the main stable. My brother trained him to be calm for me. I just can't mount and dismount on my own."

I'd worried she might dish out pity, but she just kept talking like nothing was wrong. "Han? I thought his name was Goldie."

"Goldie Han Solo."

She laughed, and I savored that sound. There'd been a famine of joyful emotions in my family since the accident.

"Do you want to ride with me sometime? I'd love the company, since I don't know the area yet."

"Sure. I know this country better than the warts on my foot."

She let out a barking laugh, and I wanted to kick myself for talking about warts. Girls probably didn't like that subject. "Then you're exactly the wart-finding partner I need."

I blushed clear down to my boots, but felt slightly better.

"How old are you, Bentley?"

"Thirteen."

"So you're in seventh grade?"

"Sixth."

"Is that in junior high here?"

17

I dug my boot into the dirt, wishing I hadn't been held back a year. "Elementary school."

"Ask your dad if it's okay if you ride with me. If so, we'll head out after supper."

Her words had made me bristle. My parents had never worried about Rawson when he'd been my age. He'd explored the hills and gullies alone at only eight. He could shoot then, too. But here I was, practically a man, and couldn't do a dang-blasted thing on my own.

I dropped an F-bomb and kicked at the dirt. "I ain't need no damn permission." I wanted to sound grown up, but my words backfired.

"Whether you do or not, I'm telling him. I don't need trouble with my boss the first month on the job. And if you talk like a crude cowboy around me again, you won't be welcome."

Her chastisement stung, though she smiled.

"I need a break from vulgar cowboys like Tony. I thought you looked more refined than him. I admired that about you."

I straightened my neck. "Sorry, ma'am." I should've known better. Mom wouldn't put up with my bad language either.

"Apology accepted. Now go."

Dad had loved the idea, so Lizzie and I had gone riding after supper. Though she was a willowy gal, Liz hadn't had any problem lifting me up and down from my horse. She'd smelled like a field of flowers, and her hands, though calloused, had felt soft against mine.

She'd let me lead, and I'd taken her to my favorite spot on the ridge, overlooking the river. She'd been super easy to talk to. I told her about the accident and how I despised people's pity. Only my legs and spine had been damaged, not my brain. Yet kids at school ignored me or acted as if I was hurt in my head. One girl, Regan, never looked me in the eye when I tried to talk to her. She searched for a friend and ditched me.

"I doubt any girl will ever be attracted to a freak show like me," I said.

"Shut your mouth. You're not a freak show. In fact, you'll be a lady killer with your dark hair and blue eyes. Those are a rare combination."

I don't know whether her sweet words or the awesome sunset had made my body tingle. For five years, my deformities had bound me, but out there on the ridge, I hadn't felt defined by my disabilities.

We returned and brushed down our horses, before saying goodnight to each other.

I headed to Dad's office. Since Liz had helped me, I wanted to return the favor.

"Yes?" Dad called when I knocked.

I cracked the door. "Can I talk to you for a minute?"

"Sure, son. What's on your mind?"

I hobbled over to a leather chair across from his desk. "It's about Liz."

18

He stretched his arms above his head. "What about her?"

"I think she should eat with us, not out with the cowboys."

"Why's that?"

"Because she's got to hate being the only girl eating in a bunkhouse full of crude guys."

Dad scowled. "Has she said they're crude?" He pounded his desk. "I told Abe to warn the boys to be on their best behavior. The last thing I need is a sexual harassment suit."

"No." Crap! Dad always jumped to conclusions. "Liz only says good things about the guys." Except for Tony. But nobody liked him.

"Then why are you here?"

Leave it to Dad to get to the point. No "How was your day, son?" or "What have you painted lately?" Just a curt "Why are you here?" Sometimes I wondered if my handicap made him uncomfortable. Before the accident, I used to shadow him everywhere. Now, he seemed in a hurry to get rid of me.

"Uh, I just thought since she's the only girl, you could let her eat with us so she'd have Mom and Addie for company. I mean, it'd be awkward for her to eat in the bunkhouse since all the guys live and sleep there. How would you like to eat in a house full of strange women and see tampons everywhere? It'd give me indigestion. Liz surely has to hate eating close to where the guys pee."

Dad chuckled and shook his head. "Good point, son. Let me sleep on it."

"Thanks." I knew better than to bug him anymore.

I hobbled to the house, concentrating on moving my left leg smoothly. Helping others felt good, and I hadn't felt good in forever because I'd been so absorbed in me.

6

RAWSON

$\mathcal{T}$HE KING-SIZED bed called to me. I dragged myself into my hotel room and stripped off my clothes. I had two days before we'd head to Florence for the next shoot but I doubted I'd get out of bed. This trip should've restarted my heart after flat-lining in California, but the last two weeks had only deepened my despair. I knew it was my own fault I explored the continent by my lonesome. The women I'd met and worked with were beautiful and uninhibited. It wouldn't take much effort or euros to claim one to walk by my side during the day and play under the sheets at night. But I'd lost my appetite for easy women.

I grabbed the remote, knowing I'd sunk to a new low. Since I was fifteen years old and Taylor Ann had pulled me into the girl's restroom at school to teach me how to French kiss, I'd been gaga over females and had determined to have fun with as many of them as I could before I died.

That'd changed six months ago.

For over three years, I'd participated in my school fraternity and earned not only the title of designated driver, but also the guy who'd never fall in love. In late November, we invited a sorority over for a party and I met Vanessa. We connected like peanut butter and chocolate. She'd been a first-year law student who'd made me march beside her in a LGBTQ parade in downtown San Francisco and attend a global warming conference another weekend. Though I thought her causes silly, I'd followed her around like a puppy, not caring if I believed in the issue or not.

I'd believed in Vanessa. That had been enough.

Me, the guy who wouldn't even pay a girl a compliment, had suddenly paid out the nose to take that goddess to fancy restaurants and sold-out concerts with backstage passes. To keep her smiling, I'd bought roses, diamond bracelets, and tickets to Maui for Christmas. I'd even let her talk me into modeling with her on the side. I'd paid my dues to the altar of love in order to win her heart.

That's why she'd grown bored.

It was so clear in hindsight. The excitement had been in the conquest. I'd known that from my own experience. Once conquered, the defeated heart held no intrigue. I'd played the vanquished to Vanessa's unholy conqueror.

I flipped through the channels twice and pulled a pillow over my head, yearning for a beer. A case would be better.

But no. I wouldn't do that again.

I must've passed out. *The Imperial March* playing on my phone woke me up a few hours later. I groaned and fumbled to find my phone in the dark.

"What the hell, Benny," I said, as the music drummed on until my groping hands found and answered it.

"Hey, Big Ben." I sounded like a frog gargling rocks. "Wuz up?"

My kid brother started singing *Happy Birthday* off key, making me wince. You know life sucks when you don't even remember your own birthday.

He finished, and I snorted. "That was truly awful, bro."

"What you gonna do to celebrate being twenty-three?" He sounded way too chipper for this early in the morning.

"I'd like to sleep for five more hours."

"Be glad I didn't call four hours ago."

I still couldn't open my eyes. "I might've thrown my phone across the room."

"Aren't you glad your favorite brother started your birthday off right by serenading you?"

I laughed, then paused. How long had it been since I'd found anything funny? Not since meeting Vanessa. She'd excelled at inciting panting, groveling, and drooling, but she'd never made me laugh. It felt cleansing to do so.

"I'll take the fifth."

Benny snort-laughed. "You'll never guess what I saw yesterday on my ride." His exuberance bubbled out of my iPhone.

"What?"

"A bull moose grazing in the shallows of the creek down Madre's Gulch."

"Did you snap a picture?"

"Sure did. Want me to send it to you?"

"Of course, bro. You should've sent it right away. It's not every day I see a moose in France."

"Not unless it's a chocolate mousse."

I laughed again. Benny's call was timely. I'd been spiraling into darkness, but hearing my brother's voice buoyed me up again.

Benny painted more pictures of his exploits, and I ached to breathe fresh air straight from heaven and ride across grass-covered hills with him. I was sick of buildings, crowds, museums, and pushy broads. I'd tired of wearing Italian loafers and French clothes that itched so bad I wanted to crawl out of my skin. I longed to be a real man, on my horse with my hat on my head, roaming the ranch with my brother.

Maybe I'd talk to my agent about getting out of my contract early. Time to stop running and face life again. Emotions had made me irrational after Vanessa's betrayal. The blow-up with Dad after graduation hadn't helped.

"Do you have to model today?" Benny asked.

"No. I have the next two days off."

"To party?"

"Party with my bed and the TV, maybe."

"You sound down."

I sighed. "Don't worry about me, kid."

"I always worry about you, homey. What's wrong?"

"Yo dawg, why you got to be all up in my grill so early?" I didn't want to talk about my problems.

Benny chuckled at my gangster lingo. "Cuz you my bro, man. Now what's eating at you, dawg? You having girl problems?"

I let loose an arsenal of swear words. Just thinking about Vanessa fired me up.

"Sorry," Benny said. "It's none of my business."

"Nah, kid. It's not that. You're the best bro-ster ever." He was just so damn perceptive it was scary. "I guess in a way, I'm having girl problems. I came here to get away from…." I bit my tongue to keep from ranting again. "A girl. But I'm over her and want to come home."

"Great. When's your flight?"

"Hold your horses, kid. I still have six weeks left on my contract."

"Oh." He sounded disappointed.

"Do me a favor though. Tell old Larry to get my horse in shape. I want to burn through those hills when I return. I don't need no fat, lazy—"

"Don't stress about Darth Bayder," Benny said. "Lizzie's taking good care of him. She rides him—"

"What!" I yelled. My eyes were wide open now. "That girl is riding my horse?"

"Well, yeah."

My fists clenched. "No one except Larry or Dad can touch Bayder. He's incredibly valuable. Why is that girl," I spat, "anywhere near him?"

"Lizzie's better than Larry with the horses. Shoot, she's better than about anyone."

My nostrils flared. "Let me talk to Dad." This had to be fixed. ASAP.

When Dad's deep voice came on the line, I ground my teeth. "Why in the hell is that new girl riding Bayder? Larry's the only one who can touch my horse."

"Not that I have to answer to you," Dad said, "but Liz is better than Larry was, even in his prime."

"You've gone soft in your old age, hiring a woman for man's work." I still couldn't believe he'd done such an asinine thing.

Dad growled. "I haven't gone soft, except where Larry's concerned. He's worked for me for over thirty years, and his heart's bad. I brought Liz in to help him since you're too caught up in seeing the world to fulfill your responsibilities."

Dad must've passed the phone back to Benny, because my brother spoke. "You there?"

"Yeah. Sorry about that." It wasn't his fault Dad had lost his marbles.

"It's all right. I can see why you'd worry about Bayder. You haven't met Liz, but trust me, she's amazing. Even Dad thinks so, and you know how difficult he is to please."

I grunted. "The amazing horse whisperer."

Benny didn't pick up on my sarcasm. "Exactly. You'll love her. She's even a *Star Wars* fanatic like you."

I rolled my eyes. "I gotta go, homeboy." No way would I listen to my kid brother praise the new hand. He loved everybody. "Thanks for starting my birthday off right with your screeching."

"Go back to sleep and dream of Mom's German chocolate cake."

"Oh, that was low, bro."

We hung up, and I closed my eyes. No way could I last six more weeks. Chatting with my kid brother made me admit what I really wanted.

For the first time in over four years, I yearned to be home.

7

LIZ

*T*HE TINKLING OF silverware contacting china sounded in the country-red dining room as I stabbed a bite of medium-rare steak.

"Can you pass the rolls, please?" Benny asked.

I set the serving basket next to him, making the adorable kid grin.

"Thank you."

"You're welcome." I swallowed a forkful of potatoes and wondered if he'd had anything to do with his dad inviting me to eat with the family. Not that I'd complain. The cuisine and atmosphere beat the bunkhouse any day.

"Are you riding after supper?" Mrs. Law asked. She was her handsome husband's opposite—gentle to his rough, quiet to his bark, and kind to his brusque manner. I liked her. So did her daughter, Addie, who'd vacated her seat to play in her mom's hair from behind the buttermilk-wood chair.

"Pretty," Addie said in a deep voice.

I tried not to let the Law's handicapped daughter distract me, but her habit of wandering around the table and touching everyone disturbed me. I wiped my lips.

"Yes. Probably out to the ridge."

A hint of a smile crossed Mr. Law's face as Addie messed up her mom's shoulder-length brown hair. At least, I thought it was a smile. He was difficult to read. Gruff and unsettling. Did he approve of me or not? I couldn't help but wonder as I ate beside him if he judged the way I held my fork or slurped my soup.

24

"We're watching *Phantom Menace* tonight," Benny said. "Can you keep Addie out of our hair?"

Hearing her name, his sister ran over and pointed to his plate. She grunted and tapped her fingers to her lips in the sign for *eat*. Benny scowled, but gave her the last of his roll, though her own plate of food sat untouched.

"Sure," Mrs. Law said.

I smiled at Benny, making him blush. Poor kid seemed to have a crush on me. Too bad the cute bugger wasn't a few years older. Mom must've cursed me to attend the one church congregation in small-town Montana, containing an eager young man determined to date.

After supper, I shoved my man problems aside and saddled up Blue Boy Renegade. I'd enjoyed getting to know Benny as we exercised horses each evening. The depth he revealed during our conversations had surprised me. Maybe being handicapped had forced him to work on inner qualities rather than relying on outward appearance alone. He was a cool kid, and fast becoming a friend.

"You going out with that city slicker from church again?" he asked.

"Yep. We're going to a movie tomorrow night."

He made a face. "Why do you like that nerd?"

"First off, he's just my friend. Mackay knows that." Knowing and believing were two different things though. I knew Mackay liked me more than he should, though I brought up horrid subjects like baseball, diseases one can get from working with horses, and all my flaws. "Secondly, he's not *that* nerdy. He's definitely not ruggedly handsome, but he's okay."

Benny wrinkled his nose. "You deserve better than okay."

I laughed. "Ah, Benny, I could kiss you for that remark."

The poor boy blushed again. "I'm serious."

I focused on the sun shining through low-lying clouds. "Looks are overrated. I'll take kindness over a pretty face any day." And Mackay was kind. He hadn't even batted an eye when I'd described how I'd thrown up for three days after my appendix had been taken out because I'd been allergic to anesthesia. Justin would've freaked.

"I think you should go for a guy who's both kind and handsome."

I had. At least, I'd thought so. Blinking back tears, I leaned down to pat Blue Boy. "That combination is rare. Do you have anyone in mind?"

He urged Han into a trot. "My brother. He's light years ahead of that fuzzball Mackay."

I laughed and urged my horse to follow. The kid was a breath of sunshine after living in a dark cave. His *Star Wars* obsession amused me. He always threw out quotes and seemed determined to turn me into a super-fan. The last three weekends, he'd made me roll dice to decide which of the six episodes in the space saga we would watch as he filled me in on crucial data only an uber-geek would know—like whether Han or Greedo shot first in episode IV's cantina scene. According to Benny, Han had shot first in the original version, but George *Almighty* Lucas had changed that in the cleaned-up wussy version because he hadn't wanted Han to come across as a cold-blooded killer.

Spending time with Benny made me feel like I had a little brother and partially filled the gaping hole in my heart. I could see past the kid's puberty-induced acne and scrawny build to know he'd be a looker some-day. His dark hair and eyelashes framed striking blue eyes, a lady-killing combination. Still, I feared his crooked neck and limp would draw the attention. It's what I'd noticed first. Now, I realized how blind I'd been, for Bentley was the most beautiful person I knew, inside and out. I only hoped his peers would recognize that.

Kids could be cruel.

8

BENTLEY

*K*EEP IT NORMAL. I smoothed my shirt as I counted, keeping my neck in the painful upright position as I watched myself in the mirror. At one hundred, I let my neck drop and walked next door to see Lizzie. It hadn't been hard to convince Dad to let her eat with us, but he'd surprised me when he'd told her she could move her belongings from the closet-sized space over the garage into Rawson's old room.

"Come in!" Lizzie called after I knocked.

I entered and found Liz primping in front of her mirror.

"Hey, Benny."

"Hey."

She curtsied. "How do I look?"

"Beautiful, as always." I didn't see the point of her trying to impress Mackay Benson though. That guy was stale as week-old bread.

"You're sweet."

"What movie are you seeing?"

"Hopefully, something light to take his mind off everything that's happening."

"What's going on?"

"Mackay's dad has prostate cancer."

"Oh. Bummer."

"Yeah." She crossed the room to grab her satchel.

"I can tell he really likes you."

She rolled her eyes. "How can you tell that?"

"He holds your hand and looks at you like you're his world."

She rumpled my hair. "You're full of it." The doorbell chimed. She

27

threw her satchel over her shoulder and leaned down to kiss my cheek. "See you in the morning." She hurried out the door.

I touched my tingling cheek. If she kissed Mackay like that, the poor guy was probably half-way in love already. And Liz had no idea.

I watched the nerd lead her to a rusty Ford Escort from my bedroom window. He wore a goofy smile. Liz really could do better.

I hobbled over to my bed and glanced up at my calendar, though I already knew exactly how many days until my brother would be home. Nineteen. That's why I'd worked hard to convert Liz into a *Star Wars* fan. No way would Rawson be able to resist a girl who rode horses as well as Lizzie and who liked *Star Wars* as well. That'd be his total dream girl.

But I had my work cut out for me, despite what I'd told my brother on the phone a few weeks ago. Lizzie hadn't even watched *Attack of the Clones* or *Revenge of the Sith* until I'd showed them to her. I'd thought every American had seen all those movies, but apparently not.

9

RAWSON

*P*INK-EDGED CLOUDS rolled out to the horizon as the taxi turned at the gate to my family ranch. The Bar-M-Law brand had been welded above a symbol of a racing horse to mark the land I called home. We drove beneath the rustic log entrance, and I looked out my window to soak in rolling hills, whitewashed fences, Angus cattle, and distant snow-capped peaks. When the green-metal roof of the arena appeared, I smiled.

Home. At last.

I directed the cabbie to pull behind the detached garage so my family wouldn't see me. It was supper time.

"Thanks, man." I tipped him for driving me out so far.

"My pleasure." He hopped out to unload my luggage.

I hauled everything inside the garage and approached the house with my carry-on. I couldn't wait to see everyone's faces when I surprised them. In the mudroom, I discarded my loafers and picked out Mom's soothing voice coming from the kitchen, followed by Addie bellowing "Mine."

I bowed my head, grateful that some things never changed.

On the upstairs landing, I peeled off my shirt as I passed Benny's room. My family had no clue I'd charmed my way out of the last two weeks of my contract. Ben would probably go nuts. I glanced over my shoulder to make sure the hallway was clear before entering my room.

Someone coming from the other direction smacked right into me. Delicate fingers splayed against my bare chest. I grabbed onto the yelping intruder and pinned her against the wall.

"What are you doing in my room?"

Wide, brown eyes stared up at me. "Your room?" Wisps of blond hair curled along high cheekbones, framing a delicate face.

"Yes. My room." I glared at the girl.

"Let go of me. Benny!" she shouted.

I stepped back, wondering how she knew my brother.

Bentley threw himself around the door, appearing out of breath. When he saw me, his mouth formed an O. "Rawson?" He hobbled in and threw his arms around my bare torso. "Rawson!"

The girl straightened her shirt and put distance between us.

"Lizzie, it's my big brother. He's back." He grinned. "When did you get here? I thought you weren't coming for another two weeks. Oh, it's so good to see you."

I perused my room...or what used to be my room. Obviously, it wasn't mine anymore. My navy blue and brown decor had been replaced by a feminine turquoise and yellow palette. My king bed still reigned below the arched windows, but a frilly, white, eyelet comforter had totally de-manned it.

I'd been displaced.

"It's good to be back." I ruffled my brother's moppy hair as I glared at the sour-faced girl with the poofy ponytail. She must be the new hand my brother had raved about. I still couldn't believe Dad had hired a female and put her in my old room. Old man must be going senile.

Benny looked between us. "This is Liz Ruthersford. She's—"

"—the new girl riding my best horse," I said.

She threw out her hand. "You must be Rawson."

My brother grinned, unaware of the tension simmering between us.

I grudgingly shook her proffered hand. "The one and only." I clenched her fingers. "Since I'm home now, I'll be handling Bayder." I lowered my voice. "You might steal my room, but you won't steal my horse."

She shook loose of my grip. "I didn't, uh..."

I tipped an imaginary hat. "Nice to meet you." Not. I marched to Benny's room. My kid brother followed.

"I can't wait until Mom sees ya."

"Settle down, Big Ben. Let me get dressed." I tossed my offending garment on the floor and retrieved a fresh T-shirt from my carry-on.

He made a goofball face. "And I just thought you were trying to impress Lizzie by flaunting your six-pack."

"Ha ha." I snapped my fingers and pointed to his bed stand. "I want my lamp back. I'm gonna need it to get out of this slimy mud hole."

He didn't miss a beat. "Mud hole? Slimy? My home this is."

I pulled him into a bear hug. "Your Yoda impression's improving."

"I watched the *Star Wars* movies with Liz. She likes them, too."

I bit my tongue at the mention of the intruder.

"I'm dying to surprise everyone." Ben's head slumped on his shoulder.

I was anxious to see the rest of the fam, too. "Let's go shock 'em, kid."

LIZ

*M*Y HEART THREATENED to pound out of my chest as I slipped into the dining room. Mr. Law glanced up from his iPhone and tossed me a rare smile.

"Lithie!" Addie boomed from across the table.

I cleared my throat. "Um, I...just ran into your son upstairs. Rawson."

All eyes focused on me.

"He seemed quite upset that I was in *his* room. Maybe I should move back out to the garage?"

"Nonsense," Mr. Law said. "Rawson gave up right to that room when he took off to Europe. Besides, Charity already redecorated. If my son wants yellow butterflies and daisies on his walls, I'll disown him."

Mrs. Law stood behind her husband and squeezed his shoulders. "I didn't paint butterflies on the walls, you goose." She kissed his cheek and grabbed Addie's hand. "Is he still upstairs?"

I nodded.

She grinned. "Excuse us for a moment. I need to welcome my boy home."

A few seconds later, I heard Addie scream "Roth-un!" at the top of her lungs. Benny and his brother laughed in a similar manner, a snorting-guffaw combination.

I took deep breaths to slow my heart rate. Rawson Law had scared the Wheaties out of me when he'd barged into my room half-naked and pushed me against the wall. I guess I would've been upset, too, if I'd come home from college to find my room given to a stranger. In my defense though, I hadn't known the Laws had put me in their oldest son's room. I mean, it'd smelled of fresh paint, but I hadn't realized why.

Mr. Law kept reading emails on his phone until the rest of the family joined us. I couldn't help but notice how handsome Benny's older brother was. And polite. He held out a chair for his mom. His brown hair had blond highlights and appeared as if a woman had playfully run her fingers through it. A sexy five o'clock shadow emphasized gorgeous lips. Dark brows and lashes framed startling blue-green eyes.

"Thanks for ruining my surprise, Miss Ruthersford." The way he pronounced my name sounded like a curse.

"Oh, don't be an ass," Mr. Law said.

Addie tried to imitate him. "Ash!"

Rawson's lips twitched as Charity frowned. "Bart, watch your language around the children, please."

He glared at his oldest son. "Let's say grace so I can eat. I have to meet with Abe before he heads out."

A short blessing was said, and we dished out food. I felt terrible for inadvertently stealing not only Rawson's room, but his thunder. No one had told me his showing up was supposed to be a surprise.

I avoided eye contact. Or tried. Rawson captivated me as he played with his sister. Addie usually tormented us as during the meal, but tonight she focused on him, climbing on his back, strangling his neck, even shoving her fingers up his nose as he tried to eat.

He caught me watching, and the playful glint in his eyes vanished. "Benny said you're from Vegas."

I dabbed my mouth with a napkin. "Yep."

"What experience do you have?"

His question felt accusatory, not welcoming. "I worked for Viktorya Lohman during high school."

He glanced at his dad. "She's our English client, right?"

Bart narrowed his eyes. "Don't ask questions you already know the answers to."

For a moment, a battle played out between them. No fists or swords, just wills swung back and forth as their eyes clashed and expressions hardened.

Rawson turned back to me, making me tense up. He might be more intimidating than his father. "So you know nothing about Western training?"

"I've been here almost two months. Seth and Larry have brought me up to speed."

He smirked. "You can't pass decades of experience onto a greenie in a couple months."

"I do just fine."

"That she does," Bart said.

Rawson folded his arms across a well-formed chest. Though I found him insanely attractive, a cloud of negativity hung over him.

I finished my chicken-fried steak and set down my napkin. "Dinner was delicious, Charity. Thank Susa for me."

"Sure thing, Liz."

I turned to Bart. "I'm leaving and will be back late, but Seth will lock up the main stable."

He waved a hand. "I trust you, kid. Go have fun. That's an order."

Without giving Rawson Law a backward glance, I exited and headed upstairs to get ready.

I spritzed myself with body spray and pinned a few curls back so they wouldn't harass me all evening. Then I walked outside to wait for Mackay. With the prodigal son home, I didn't dare wait for my date inside.

I frowned as I spotted a trail of dust in the distance. Not *date*. Mackay and I weren't a couple. He just needed someone to distract him from his dad's declining health, and I needed a friend to keep me from thinking about the condescending way Rawson Law had addressed me during supper. I growled. That man certainly had pompous and arrogant down to an art.

Mackay pulled up to the house. "Sorry I'm late," he said, helping me into the passenger seat.

"You're perfect."

Mackay reached for my hand.

"Uh, I mean it's perfect you showed up when you did, not that you're, um….It's such a perfect day, isn't it?" Oh stink. Open mouth, insert boot.

His fingers squeezed mine. "It's perfect now that I'm with you."

Oh help. I felt a twinge of indigestion.

Mackay launched into a detailed account of his day at the hardware store. My hand began to sweat. For the love of all that was holy, didn't he realize hand-holding in July just wasn't right, even if I liked him, which I didn't. By the time we reached the dollar theater, Mackay felt he had a legal claim to my hand. I wanted to protest on grounds of clammy fingers, but that'd be mean.

The lights dimmed in the theater, and Mackay leaned over to whisper. "Thanks for coming. I've been dying to see this."

Yeah, right. Every guy dreamed of seeing *27 Dresses*. I doubted Mackay had a clue what the movie was even about. But I wouldn't complain. James Marsden was dark chocolate to my heart.

Mackay leaned across the arm rest again. "You look really nice."

"Um, thanks." Talk about awkward. He had it in spades.

"I love your hair down like that. It's real pretty."

I gave him a playful shove. "Hush. The movie's starting."

34

During the opening scene, I wondered how to extract my fingers. Minty praise and comments about my appearance had warning bells ringing in my head. When would I learn to stop being so dang nice? The last thing I wanted was a boyfriend.

When the movie ended, Mackay drove me home. Though midsummer, hot air blasted through the vents. When the temperature gauge spiked in his piece of crap car, he flipped on the heater to draw heat away from the engine.

"Sorry about this." His gaze flicked hopefully to my face as he placed his right hand on the selector lever between us.

I folded my arms, determined to avoid another sticky-finger calamity.

The headlights illuminated the Bar-M-Law sign, and I relaxed. Almost done. Mackay pulled into the circular driveway and cut the engine.

I unfolded my arms. "Thanks for the...uh," I bit my lip as he found my hand. "...movie."

"I had a wonderful time." His thumb caressed my knuckles. "Of course, I always have fun with you." His gaze dropped to my lips.

Not good. I tried to pull away, but all I managed to do was prompt him to lean over like one of those Dippy Bird contraptions I'd played with as a girl. Caught off guard, I didn't react in time to dodge his lips that sought mine like a missile. When his head jerked back up, I yanked the door handle and made my escape. Ugh.

Mackay caught up to me at the porch. Dang it. I'd come to the middle of Nowhere, Montana to get away from this kind of drama, not dive into more. I wasn't ready to deal with another relationship. Maybe I never would be. It didn't matter how nice Mackay seemed. I was the Tin Man. I had no heart.

His thumb rubbed my jaw, reminding me of the imminent danger of him kissing me again. "Can I see you tomorrow?"

I shook my head. "I promised to take the kids to a movie."

He shuffled his feet. "I could meet you there."

"No. Bennie would be upset if I brought someone else. He's funny that way."

He frowned. "Okay. I guess I'll pick you up Sunday for church then?"

I threw out a "Sure," mumbled goodnight, and forced my way inside. When the door closed, I leaned against it and shuddered.

Freak. That had been a disaster. I liked Mackay, but not in a hand-holding, kissing sort of way. He was my friend. That's all. Justin had ruined me and taken my heart with him to his grave. I wouldn't be handing it out to anyone ever again.

BENTLEY

*A*FTER LIZ LEFT on her date and Dad excused himself to go talk figures with the foreman, Rawson became more animated. He made Addie laugh so hard I thought she might pee herself.

Mom rubbed her side. "I haven't laughed so hard in ages."

Five years to be precise. We hadn't had much to laugh about since the accident.

Rawson kept telling us about his international travels. "In Madrid, there was a goat head in a window of a butcher shop that someone put sunglasses on. Cracked me up. I also found a *marihuana* store."

Mom frowned. "I hope you didn't go in."

I could tell by how his eyes sparkled that he was messing with her. "Oh, I went in. How could I not? The sign was big and legal, screaming at me to try its wares. M-A-R-I-H-U-A-N-A."

My mind tripped on the spelling. "I thought marijuana has a J in it."

Rawson ruffled my hair. "You're sharp, kid. It does when it's a drug. For a regular clothes store in Madrid though, it's spelled like I said."

Mom visibly relaxed. "So it wasn't a drug store?"

Rawson chuckled. "No, *mamacita*. I didn't get high, but I did buy a couple of awesome shirts."

Addie groped his face. He kissed her cheek. "Love you, princess."

"Me princess!"

I rolled my eyes. "*I'm* a princess, not *me*."

She stuck her lips out. "Me princess!"

My brother snorted. "Addie's right. She's the beautiful princess and Benny's the ugly adopted step-brother."

Addie broke into a fit of giggles. "Benny ugly!"

I made a scary face. "All the better to break your mirror, little girl."

She shrieked and launched a handful of potatoes from Rawson's plate. Mom grabbed Addie as I wiped mashed potatoes off my forehead.

"Time to bathe this food-flinging princess." She kissed Rawson's head. "I'm so glad you're home, son. Put your stuff in the basement guest room. There are clean sheets in the closet." She faced me. "Help Susa with dishes."

"Ah, Mom. I want to help Rawson."

"*After* you help Susa." Her stern look sent me scurrying from the room.

When I finally made it to Rawson's new room, it looked like a bomb had gone off in it. He'd opened every box shipped home from college and had dumped clothes and books all over the carpet.

"Want to come up to my room and see my paintings?" I asked.

"Sure. Let me change first."

I smiled, finding comfort in his weird unchanging ritual. Clothes made my brother sort of loony. When I was younger, he'd explained that shirts, especially anything made of cotton, made him feel like ants were crawling all over and biting him. The sensation intensified when he perspired. So, he special ordered shirts made of super silky material. Even with his soft shirts, it wasn't unusual for him to change half a dozen times a day or more.

Rawson raved over my paintings, and we ended up talking until almost midnight.

"So what have you been doing to keep busy, bro?"

"Lizzie's taken me riding almost every day."

He frowned. "You don't need to ride with her anymore. I'm home and can take you out tomorrow."

"Liz is already taking us to the movies."

"What?"

"Addie's bugged Liz to take her to see *Coco*. She promised we'd go tomorrow, before we knew you'd be here. We can't back out. You know how Addie can be."

"I thought Miss Ruthersford was hired to work the horses, not nanny."

His words filled me with doubts. Did my parents pay Liz to take care of Addie and me in her free time? I'd thought she enjoyed hanging out with me, but maybe all I was to her was a way to pad her pocketbook.

"Why don't you come with us?" The thought of being a charity case like that lame Mackay Benson made me ill.

"Nah. I need to talk to Dad."

I chewed my lips. Now that I knew Liz only dished out pity, I wondered if I could come up with an excuse as well. Why had I thought a pretty girl like her would want to spend time with a handicapped freak like me?

I had to be the world's biggest fool.

12

RAWSON

HE NEW GIRL already sat at the table like she belonged there when I entered the dining room for breakfast. Just one more grievance against her. Acting like one of the family was a clear case of the camel sticking its nose in the tent until the Bedouins were ousted.

She hadn't noticed me yet. When my brother had told me about the new girl while I'd been in Europe, I'd conjured up a big-boned, plain-faced heifer who could work as hard as he'd described. I hadn't envisioned this petite, long-legged creature with her doe-brown eyes and luxurious, ashy-blond curls. But her cute facade didn't fool me.

Mom entered with a plate of scrambled eggs. "Morning, son."

The girl jerked her head up with a deer-in-the-headlights look. Too bad I couldn't run her off the road.

"Morning," I mumbled as I sat across from her.

Mom planted an embarrassing kiss on my cheek. "How did you sleep, baby? Was that bed all right?"

"It was fine." Not as comfy as that soft king the girl had stolen from me though.

Mom headed back the way she'd come. "I need to turn the sausages. Let me know when your dad arrives."

I grunted and scooped eggs onto my plate. When I looked up, I caught the girl watching me.

"Why aren't you eating with the other hands? You're not part of this family."

Her cheeks turned bright pink. "Uh, I, uh…"

"Do you think you're special or something?"

She began to inhale pancakes and eggs as if it was her last meal.

Dad entered, brushing off his jeans and throwing his hat onto a peg on the wall. I called to Mom, so she'd know he'd arrived.

He scowled at me, before turning to the intruder. "Morning, Liz." She received a smile.

"Good morning, Mr. Law." Miss Kiss-up stuffed more eggs in her mouth and set her napkin on her plate. "I'd better get back to work. Thanks, Charity," she said as she passed the kitchen.

Mom ran out. "Are you rushing away already? The sausages are almost done."

"I need to get started since I'm taking the kids to the movie later."

"Oh, that's right." Mom grinned. "Have fun, sweetheart."

I scowled at Dad when the door shut behind her. "Did you go and adopt a new sister for me while I was away? Since when do you let hired hands eat at our table?"

His eyes flashed, but I didn't care. It irked me how he hadn't bothered to greet me, yet he'd welcomed and smiled at the girl. He never smiled at anyone but Mom and Addie.

Mom bustled into the room, holding a plate of sizzling sausages. She stopped to hug me. "Oh, I've missed you."

I stabbed three sausages from the plate and pulled them onto mine. "Spoken like a true mom."

Benny entered. His dark hair stood on end and his eyes appeared goopy with sleep. He winced as he stepped, making me frown. Mom had informed me that with his growth spurt, his legs ached worse than ever.

"Hey, Big Ben. You look like hell."

He laughed as Mom swatted me. "Did Lizzie already leave?" he asked.

"You just missed her." Mom set a loaded plate in front of Dad and started piling another with pancakes for my brother.

"Shucks. I wanted to catch her before she headed out."

Pancake lodged in my throat. Ever since I'd returned, I'd felt a tangible difference, but hadn't been able to put my finger on it. Now the truth hit me. I usually occupied the center of Benny's and Addie's universe, but my orbit had been shifted by that meddling girl.

"She inhaled breakfast like a beached whale given water."

Dad hissed and shook his head. That's how he showed displeasure. I should know, since I'd been the cause of that reaction all my life.

Benny grabbed five sausages. "I don't think I can go to the movie. My leg hurts super bad."

Mom frowned. "Your sister won't be happy about that."

"Maybe Liz could just take her."

Mom did one of her "Hmms" that meant *probably not*.

I headed to Dad's office after breakfast and dropped a blue folder onto his desk.

He raised his head.

"It's a print-off of my plans for getting a higher margin back on the cattle. I've also outlined a proposal for a horse-racing venture to phase in over the next few years." I didn't bother with a greeting. The less said between us, the better.

Dad folded his arms over his chest. "What makes you think I need to change anything? The ranch had a gross margin return of thirty-three percent last year with all land owned. Our profit was the highest it's been in a decade."

"Did you figure in opportunity costs? If you'd charged opportunity interest on the value of the cattle, that would add more direct costs and cut your return on the beginning inventory by maybe ten percent. Then there's opportunity rental that—"

"Son, I don't have time to discuss made-up economic scenarios. You're not in class anymore. There's real work to be done."

"But you're under-utilizing—"

"You're not the only Law who graduated from college. I have my degree from Stanford, too."

"But you're stuck in the past. At least, look this over." I touched the thick file I'd invested countless hours of research on over the past few months. "These could put the Bar-M-Law Ranch on the map."

"Son, you have big dreams but no experience to back them up. Put in a full day's work before you perform slick tricks on a spreadsheet."

My nostrils flared.

"You haven't spent more than a couple weeks here since you left four years ago. Maybe we'll talk after you've broken a sweat and dirtied your boots. Right now, you're a liability on the books with all I've dished out for your education."

"You forced me to go to Stanford."

The way his eyes narrowed warned that I tread on thin ice, but it frustrated me that he wouldn't even take a peek at my work.

"My ideas would more than pay back my debt. For starters, your cattle reproductive performance could be improved. Implementing my procedures would increase calving and weaning rates—"

"Book smarts won't save this ranch." He nudged the folder back to me. "Hard work and commitment will. And has. You haven't dirtied your hands since high school. If I turned you loose, you'd supplement the cattle and run this operation into the ground before winter's end."

My hands fisted at my sides.

"They don't teach you everything in business school. There are practical lessons you only learn from years of hard work and comparing notes

41

with other producers and regional Ag groups. Maybe in a few years we'll talk, when you've had a chance to impress me."

"You're impossible to please."

"I didn't say please me. I said impress. Show me you have what it takes to run this ranch. Intellectual research isn't enough. Any city slicker can make things work on paper. I know you're smart, but your genius has landed you in trouble in the past. I haven't seen evidence of change. I don't want smarts. I want commitment, which means you make wise choices in your time, family relationships, and friends."

"Not this again." I grabbed my folder and smacked it against his desk. "Are you going to hold Damon over me forever? It was a mistake. He paid the price. Let it go."

"You're a smart kid, Rawson, but—"

"I'm not a kid. I'm a man."

"As long as you live under my roof and subsist on my money, you're a kid. And if you even sniff in the direction of that loser friend of yours, I'll never trust you to handle even the chicken coop. Do I make myself clear?"

"Crystal." I aimed my middle finger at him around the folder, and marched out of his office.

13

LIZ

*A*T THE BOTTOM of the stairs, I yelped as I ran into a steel-hard chest. "Oh, I'm so sorry." I stooped to gather papers I'd caused Rawson Law to drop. "I didn't see you there." Crashing into each other had become a nasty habit.

"Obviously." He yanked the papers from my hands.

A charged cloud of toxicity had hung about the ranch since he'd shown up last night. At first, I'd felt sorry for him. But no more. The man had been nothing but rude to me. I could read dislike in his gorgeous eyes as plain as if it'd been written there in permanent black Sharpie.

"Are you going to stand there and stare at me, Miss Ruthersford?"

Too late, I realized I'd done just that, but not for the reason the cocky man insinuated. I'd only wished to know what I'd done to earn his scorn.

"I-I need to speak to your father."

He snorted. "Enter at your own risk. He's in a foul mood."

That was certainly calling the kettle black. I started up the steps, rubbing my arms. Negative vibes clung to Rawson Law, shocking everyone he came into contact with. Even sweet Benny had a chip on his shoulders this morning when he'd ditched out on our movie adventure.

I took a deep breath and knocked on Mr. Law's office door.

"Come in," he called.

I entered with a smile, the best weapon against bad moods. Or so I hoped. "Larry said you needed to talk to me."

Mr. Law motioned for me to take a seat. "He told me what you did with Fargo Noon. I wanted to pick your brain about some of the other horses."

43

Oh, good. He wouldn't fire me. I'd worried he might, now that his son had returned. I leaned forward to talk about my favorite subject, and time ceased to exist as we discussed all of my equine charges. Mr. Law shared some ideas for the future, and I became overconfident and shook my head.

"I don't think that'd be wise."

He frowned, and I wished to snatch back my words.

"What do you have against selling off the two-year-olds?"

I squirmed in my seat. "I just think you could get more back on your investment if you put in another year of training."

His fingers tapped together. "Remind me of your credentials. You went to Utah State, correct?"

I ducked my head. "Only for a semester. I don't have any formal equestrian training. It's just a hunch, but I feel strongly it'd be a win-win for you and your clients."

"Well, your hunches have been dead-on up to this point, so work up a training schedule with Abe and Larry. Run it past me when you're ready. I think you could be onto something."

"Are you kidding me?"

I flipped around to see Rawson Law standing in the doorway, looking like a pissed-off bull in a rodeo chute.

"She has a *hunch* and you fall all over it, yet you won't even read my plans I spent months researching?"

"Why are you eavesdropping on a private conversation?" Mr. Law said.

"Trying to keep one step ahead of you so you don't run this ranch into the ground before I have a chance to manage it. I can't believe you're listening to this *girl*."

My jaw dropped. Girl had never sounded so derogatory.

"Get out!" Mr. Law stood and pointed to the door.

I wished to disappear as Rawson glared at me before storming out.

Mr. Law's fists relaxed as his son's heavy footsteps descended the stairs. "Sorry you had to witness that."

"I'll get that schedule to you by Friday." I started for the door, only to pause when he called after me. "Yes?" I looked back at my boss.

"Don't let what my son said get to you. In my opinion, hunches backed by hard work are worth more than educated research backed by arrogance."

"Thanks, sir."

"Call me Bart. You've earned the right."

I grinned. "Thank you, Bart."

I made my way downstairs, a huge grin on my face. My job was safe. I might not have much formal training, but I knew horses better than the freckles on my nose. Mr. Law had admitted that he valued my contribu-tions, even if his jerk son didn't.

I could live with that.

14

BENTLEY

𝓜UD KEPT ITS form as I pulled the miniature loaf pan away. I wiped my hands against my jeans and surveyed the new bricks drying on the old blue tarp.

"Are you going to build a high-rise with those?"

I almost jumped out of my skin as Lizzie approached, leading Han and Kisser behind her.

"I've never seen your magical kingdom." Her gaze traveled across the four buildings taking shape. "You have quite the setup here."

The last thing I wanted was for her to see me playing in the dirt. "It's for Addie."

Liz tethered the horses. "I'm tempted to join her. Looks fun. If you dug a trench down the middle, you could fill it with water from the hose and have a river through town."

I chewed my lip, not wanting to appear eager about her suggestion.

"How much taller are you going to make your building?"

"Addie's building," I said. "Maybe another foot."

"Can I help?"

"I'm sure you have better things to do."

She leaned down to touch one of the bricks. "Want to take a ride while these dry? I saddled Han for you."

I wanted nothing more than to go riding, but the thought of being her project kept me from accepting. "You go ahead. I have things to finish."

"We could just do a short ride."

"Rawson can take me."

She frowned. "Have I done something to upset you?"

"No."

"Then why have you avoided me all week?"

I rubbed my hands to flake off mud. "I'm not a little kid, like Addie."

Her brows drew together. "What?"

I kicked a mud clod to the side. "I can take care of myself."

"I thought you liked hanging out."

"Well, I don't."

She reared back as if I'd slapped her. "Okay. Guess I'll see you later." She marched the horses back to the stable. I almost called after her, but words stuck in my throat.

I headed to the office. Right step. Left leg-lift, swing-out, step-down and wince. Right step. I focused all my energy into walking smoothly as I made my way upstairs and barged into Dad's office without knocking.

He looked up from his desk. "What is it, son? I'm busy."

"Are you paying Liz extra to take care of me and Addie?"

He gave me a strange look. "Why in Sam's hill would I do that?"

"Well, she hangs out with me. I thought maybe she did it 'cause you asked her to."

He shuffled papers. "I don't tell any of the hands what to do in their free time. If Liz spends hers with you, you should be thankful. It's a gift.

Crap, crud and cowpies. I left before Dad could see the stupid tears slapping my eyes. Liz hadn't been handing out pity. At the bottom of the stairs, I ran into my brother.

"Hey, Big Ben. What's the rush?"

I sniffed and tried to man up, but Rawson still noted my glistening eyes.

"Whoa." He grabbed my shoulders. "Did Dad get after you?"

"No." I rubbed my eyes against my sleeve. "It's just allergies."

He frowned, but didn't call me out. "Want to go riding?"

"Nah. I need an allergy pill." It didn't feel right accepting a ride with him after rejecting Liz.

"We could watch a movie. I need a *Star Wars* fix."

"Rain-check?"

"Is your leg paining you?"

"No. I'm just worn out."

Rawson walked me back to the house. "You sure you're okay, kid?"

I bristled. "Don't worry about me."

"I'll always worry about you, homey. You my bro."

We sounded stupider than a hick on Wall Street when we used our ghetto lingo, but it made me smile. "I love ya, dawg."

"Ditto, homeslice." He rubbed my hair. "Get feeling better."

Was that possible after how I'd treated Lizzie? I noticed her closed door and wanted to cry. Why had I allowed my insecurities to rule me?

47

RAWSON

SOMETHING BOTHERED MY brother. I watched him trudge upstairs, wondering what had upset him. I almost walked away but stopped when I saw him pass his door and disappear down the hall. Probably heading to that girl's room. Hearing a light knock, I crept upstairs and stood outside her open door.

My brother's wavering voice carried to me. "I'm sorry, Lizzie."

"What happened?"

There was a long pause. "I thought you were being paid to babysit me."

"What? How could you think that?"

My brother sniffed. "Sorry."

Silence made me peek around the corner. The girl had pulled him into a hug and wasn't letting go. I eased back so as not to get caught.

"Now that you're not confused, should we take Addie to *Coco* on Saturday?"

"For sure."

"Okay. I'll make arrangements with Seth to teach me how to drive that old truck your dad said I could use. I'm kind of scared to learn stick shift."

"Ah, it's simple."

"Easy for you to say. You've never driven."

I slipped away. Reminders of the normal things my brother had lost always depressed me. The girl was wrong. Benny had driven before the accident. I'd actually given him lessons on Dad's 1998 Ford Super Duty truck. Even at eight, he'd been a natural, besides being short and having to sit on several books to see over the steering wheel. If the accident hadn't messed him up, he'd be a better driver than me.

Unbalanced by memories, I hurried outside and crawled into the hammock I'd set up last night, like the one I'd claimed in high school after fights with Dad. The blue spruce had grown and now sheltered my hiding spot from the deck.

I gazed up at the stars and thought about Damon. I'd found him in town two days ago skunk drunk and shooting off his mouth to some bikers. I'd schmoozed them into not beating him up and had driven him out to the old homestead to sober up. The shack wouldn't be used until calving season, so the chance of Dad catching wind that he was holed up there was minimal.

Damon needed a time-out from life.

I heard the rumble of the sliding glass door and peeked over the edge of the hammock. Someone paced back and forth on the wooden deck.

"Sure." It was that troublesome girl, talking on her phone.

I settled into my hammock, content to eavesdrop.

"Don't worry. I'll get the money. You know how tenacious I can be."

When she laughed, I frowned.

"It shouldn't be hard. You taught me well." She laughed again. "That's why I love you."

Whoa. Was she talking to a lover?

"They'll never know what hit them. I'll arrange everything and have the money transferred to you soon." She giggled. "Oh, yeah. They're gullible."

Was she talking about my family? Did the conniving impostor plan to embezzle from Dad? He'd certainly fallen for her charms and would probably give her whatever she asked for, including access to his bank account.

"No, don't do that. Last time, things didn't end well when she got involved. Leave it to me. I know how to work them." She gasped. "Don't compare him to me. That's mean. He has a thing for old widows who are dying to leave him their inheritance."

It took all my self-control not to jump up and strangle her.

"Me? I wish. I do better with horses. That's why I'm here."

And that's why I'd make sure she left.

"No. It depends on how much money I get from them. Maybe a Mediterranean cruise." Pause. "No, I love you more. Call you later." She shoved her phone into her back pocket and disappeared back inside.

I threw my legs over the hammock and scratched my head. What to do? Going straight to Dad would be a mistake. I didn't have evidence, and he would never listen. Mom didn't need anything else to worry about, so she was out. Benny wouldn't believe me. The girl already had him

49

bamboozled. The only way to save my family would be to make life so miserable for Miss Ruthersford that she'd leave of her own volition.

I rubbed my hands together. The drive to the movies on Saturday would be the perfect opportunity to initiate my Get-Rid-of-Con-Artist plan. All I had to do was get invited along.

That shouldn't be difficult to accomplish.

BENTLEY

*N*OT ACTING EXCITED took every ounce of acting power I possessed. I hid a smile as Lizzie secured Addie's seatbelt and told my sister not to unbuckle it. Addie grunted and mimicked the way Liz wagged her finger at her. Once Lizzie hopped into the driver's seat, I stuck my arm out the window and motioned to my brother.

Rawson opened the passenger side door, and Liz turned to glare at me. "You didn't tell me your brother was coming."

Rawson climbed inside. "Sure am, sweetheart. Don't let your heart race too hard."

She frowned. "Uh, you can take them then. I, uh…want…need to stay and work a new foal."

Rawson smirked. "Are you scared of me, Miss Ruthersford?"

She huffed. "No."

"You will be. You. Will. Be."

I snorted at the *Star Wars* reference he so smoothly slipped into the conversation. "Yoda," I said. "*Empire Strikes Back.*"

He gave me a high five. "Great, kid. Don't get cocky."

I laughed. "Han. *A New Hope.*"

Lizzie undid her seatbelt. "I'll leave you two to your trivia game."

"But Liz," I whined, "I thought you enjoyed spending time with me and Addie." I wasn't above guilting her into staying. She'd have fun with my brother if she just gave him a chance. "You promised to take us."

She chewed her lips, but then sighed. "Oh, all right. But your brother should drive."

Of course, Rawson would drive. He never let anyone else behind the wheel.

But he surprised me by waving a hand. "Go ahead and let me catch some zzz's, will ya? I'm still suffering from jet lag. Besides, I hate this old clunker."

Whoa. Rawson must really like her to give up the driver's seat. That'd never happened, at least that I could remember. I gave Liz a thumbs-up.

She didn't look happy, but when my brother leaned back and pulled his Stetson over his eyes, she put the truck into reverse and backed out.

I rubbed my hands together. Rawson was home and things were right with Lizzie again. Life couldn't be better.

But ten minutes down the road, Rawson shifted in his seat and slammed all my illusions to pieces.

"You're driving slower than my ninety-four-year-old granny. Can't you go faster?"

"Faster! Faster!" Addie boomed.

Rawson turned to wink at our sister as Liz sped up. Slightly. He didn't speak again until we reached the junction to the highway. It wasn't an actual highway. We were still twenty minutes from any paved roads, but this section of dirt was graded smoother so she could pick up speed without rattling our teeth. She shifted roughly into second gear, making Rawson drop an F-bomb.

Liz winced when Addie tried to copy him. "Duck!"

"I'd appreciate if you watched your language around your sister," she snapped.

"Oh, appreciate my language clean, you would?" he said in a Yoda voice.

Addie giggled, feeding his dark side.

"Well, get used to disappointment, darling. I'm not my dad and won't give into your—" Lizzie's cheeks and neck flamed red as he shot off literary bullets.

"Rawson, knock it off," I said. "You really do swear too much."

He glared at Liz as if she'd spoken instead of me.

We started up the steep section that climbs up from the creek. I'll admit, Lizzie wasn't very good at driving a manual transmission. Seth had given her lessons, but she must not have realized she'd decreased speed and needed to downshift. The truck sputtered and lurched. She grabbed the shifter and yanked, but her foot slipped and the ten-year-old Ford died with a huge groaning bounce.

"What in the hell are you doing?" Rawson yelled.

Lizzie's natural grace became lost in jerky movements as she tried to restart the engine while the truck rolled backward. Hitting the brake, she jolted to a stop. Her eyebrows scrunched as she engaged the engine again and pressed the clutch. But she forgot to put the truck into first gear, so it died.

My brother's nostrils flared. To him, there's nothing worse than a bad driver, and Liz wasn't making a positive first impression. If we hadn't been on a steep incline, she might've managed, but with Rawson snorting and swearing beside her like a Brahma bull, she forgot once more to downshift and killed the engine. The truck rolled closer to the ledge.

Rawson started swearing all sorts of terrible as he shoved her hands off the wheel and crushed her into the door. He braked to stop our backward momentum and moved his other foot over to the clutch to switch gears.

"You'll destroy the transmission doing fool things like that, woman. You have to put the gear into first to engage."

My mouth hung slack. It wasn't as though Liz had meant to kill the truck. She was simply flustered. I would've been too if Rawson had yelled at me.

He cut the engine and slid back to his side. Liz squirmed in front of the steering wheel. "Why don't you drive."

"Just do it right," Rawson said between clenched teeth.

She started the engine and gradually released the clutch. We moved forward, only lurching once before she switched into second and made it over the rise and onto level road. Hallelujah.

Still, my brother couldn't leave her alone. "We're going to miss the movie if you keep this turtle pace."

Lizzie ignored him.

"Seriously. Give it some gas, Goldilocks."

Anger must have been smoldering under her calm facade because Liz slammed on the brake, making Addie hit the front seat. She'd unfastened her seatbelt without me noticing. I reached out to grab my sister.

Rawson smacked the dashboard. "You're going to kill us all, you—"

Lizzie hopped out the door as he spewed out curses. "Drive it yourself, you arrogant pig!" She slammed her door and stormed down the dirt road as fast as her two legs could carry her.

Numbness claimed me as I watched her go.

Rawson snickered. "Woo-whee. She sure told me."

"Woooo Wheeee!" Addie copied him and laughed.

I opened my door, not wanting Lizzie to go off alone.

"Come on, little bro. You have to admit, that was funny."

I glared at him and my foot missed the runner, making me fall awkwardly into the gravel.

Rawson leapt out after me as I started to cry. I couldn't help it. There I sat, five weeks away from being fourteen, and I couldn't even act like a man.

Rawson gushed out sorrys as he helped me to my feet, but I flung his hands away. "Go see the stupid movie with Addie." I rubbed my eyes. "I don't want to go nowhere with you."

He caught my arm, but I shrugged him off. Right step. Left leg-lift, swing-out, step-down. Right step. Left leg-lift, swing-out, step-down.

"Ben, I'm sorry." My brother's desperate plea made me pause my awkward rhythm.

"Lizzie's a good driver," I said.

"I was only playing. I didn't think she'd get upset."

Adrenaline made me shaky. "You were rude. She only learned to drive stick yesterday."

"Sorry, Big Ben."

"You need to be sorry to Lizzie." I glanced down the road. She'd already disappeared over a rise.

"Okay, I'm sorry to Lizzie." He huffed. "Now will you get back in the truck and stop being stubborn? I can tell your leg hurts."

It hurt like the dickens, but I refused to admit that. "I'm not going anywhere with you until you get Liz."

"Come on, Benny. Stop horsing around."

He tried to grab me but I lashed out with my fist. Rawson didn't expect me to act like a bully. That's the only reason I connected. In a real fight, no one whips my brother. He's the strongest guy around. Never had I punched him. Shoot. I hadn't even back-talked him. To say I'd surprised him would be a huge understatement.

He swallowed and rubbed his cheek. "Great shot, kid. That was one in a million."

My knuckles stung as if I'd batted a wasp's nest. Note to self: punching hurt the puncher worse than the punched. "So go get her."

He frowned. "I'm not leaving you on the side of the road."

"And I'm not going anywhere unless you apologize and make things right with Liz."

His jaw clenched, but he turned to Addie in the back seat. "Stop crying." He leaned in to refasten her seatbelt. "Keep this on and I'll get you jelly bellies at the theater. Kay?"

He climbed in the truck and slammed the door. After turning the old Ford around, he pulled up beside me and rolled down the window. "I'll be right back. Stop walking and sit and wait. You're aggravating your muscles."

Before I could reply, he peeled out, leaving me choking on dust. Tears streaked my cheeks as the truck disappeared. I rubbed them against my sleeve and sat to relieve the pressure on my muscles.

Hurry, I thought.

LIZ

*C*OULD TWO BROTHERS be more different? If Rawson Law didn't resemble his sweet brother physically in so many ways, I'd find it impossible to believe they were related. They were the do-gooder Dr. Jekyll and the monstrous Mr. Hyde.

"Goldilocks." I kicked a rock off the road. "What a jerk."

I wondered how many miles loomed between me and the ranch. My jaw hurt from clenching my teeth. I put my hands together and tossed words to the sky.

"Please, let Rawson Law work with the cows, not the horses. And let him step in manure every day."

The sound of a gunning engine shattered my irreverent prayer.

The old, white truck barreled over the hill at a breakneck speed. I moved off the road, figuring the jerk would throw me a taunting wave as he passed. Instead, he slammed on his brakes and spun out, flipping the vehicle around in a half circle and teetering on two wheels before coming down on all four tires to face me.

I closed my eyes as a cloud of dust enveloped me. A door slammed and I coughed as heavy footsteps approached. I flinched when I peeked to see Rawson scowling at me through the settling dust. His eyes had been green this morning but appeared icy blue now. His face creased in threatening lines, but my temper detonated first.

"Are you nuts driving like that with children in the car?"

"Addie's got her seatbelt on. She loved it."

"What if she'd unbuckled it, you psycho?"

He threw back his head and laughed.

I marched away, sick of his games.

"Oh, no you don't." He caught my arm.

"Let me go, jerk."

"Get in the truck."

"No way. I'm not going anywhere with you."

He twisted my elbow behind me, making me yelp as he scooped me up into strong arms.

"Put me down!" I lashed out with a fist. A reflex move. My knuckles stung as they connected with his nose. For a moment, I feared he might drop me. He staggered but held me steady long enough for blood to gush down my gray T-shirt. Ick.

I grimaced and cradled my throbbing hand.

"Roth-un!" Addie climbed down from her seat and ran to him, signing something with her hands.

"Yep. I'm okay." He squeezed the bridge of his nose.

I jogged away to put distance between us. Though winded, I didn't dare pause or check over my shoulder to see whether he followed. I'd gladly jog-walk all the way back to the ranch if I didn't have to see his smug mug any time soon.

But no such luck. I heard the diesel motor and mentally prepared for another confrontation. At least, he wasn't speeding now. But he was probably fuming mad.

The Ford inched up beside me, and Rawson rolled down his window. "Miss Ruthersford?"

I kept walking.

"I'm sorry, okay?" His apology sounded like sour milk in his throat. "Please get in. Benny's ticked and refused to ride with me until I apologized and brought you back."

I turned to stare at the thoughtless man hanging out his window. "You left your crippled brother on the side of the road?"

A storm brewed behind his sapphire blues. "It's your fault for heading off by yourself. If you'd stayed, he wouldn't have snapped."

"My fault?"

"Yeah. I only teased, but you had to get bent out of shape and cause a scene. Benny has a tender heart. You upset him."

I shook my head, horrified that he'd left Benny behind. He really was a cad. "Get out."

His eyes narrowed at my command.

"Either let me drive or go away."

I expected him to argue, but he hopped out and gestured for me to switch places. I climbed inside the cab and shut the door as he walked behind the truck. Before I could talk myself out of it, I pressed my foot to the clutch and punched the gas.

Rawson ran alongside the truck, beating the passenger door. I locked the door, making him cuss to high heaven when he jiggled the door handle. "Stop, you—" I tuned out the rest of his shouting. For being a brilliant Stanford graduate, he spoke like a caveman. "Let me in, you—"

"La la la la," I sang as he hit the window.

Shifting into second, I increased my speed and pulled away from the maniac. He jumped, screamed, and shook his fist in the rear view mirror as I left him in my dust...right where his potty mouth belonged.

I drove far enough up the road where I could stop and perform a three-point turn without him catching up to me, then I headed back the way I'd come.

"I think your brother needs a time-out so he can learn some manners," I said to Addie in the backseat. "Let's go get Benny."

"Benny!" she bellowed.

I focused on shifting gears correctly. Killing the truck right now would be mortifying, not to mention dangerous with psycho cowboy in the vicinity.

Speaking of psycho cowboy, Rawson planted himself in the middle of the road.

"Don't be a fool," I muttered, gripping the steering wheel tighter.

He folded his arms over his muscular chest. I chewed my lip. Would he be dumb enough to stand there and get run over?

Probably.

At the last second, I swerved into sagebrush, jarring the teeth out of my head as I fought for control and prayed I wouldn't stall.

"Please, don't die," I chanted to the hormonal truck.

It lurched like a bucking bronco as I downshifted into second and maneuvered back onto gravel. My fingers tingled from clutching the steering wheel so tight. The engine made scary sounds, but Addie's booming laughter from the backseat made me grin.

"More." She tapped her fingertips together.

"Maybe later." I glanced in the rearview mirror and snorted as I saw Rawson Law throw his hat on the ground and kick it. "Too much of a good thing can make you sick."

18

RAWSON

*B*LACK SMOKE POLLUTED the air as Juan's ancient Chevy pulled away from the garage. After walking for an hour in the heat, Susa's grandson had happened to drive by on his way to visit her and had given me a lift, saving me five more miles of walking. I stomped into the four-car garage and threw the air pump into the back of my new truck. I stripped off my sweaty shirt and grabbed a fresh one from the duffel bag behind my seat.

That girl would pay.

Soon, a trail of dust flew behind my F-350 SuperCab as I sped toward town. If I booked it, I'd arrive before the movie ended. My grip tightened on the wheel as I recalled her cold-hearted trick. No one pulled one over on me, yet my blistered feet and sore nose proved I'd been bested. Of course, I was up against a professional, since the woman conned people for a living.

I reached town in record time and cruised up and down the rows of the theater parking lot until I found Dad's old Ford. Parking on the next row, I grabbed a pair of gloves and sauntered over to release the air on the back two tires. I finished just as movie patrons began pouring out of the theater.

Sauntering back to my truck, I watched and waited. If the blasted woman didn't have my siblings, I'd just leave her stranded.

It didn't take long to spot the traitorous wench with my brother and sister. Addie held a licorice rope in one hand while holding onto Miss Ruthersford with the other. Benny talked nonstop, a cheesy grin on his face. I hated how she'd wormed her way into their innocent hearts.

Miss Ruthersford stopped abruptly and covered her mouth when she registered the flat tires.

I hopped out of my truck. "My, my. It seems you have a predicament."

She whipped around to face me. "You!"

Addie jerked out of her grip to clobber me with affection. I swung her around before setting her down on the asphalt. Out of the corner of my eye, I noticed Benny sulking.

"How was the movie?" I asked.

"Member me!" Addie barked.

I patted her head. "You forgot something on the side of the road," I said to Miss Ruthersford, "so I brought it to you."

"Member me!" Addie bellowed again.

"You let the air out of our tires," Benny accused.

"Ah, why would you think I'd do something mean like that?" I smirked. "I just happened by and noticed your dilemma. Thought I'd offer assistance."

The girl glanced at Benny and folded her arms. "We don't need your help."

I tipped my hat. "Suit yourself. I'm waiting for a client to call me back. If you need a hand before I leave, let me know."

Back inside my truck, I leaned into my seat and pulled the brim of my hat down to shade my eyes. A couple minutes passed before someone knocked on the window. I tipped my hat and stared down at Benny, who looked like he'd eaten stinkweed.

I rolled down the window. "How'd you like the movie, Big Ben?"

He pouted. "You going to be nice to Liz?"

I shrugged. "I'm here, aren't I? Would you like me to pump up the tires for your girlfriend?"

He scowled. "I want you to fix what you broke."

"How many times do I have to tell you it wasn't me?" Seeing doubt cloud his eyes, I slathered on charm. "Why would I let the air out of your tires and offer to fill 'em up as well? That'd be stupid. I'll be over in a second with my air pump. You're lucky I drove by and saw you guys."

His expression turned skeptical. "Why do you have an air pump?"

I'd forgotten how sharp my brother was. "I always carry one with me, along with a chain for pulling cars out of ditches in the winter. I like to be prepared."

He sighed and motioned me to follow. I grabbed the pump and swaggered over to play hero to tick off the girl.

"Member me!" Addie yelled as Benny tried to wrestle her into the cab.

"Yeah, I'll remember you, Addie. Now get in your seat and stay put."

I plugged the pump into the charger and turned the ignition key. "Sit in there with her so she doesn't run me over, Benny."

He awkwardly climbed in, and I carried the pump to the back and set it next to the tire. I unscrewed the valve and inserted the end of the hose into it, while the girl watched.

"I feel like we got off to a bad start," she said. "Sorry I inadvertently stole your room and left you on the side of the road."

"That wasn't inadvertent."

"Well, no. But in my defense, you acted like a jerk."

I threw her a glare over my shoulder. "Your apology sucks."

She huffed. "Look, I know you did this, so that makes us even."

I checked the pressure gauge. "When you've walked five miles back to the ranch, we'll call it even."

She frowned. That combined with her hair pulled back in a tight bun made her appear like a stern librarian.

"Am I going to have to watch my back now?" she asked.

"Every second, lady. Your innocent act doesn't fool me."

Her brows scrunched together in a way I might find cute if I didn't hate her so much.

"Consider this your warning, Miss Ruthersford, if that's even your name. Don't mess with my family. I'm onto you and will be watching your every move. You should leave while you're ahead."

She marched to the front of the truck.

Had I gotten through to her?

Her door slammed as I began filling the other tire. The girl was a good actor, I'd give her that. But maybe now that she knew I was onto her, she'd vacate our lives. Con-artists needed the element of surprise, and she didn't have that anymore.

19

BENTLEY

A HIGH-PITCHED TRILL sounded above me. I looked up and spotted the iridescent blue-green feathers of a male tree swallow, perched on the nesting box Dad had fastened to the aspen. His white belly jutted out as he chirped, gurgled, and whined a love song. I admired his forked tail and turned back to my pail of slurry. It needed more water.

Right step. Left leg-lift, swing-out, step-down. Wince. I hobbled to the stable to fill my bucket, concentrating on being as fluid as water. Dr. Bowler and I had made dozens of goals over the years, the first being just getting out of bed. That'd taken months to accomplish. I'd worked on walking smoothly for over six.

I set the bucket under the tap and filled it with water. As I stepped and dragged, stepped and dragged, another bluebird flew around the nesting box. I placed the pail down and brushed my hands against my jeans just as my brother emerged from dad's office, looking angrier than a mama grizzly.

"Hey, Rawson." I waved.

He marched over and slammed a fist into the tree, making the swallow fly away. "That woman's nothing but trouble."

"What happened?"

He paced in front of my tarp full of drying bricks. "Dad's gone and put her in charge. He wants me to work as her *apprentice*." He punched the tree again. "He's freaking lost his mind."

"Lizzie has a gift with horses."

He whipped around and fixed me with a scary glare. "Whose side are you on? Don't you get it? Dad put a stranger over me, and a girl to boot."

Liz appeared in our peripheral vision. Rawson hissed and crouched behind a bush. I knelt next to him.

"Dad lit into me like a load of buckshot, telling me to treat her with respect or I'd spend the winter with the cattle."

"Give her a chance. I think you'd like her." Liz was the nicest girl ever.

"Not likely." He tousled my hair.

"Knock it off." I shoved his hand away.

"You're a good kid. I wish I was more like you."

"With a bent neck and spastic leg?"

Rawson's expression shattered before my eyes. "I'm real sorry, Benny."

Ah, crud. I felt like cow dookie for stirring up painful memories. "Don't be." When he looked away, I said, "It's not your fault."

He studied my buildings. "These look futuristic."

Why did he always change topics when we tread too close to sensitive subjects? It'd do us a world of good to delve into them, like a dive into that pool beneath the waterfall was medicine to my sore body after a long ride.

"It's Coruscant," I said.

"I can tell. We should watch *Phantom Menace* tonight to get more ideas."

I refused to discuss trivialities. "Lizzie told me I won't have this bent neck and crooked leg forever. She says after I die, I'll be made whole and—"

"What would she know about the afterlife?"

"She knows plenty since she goes to church."

"You don't need that broad filling your mind with religious fairy tales."

A lump formed in my throat. "You think I'll be like this forever?"

"No!" He swiped a hand over his head. "We don't know the answers to things like that." He growled. "I don't want to talk about her. She's no good."

"Lizzie's all good."

"It's an act, little brother." He stood and dusted off his jeans. "She's trying to wheedle her way into your life so she can take advantage of us." I shook my head, but he patted my back. "You'll see I'm right. I just don't want you hurt when that happens. Be careful."

"Be nice."

Rawson flicked my chin. "Am I ever anything but?"

"You've definitely been a butt lately."

He laughed and messed my hair again.

"Gah!" I pushed him away.

"Mom needs to cut this mop so I don't confuse you for a Wookiee." He sobered. "Serious, Ben. Stay away from Miss Ruthersford. Trust me on this."

My stomach churned as I watched him go. He was the coolest big brother ever, but how could he make me choose between him and Liz? It was like asking me which hand I wanted chopped off. I didn't want to lose either.

20

LIZ

*L*AUGHTER, THE LIKES of which I'd never heard, diverted me from walking out the door. I turned up the hallway, following the sound of infectious giggling. Was Benny playing with his sister? I tiptoed up to the arched entrance of the living room and peeked. My eyes widened. Benny wasn't playing with Addie. His jerk brother was. Rawson was on all fours, encouraging his sister onto his back.

"Now don't let go. Hold on tight."

"Tight!" Addie giggle-grunted.

"Give your horsie a name."

She ran her fingers through his highlighted hair, and Rawson gave her a tender look.

I pulled back sharply. What the heck? I'd worked with him for almost two weeks and had never sensed a hint of kindness in the man. Staying hidden, I bent to watch more of the baffling scene.

"Horsie!" Addie licked a finger and stuck it in his ear.

"Give me a neighhhm."

I cracked a smile. If he wasn't such a poop, I might find the way he treated his handicapped sister sweet. But Rawson was worse than poop. Since Larry had resigned for health reasons and Mr. Law had placed me in charge of the yearlings, Rawson had tempted me to swear daily. He'd been assigned to be my assistant, but so far, he'd only acted like the first three letters of his title. He showed up only half the time and with a belligerent, argumentative attitude. He sabotaged me at every turn. Whatever could go wrong had done so this week, and in a highly suspicious manner. The tack had been moved to the wrong pegs. A truckload of manure had spilled onto the arena. Pine sap had been smeared inside my riding gloves. Cooking oil, reeking of burnt bacon, had replaced the water in my bottle. I still hadn't rid my mouth and nose of that foul taste and odor.

"Barf...Bayer!" Addie must be hard of hearing. She yelled everything.

Rawson snort-laughed. "Call me Barf, sis."

I wanted to call him Barf.

He brought her hands around his neck. "Ready for the ride of your life, cowgirl?"

She giggle-grunted.

"Hold on tight." He reared back on his knees and made realistic horse sounds as he waved his hands in the air like a show-off stallion. Pawing the carpet, he covered the room on all fours in a wild bronco ride that left me envious. I'd been raised as a grown-up from the time I was born— getting pedicures, having my hair styled, going on mall trips for fun. What would it have been like to get a ride like that instead?

Rawson eased to a stop and shuddered like a horse. "Barf's tired. Ready to cool me off? Get the brush."

She climbed off his back and ran to the couch. Hairbrush in hand, she combed not only Rawson's hair, but his face and clothes as well. He stayed on all fours, patiently letting her be Addie.

He winced when she jabbed his eyes with the brush handle. "Don't brush Barf's eyes. Horses don't like that crap." Except he used the naughty word.

"Ship!" And his sister tried to copy him, which made him laugh.

Addie dropped the brush and stretched out below him. She reached up to explore his face, pulling his mouth in weird angles and laughing when he talked through squished lips. When she stuck her fingers up his nose, Rawson grabbed her and rolled onto his back, pulling her on top of him.

"You want a piece of me?"

Addie's whole face smiled. "Piece a me!" Her rough, invasive tickling made him roar with laughter.

I should've given them privacy, but I couldn't tear myself away from the sweet scene. How many adult men played with their sisters like this? It was adorable.

Rawson glanced over his shoulder and spotted me. The scowl he leveled at me sucked happiness from me like an industrial strength vacuum.

I scurried away, chiding myself for being stupid. Now he'd hate me even more, though I didn't know how that was possible. The guy pretty much despised me completely already.

21

RAWSON

*M*Y EYELIDS GREW heavy as I watched the girl from my hiding spot beneath the bleachers. For being a lying, conniving schemer, Miss Ruthersford had an intense work ethic. What I couldn't figure out was why she hadn't gone to my dad and ratted me out yet. I'd been less than the ideal employee since I'd been assigned to work with her, skipping out early and pulling some kick-butt pranks. Yet, she hadn't said a word.

She turned off lights and left the building. I crawled out from under the bleachers and flipped on my flashlight. At Blue Boy's stall, I unlatched his gate and dropped one of the girl's gloves in the aisle. Dad would go ballistic when he discovered that Miss Ruthersford had been careless and forgotten to lock up one of the horses.

"What are you doing?"

I whipped around to be blinded by the beam of another flashlight. "Oh hey, Benny." I shielded my eyes.

"What are you doing?" he repeated.

"I'm just—"

"You're trying to get Lizzie in trouble, aren't you?"

"No." I stepped to the side to dodge his blinding beam. "What are you doing out so late, kid?"

He pointed his flashlight at the ground. "If any horse escapes, I'll know who to blame." He lifted an eyebrow. "And I'll tell Dad what I seen."

Sometimes I hated how sharp my kid brother was. Nothing got past him. "I'll double check all the gates to make certain they're secure."

"Promise?"

"I promise, Sherlock."

He hobbled out, and I relocked the stalls, but felt too keyed up to hit the sack. Damn my sneaky brother. He'd ruined my plan.

I headed to my hammock to blow off steam. Without the moon to light the way, I didn't notice Miss Ruthersford until I almost stepped on her. Luckily, she spoke into her phone and I slipped behind a blue spruce.

"I know. It's just hard." She sniffed as she paced the grassy area below the deck. "No, Daddy. I'm a big girl and can fix my own problems."

I smirked. Big girls didn't call their dads *Daddy*.

"I don't want to discuss it." She sniffled. "I'm not crying. It's allergies."

I'd never noticed her use so much as a Kleenex.

"Fine. I'll tell you, but this doesn't mean I want to come home. The boss's son returned and he's been a big pain in the you-know-what." I grinned. "No, he's not hitting on me. A different kind of pain. He's lazy, rude, and makes tons of work for me." She huffed. "If he liked me, he might be a tiny bit nice, but I just told you—he's a big jerk. His parents stuck me in his room and he didn't know and came barging in— No!" she cried. "Settle down, Daddy. Of course, I was dressed."

I scoffed into my hand.

"No! He's never touched me." She sighed. "Don't worry. Besides him, I love everything about this place. I haven't had time to be sad."

I clenched my teeth. That wasn't what I wanted to hear.

"While I have you on the phone, let me fill you in on my progress."

I pulled out my phone to record her in the darkness. Maybe I could get proof of her scheming to give to Dad. Then he'd have to fire her.

"Aunt Marge and Uncle Floyd are in. They sent three hundred dollars toward the cruise. Aunt Edna only sent a hundred." She giggled at whatever her *daddy* said. "Maddy and Roy promised to send a thousand. I still haven't talked to Uncle Les, but I'm sure I can wheedle a good sum from him, especially if I let it slip how much Maddy and Roy contributed."

She paused. "Don't ask me to do this ever again. A reunion at the park is more my style. But I know Grandpa and Grandma haven't been on a real vacation. Hopefully, they like this. Are you and Mom still planning to go with them? Okay. Yes. I'll try to have the money to you by the end of the month." She groaned. "No. You book the tickets." Pause. "I'm not lying. I really do love it here. Miss you, too, Daddy, but I'm almost twenty. I can't be your little girl forever." She giggled. "Love you more."

As the woman—no girl! She was only nineteen for criminy's sake— crept back inside, I stood next to the spruce, comparing everything she'd said last time to what she'd said tonight and realized I'd jumped to the wrong conclusion. Big time. Miss Ruthersford wasn't the monster I'd imagined.

Still, she'd turned everything upside down around here. I refused to make life easy for her. She'd either earn her position of trust Dad had given her or she'd run back to her daddy crying.

I hoped for the latter.

2 2

BENTLEY

𝒶 POWERFUL GUST OF wind lifted the brim of my baseball cap. Again. Should've worn my Stetson. I pulled it down and urged Han to catch up to Lizzie's three-year-old paint on the hill.

"How much further to the creek?" she asked.

"Quarter hour that way." I pointed east.

We headed up the hill, chatting all the way, and Liz let it slip that it was her birthday.

"Are you kidding?" I said. "Why didn't you say something so I could get you a gift?"

"Your friendship's my gift."

I rolled my eyes. "That's a copout. I'll paint you a picture."

"Deal. I love your art."

"How old are you now?"

She grinned. "I'm not a teenager anymore."

"You're twenty?"

"Yep. I've officially been alive for decades."

I laughed. Talking to her was easy. We discussed ways I could change my status when school started. I didn't want to be known as the handicapped kid. Junior high would be a new beginning. I meant to grab hold of that and ride it hard. Liz encouraged me to get outside myself and help others. Be proactive in doing good and making friends.

I loved being around her—not in an *I want to kiss her* kind of way, although I wouldn't turn one down if she offered. She just felt like a bosom friend, which sounded sappy, but Mom had put on *Anne of Green Gables* for

Addie a couple weeks ago, and I'd been bored enough to watch with her. Sappy words stick to you.

Liz helped me dismount at the stream. I took my boots off to soak my feet while the horses watered. She stretched out beside me and closed her eyes. Strands of hair curled about her face. I loved her hair. I'd only seen her wear it down a few times for church, and she'd looked beyond gorgeous then.

"You think I could go to church with you? If Rawson lets me?" For the past three months, I'd noted her Sunday routine and had hoped she'd invite me to tag along. I'd love any excuse to leave the house.

"Why do you need your brother's permission?"

I shrugged. "He's my bud."

"Well, your bud hates my guts. H-E-double toothpicks will freeze over before he okays that."

How could I change that? Rawson and Lizzie were my two favorite people. They needed to like each other.

"I'd love you to come," she said, "but I don't want to come between you and your brother. If you work it out with him, let me know and you can drive to town with Mackay and me."

She helped me onto my horse, but a gust of wind grabbed my cap. "Crud," I muttered as I watched it perform a Mexican hat dance on its way over a rise. "That was my lucky Red Sox hat."

"I'll get it." Liz mounted the young paint and dug her boots into its side. Shoshone balked, but she brought him under control and guided him after my evasive headgear.

I rode to catch up to her, and saw that she'd managed to corner my cap against a tree near the old homestead.

A loud voice from the shack startled both of us. "Hey, baby."

Lizzie spun around and yelped.

I didn't blame her. The old homestead was creepy. And my brother's friend, Damon, stringy hair hanging to his shoulders, thick mustache drooping over his sneering mouth, ratcheted up the horror element.

What the heck was he doing out here?

Liz grabbed my cap and Shoshone's reins.

"Now, hold on. Don't go." Damon draped himself over the rickety porch railing. "You just got here, sugar. Come on in and stay a while. I'll show you a good time."

Not liking how he looked at her, I nudged Han's side with my boot to move in front of Liz.

"Howz it goin', Benny-hana?" He snorted, as though he'd said something funny. "Who's yer purty friend?"

"Is Rawson here?" That was the only reason I could think for this loser being where he didn't belong.

He pointed at the cabin. "He's still nappin'. We got a bit wild last night, if you know what I mean." He wheeze-laughed.

"Let's get out of here." Liz handed me my hat and mounted her horse.

I spotted my brother and nudged my horse closer, so he'd know I knew he was hiding garbage out here.

"Big Ben." He walked onto the porch and scratched his crotch. "What brings you out to this neck of the woods?"

"My hat blew away. Lizzie chased it."

His enthusiasm cooled as he turned and noticed her by the fence. When she saw him, she turned Shoshone around and began a slow return.

"Roz, ask Benny's gal to stay," Damon whined. "She looks fun."

My brother marched down the steps like a tornado touching down in Kansas. "As fun as falling into a cactus," he muttered.

I cringed in my saddle as he yanked the reins from my hands and tugged Han in front of Damon. "Hold him." He shoved the reins into his friend's hands. He stalked over to Liz. "You have no business being out here. Leave. Now."

I bristled at his angry tone. "Don't talk to her that way. It's her birthday." I struggled to grab the reins from Damon, but he held them out of reach.

"What about Ben?" I heard her ask.

"I'll bring him home. Now shoo." Rawson whacked Shoshone's buttocks. "Yaw!"

Lizzie's touchy mount lunged, making her scramble with the reins and hunch over to keep from falling. I fisted my hands as I watched her disappear into the trees.

"Jerk!" I kicked at Rawson as he took my reins from Damon. "Let me go. I don't want to stay here."

"Settle down, kid." He tied the rope to the railing.

"Why'd you make Liz go?"

He hissed under his breath as Damon repeated her name. Wrapping an arm around his loser friend's shoulders, he led him up the stairs. I glared at his back, wishing I could dismount. But no, I had to sit and wait for him to untie my horse and lead me home, like a kid at a pony party.

On the ride home, he made excuses. "Damon and I just met up this morning. Thought we'd hang out for a while, for old time's sake."

I didn't respond.

"Come on, Benny. Don't be mad."

I refused to speak to him. At the house, he lifted me from my horse and held my shoulders. "I wish you'd talk to me, kid."

My lips curled. "I can't believe you're still hanging out with that doo-doo head." I shrugged out of his arms and hobbled to the porch.

71

"Benny?" I almost turned, but his next words stopped me cold. "Damon's always had my back. Please don't blame him."

My jaw felt like it might snap. "I'll always blame him." I hobbled through the door, furious that he dared ask such a thing after what his stupid friend had done to our family.

23

RAWSON

$\mathcal{M}$Y BROTHER WAS ticked at me, and Miss Ruthersford was to blame. Everything had been fine until she'd started working here, and now nothing was right. So, she wasn't a con-artist out to swindle my family. But she'd snooped where she shouldn't, and now Damon had become obsessed with her.

What a nightmare.

Before I'd left the homestead, I'd told Damon to stay put, promising to send Chance out with a sack of groceries and a case of beer. "That'll get you by until we can rustle up some gals for the weekend." I'd promise him anything to keep him away from the crank.

"I want Benny's girl," he'd said.

I'd cursed the lousy timing of her and Benny showing up. "She's a hired hand, dude. Leave her be. We don't need Dad catching wind you're out here." His leer as I'd ridden away still haunted me. He'd probably been lusting after that troublesome girl.

What if she ratted me out to Dad? Just another reason, on top of a mountain of others, why she needed to go.

I entered the arena and spotted the object of my irritation. Miss Ruthersford glanced up from brushing a horse.

"So you decided to show up. What gives?"

"You may dispense with the pleasantries, commander." I paused to breathe heavy, like Darth Vader. "I'm here to put you back on schedule."

She didn't crack a smile. "I could've used your help the last two weeks, but I'm fine now. Maybe your dad can utilize your on-again/off-again skills with the cattle."

Time to lay on the charm. "Sorry about yesterday." She scowled. "My friend gets crude around pretty girls. I was afraid he'd mouth off and offend you. That's why I asked you to leave."

"Asked?" She huffed. "You ordered me to leave and almost made me fall off Shoshone by swatting him."

"Nah. You're too good a rider for that." Flattery worked wonders with the weaker gender. "But will you forgive me?" Humility worked where flattery didn't.

She averted her eyes, making me realize I'd gone about getting rid of her all wrong. Instead of fighting her, I should embrace her. After all, females tended to lose their heads around me. She didn't appear any different.

I swaggered over and grabbed the curry comb from her hand. "Let me finish brushing him. I owe you for slacking off."

Her big, brown eyes met mine. I swallowed and reminded myself how Benny had acted on the ride home. He hadn't said one word, except to lam-blast my friend. Puberty had made him stubborn, but Librarian Liz had magnified his negative traits.

"I'm taking Benny kayaking this Saturday for an early birthday present. He mentioned it was your birthday yesterday. Want to join us?"

"Uh, I don't think so." Her bossy, serious attitude had disappeared.

"Oh, come on. Benny would love it." He really would. I could already imagine how the day would play out. My brother would throw all his attention her way, and I'd be left with nada, zip, zilch.

She still acted hesitant, so I tossed out more crumbs. "The lake is one of the most spectacular settings within two hundred miles. You haven't really lived until you see it." I kept brushing the mare's glistening coat.

"Are you sure?" She chewed her lips. "I don't want to take away from Benny's special day."

"You won't. He'll be thrilled to have someone around to show off for."

Her lips twitched, and I saw a hint of a smile. "Okay. If you're sure. I'm a sucker for beautiful places."

And faces, I added silently.

74

24

LIZ

*D*ARKNESS STILL BLANKETED the ranch as I approached Rawson's massive black beast. Benny had said his brother had purchased the decked-out truck as a welcome home present for himself. Who did that? Though I found the man extremely vain, I had to admit he struck a powerful image in the vehicle.

"Morning, Miss Ruthersford." He leaned out his window on a muscled arm.

His greeting sounded condescending, but I imbued mine with cheer. "Good morning." I hoped to get past our earlier enmity and become friends, or at least non-fighting acquaintances.

"Did you get the mucking done?"

I sensed subtle mockery. "The arena's done. Chance will finish the rest after breakfast."

"I wish I could bat my eyelashes and get someone to do my chores," he said with a mischievous twinkle in his gorgeous eyes.

Irritating man. "You don't have to bat your eyelashes, Mr. Law. You just get in your truck and drive off to who knows where to get out of work."

He smirked. *"Touché."*

I hopped in the backseat to avoid any more conversation with the unsettling man.

"Hey, Lizzie." Benny hobbled toward us.

"Hurry up, slowpoke," Rawson called.

I thought Ben would get in front with his brother, but he climbed in the back with me.

"What am I? The chauffeur?" Rawson quipped. "There's plenty of room up here."

"You can sit with your brother," I said to Benny.

"I want to sit with you." He made a goofy face, making me laugh.

Rawson bristled in the front seat. My first experience with him as the driver had been awful. Today wasn't much better. Even hauling two kayaks, the speedometer needle rested above seventy on the dirt road. To take my mind off my teeth jarring into my nasal cavity, I made small talk.

"How far is this lake?"

Rawson shrugged. "Maybe forty miles as the crow flies."

"It'll take us a little over an hour to drive there." Benny's answer was more helpful. "The last twenty miles aren't much more than a game trail."

My stomach protested. Maybe I should've found out those details before I'd agreed to this trip.

"It's my favorite spot," Benny said. "The lake's surrounded by snow-covered mountains. The water's crystal blue and beyond beautiful. Isn't that right, Rawson?"

"Sure, kid."

"How long will it take to kayak across it?" I asked.

"As long as it does," Rawson said.

I gritted my teeth. He sucked.

"It's been a few years," Benny said, "but if I remember right, it took us an hour or two. Isn't that so, Rawson?"

"I guess." Mr. Vague didn't seem interested in conversing.

I focused my attention out the window. With the temperature dropping at night, leaves had started changing. I couldn't help but compare this majestic Montana autumn to the monochromatic Vegas ones I'd known. I dozed since I'd been up since four to muck stalls.

When the truck stopped, I sat up and looked out the window. Benny hadn't been lying. The setting was gorgeous.

Rawson unlashed the kayaks and dragged them to the shore. His contagious grin energized me as I stared at the serene lake. Benny and I took the double kayak. Rawson followed in the smaller one. It took us about an hour to paddle to a distant island.

Rawson beached his kayak and helped pull ours up onto the bank. He even helped me out so I didn't get wet. Maybe he wasn't the arrogant jerk I'd judged him to be.

The brothers traded jokes while we ate cold chicken and potato chips. Rawson unfastened his watch and set it on the blanket next to a pocket toolkit. Both brothers started stripping, and I found it impossible not to stare. Rawson's toned arms and chiseled abs did weird things to me.

"Want to jump in with us, Miss Ruthersford? There's nothing more refreshing than a dip in a mountain lake." He waggled dark brows.

My whole body seemed to blush. "I'll pass."

To resist gawking, I stretched out on the blanket and listened to the brothers splash and play like little boys. When I heard them getting out, I carried towels over to them.

"How was the water?"

"Fr-fr-freezing," Benny said with a blue-lipped grin.

Rawson puffed out his chest. "You should've joined us."

I studied the wildflowers at my feet. "I don't do freezing."

"What about hot?" When I glanced back at him, he winked and flexed his biceps.

"Uh, no. I like things just right."

"Like Goldilocks?" He tugged a frizzy curl loose from my ponytail.

"Stop." I batted his hand away.

He smiled, and dang. Just dang! My insides melted like butter on toast. His expression combined adorable, sexy, and mischievous all together.

"Do you mind taking the single back?" he asked. "I'd like to spend time with my brother, since you got him on the way here."

It sounded fair. "Sure."

Within minutes, he had Benny in the double kayak and pushed off into the lake. I watched them go, admiring Rawson's wide, muscular shoulders as he paddled. He reminded me of a strapping island warrior.

I grabbed the blanket. A watch and toolkit tumbled to the ground. Rawson's. He'd forgotten them. I chucked them into the hatch and positioned the kayak so the end rested in the grass. Rawson had done that. I crawled inside and dug my paddle into earth, but I might as well have pushed Mount Everest as to move my kayak off the embankment.

I crawled out and moved the boat all the way into the water. Jumping, as I'd seen Rawson do, sent me toppling over the other side.

Fr-fr-freezing, as Benny had put it, didn't come close to describing the needling pain as I sputtered and floundered against the steep bank for a foothold. My kayak floated gracefully into deeper water.

I pulled myself up onto the grass with the grace of a beached whale and heard Rawson's bellowing laughter in the distance.

That's when I knew the no-good cowboy had planned this and wouldn't return to my aid. So much for him being an honorable island warrior. The man had embraced the DRK-SID, as his personalized license plate attested.

I recalled his excitement as he'd pulled the kayaks off the truck earlier. He hadn't been thrilled about the alpine scenery or spending quality time with his brother. He hadn't been anxious to use his muscles in sport, either. And he most certainly hadn't been eager to spend time with me. Why had I even considered that a possibility? He'd only been waiting for the right moment to exact revenge, and I'd fallen right into the dumb jerk's trap.

I jumped back into the frigid lake to retrieve my escaping kayak and drag it back to the island. It took two more attempts before I managed to stay inside. Sadly, I left my paddle behind and had to hand-propel the boat back for another attempt.

On my last jump, I stayed in the kayak and kept hold of the paddle. I thought I was home free but discovered Benny must've done all the steering as we'd navigated to the island, because with me at the helm or paddle or whatever one called the steering mechanism of a kayak, I traveled in circles. When I did manage forward progress, the kayak moved in inefficient zigzag lines.

The kayak with Benny and Rawson disappeared around a bend, and I freaked out. Never had I been alone in the great outdoors. In a lake!

I jabbed my oar into the water, trying to row faster. Rawson might leave me if I didn't catch up. My mind conjured up crazy scenarios of bears swimming out to eat me. Or a giant fish capsizing my kayak. No way could I doggy paddle to shore. I despised Rawson for putting my life at risk, but I was even more annoyed that I'd been gullible enough to make this moment possible for him.

I finally rounded the bend and whimpered. The shore where we'd parked looked miles away. And now I fought a headwind. Maybe Rawson had summoned it with his evil powers. Waves made the earlier lake of glass a choppy assembly line of death. I tried to steer into them but kept getting turned sideways and wobbling as each crest took my kayak up and threw me down into a trough of icy terror.

Rain pelted my face, and I knew the man must control the elements. I dropped my paddle and buried my face in my blistered hands. Sobs racked my body until I imagined Rawson Law laughing at my predicament.

Adrenaline shot through my limbs. I swiped at tears and raised my paddle. Glaring at the ominous sky that reminded me of Rawson's stormy eyes, I yelled, "You won't stop me."

Hail began falling, as if to punish me for my defiance. I cringed and yelped as ice pellets battered my tender skin. If I ever made it back alive, I vowed to never be gullible again. Going by how every muscle in my body screamed, that was a very big IF looming over me.

The hail stopped soon after it started. Thank heavens. Chaotic curls wedged between my cracked lips. I spit them out and shoved the paddle down right, then hard left.

I almost cried when I spotted a miniature Benny on the shoreline. But I refused to give Rawson the satisfaction of seeing my emotions. With each circular arm motion, muscles screamed, but at least, with my destination in sight, if I died, someone would know my watery fate. Better than being eaten by a bear or drowned in the middle of the lake alone.

Perspective.

25

BENTLEY

*a*s Lizzie's kayak approached, I could tell she'd been crying. Glancing at my brother napping under a tarp, I wished to kick his sorry backside. I waded awkwardly into the shallows to grab the carrying handle of her kayak. Though my leg and neck ached, I gritted my teeth and lugged her to shore.

"Rawson wouldn't let me go back. I tried to stop him, but—"

"It's all right, Benny." She wobbled on her legs. Red welts dotted her arms from that freak hailstorm earlier.

"I didn't know he'd leave you. I should never have gone with him."

She touched my cheek. "Don't worry about it. I'm here."

"What took you so long, Miss Ruthersford? We've been waiting for hours." We flinched at Rawson's sarcastic voice.

"I didn't know we were on a timeline, Mr. Law."

I grinned at Lizzie. Rawson liked sass in his women.

"You look like a drowned kitten."

"Someone told me there's nothing better than a dip in a mountain lake." Pushing past him, she headed to the truck.

Rawson took hold of the kayak and dragged the orange beast behind him with ease. "Miss Ruthersford?"

She stopped, but didn't turn around. "What, Mr. Law?"

He held up his knife. "Was my Leatherman on the blanket?"

"Yep."

"Was my watch with it?"

"Yep." She opened the back passenger door of the truck.

"Well, where is it?"

"Don't know, don't care."

Judging by how red my brother's face turned, he didn't like her answer. "Where's my freaking watch?" he said, except he dropped a nuclear F-bomb.

"I threw it in the lake." She didn't sound sorry.

I gnawed my lower lip.

"You threw my Swiss watch in the lake?"

She gave him a gloating smile.

"Do you have any idea how much that cost, you...?" I thought he might call her a nasty name, but he bit his tongue.

"No idea. But it couldn't have been worth much if you left it on the blanket and took off like you did."

Rawson's jaw twitched.

"I'm sure your daddy will buy you another next time he goes to Walmart," she cooed. "If you're a good boy, maybe he'll throw in a *Star Wars* figurine for your collection, too."

I snickered.

Rawson kicked the kayak. "You can walk home, Miss Smart Ass."

I hobbled over to stand beside her. A united front. "If Lizzie walks home, so do I."

"Either shut him up or shut him down." I recognized Han's quote about C-3PO but didn't say so. Rawson seemed ready to erupt. "Get in the truck, Benny."

"Go to hell."

Lizzie squeezed my arm. "Watch your language."

"Sorry." I lifted my sore neck and met my brother's angry gaze. "The devil wouldn't want you, you're so mean. Go ahead. Leave." I grabbed Lizzie's hand. "We know the way home."

I dragged her though tall grass to reach the road. No doubt we'd have to do a tick check when we got home in a week.

Right step. Left leg-lift, swing-out, step-down. I bit my lip to keep from crying. Maybe Liz would be kind and bury me along the journey. Each step sent razor sharp pain shooting up my thigh and into my back. I'd overdone it. But Liz needed me, and I absolutely refused to leave her.

After a dozen steps, she dug in her heels. "Ben, go with your brother. I can tell you're hurting."

"I'm not leaving you again."

"She's right, bro." Rawson said. "You need to get off your leg." I turned to glare at him. "Miss Ruthersford can come, too. You don't think I'd really leave her, do ya? Though that watch cost more than she'll make all year."

I crawled inside the cab, my leg throbbing so bad I didn't know if I'd make it home without crying. But my feelings hurt worse. I hated my brother for ruining my birthday trip with that dirty trick on Lizzie.

Why was he such a big dummy-head?

2 6

RAWSON

*E*NTERING THE STABLE, I spotted the girl leading that new black
around the arena. Chance, one of the hands, held up the walls,
watching her with a goofy grin. I marched over and slapped his back.

"Hey, Rawson." He straightened and showed more teeth than I
thought possible. "Didn't hear you come in. What's up?"

The girl's gaze flicked my way, but she turned up her nose and ignored
me. She'd mastered that move.

"The sky." I approached my stubborn boss. "I'm here. You can hit the
play button now and let the good times roll."

"Your head's going to roll if you don't get to work," she said. "You're
three hours late."

"Needed my beauty sleep." I waggled my brows. "Looks like you
could've used more yourself."

She snapped the lead rope a little harder. "Grab Yakama Yoda."

I frowned and left to saddle the two-year-old roan. If I wanted a chance
to show Dad what I could do, I needed to ramp up my game to get her to
throw in the towel. The girl had surprising tenacity.

For the next hour, I made rude comments and argued constantly, but
she didn't bite. Desperate to get a rise out of her, I strode over to the tall
gray's stall and unlatched his gate.

"Let's work this guy." We'd purchased Sidekick Shooter weeks ago.
The stallion was wilder than a cougar on crack.

"Absolutely not. He's still adjusting. I sense so much anger in him."

I snorted. "You sound like Yoda. The only thing I sense is that he needs
boundaries." I held up an arm and flexed. "Muscle can tame any horse,

but a delicate thing like you wouldn't know that, would you? Why, you can't even steer a kayak in a straight line."

Her scowl revealed I was getting under her skin. Finally.

"With my skills and these bad boys," I paused to kiss each bicep, "I'll be riding this cuss in under ten minutes."

"Do you have a death wish?" she asked as I led Shooter from his stall. "Put him back."

I waved a hand in front of her. "Your mind powers won't work on me. Now watch and learn, you will." I began saddling the stallion. Shooter took a chunk of skin off my arm as I brought the bit to his mouth.

"You're making him angry."

"You're doing the same to me, woman. Either help me saddle him or zip it."

She folded her arms. "I'm ordering you to put him away."

"Don't pull the boss card on me, Goldilocks."

I maneuvered the headpiece over the stallion's ears and yanked the gray to show who held the reins. He only needed a firm hand. Leading him into the arena, I mounted and held on as the wild cuss reared in an attempt to dislodge me.

"Rawson!" Miss Rutherford yelped.

I grinned and brought the reins back sharply, reminding the spirited stallion who was in charge. He shuddered and settled into a gorgeous canter.

"See. There's nothing to it if you have some force behind your commands," I yelled over my shoulder.

Shooter had an energetic gait. I loved my horses and women a little on the wild side. We rounded the last corner and Shooter reared up and bucked simultaneously. The athletic move, combined with the element of surprise, displaced me like a rodeo pro.

I caught a blur of movement from Lizzie's direction as I hung suspended in air, before smashing into wood shavings. My life flashed before my eyes as air whooshed from my lungs and hoofs thundered next to my ears.

This is it! I thought as twelve hundred pounds of horseflesh struck the ground beside me. *I'm a dead man.* Any second a hoof would crash through my skull.

"Easy, boy." Lizzie's soothing voice entered the chaos of whirling dust and kicking legs. I heard a shrill neigh and a thudding whump against the gate, followed by a grunt.

Had the loco stallion crushed her?

"It's all right, boy," she soothed. "I'm not going to hurt you."

My frozen lungs relaxed as the stallion moved away from my fetal form. I lifted my head to see Miss Ruthersford lead the skittish beast to the gate and secure him. She turned, and I noticed blood streaming down her forehead. I rolled into a sitting position and opened my mouth to ask if she was okay, but my tongue wouldn't work.

"Are you hurt?" Her voice sounded small and scared.

I still heard beating hoofs in my ears and felt a taunting death dance in my heart, but she was the one bleeding. I struggled to form words, but there was too much to say. I wanted to apologize for being a world-class jerk. Needed to thank her for risking her neck for me. Mostly, I yearned for a do-over. But all I could manage was to raise a feeble thumb.

Her brown eyes glistened in the florescent light as blood trickled down her cheek. She huffed and grabbed the reins, marching away with the horse from hell.

As I considered how close I'd come to going there myself, I began to tremble. If Liz hadn't read the signs and raced to my aid as quickly as she had, I'd be dead. I knew it. The courage she'd displayed filled me with shame for every mean thing I'd ever believed, done, or said to her. I glanced around to ensure I was alone before standing on wobbly legs.

Somehow, I made it out of there and saddled Bayder. Once my trusty steed was ready, I dug the heels of my boots into his sides and galloped into the hills to escape my prickling conscience.

SHAPING HOPE

Let your hopes, not your hurts, shape your future.

~ Robert H. Schuller ~

BENTLEY

*A*s Lizzie and I finished breakfast, Rawson ran out and caught us in the hallway. I didn't even know he was there until Liz stopped talking and glared at someone behind me. I looked over my shoulder, and there my brother stood, holding his Swiss watch.

"I found this in your kayak," he said. "Stuck in the back compartment."

Lizzie made a face. "Guess your daddy won't have to drive to Walmart to replace it."

I thought Rawson might get mad, but he only chuckled. "No, he won't, though I still wouldn't mind a *Star Wars* action figure." He grabbed her hand.

She growled and tried to pull away, but he pried her fingers open and placed the watch in her palm.

"I want you to have it."

A fly could've flown in my mouth. Rawson loved that watch. It'd cost him eight grand in Switzerland and was his favorite souvenir he'd brought home.

"I don't want your stupid watch," Lizzie said. "I wish I'd thrown it in the lake."

Maybe she didn't realize how much it cost.

Rawson grinned. "Would've served me right."

Liz gave me a look that seemed to say *What in the heck's wrong with your dumb brother?*

I shrugged to say *Beats me.*

"Look," he said, "I'm real sorry for leaving you stranded in the kayak, and I'm super sorry for yelling at you about my watch. I was out of line."

"You're always out of line."

He gazed down at her and smiled. "The watch is yours."

"Why in the world would I want a man's watch?"

"Keep it to remember how stupid I am."

Her lips twitched. "I don't need a watch for that. I just have to look at your face." She tried once more to hand it back, but he shook his head

"Keep it as a token of my apology. And a thank you for saving my life," he added as he glanced at the bandage above her eye.

I perked up. Lizzie had saved his life?

"I'm calling a truce."

She rubbed the stainless steel band. "It's too big for my wrist."

He turned to leave. "I don't expect you to wear it, Miss Ruthersford. Just keep it to remember I'm truly sorry for how I treated you. I promise to behave better in the future."

When we were alone, she whispered, "Your brother's an idiot."

I snorted. "Tell me something I don't know."

LIZ

*M*Y PHONE VIBRATED in my back pocket as I ran Peaches in the round pen. "Who in the world's calling me?" I muttered as I brought the mare to a halt. I grabbed my phone, but frowned at Rawson's face on the screen. What did he want?

"Hey." I lifted my arm to wipe sweat from my brow.

"Dad just called and wants us to show some horses to a friend of his from back east who's flying into Bozeman this afternoon. He reserved the MSU arena for us, so meet me at the big stable in fifteen minutes."

"Why can't you take Seth or Chance? I'm busy." I'd never met out-of-town clients and didn't relish the thought of starting now. I worked well with horses, not people.

"Too busy to do what the boss-man says?"

I chewed on my lips, not knowing what to say to that.

"Dad wants to unload Arabella off on him. Guess the guy's loaded. You need to come in case Bella gets in one of her moods."

I didn't want to drive to Bozeman and blow my schedule to pieces for a high-pedigreed hormonal mare...or man. Rawson Law made me crazy. One minute I wished he'd break a leg so I wouldn't have to work with him, the next, I'd saved his sorry hide from certain death. That tall gray would've made mincemeat of him three days ago if I hadn't intervened. Those hooves had stamped right next to his handsome face, yet he'd walked away without a scratch. I hadn't been as lucky. Shooter had thrown me against the gate and had split my eyebrow open before I'd been able to get a firm grip on his reins.

I'd thought my heroics and blood donation would've earned a simple

Thank You from the arrogant cowboy, but Rawson Law refused to stoop to such civilized behavior. The jerk had disappeared, leaving all the work to me again, and then had handed me his glitzy watch two days ago and considered us even. As if a stupid watch equated to saving his life. He'd probably planted the showy timepiece on me so he could have me arrested for stealing it.

"I'll be done loading horses soon, so get a move on it, boss." The dang ornery cowboy hung up before I could protest.

I stomped my boot.

Fifteen minutes later, when I met Rawson at his truck, he raised a brow. "Guess I should've told you to spruce up a bit."

I shoved past him. "We're not heading to a beauty pageant."

"Yeah, but Dad said this guy's big in the horse world."

I opened the passenger door and climbed inside. "Then he'll understand manure on my boots." I slammed the door.

He jumped in beside me. Silence tensed like a balloon too full to hold one more puff of air. I peeked to see why he hadn't started the engine and found him staring at me.

"What are you looking at?" I tried to sound tough, but failed, judging by his laughter.

"You're adorable."

"Shut up. You just told me I looked like crap."

"I said no such thing."

"You said I should've spruced up."

"You're a mite dusty, but nothing a little brushing off won't fix." He winked. "I'll volunteer for the job."

I folded my arms. "Just drive, will you?"

He pulled away from the ranch, and I sighed. This would be a long ride. A few miles down the road, I cringed when he opened his mouth again.

"When I mentioned sprucing up, I didn't mean you looked bad."

Breathe in...hold. Exhale all doubts. Breathe in the good...hold. I focused negative energy into each exhalation since the man beside me wouldn't shut up.

"You look great, except for the ponytail."

I narrowed my eyes. "And what else do you find wrong with me, oh, mighty model boy? I'm waiting with bated breath to hear my faults."

He had the decency to squirm. "Just your ponytail."

The deluge I'd been holding back spewed out in a flood. "Let me give you the rest so you don't feel the need to remind me of them later. I'm too skinny, I have big feet, I bite my nails, I'm small-chested, my hair frizzes, my lips are too thin, my chin's too pointy, I have an obnoxious laugh."

His hand covered mine, and I realized he'd stopped the truck in the middle of the road.

"Where is this all coming from?" He tilted my chin. "I don't know who told you all that, but they must've been jealous. I'd call your chin perky. And you're not skinny, you're willowy. I've never noticed your big feet, but don't know why I'd care unless I was a bug about to be squashed by your boot."

I bit back a smile.

"What else did you say?" His grin turned mischievous as he looked south. "Your girls are just fine, like your chin."

I sputtered and pushed his head up into a proper position.

He chuckled. "Your lips," he traced them, making goosebumps form all the way down my arms, "are just right. You don't want no Angelina Jolie's hanging out there to catch flies, do you?"

I laughed, and he gave me a tender smile that stopped me cold. It wasn't the cocky one he usually sported or the mischievous one. Not even his sexy one. I'd only seen him smile this way at his sister. He ran a finger over the bandage above my eye, the one I'd earned saving his stupid life.

My body went nuts, tingling and jingling like a Vegas casino. If I'd been thinking straight, I would've smacked his fingers and not been tempted by the devil. I'd always believed Satan was real, and if he showed himself to mortals it wouldn't be in some demonic form with horns and a creeper-stache. Rather, he'd take on the form of the hottest man alive, one like Rawson Law with his luscious lips, captivating Caribbean blue-green eyes, and just enough stubble to make a girl all weak-kneed. Who could say no to temptation like that? You'd have to be saint-sitized to resist a man who looked like Rawson Law when he acted all tender and sweet, which I'd never been on the receiving end of so far.

"I like your laugh and your nubby nails. And when you get on a horse and ride, I think you're the most beautiful sight I've ever seen."

My breath hitched in my throat as he pulled the elastic from my hair, letting crazy curls tumble over my shoulders. I self-consciously smoothed them back to pen up again.

He caught my hands. "No, leave it. Your hair's gorgeous."

He had to be kidding. Suddenly, it dawned on me that he was totally messing with me. His words were a joke.

Mortified that I'd been played, I pulled away from his taunting hand. "We're going to be late." I folded my arms over my small, non-perky, chest.

"You okay?" he asked as he accelerated. He almost sounded like he cared, but I wouldn't be fooled twice.

"Where's my elastic?"

He lowered his window, making curls whip about my face.

"Give me my hair band."

Rawson waved my elastic in front of me. I reached for it. But he tossed the black band out the window before I could snatch it from him.

I punched his shoulder. "I needed that to hold back this mess."

"Believe me, I did you a favor."

I huffed and ignored him until we arrived at the campus. We met the Lincolns—father and daughter who owned a horse-racing business in Kentucky—and set to work. Or rather I did. Rawson preened like a peacock for Mr. Lincoln's daughter, who had to be thirty, if she was a day. Though she claimed to be country, her thick makeup, stylish clothes, and gaudy jewelry screamed city-bred princess. Mom would've loved her.

I had the unfortunate luck to stand beside her as Rawson rode past on Admiral Rackbar, an athletic black gelding I adored. She clapped and squealed like a high school cheerleader hyped up on Mountain Dew.

"That man is so scrumptious. I'd love to—" I won't repeat the rest of her crude monologue. I must've hissed, because she turned to me. "Oh, sorry, honey. Are you two a *thang*?"

"Most definitely not."

Her tittering laughter was phonier than her eyelashes. "I knew that, hun. I'm just playing." Her snide jab stung.

Rawson rode up to us and stopped. She fluttered her eyelashes and kicked into cougar mode, rubbing his leg and speaking in a breathy voice.

"I love the horse, but I only want him if it comes with you attached, sugar." Her hands moved up his powerful thigh. "Seriously, if you want a change of scenery, you have a job at our racing facility…and whatever else you want."

I made a hasty exit and began to saddle Houdini to be ridden next. Rawson sidled up behind me, scaring me out of my boots as he grabbed me around the waist.

"Play along," he whispered. "This woman's a nightmare." He kissed my cheek and stood tall again, clasping my hand in his.

The busty blonde gaped at us.

"Hey, sweetheart," Rawson said, "come on back and keep Kelsey company while I talk business with her father. We're done looking at horses. He wants Admiral and Bella."

The blonde's eyes narrowed. "You told me you two weren't an item."

Rawson's hand clenched mine.

"You asked if we were a *thing*," I said, trying to help him for some inexplicable reason, "and we're not. *Thing* implies an inanimate object. We don't use such sterile words to talk about relationships out here in the West. We're a couple."

He wrapped an arm around me and chuckled. I froze, even as my body buzzed as though an electrical current zipped through my veins. His hand dropped to my waist, keeping the current alive.

"Lizzie's an English major. Takes words way too literally. Drives me bonkers." He leaned down to plant another kiss on my cheek. "But I love her, crazy, analytical mind and all."

I scowled. He'd totally used me to save his arrogant neck, and now had the audacity to mock me? I wanted to smack him, but instead, found myself enduring the bimbo's company as Rawson finalized the sale with Mr. Lincoln in an air-conditioned office downstairs.

Miss Hoochie ramped up the crass factor once we were alone. "How's that man in bed, hun?" She fanned herself.

I pushed an obnoxious curl behind my ear. "We don't believe in premarital sex. We're saving ourselves until marriage."

A wicked gleam sparked in her overdone eyes. "You mean Rawson Law's a virgin?"

"A virgin piña colada." It was the only drink I could think of offhand. "I need to start loading horses. Nice to meet you, Miss Lincoln." A bold-faced lie if ever I told one.

I'd finished loading the last horse when Rawson wrapped his arms around me again. I jumped as he nestled his stubbled chin into my neck.

"You ready to go, babycakes?"

Goosebumps erupted as he rubbed his chin against my neck. I tried to escape, but Blondie stood nearby and Rawson acted for all he was worth. Twisting me, he pulled me close and leaned in for a kiss. Before his lips could make contact, I covered my mouth. At this angle, the bimbo couldn't tell he kissed the back of my hand quite passionately. Thank goodness, for small mercies. I might've passed out if he'd gone at my lips with such gusto.

He paused to wink at me.

"I hate your guts," I whispered.

"I know." He grabbed my slobbery hand and said over his shoulder, "Pleasure meeting you, Miss Lincoln." He doffed his hat and opened the door of his flashy truck. "There you go, sweetheart."

When he climbed in beside me, I hauled off and punched his leg. "I can't believe you kissed my hand like that."

"I was going for your lips."

"Gross!"

He glanced out the window. Catching Kelsey watching us like lab rats, he leaned over to peck my cheek.

"Kiss me again and I'll deck you," I said between clenched teeth.

"It might be worth it, especially if you move your hand."

I huffed.

He pulled away from the arena. "I owe you big time for saving me from that blond nightmare. Thanks for playing along."

"You kind of forced me to."

"Did you see her face when you said all that garbage about what thing implied? I found it difficult to keep a straight face."

I stuck my tongue out, making him chortle.

"Ah, Lizzie, you're all right."

"And you're an idiot."

He grabbed my hand. "How about we stop for ice cream? You deserve something decadent for your acting skills."

I pulled my fingers away. "Just get me home."

He pouted, which looked extremely good on him.

We left Bozeman behind, and I couldn't help but notice how he squirmed like a five-year-old needing a bathroom break. Maybe he did. I certainly wouldn't ask.

I stared out the window, pretending he wasn't there. Unfortunately, he was like a scratch on a disc. I couldn't stop replaying how arousing his stubbly jaw had felt against my neck. An evil part of me wished I'd let him kiss me for real. I doubted I'd get a chance like that again.

The truck pulling onto the side of the road snapped me out of my wicked trance. Rawson threw the truck into park and hopped out. He stood in the middle of the road and ripped off his shirt.

I gasped. "What are you doing?"

Air stuck in my throat as he glanced up at me. The sight of his wide shoulders, muscular arms, and toned pecs flooded my body with delicious warmth. Wicked warmth, surely. Yet, I couldn't tear my gaze away.

"I need to change shirts or I'll lose my mind. That's why I wanted to stop at DQ." He pointed to my boots. "Reach under your seat and grab my duffel."

What a strange man. I handed him his bag, keeping my focus on his face, not his hot body. He pulled out a silky red shirt. Although the material seemed feminine, it looked amazing once it outlined his ripped muscles.

"Why do you change so much?"

He shrugged. "A glitch in my system. Clothes itch. Sweat magnifies the sensation. Trust me. I'll drive safer with a fresh shirt."

"So you're not just vain?"

He snort-laughed. "Oh, I'm vain. But my body also has a psycho sensitivity to detergents and materials. I'm afraid right now, this is necessary for my sanity...and your safety." He gestured to the new shirt he wore.

"Sounds horrible."

"I'm used to it." His dazzling eyes took on a mischievous glint. "Did you really tell Kelsey I was a virgin?"

Heat licked my cheeks. How had he found out about that?

He laughed. "No wonder she pulled me aside all hot and bothered. You made me that much more enticing by telling her I was an innocent."

I turned to look out the window.

"She wanted to dig her claws into a fresh slab of meat."

"Shut up." I smacked the seat between us. "You're such a fruitcake."

"A fruitcake?" He laughed. "I've never been called *that* before." He hopped back in, and I relaxed. Saving his life had reaped some benefits.

BENTLEY

*T*HE SUN WELCOMED me with a spectacular color show. Today, I was going to church with Lizzie. And Rawson. I still didn't know what to think about my brother joining us. He'd never showed an interest in church before, so why had he offered to drive us?

I waited in the entryway for Liz and heard the rumble of Rawson's diesel truck as it pulled up to the house. Good timing. I adjusted my red power tie and caught a flash of blue on the stairs. Lizzie descended in a turquoise-colored dress that hugged all her curves.

"Yowza."

She pushed curls over her shoulder. "You look handsome, Ben. I've never seen you all gussied up like this."

"Thanks." I took her hand and walked outside. At least, with Rawson driving, I didn't have to endure a boring ride with that lame Mackay Benson.

I climbed into the middle seat, and Rawson smirked.

"Don't you look like a silly fool in your ape suit."

"Who's more foolish? The fool or the fool who follows him?"

"Good one." He raised his hand for a high five.

Lizzie's dress snagged on the seat as she climbed in, revealing her upper legs. I turned my head like a gentleman, but Rawson grinned as she scrambled to get modest.

I tried to distract him. "What are you? One of Jabba's sideshows?" My brother's Wranglers, burgundy dress shirt, and shimmery silver tie were quite gaudy. "I told you to wear a white shirt and slacks."

"I liked this better. And you have to admit, this tie is amazing. I picked it up in Italy." He pulled out. "And these are my good jeans. No holes."

"Because you ain't holy."

"Ha ha." He slugged my arm.

He turned onto the dirt lane and began driving like the devil chased him. Or the cops.

Lizzie clutched the hand hold. "Slow down."

Rawson increased his speed. "Traveling through hyperspace ain't like dustin' crops, girl." When he winked, I chuckled.

"You're freaking me out."

"Loosen up, sweetheart. I'm the best driver this side of the Mississippi." To prove his point, he slammed on the brakes and spun us in the middle of the road. Dust stirred up like a cyclone as we came to a stomach-lurching stop.

I laughed, loving my brother's wild stunts.

Lizzie's seatbelt flew back and almost hit me in the face. She opened her door and ran from the truck, like a bat released from Hades. She didn't make it far before she emptied her breakfast on the side of the road. And worse, she started to cry.

My brother cursed, then jumped out to help her. Liz pummeled his chest, but Rawson pulled her into a tight rocking-hug. "Sorry. Most girls like my stunts."

She stiffened. "I'm not most girls." She pushed out of his arms and marched away. At the hood, she turned. "I refuse to drive with you."

"I'll go slow. Promise."

She shook her head. "I don't believe you."

"Well, you should. I don't want you upchucking in my new truck. That was nasty."

She scowled.

"Cross my heart. Hope to die. I promise not to go over sixty."

My brother didn't make promises he didn't keep, but Liz didn't know that. "I believe him, Lizzie."

She rolled her eyes. "Fine. But I'm watching the speedometer."

Rawson reached behind his seat. "Here." He tossed her a water bottle.

She didn't thank him, but she did turn around to drink and spit.

My brother kept his lead foot under control. Mostly. Liz called him out a time or two when the needle inched upward. He grumbled, but otherwise didn't argue.

At the church, Liz looped her arm through mine and walked at my hobbling pace across the parking lot. Having a girl on my arm made me feel like a man.

"Liz!"

My lips puckered on an invisible lemon when I saw Mackay jogging our direction. Of course, Lizzie paused to wait.

He reached us and leaned in to peck her cheek and take possession of her hand.

"What the hell?" Rawson muttered.

I thought his swearing sacrilegious, being next to a church and all, but didn't blame him.

Liz squirmed. "Uh, you know Ben."

It wasn't a question, but Mackay answered like it was. "Yes, I know Benny. How could I forget my little partner at the rodeo?" He spoke as though I was eight, instead of fourteen.

"Judge me by my size, do you?" I muttered.

Rawson nudged me to acknowledge my Yoda wisdom.

Lizzie continued her introductions. "This is his older brother, Rawson. I don't know if you've met."

The smile slid off Mackay's face. "I know Rawson." His eyes narrowed. "I never thought I'd see the day you darkened a church." He steered Lizzie past us.

My brother's nostrils flared. "Never thought I'd see you get a girl."

Liz scowled over her shoulder.

I elbowed my brother. "Hush."

We followed them into a chapel, where several people stopped to introduce themselves. Most already knew Rawson. No matter where we went, he always knew how to fit in and belong. I wished I could be even one-tenth as cool as him. I didn't fit in anywhere.

Mackay motioned for Rawson to slide into a pew. I squeezed in next. Liz sat beside me. Mackay ruined it by draping his arm across her shoulders. With his fingers so close, I wanted to bend one back until he cried *Uncle*.

Rawson turned to a man behind us and chatted about the new thoroughbreds.

I patted Lizzie's hand and whispered, "You want me to switch places so you don't have Doofus's arm around you?"

Her lips twitched. "I'm fine, Ben."

"But you don't like him."

"Shh. I never said that." She sat up straight.

Mackay stroked the top of her arm. "How did you get Rawson Law to come to church?" he asked.

She shrugged. I wanted to deck him. Why did he care whether my brother came or not?

His fingers pushed under Lizzie's gauzy sleeve, getting fresh. I leaned into her and smashed his naughty appendages. When he withdrew and folded his arms, I smirked. Liz could thank me later.

The organ stopped playing. The pastor, bishop, or whoever he was started the service. Liz grabbed a hymnal. As we sang a hymn, I felt the same as when I'd watched the sunrise this morning. Warm and happy.

When a closing prayer was offered, Rawson jumped to his feet, anxious to leave. I informed him I wanted to stay for Sunday School. He dug a finger beneath his collar and looked like I'd just stolen the last bit of chocolate from Mom's secret stash.

"You're kidding."

"Please."

I think he would've called it a day if Liz hadn't intervened. "Benny's looked forward all week to meeting kids his age."

"All right," he growled. "But you owe me big time for this, bro."

Liz helped me find the right classroom. Sweat rolled down my spine as I prepared to leave her. It turned out I didn't have to worry. Sunday school was way better than regular school. The teacher made me laugh and gave us chocolate-covered cinnamon bears to chow on during his lesson. There were seven kids: two boys—Sam and Erik—and four girls. Alice was the only girl I remembered. She never stopped talking and didn't seem bothered by my crooked neck, like the others.

I met up with Rawson and Liz after church ended.

"How did you like class, Ben?" I loved how she'd started calling me Ben instead of Benny. It sounded grown-up.

"It was great. I already know one kid from school, but now I'll have other friends." I grinned, but as Octopus Mackay sauntered onto the scene and wrapped his tentacles around Liz, my lips puckered.

"Mackay, not here," I heard her whisper.

Rawson rolled his eyes. "Let's blow this taco stand. My butt hurts from sitting so long. Who's up for chicken at Freda's?"

"I am. Come on, Lizzie." I took her hand to pull her away.

"I'm taking Liz home." Mackay put an arm around her, reeling her back.

"No need to waste gas, Macky." Rawson purposely slaughtered his name. "Liz is headed to the same place we are."

Liz came to Mackay's rescue as he bristled. "You two go ahead. I'm having dinner with Mackay's family." She stepped over to hug me. "See ya later."

She left, and I wanted to kick a wall. I'd hoped that she would start liking my brother, not get closer to that boring Mackay. He was all wrong for her.

Rawson grilled me as we filled up on greasy chicken at Freda's. "So the other kids were nice to you?"

"You sound surprised. Did you expect them to strap me to the wall and throw darts?"

He bit into another drumstick. "Kids can be cruel."

"They were great. This one girl, Alice, even invited me to eat lunch with her and her friends so I won't have to eat alone."

Rawson set down his chicken. "Did you used to eat alone?"

I bit into my drumstick. "Sometimes." *Always* would be more accurate. The other kids had treated me like a disease after the accident. I shifted the conversation back to him. "Did you feel all warm and tingly during the sermon?"

He raised both brows. "You sound like you're asking if I wet my pants."

"It's just, uh…" I searched for words. "I felt so good. Warm. I don't know how to explain it."

"Maybe they had the heater cranked up."

I raised my neck. "Liz told me it's the Spirit."

Rawson licked his fingers. "I didn't feel no spirit or any other warm, fuzzy feeling…except when I saw Lizzie's legs as she got into the truck." He whistled. "Those were sizzling hot."

I glared, making him chuckle.

"Just kidding, kid. Church wasn't too bad, though my shirt and tie had me crawling out of my skin." He'd changed when we'd arrived at the diner.

Rawson threw a tip into the jar on the counter as we left. I was dog-tired from trying to look semi-normal for so long. All that greasy chicken and mashed potatoes hadn't helped. I dozed on the ride home and awoke when we pulled into the garage.

We shed our shoes in the mudroom. Rawson followed me to my room, where he stripped off his shirt and plopped down on my beanbag.

"How long has Liz been going out with Tacky Macky?"

"Don't call him that. I hate when kids call me names like Bent-head."

"Who calls you Bent-head?"

"Doesn't matter. Just don't call people names."

"Tell me who calls you that."

I frowned. "No way. You'd kick their butt."

He smashed his fist into the beanbag. "No one calls you names without answering to me. Now who is it, so I can kick some ass."

"You need to stop cussing, dude. She's been going out with Mackay since she got here in April."

Rawson's brows furrowed.

"How do you know Mackay?" I asked.

"I tortured him in high school."

I laughed but stopped when he didn't crack a smile. "Serious?"

"As a heart attack."

A tremor shook me. "What did you do?"

Rawson looked at the ceiling. "Face-dipped him in garbage cans, tripped him in the halls, punched him when he passed, you name it."

"You and Damon?"

"Yeah. I was stupid back then. Let a girl get to me."

"You bullied Mackay because of a girl?"

"His sister."

"No way."

He nodded. "Sarah Benson. We had seventh grade art together. I crushed on her but was scrawny and had acne. I didn't have the confidence to make a play for her." He propped his hands behind his head. "Ninth grade changed all that. My hormones and muscles kicked into turbo-drive, and I became popular overnight. Fame kind of went to my head. It seemed I could have any girl I wanted...except Sarah. I asked her out repeatedly, but she refused on grounds that I wasn't of her faith. That's why Damon and I started messing with her little brother."

I gulped. For five years, I'd been pushed around and mocked by others. To learn that my own brother fit in the bully category made me sick.

"That wasn't very nice." It came out a whisper.

"I'm not like that anymore."

"You called Mackay names today."

He grimaced. "Sorry. It felt like high school again. I was ticked that girls like Liz and Sarah Benson will only go out with..." he put his fingers in the air like quotes, "...*men of faith*, instead of giving us regular guys a chance."

I blinked. How could my own brother be one of the bullies I hated so much? I hobbled over to my bed. "I should take a nap before dinner."

He gave me a weird look. "You okay?"

"Yeah," I lied. "I just think I overdid it today."

"No doubt. Get some rest, kid. I'll talk to you later."

RAWSON

*J*RAPPED THE WOODEN door. "Boss? You out here?" I peeked into the tack room to find Liz with her arms full of gear. The woman worked like a Clydesdale but had the grace of a Lipizzaner. "What horse do you want me to work this morning?"

She pushed past me. "Grab Millennial Eagle."

"Now you're talking. I thought I was doomed to work with those brainless geldings the rest of my life."

"That's only for the days you show up late."

I laughed. "So you were punishing me?"

She began saddling Blue Boy Renegade. "Maybe."

I bridled the majestic sorrel stallion and joined her in the arena, where she was lungeing Blue Boy in a four-beat walk rhythm.

"I have a question for you," I said as I led Eagle in a circle.

She clicked her tongue to switch Blue Boy into a two-beat trot.

"Why Mackay?" I flicked the rope to increase Eagle's tempo, focusing on his hindquarters. "Seriously, Lizzie. Mackay?" I still couldn't believe she'd been with that pimply-face kid yesterday.

"What? He's a good guy."

"So's the Pope, but I don't see you dating him."

She kept watching Blue. "What do you care who I date?"

"You saved me from being crushed by Shooter's lethal hoofs and meeting my Maker, so I kind of owe you."

"You don't owe me." She whistled to signal Blue into a three-beat canter.

"Yes, I do. And believe me, you can do a whole lot better than Mackay Benson. He's like ordering vanilla at an ice cream parlor. Boring."

She slowed Blue to a walk. "I happen to like vanilla. What's the deal with you two anyway?"

"Expensive vanilla bean isn't bad, but Macky's a tub of generic vanilla. Icky."

She scowled. "Be nice."

I tipped my hat. "You shouldn't settle for a tub of boring when there are better flavors to try. Like Chance or Seth."

An unladylike snort came from her throat and nose. "They're just friends. Seth is teaching me to barrel race, and Chance just helps out when you're missing in action."

"I can assure you Chance never bothered asking old Larry if he needed help. He likes you. And he's a great guy, even if he doesn't go to church. I can vouch he's no vanilla." I brought Eagle to a halt and reached into my pocket for a sugar cube. "What ice cream flavor would Chance be?"

She laughed.

"I'm serious. Name a flavor."

She stroked Blue. "Rocky Road?"

"Ah. I wanted to be that."

Her lips twitched, creating a cute dimple in her cheek. "You're more like blue bubble gum ice cream. Flashy, but not much substance when you dig into it."

I clutched my heart. "You wound me."

She grinned. "Nothing can hurt your ego. It's steel-plated and Kryptonite proof."

Eagle nibbled at my neck. "Let's say Chance asked you out. What would you say?"

She rolled her eyes. "No. I'm dating Mackay."

"But you and Macky don't have the slightest snap, crackle, or pop. Believe me, I would've noticed if you did."

She rubbed Blue's ears. "We were at church. What did you expect us to do? Make-out during the sermon?"

I patted Eagle and lifted the rope to run him again. "That would've been a whole lot more interesting. But you don't need to kiss to have snap, crackle, and pop. It's noticeable in a couple even if they're just sitting by each other. And believe me, you and Macky don't have the slightest zing."

"His name's Mackay. And stop comparing our relationship to a box of breakfast cereal."

"Not just any box of cereal. One that's been in your grandma's cupboard for fifteen years."

Her brown eyes flashed. "Stop badmouthing Mackay."

"He's freezer burnt vanilla. I'm surprised you didn't sleep during the service, sitting beside him. Now Chance, you said yourself he's Rocky Road. No one gets bored with that."

She waved me away. "This is a ridiculous conversation. Check Eagle's collection."

I saluted. "Yes, boss."

I rode Eagle around the arena while Liz took notes, then we traded places so she could ride Blue Boy as I rated him on the training scale. When she finished, she led him over to me.

"What do you think?"

"His rhythm's off."

She wiped a bead of sweat from her brow. "That's what I thought."

We led our charges down the aisle to their stalls. "You and Mackay's rhythm is off as well." I locked Eagle up and met her at Blue Boy's stall. "Let's pretend I'm Chance, asking you out."

She shook her head. "Not going to happen."

"Humor me."

She narrowed her eyes. "No kissing."

I gasped. "Miss Ruthersford! I'm not that kind of guy. All I wanted was to ask you out, not make-out."

She laughed. "You know what I mean. My hand still hasn't recovered from all that slobber you left on it."

I grinned and waggled my brows. "It could've been your lips, baby. Remember that on cold, lonely nights."

She laughed again.

I sidled closer. "Ready to role play?" I pulled back, surprised by how good she smelled. Ironically, she smelled of vanilla. "I'll be Chance." I puffed out my chest, licked my fingers, and played with the front of my hair.

She giggled, and I knew I'd imitated the guy perfectly.

I grinned, showing all my teeth like he did. "Hey there, Liz." I made my voice higher. "I wondered if you could do me a favor." I slicked back my hair. The real Chance did that constantly.

Her eyes crinkled.

"A couple guys from high school are getting together to see a movie. Haven't seen them in ages..." I switched to my real voice. "Which means about two weeks in Chance's lingo." I raised my voice to his level again. "But never mind that. We were tight back in the day. So I wondered if you'd go with me since I don't want to show up stag. They'd razz me or maybe even think I bat for the other side. Can't have that. Please say you'll go. Pretty please?"

She walked toward the tack room. "You play Chance better than Chance. But believe me, I'm not his type."

"I disagree. You're pralines and cream. All soft and delicate, but a little nutty. You'd mesh well with Rocky Road."

"Who are you calling soft, Bubble Gum?"

I snickered, liking her sharp wit.

The rest of the morning passed pleasantly as we joked and worked with the other horses.

At noon, I teased her again. "We've discussed two flavors—Vanilla and Rocky Road. But we never discussed the third. What flavor would Seth be?"

"He's not a flavor. He's only doing me a favor by training me on the barrels."

"And why do you think he's so anxious to do that?" When she didn't reply, I said, "Let me assure you, if I wanted training, he'd be too busy. But then, I guess he doesn't want to get all close and personal as he shows me how to sit the saddle just right."

A blush crept up her cheeks. "He's just nice."

"Like Mackay?" I stuck my finger in my mouth and gagged. "Except if Mackay is bargain bin vanilla, Seth is pure-aged vanilla at its finest, since he's a cowboy."

"He's definitely aged."

"He's only four years older than me, and I'm twenty-three. Besides, don't you think older guys like younger women?"

"He doesn't like me."

Surely she couldn't be as clueless as she pretended. "Seth is probably mooning over you right now, trying to figure out how to get you training more with him."

"Oh, hush."

"You should branch out and give one of those flavors a chance. Pretend I'm Seth."

"Not this again."

I stood bowlegged and slouched. Bobbing my head, I swallowed several times before speaking in a raspy tone. "Howdy, Liz. I saw you out on Blue Boy. Looks like he's coming along fine, real fine." I mimicked his slow drawl. "Have you had any more time to work on that last move I taught ya?"

She nodded to humor me.

"Well, that's great, just great." Seth had a habit of repeating himself. "I have some time tonight if you want to learn the next move, the hitchy-kitchy."

She snorted at my made-up word.

"Thought maybe we could take a drive. Supposed to be a super moon tonight. Don't even need a flashlight, no sir-ee." I bobbed my head and swallowed, making my Adam's apple pump up and down.

She covered her mouth to stifle laughter.

"We could practice the hitchy-kitchy under the moonlight. That'd be fine, just fine." I waggled my eyebrows in a very non-Seth like way, sending her over the edge. A series of seal-like barks erupted from her, making me laugh. I'd never heard anyone laugh like that before.

"Stop it," she gasped.

"I'm pretty sure Seth wants to do the hitchy-kitchy with you rather than barrel racing."

She barked like a seal and sucked in a deep breath. "I mean it. Stop talking. You're making my side hurt."

"No one with a laugh like yours should be stuck with plain old vanilla, even the pure-aged stuff."

She narrowed her eyes.

I raised my hands. "That's not a jab, just the truth. Has Mackay ever made you laugh like that? And I take back what I said about Seth. He's a great guy, but he'd bore you stiff in less than a week."

We entered through the back door and headed to the washroom.

"Stop belittling those guys."

"All right, Praline."

She elbowed me. "Shut it, Bubble Gum."

I snickered, loving her sharp wit and elbow. The girl wasn't perfect, but I was beginning to appreciate why my brother liked her so much. She was cooler than I'd expected her to be.

31

LIZ

*S*ETTING MY NAPKIN on my plate, I stood. "Breakfast was delicious, Charity." Rawson stood as well.

"Are you feeling sick, son?" Charity asked as I left the room. "You still have food on your plate."

"No. I just..." I didn't hear the rest of his response, but hoped he wasn't ill. He was our ride to church again.

"Hey, wait up," Rawson called after me.

I turned and smiled. Since he'd given me that flashy watch, he hadn't been such a pill. He'd made me laugh and had turned out to be an excellent assistant, making me wonder why his dad had put me in charge. Rawson was strong, intelligent, and possessed more people skills than I did. Charm oozed from his every pore, while I stumbled over words and froze up in front of clients.

"What do you need?"

He wrinkled his nose. "Could you maybe back off on this whole church thing with Benny? He's getting too into it, and I don't want to keep losing sleep each Sunday to drive you guys there."

"No one's forcing you to come. If I remember right, you asked to take us, not the other way around."

Furrow lines formed between his mesmerizing eyes. "I know. But I thought it'd just be a one-time thing and he'd want to sleep-in after that. Benny's too easily swayed. I feel I have to go to keep his head on straight."

I winced at his poor choice of words. They sounded terrible in connection to his brother's crooked neck.

"That came out wrong. I didn't—"

106

"I'm sorry if worshiping God offends you. I'll make sure to offer your brother drugs or some sleazy porn in the future instead."

He ran a hand through his hair. "That's not what I—"

"Just go back to bed. When you wake up, get out on the right side so you're not such a grump. I'll call Mackay for a ride." I pushed past him.

"Vanilla?" Unlike the other day when he'd teased, he sounded down right mean.

I scowled.

He shook his head. "Sorry. I'm not trying to pick a fight."

"I find that hard to believe. If I've learned anything about you it's that you love to argue."

"True, but I gave you my watch, so I should probably concede." He threw me a small smile. "It's just that Benny's good heart makes him gullible. I don't want him to—"

"Fine. Talk to him and stay home. I'll call Mackay for a ride."

He hissed. "You don't need to call Macky. I'll still take you."

"Don't bother. I don't want to risk filling your head with rubbish, like how God loves you and can save you from hell and horrible ideas like that." I marched down the hall, but he caught my arm and turned me around.

"Stop being so sensitive."

Electricity seemed to shoot up my arms where he held me. My heart beat like hummingbird wings as I stared up into his eyes. Light green flecks burst from his pupils, like rays into the startling blue of his irises.

"I'm not being"—he backed me up against the wall—"sensitive." I squeaked as his body pressed against mine. I'd lied. Right then, I was the very definition of sensitive. Warmth flooded my body and the sensory receptors in my skin exploded where our bodies touched. His cool breath caressed my cheek, and I feared I might faint.

"I'm taking you to church." His eyes dared me to disagree.

"Okay?" It came out a question because my body was busy putting out internal fires.

"All righty then." He released me and stepped back. "I need to get ready for church. And you need to spruce up."

His snarky words shattered the evil spell I'd fallen under. Grr. "Yeah, I'm sure you need to change at least six more times."

I know. Lame. But my brain didn't operate at optimal performance. He'd thrown me off my game. Shoot! He'd thrown me out of the ballpark.

He chuckled as he walked away. "At least."

I dreaded the drive to town.

When I met him at his truck, I shook my head. Rawson wore black jeans, a lime green dress shirt, and a black blazer with a bolo tie. So Montana. Not the green shirt, but the bolo. He also sported a black cowboy hat that looked fresh off the rodeo circuit. Sadly, the whole get-up looked amazing on the primping peacock. So unfair.

"Wow," Benny said as he hobbled to the passenger side. "I thought last week's outfit was crazy, but you topped it with the Kermit the frog shirt."

I snickered into my hand.

"Glad you like it, kid."

"I hope you aren't planning on wearing that hat in the chapel," I said.

He tipped the brim. "Wouldn't be caught dead without it, darling. This here's the genuine El Presidente by Stetson. It'll keep religious rubbish from getting into my head."

I almost laughed but caught myself. No way would I feed his inflated ego.

When we arrived at church, I could tell Rawson's garish outfit irritated Mackay.

"Doesn't that guy possess an ounce of respect for others?" he complained.

I bumped his shoulder, trying to distract him from our pew mate. It worked. Mackay wrapped an arm around me and didn't glance at Rawson again.

I carefully evaluated my emotions, wanting to feel a spark of something. If Mackay elicited any yearning—even the smallest atom—I'd know I could build on that and cast the no-good Kermit cowboy from my head. Mackay's fingers caressed the top of my arm, but didn't create the slightest zip, bang, or spark, unlike the crazy ruckus Rawson's contact had produced this morning when he'd trapped me against the wall. My cheeks heated like a burner above a gas flame at the memory.

"Are you feeling well, Miss Ruthersford? You look a little flushed."

I gulped. Rawson's hand on my skirt brought me back to the present and provided stark contrast to Mackay's platonic touch.

"Uh, it's hot in here?" Again, it came out a question. Dang him and his brain-frying magic.

"Are you crazy?" Benny said. "I'm freezing."

Thankfully, the service began and I didn't have to justify my red cheeks and sweaty neck to them. Mackay kept stroking me as I struggled to stay awake. My head bobbed again, and I almost wished Rawson would lean over to touch my knee. I needed a good spark to jump-start my system.

The meeting ended. Benny took off to the youth class. As I waited for Mackay to discuss a service project with the pastor, a well-endowed brunette slid into the empty pew in front of us.

"Rawson Law? I haven't seen you since high school," she gushed.

"Well, well," he drawled in that sexy bass he pulled off to perfection, "look at you." He did just that, giving her a once over that would've made me blush. "Has it really been five years, darling? You haven't aged."

I noticed he didn't say her name, making me wonder if he remembered it. He dropped pet names like sunflower seeds.

The woman beamed. "You haven't, either. You're still the hottest guy around."

"Yeah."

I snorted, the loud, obnoxious kind. Seriously. If I'd burped, I couldn't have drawn more attention to myself.

The flirting duo turned to stare. I stood and pushed Mackay down the aisle. "Time to get to Sunday School."

We worked our way into the flow of people, and I overheard the brunette say, "We should get together and catch up."

Mackay led me out of eavesdropping range, and I cast the Casanova from my mind. I didn't need to be thinking about Rawson at church. That was like courting Satan at St. Peter's gate.

The ladies' man caught up to us at the end of the hall. I felt as wicked as the children of Israel when they worshiped the golden calf as I stared at him. Only Rawson could wear a bolo tie and make it look sexy, not geriatric. Averting my gaze, I followed Mackay into the classroom and sat next to him.

A deep frown creased Mackay's face when Rawson sat on the other side of me. I wished I knew the reason for the bad blood between them. Rawson snorted to irritate me.

I stuck my tongue out, making the idiot snicker. "You didn't know that girl, did you?" I whispered.

"Not at all." He leaned forward and turned to face me. Unfortunately, that gave Mackay a better view of him waggling his eyebrows.

Mackay stiffened and pulled me closer.

The teacher introduced the lesson. I leaned down to retrieve my Bible from my satchel.

"Here." I set it on Rawson's lap. "We can share since you don't have your own." I caught of whiff of cologne as he leaned closer. Rawson always smelled divine, but dang, whatever he'd put on today was positively sinful. I'd name it *Temptation*, *Enticement*, or *Rapture*. It was all of those and more.

"Don't give me my own either."

I frowned. "Don't worry. I don't throw pearls to swine."

He snorted again, drawing looks.

I elbowed him. "Will you drop it already."

"Snort again," he whispered. "Please." His luscious scent wrapped around me, sapping me of much needed wisdom. Why couldn't Mackay affect me this way?

I pinched his leg.

"Ow!"

Everyone in the room, including the teacher, turned to stare.

"She just pinched me." Rawson sounded authentically shocked as he pointed at me. The man should work in Hollywood.

My IQ surrendered, leaving me speechless.

The elderly instructor chuckled. "She's probably trying to hush you, Mr. Law. You haven't stopped whispering since class began."

Of course, he knew Rawson. Everyone did. The class enjoyed a good laugh at my expense, making Butthead's grin grow. Mackay's frown, in contrast, touched the floor and his arm trembled on my shoulder.

The teacher chortled. "I recall you doing the same thing in history class, always flirting with the ladies."

Mackay's fingers dug into me as he handed Rawson his large print Bible. "Use this. I'll share with Liz."

The teacher had us turn to a verse in the Old Testament. Rawson touched my arm. "Where's Isaiah in this mess?" he asked irreverently.

I leaned over to flip to the right section.

"You spruced up real nice, Miss Ruthersford," he whispered.

Goosebumps formed on my arms. I rubbed them as Mackay leaned into my other ear. I willed my body to react, but his breath did nothing.

"Is he bothering you?"

"He just needed help finding Isaiah." And I needed help finding my common sense.

Rawson leaned forward and winked, making Mackay tense up like a coiled spring. I ignored him. The safest option, considering the state of my mind and the power of his cologne.

"You're adorable when you're flustered, Miss Ruthersford."

"Shush," I hissed. "I don't want to be called out again."

"Ah, Mr. Larsen's a softie. He never once gave me detention in high school, and I more than deserved it."

Mackay pulled me back firmly. "Tell him to be quiet. He's being very disruptive."

"Sorry."

"Are you?"

I cringed, feeling like a naughty child. Why did guys always make me feel this way?

Class ended, and Mackay's eyes narrowed like a boxer as he took my hand. "See you later, Benny." He didn't acknowledge Rawson as he marched me out the door.

Silence settled between us on the drive to his house. Without Rawson's irresistible scent blocking my brain, I realized how foolish I'd behaved. Rawson didn't like me. He just liked to tease me. Stupid man. I hated how I loved the smell of his cologne. It irritated me how my whole body warmed whenever he smiled. The fact that I appreciated his outlandish clothes that enhanced his physique and had every female at church gawking at him irked me also, because everyone was drawn to Rawson Law. I didn't want to be another of his groupies.

After dinner with Mackay's family, I reached over and squeezed his hand under the table. Mackay turned with hope in his eyes, and my heart wanted to cast up walls, but I couldn't keep being so cold. Mackay deserved more. Rawson was wrong. Vanilla was safe and solid, a staple in the ice cream world.

"We'll stop by to visit Dad before I take Liz home," he told his mom.

"Be home by nine."

He leaned over to peck her cheek. "I'll try, but it's a long drive. It might be closer to ten."

She threw me a scowl, as if it was my fault I lived in the boonies.

"Thanks for dinner, Mrs. Benson."

We drove to the hospital, and my mood plummeted. Mackay's dad was so heavily medicated he had a hard time speaking. Mackay put on a brave face, but I could tell his dad's deteriorating health upset him. I felt even worse about my earlier games with Rawson and determined to cheer Mackay up when he took me home.

I owed him a kiss.

Maybe I owed him my heart.

By the time we pulled up to the ranch house though, doubts tied my stomach into knots. I endured another Dippy kiss and waited for gravity to pull Mackay upright again. As kind as the guy was, I still only liked him as a friend. Affection between us felt wrong, like kissing a brother. Not that I had a brother, but kissing Mackay felt like what I imagined that'd be like. Yuck. Maybe Justin had jaded me so I couldn't feel anymore.

I felt insta-guilt for thinking negatively about the dead.

"Thanks for dinner," I said as Mackay straightened. "I better go in. I have an early day tomorrow."

"Night, Liz." The look of adoration in his eyes stirred up more guilt.

I slipped inside and let out a weary breath. How had things come this far? But what were my options? Rawson Law? Heaven forbid. He probably had mega-models lining up to date him. And as much as he teased me about Chance and Seth, they really were just friends.

It seemed the devil dangled Rawson on the side of a cliff to tease me, while God hoped I'd choose Mackay on safe, sturdy ground.

So, why did falling off a cliff suddenly seem so enticing?

32

RAWSON

*A*s I ROUNDED THE corner of the tack room with two saddles, Lizzie collided with me and yelped. I took in her work attire—dusty jeans, a button-down flannel shirt that hid her assets, and an abominable bun that gave her ponytail a run for its money. I wanted to yank the pins out to free her curls. It seemed a criminal offense to hide them from the world and torture her cute face by pulling her cheeks and forehead back so severely.

"I was looking for you."

She frowned. "Are one of those mine?" She reached to take a saddle and blanket from me.

"I have it." I swung out of reach and headed to the stalls. "Which horses are we working this morning?"

She followed. "Millennial Eagle and Sidekick Shooter."

I hissed. "I suppose you want me to work with Shooter."

"Yeah, but stay off him."

"Don't worry. I learned my lesson." I stopped, and she bumped into me. "Hey, I wanted to apologize for yesterday."

Her cute face puckered—well, at least as much as it could pulled back by that infernal bun.

"I didn't mean to embarrass you in Sunday School."

Her pouty lips made me all hot and bothered, especially when she licked them. I looked up at the rafters, knowing no good could come from crushing on my boss. She was too uptight and innocent, nothing like the women I normally went after.

"No hard feelings?"

She shrugged. "As long as you stop harassing Mackay."

I set the saddles on a hay bale. The last thing I wanted was to hear her gush about her tub of vanilla. "I still think you should give Chance a chance."

She rolled her eyes and entered Eagle's stall.

"His name demands it. Besides, the guy thinks you walk on water" I stifled a grin. "But we know from the lake incident that you don't. Why you can't even steer a kayak."

Thankfully, she laughed instead of getting all huffy. I never knew quite which way she would swing when I teased her.

"I sink as much as the next fellow."

"No, you'd kick and flail yourself to shore. You don't need to walk on water with determination like yours."

Pink blossomed in her cheeks. "Thanks…I think."

I followed her and Millennial Eagle into the arena, admiring her long legs. Unlike her upper body, which she camouflaged in baggy shirts, her jeans fit like a glove.

I worked the idiot horse for about an hour before Liz told me to switch out for Yakama Yoda.

I patted the two-year-old stallion as he nibbled my chin. "Who's the man? Yoda man."

Liz let out a barking laugh. "You surprise me."

I reached up to rub Yoda's neck. "Why's that?" A rosy blush colored her cheeks, making me want to reach out and touch her instead.

"When your dad put me in charge, I figured you must not know squat about horses. But the more I see you in action, I realize that's not true."

Her words picked at a festering scab. "Maybe I've just fooled you."

"No." She led the newest gelding past me. "You might fool me, but you can't fool horses, and they all like you."

"Except Shooter."

"Shooter's not right in the head. He doesn't count."

"I'm surprised to hear you say that. I thought you were the equine Mother Teresa."

"Even Mother Teresa had to admit there were crazies in the world."

I reached up to massage Yoda's velvety ears as she mounted Moonshine and walked him around the arena. Minutes later, I caught up to her and slowed Yoda's pace so he wouldn't bite at her mount in a display of dominance.

"It's ridiculous for me to be your boss," she said. "You know way more than I do."

"Don't sell yourself short. You have a gift I don't. Sure, horses like me, but they like anyone with half a brain and a sugar cube. You, though, are a horse siren. When you speak, they listen."

She snorted, like she had in church the other day when I'd inadvertently said "Yeah" to that Trina-girl's comment about looking hot. I hadn't really been listening. Until Liz snorted, I hadn't realized what I'd agreed to.

Her index finger shot up. "Don't say a word."

"My lips are sealed, Miss Snort-boss."

She huffed. "I'm going to talk to your dad about sharing responsibilities. You're so good with—"

"Drop it."

Tension prickled between us as she led Moonshine into his stall. She'd tried to do me a good deed, and I'd thrown it back in her face.

"Really, I'm content with how things are," I said.

She latched the stall. "Okay. But if you change your mind, I'm willing to step down and let you take charge."

"That isn't your call to make." I locked up Yoda and joined her in the tack room.

She pursed her lips. "I never set out to be your boss. When you returned, I feared your dad would let me go since he had you."

"Dad has never needed me."

"I don't believe that. You obviously clash like brass cymbals, but I can tell he loves you very much."

"That's girl talk."

"Good. Because last I checked, I'm a girl."

I allowed my gaze to drop and check her out. "Oh yeah. You're definitely all girl."

She punched my shoulder. "Stop it."

"What? I'm making an observation. Chance is definitely going to ask you out one of these days. Then maybe you'll experience that snap, crackle, and pop I keep talking about."

She snorted again, making me laugh. The girl was adorable. But so were bunnies, and I'd shot my fair share of them. Maybe I needed to take Damon to town to shoot Liz out of my head. There were plenty of women there who'd be happy to help me forget my troubles. No sense being tempted by my boss, no matter how well she fit into her jeans.

114

LIZ

REAKFAST WAS A quiet affair. I chewed bacon, not really tasting it. A new low. When you don't taste something as delicious as bacon, you might as well be dead. My mind kept hiccupping Rawson Law, and like real hiccups, I couldn't make him go away no matter how many strange internal rituals I attempted. I downed some milk to wash that man from my thoughts, but my mind hiccupped again, recalling how easily we'd gotten along recently. We'd made great strides in training several of the harder horses, even Shooter.

"Can you pass the muffins, Liz?"

I transported muffins to my boss at the head of the table as my mind stewed on how to deal with his son. Rawson had shown up hours late for work the last week and had skipped out completely this past weekend. I couldn't keep covering for him. Eventually, Mr. Law would notice.

I emptied my glass and stood. "Thanks for breakfast, Charity." I patted Benny's back. "See you later."

"Count on it," he said through a mouthful of muffin.

I slipped out the door and crossed the pasture, thinking of Rawson again. A week ago, I'd wanted to make him my partner. Today, I seriously considered filing a complaint about him to Bart.

What was up with him?

I was halfway done sweeping stalls before my inconsistent apprentice showed up.

"Hey," he called from the other side of the arena, sounding out of breath, "sorry I'm late. I got here as fast as I could."

He disappeared into the tack room as I guided Whiskers in a circle.

"Which horse do you want me to get?" he shouted.

"Taco Twister."

He swore.

Rawson couldn't stand the two-year-old dun. The magnificent gelding possessed no focus, like him. Maybe that's why I paired them together. I expected an argument, but Rawson marched to Taco's stall and tacked him up. He worked as if his life depended on it, and in a way, it did.

The lunch bell rang. I led Whiskers out of the arena, but Rawson stopped me. "Tie him to a post. I'll finish with him while you eat."

"You're not coming?"

"Nah. I'll work through lunch since I started a little late."

"Three hours is more than a little. And what about this weekend?"

His Caribbean eyes appraised me. "Sorry. I promise—"

"Please don't make any more promises." No way would I let him sweet talk his way off my bad list.

He ran a hand through his hair. "Let me make it up to you. How about we go for a ride and have a picnic?"

"I'm already behind."

"Taco and Shooter need time in the saddle. It'll be a working lunch, except more pleasurable."

"What would be more pleasurable is if you'd get your sorry butt to work in the mornings instead of—"

"I know. I really am sorry." He ran his hand through his hair again, making my hands jealous. "I'll level with you, Liz. My friend's trying to quit drugs. Withdrawals have been ugly. Mornings are the worst. He needs me so he doesn't do something stupid." His blue-green eyes crinkled at the corners, working their magic on me. Dang him.

"Fine," I huffed. "Just try to get here earlier. I'm getting behind."

"Deal. So, how about that ride and picnic?"

I rolled my eyes. "You better pack a mean lunch. I'll saddle the horses."

He saluted as I brushed past him. "You won't know what hit you, boss."

I didn't look back as he chuckled because I feared I might laugh. Curse him for being so dang funny.

By the time I had the horses saddled, Rawson returned with a backpack loaded with food. He mounted Taco Twister. I climbed onto Sidekick, and he winked at me.

"Stop staring." I urged Shooter into a trot.

"Why? The view's nice."

"You're such a liar."

He caught up to me and grabbed my reins. "Hold up. Why do you always accuse me of lying when I'm only telling the—"

I covered my ears as he used the Lord's name in vain. "Please don't use His name that way."

He gave me a weird look.

"I hate how dirty I feel every time you open your mouth, especially when you use God's name as if it's worth less than an inflated Mexican peso."

"Fine. I won't swear around you if you stop thinking you're plain and deficient around me."

"I don't think I'm deficient. And who uses words like that anyway?"

He grinned. "Have to put my college degree to use. And you do think that. You gave me a whole list of deficiencies on the drive to Bozeman the other day. And just now you accused me of lying when I said you looked nice."

I squirmed in my saddle. "Give me my reins."

"Not until you make the deal." He held out his hand. "Shake on it."

I rolled my eyes but gave him my hand. The horses bit at each other as Rawson squeezed my fingers, sending fiery pulses up my arms.

"Tell me three traits you love about yourself."

"What?"

"We made a deal. The Love Triangle is how I'll know you're keeping your end. You can hear whether I'm keeping mine, but I won't know if you're listing deficiencies in your head. So tell me three things you love about yourself. I'll give you ten seconds before I pull out the big guns and let you hear the names I call the cattle."

"That's stupid." I pulled my hand from his.

"Ten, nine, eight…"

"All right. Shush. I can't concentrate if you're counting."

He held up his hand and dropped a silent finger. As he lowered the second to last one, I pushed his hand down.

"I like my hands."

He grabbed mine again. "Me, too. They're delicate and soft. Very soft."

I yanked my hand out of his grip. "They're calloused and scratched up more than a cat tower."

"Damn it, Lizzie. You're not supposed to tell me deficiencies."

I puckered my lips. "Okay. I like my hands because they're calloused and scabbed. Are you satisfied?"

He winked. "That's one. Give me two more."

"You cussed. We're done."

"I cussed because you lashed out at yourself. Fair's fair. You tell me a negative, I'll throw out an ear-scorcher. Now hurry before I lose my patience. You're as infuriating as a heifer."

I propped my hand on my hip. "Did you just call me a cow?"

He laughed. "No. I likened you to a heifer. Big difference. A cow has had calves. A heifer has not. Therefore, as a single adolescent female, you wouldn't be a cow, unless you had a teen pregnancy and gave up a child for adoption I don't know about. In that case, you'd be a first-calf heifer."

I scowled. "Don't ever call a woman a cow or a heifer, or you'd be a first-class idiot."

He snorted. "Stop chewing your cud and tell me a second thing you love about yourself." He walked Taco ahead, which was good, because I wanted to kick him.

Closing my eyes, I tried to block out the man ahead of me.

"Seriously, Liz. You're acting as though I asked for the mysteries of the universe. You're a beautiful, talented woman. This shouldn't be hard."

I blushed. "Be quiet. I'm thinking."

"I hadn't thought this was any kind of a challenge."

"Um, I can whistle?"

His lips twitched. "You asked that like a question. I don't know. Can you whistle?"

Irritating man. I stuck two fingers in my mouth and produced an ear-piercing whistle that startled Shooter into a trot.

Rawson hooted and clapped when he caught up to me. "Incredible. You're definitely a master whistler."

I chewed my bottom lip. "Mom says it's not very ladylike."

"I disagree. Whistling might be the sexiest thing a woman can do. I'm not saying you should haul off and whistle in church or at a swanky black tie event, though it'd sure liven those venues up, but I see nothing wrong with whistling anywhere else. In fact, it's a huge turn-on."

I reached over to slug him. "Liar."

He raised a chiding finger.

I huffed. "You are. Men want big boobs and curvy bodies. They like girls who drape themselves all over them and giggle at whatever stupid thing they say. They don't care about girls who can whistle. They just laugh at us behind our backs or tease us to our faces, like you do."

"Wow. Someone's done a number on you. All right, you're being honest. So will I. Yes, as a man, I like boobs and curves, but they don't have to be big. In fact," he dropped his gaze, "small and perky might be my favorite."

I blocked my chest behind my arms.

He smirked. "As for giggly girls, I disagree. I like girls to be real. There's nothing more annoying than some ditzy blonde like that Kelsey from Kentucky hanging on me." He raised an eyebrow. "Finish the triangle. Tell me something you really, really love." He reached down to pat Taco's dark coat, giving me time to reflect.

"I like my ears." I knew I didn't have Dumbo ears. Mom would've told me if I did.

Our legs touched between the horses as Rawson reached out to finger my earlobe. "They are lovely. Perfect for nibbling." Heat flooded my body as his gaze zeroed in on my neck and slowly traveled back up to my face. What did he mean by nibbling?

I swatted him when he leaned closer.

He straightened in his saddle. "You know, I was ticked at first that Dad put you over me, but if I have to work under anyone, I'm glad it's you so I can see your cute ears."

"Are you ever serious?"

"Just because I say things to make you laugh doesn't mean I'm not serious."

I shook my head and urged Shooter into a trot. Rawson followed and hollered, "I love the view from back here."

"I hope Shooter passes gas."

"It'd still be worth it."

We stopped in a grassy spot with wildflowers. I breathed in the peaceful setting but flinched when a heavy metal song blared from Rawson's pocket.

He checked his phone and cursed. Must be his cruddy friend.

"Don't answer," I said. "You promised to help me work the horses this afternoon. You were with your friend all morning."

He frowned but shoved his phone in his pocket.

I grinned. Maybe there was hope for him.

We made it to the next knoll before the annoying song played again. Our gazes locked. His hands clenched, but he dug his boots into Taco Twister and took off down the hill.

I let out a "Yeehaw" and galloped after him.

At the meadow, the irritating song began playing a third time.

Rawson gave me a pleading look. "Let me answer so he'll stop calling."

"Just turn off your ringer." He'd short-changed me all week. This was my time.

"Not a chance. I'm Damon's only friend." He brought his iPhone to his ear. "Yo. This isn't a good time. Can I call you back—"

Even a few feet away, I heard the scream. Rawson winced and pulled the phone away from his ear.

"Damon man, you're fine." He rubbed his forehead. "Calm down. You're hallucinating. There aren't any shadow men."

I don't know what he heard next, but he stiffened. "Damon? Damon! Talk to me, man." The color drained from his face as he yanked his reins to the side and turned Taco Twister. "I have to go," he said without looking back at me.

I watched him gallop away until he disappeared over the rise. That's when I remembered that he had the bag with our lunch in it.

119

"Dang, stupid, no-good cowboy." I growled. I'd been stood up in the middle of nowhere in exchange for a sorry waste of manhood.

Men sucked.

34

RAWSON

OUR DAYS HAD passed since Damon had ruined my ride with Lizzie. All over a false alarm. Now, Liz was giving me the freezing shoulder. Not that I blamed her. "There you are," I said, acting as if I didn't already know where she'd been hiding. I held up my phone. "Bryce Levanson's having trouble with the sorrel mare we sold him. I told him we'd drive over to help."

Her face scrunched into an adorable pout. "You go. I'm kind of busy."

"We're all busy, but customer relations come first. He asked for you by name, said you're the best."

"Oh, Mylanta," she muttered.

"Stop talking about antacids and go spruce up, boss."

She shook her head, but I caught a smile.

By the time Liz crawled into the cab of my truck, I was twitchy as a mouse in a cheese factory. "My, my. Don't you look nice."

"Stop being a ding-dong."

Lizzie's dated slang cracked me up. I pulled away from the stable. "I haven't cussed once in your presence since we made our deal."

"How many times have you cussed outside my presence?"

"I believe they use a symbol that looks like an eight turned sideways to count that high."

She giggled.

"I've held up my part of the bargain. What about you?"

"I've done a stellar job not listing my deficiencies."

"Tell me three new things you love about yourself."

Lizzie groaned. "Not this again."

"Hell-ck yeah."

"That counts. You lose."

"You can't count *helk*. You'll never find it in a dictionary."

"No, but you'll find hell in there, and that's what you said before you added a hiccup at the end."

"Hellll-o. Did you just swear?"

She laughed. "Stop being a goober."

"Goober? No one's ever called me that before. Now loober, toober, boober."

She leaned over and covered her mouth. "Stop."

"Why? I'm hoping the seal escapes."

She half barked-half huffed, making me pull over onto the side of the road because I laughed so hard.

"You did *not* just call me a seal." She swatted my head.

I lifted my hands to protect myself. "Hey, it's better than heifer." I chortle-snorted.

That did what my words couldn't. Lizzie's full inner seal escaped. More of my snorting guffaws followed, feeding the cycle. The harder we tried to stop, the more we laughed until she added hiccups between barks that made tears roll down my face. Who knew laughing could be such a workout?

Lizzie blew out a long breath. "I'll never laugh again now that I know you think I sound like a seal."

"That'd be a travesty."

She folded her arms.

"Has Chance asked you out yet?"

An eye roll. She had those down to an art. "He's not going to ask me out."

"That boy would be all over you right now if he was here. Pretend I'm him." I slid across the bench seat to wrap an arm around her. She stiffened as I leaned in close. "Play along. You don't want to hurt Chance's feelings. It takes guys a truckload of courage to ask a girl like you out."

She swallowed hard as I ran my fingers along the top of her arm. Goosebumps flared clear down to her wrists. And there was no mistaking the hitch in her breath. My touch had already put Mackay's to shame, and I wasn't even trying.

"Show me how to let a guy down easy."

"Rawson, uh—"

"I'm Chance."

"Chance, I'm, uh…flattered, but not comfortable with your…ahh!"

She choked as I blew gently in her ear.

"I don't think Chance would do that," she wheezed.

"Me neither." For some odd reason, I had the strongest urge to pull her close and work my way down from her adorable ears to her graceful neck. I pulled back slightly. "It might be good for you to practice with a pro."

"You?"

I winked. "Can you think of anyone better?"

She gave me a deer-in-the-headlights look as I brushed my thumb along her jaw. "You have the most gorgeous brown eyes."

She blushed as though I'd complimented her perky chest, which I'd totally do if I didn't think she'd slap me. But she took everything so serious.

"I could get lost in them."

She scoffed. "They're just plain brown."

"Nothing's plain about you, Lizzie. There are flecks of gold in your irises."

"Liar, liar, pants on—"

I lowered my lips to silence her. A natural reflex. Her lips were as soft as I'd imagined, but I'd barely sunk into them before she shoved me back. Hard.

"What are you doing?"

I shook myself out of my trance as she clambered out the door.

I jumped out after her. "Wait up."

She scowled. "Why did you kiss me?"

"Because you looked like you needed it. Vanilla didn't do it for you. Rocky Road's too shy to make a move. So Blue Bubble Gum to the rescue."

"Bleack, agh, ick!" She made spitting sounds and wiped her mouth. "Does that look like I needed it? I'll have to scour my mouth for germs."

"Save it, sweetheart. I could have Ebola and you wouldn't have contracted it from that pathetic contact."

She put her hands on her hips.

"Not saying your kiss was pathetic, but our lips hardly touched. That's the pathetic part."

"And they're not going to. I'd rather kiss a Wookiee."

I threw my head back and laughed.

Just then, a white Ford F-350 barreled over the hill and pulled up beside us. The ranch foreman stuck his head out the window.

"Anything the matter?" Abe glanced at Liz and tipped his hat.

I answered before she could humiliate me. "Liz dropped one of her headbands out the window. We're looking for it."

"Need help?"

"Nah. We're good. Don't want to keep you."

Lizzie huffed when Abe drove away. "A headband? That's the best you could come up with? I'm still wearing mine. Why didn't you tell him the truth—that you pulled over to seduce me?"

I smirked. "Why didn't you beg a ride off him to escape?"

She pouted. "I didn't think about it until he drove off."

"Stockholm Syndrome. You've become attached to your abductor and secretly want to kiss me." I waggled my eyebrows to make her laugh. "Most girls do."

"You're way out in left field."

"You want to make-out in the field?" I pointed to a crop of alfalfa. "I'm allergic to grass, but I'm willing to brave it if you are, baby." I stepped toward her, but she stomped her boot.

"Be serious!"

I made smoochie sounds. "Oh, I am, darling. I am."

She pushed me out of the way. "Don't we need to get to Mr. Levanson's?"

I sighed. Lizzie was no fun. "That we do."

We climbed in, but she stayed glue to her door and glared at me. "Keep your hands and lips to yourself, fresh guy."

"Whatever, Stockholm. All I was doing was prepping you for more flavor when Chance makes his move."

She stuck out her tongue.

I chuckled, but felt somewhat befuddled. All I'd done was give her a simple kiss. It hadn't meant anything. Yet she'd reacted as if I'd tried to steal her virginity.

The drive to town produced all sorts of awkward. I didn't know what to say after she'd made an atomic bomb out of a sparkler.

Somehow, we managed to pull off normal while we worked with Bryce and his new mare, but as soon as we sat in the cab of my pickup again, tension sparked between us like a downed power line.

"Want to grab a bite to eat?"

"I don't think we—"

"Look, can we forget about earlier?" My bruised ego sure wanted to. "I'm starved, and by the time we get back, supper will be over."

"All right, but I'll pay for my own meal."

I took her to my favorite hamburger joint and let the stubborn woman buy her own meal. When I sat next to her in the booth, she squirmed into the corner.

"Rawson, this is inappropriate. You and me—"

"It's dinner, baby. Everybody does it." I scooted closer, trying to tease her out of her foul mood.

"Stop messing around. You're acting like this is a date."

I waggled my brows. "It is. August eighteenth to be exact."

"Stop crowding me."

I scooted closer. "But I like you, *boss*."

"I'm ordering you to leave me the heck alone."

The way she diluted swear words made me grin. "Don't try to act tough. It doesn't become you." A lie, if ever I'd told one. Truthfully, I found her very appealing right then, even with her librarian bun.

"I don't care what becomes me. I'm not trying to impress you."

"Obviously, or you'd wear a more form-fitting shirt."

Her crestfallen expression lasted only a fraction of a second but made me feel like a heel. I took her hand, but she yanked it away.

"Stop fooling around. I'm dating Mackay. This doesn't look good."

I gritted my teeth. "What doesn't look good is you and Macky."

"Stop calling him that. He's the kindest man I know."

"Kindness only goes so far in a relationship, Stockholm. You need passion, too."

"We have passion." She shoved me. "Now get on your side."

I rubbed my face as I moved to the bench across from her.

"Thank you," she said in a prim and proper voice.

"You're welcome, little liar."

She shoved fries in her mouth.

"The day you and Macky have passion is the day the Pope wears a Speedo in public."

She ignored me. We finished our meals and walked to my truck. I opened her door and spotted Mackay pulling into the parking lot in his rusty heap of metal. He climbed out and noticed us together.

I pulled Liz close. "What's in your hair?"

She squirmed to escape.

"Hold still. I think it's a spider."

She tensed, but to her credit, she didn't squeal.

I ran my hands over her head and pulled out several bobby pins, freeing her gorgeous curls.

"It's tangled. Hold still." I took advantage of her ignorance to pull her nearer. "There's another one. You must've run into a nest of webbies."

She shuddered.

"Almost have it." I lowered my head to inhale the smell of her shampoo. Tropical, with a hint of coconut. I let my fingers explore the wild curls that'd escaped, hoping Mackay was watching.

A door slammed, and I knew I'd kept her preoccupied long enough that Vanilla had received my message loud and clear. She'd thank me someday.

"Got it." I flicked my fingers so she'd think I was getting rid of a nonexistent arachnid.

"Thanks," she said breathlessly into my chest.

I kissed her brow, smoothing the stress lines there. "You're welcome, Little Miss Muffet." I pulled back to look at her. The girl was completely adorable. That's why I didn't feel guilty for sabotaging her relationship with Macky. She deserved better than vanilla.

35

LIZ

*M*EN WILL SEND me to my grave. I'd come to Montana to escape them, but between Rawson Law and Mackay Benson, I'd had more trouble than I ever had in Vegas. I'd looked forward to going out with Mackay tonight after that uncomfortable drive to Levanson's yesterday with Rawson. Maybe Mackay would get my head back in whack. Rawson had thrown me for a double whammy when he'd kissed me.

Mackay helped me into his car. I thanked him and gave myself a pep talk. It didn't matter what Rawson said. Mackay was the purest vanilla bean ice cream ever created. So what if he was predictable? Who wanted to build a house on an unstable foundation? Not me. I'd almost done that. Steady and reliable worked for me.

On the drive to town, I made a mental list of all Mackay's positive traits.

He volunteered at the Food Bank.

He was a faithful church man.

Smart, kind, thoughtful. He'd never belittled me.

I frowned as I thought of Rawson, who'd called me a heifer and had laughed about it. Dumb man.

Mackay was a good listener, even when I'd brought up horrid subjects or had tried to bore him in the early days of our relationship.

He was blind to my faults. Honest. Responsible. Hard worker.

Everything Rawson was not.

We reached the junction to turn, and I realized Mackay hadn't spoken. I'd been so lost in my thoughts I hadn't even asked about his day.

"How was work?"

"Fine." His hands clenched the wheel. Was he stressed about his dad's health?

"How's your dad?"

"About the same."

Silence occupied the space between us, which was odd. Mackay usually filled it with friendly chatter. I tried a few more times to draw him out but gave up after his fourth one-word response. Obviously, he wasn't in the mood to chat.

Mackay pulled into the same diner Rawson had chosen last night. What were the odds?

He raised a brow. "Have you eaten here recently?"

I nodded. "Last night. But I can order something different. I don't mind." There weren't many options in town.

"Who were you with?"

I stared at him. Was he interrogating me? "I stopped here with Rawson Law after a work call."

He scowled. "He's very charming when he wants to be."

I rolled my eyes. "He's a tease."

"Was he teasing when he played with your hair and kissed you?"

"What? I've never kissed Rawson Law," I said, but blushed when I recalled I had. But he'd surprised me. I'd pushed him away. My pesky conscience reminded me that though it'd been the shortest kiss of my life, I'd relived the moment dozens of times in my dreams.

How did Mackay know about that?

"But you like him."

"No!" When he gave me a hard stare, I lowered my eyes. *Maybe a little,* I thought.

Mackay took a deep breath. "I saw you two last night. You looked quite cozy."

"What?" I certainly hadn't kissed Rawson here.

"He doesn't care about you, Liz. I know you work with him and it's probably easy to get caught up in the moment, but you don't know him like I do. The man's a predator. I saw him do this in high school, move in and get some girl to like him, then use her all up and cast her aside. He doesn't care about anyone but himself."

Whoa. I hadn't thought Mackay possessed a mean bone in his body, but he must've ingested calcium-fortified fury for breakfast. "He's not like that." I don't know why I defended him.

"You're naive and gullible, like all the other girls who had their hearts broken by him."

"Now wait just a confounded minute. I resent being compared to some high school cheerleaders who wanted the big guy on campus." Which I'm sure Rawson was. I mean, all I had to do was look at him to know he'd been Mr. Popular.

"You're nothing like them," Mackay said. "If you were, I wouldn't care. But I like you, Liz. A lot! I don't want you to get hurt."

His concern touched me. Though Mackay thought I'd cheated on him, he still cared. "It wasn't what you think."

"I'm not mad, but—"

I placed a finger on his lips. "Rawson was trying to get a spider—two spiders, actually—out of my hair." I shuddered, thinking about creepy crawlies invading my personal space. Thank goodness Rawson had extracted them for me.

"I saw him kiss your forehead."

"That was just a friendly kiss." *Like ours*, I wanted to add. "It meant nothing."

"I don't like you hanging out with him."

"We work together. We have to hang out at times. But we're only friends. Nothing more."

"You said you like him."

My eyes widened. Had I said that out loud? Oops. "It's the kind of *like* I feel for Matt Damon. He doesn't like me back. In fact, he's always trying to convince me to go out with other hands at the ranch."

Mackay tapped the steering wheel. "Because he hates me. He saw us together at church. Now, you're a target. He bullied me in high school and now wants to steal you away to make some macho point."

"Really, Mackay. If Rawson wanted to steal me, he'd try a little harder. He mostly pokes fun of how bad I look."

"You've never looked bad a day in your life."

"You haven't seen me mucking stalls at four A.M."

"You're the prettiest girl I know. And the nicest. Rawson would be a fool not to make a play for you."

"Look. I'm sorry he bullied you in high school, but he's an adult now. Not a stupid kid."

"He's an actor, showing you what you want to see. He did this with every pretty girl in high school, acting like Prince Charming until he had them wrapped around his finger, then throwing them off with his middle finger when he was onto the next flavor of the week."

The mention of flavors made me cringe. Had Rawson teased and kissed me yesterday because of the challenge of it? Would he ignore me once he got a taste of how boring and plain I really was? He compared Mackay to vanilla, but if anyone resembled that flavor, it was me. Besides horses, I didn't have any cool hobbies. I liked to read and cut things out with a scroll saw. I could whistle, change the oil in a truck, and take gadgets apart. But no man wanted a girl like that. Men wanted helpless beauties who made them feel manly. That wasn't me. I knew I wasn't ugly, but I wasn't anything special, either. To guys, I was a pal, not a gal.

He heaved a weary sigh. "Maybe we should take a break from seeing each other."

My eyes widened. Was Mackay breaking up with me?

"I think the world of you, Liz, but I can tell your heart's not in this relationship"

I opened my mouth to protest, but he continued in a rush.

"With everything going on—Dad's health and Mom worrying about medical bills—I can't do this. We've been going out for four months. I'd like to take things to the next level, but I don't think you're ready. Maybe if I give you space, you can decide whether you're all in…or not."

I twisted my hands in my lap, feeling like the worst girlfriend ever.

He tipped my chin. "Don't let down your guard around Rawson."

"I won't."

He blew out a breath. "Guess we better go inside and order."

"Can we just go through the Wendy's drive-thru?" I couldn't fake happy right now and wanted this breakup date over sooner, rather than later.

He drove down the road to my take-out Mecca, where I ordered a chili to warm my cold, dead heart.

The drive home seemed to take twice as long as normal. It must be an unwritten law of physics that awkward tension drew out the distance between any two points. When I spotted the log entrance to the ranch, I almost cheered—not because I wanted away from Mackay, but because I felt unworthy of such a decent man. God had given me a second chance to get it right, and I'd thrown a future with Mackay away by only thinking about myself. Who did that to such a nice guy?

Me, that's who. I seemed to ruin everything.

RAWSON

*M*ONOPOLY RANKED HIGH on my list of most hated games. Yet, I sat on the rug in an uncomfortable position playing the time-waster of my own free will and choice. When Benny had asked if I'd play with him and Liz, I'd shocked him by agreeing. The game took too long, but with Liz on the other side of the board, that suddenly didn't seem so bad.

Benny finished his turn. I rolled the dice and moved my boot to Board-walk. "I'll buy it."

"Are your feelings on this matter clear, Lord Vader." Benny was the smart-aleck banker.

"They are, Master." He snickered as I handed over four hundred Monopoly dollars.

Liz rolled the dice next. She moved the thimble to Baltic and bought it.

"If you're trying to buy up the cheap sh—" I caught myself, "crap and bankrupt us at the end with hotels, you might want to rethink your strat-egy. With doofus here buying everything he lands on, we're both in trou-ble." I rubbed Benny's head hard to make his hair stand up straight.

"Stop it!" He pushed me away.

"How was your first day of junior high?" Liz asked.

My brother's brows scrunched together and he forced a smile. "Good. Couldn't be better."

I bit my tongue to keep from interrogating the little liar. There'd be time to pull the truth from him later.

Benny rolled a seven. When he put money into the bank and snatched up Park Place, I threw Boardwalk across the board.

"Are you kidding? Now what good will this do me?"

Liz touched his hand. "I suggest a new strategy, R2: let the Wookiee win."

I whistled. "So I'm a Wookiee now?"

"If the fur fits, wear it." She concentrated on the board, fighting a grin.

I waited until she glanced up at me. She always did. "If I recall correctly, you said the other day you'd like to kiss a Wookiee."

She rolled the dice. "I said I'd *rather* kiss a Wookiee, meaning the creature ranks higher than you if I had to kiss something nasty. But Mackay ranks higher than you both."

Benny gave her a weird look. "I thought you said you broke up—"

"I'll buy it!" she shouted over his enlightening announcement.

"You broke up with Macky?"

Crimson splotches flared up her cheeks.

"I knew you'd come to your senses soon and dump that bin of vanilla."

She glared. "For your information, he dumped me."

"Then he's stupider than I thought."

She huffed and grabbed her property.

"Your turn, bro." Benny jabbed my side.

I rolled the dice and moved. Benny had one of every property, so I had no chance of winning. "New rule. Junior high punks aren't allowed to play."

His bottom lip jutted out. "You're just sore about Park Place."

"Damn straight."

Liz threw me a stern librarian scowl.

"Oops. I mean, *Dang* straight."

"Yeah, yeah," she mumbled.

"Since you're not stuck with vanilla, are you ready to try a new flavor?"

"We haven't completely broken up."

I smirked. "You're either together or you're not. Which is it?"

The dice were forgotten. Benny held them in his hand as he stared at us.

"We're just taking a break from each other," she said.

"Did you hear the key word in there, kid?"

He grinned. "Break, as in break up."

Lizzie pouted. "No. Break, as in rest. We're getting our lives in order before we get back together. With his father so sick—"

"Stop making excuses. If I were Mackay and you were my girl, the world could be falling apart and I would never...ever!...take a break from you. The worse life got, the tighter I'd hold onto you."

She looked at the carpet. "Ben, it's your turn."

I squirmed to get blood moving into my crossed legs.

131

"Do you have any classes with the kids from church?" she asked Ben.

"Yeah," I piped in, "because if you don't, the devil will get you."

Benny snickered as he collected fifty dollars rent from Liz for landing on one of his railroads. She gave me the evil eye. I hissed and crossed two fingers to ward off her spell. The corny act elicited an unwilling smile and a hard eye roll from her.

"I wish," Benny said. "But Alice saw me in the lunch line and invited me to eat with her and her friends."

Liz smiled. "That was nice of her."

Benny blushed, and I realized my kid brother was growing up. If the accident hadn't happened, he'd be in eighth grade, instead of seventh. That's when I'd started noticing girls.

"Are you sweet on this Alice chick?" I asked.

Benny turned beet red.

Liz elbowed me. "He's only fourteen."

"So? I liked girls at his age."

Benny snorted. "You were born liking girls."

"True that."

Liz folded her arms. "Well, normal boys his age think girls have cooties."

"I knew girls had cooties back then. They still do. But having a scientific mind, I've always enjoyed studying cooties up close." I winked.

They both made gagging faces, making me laugh. Monopoly had never been so fun.

Liz shoved me. "You're terrible."

"And gross." Benny handed me the dice.

"Gross and Terrible." I shook the dice and let them fall. "That was my nickname in junior high. That and Cootie Catcher."

Lizzie groaned as Mom peeked in at us.

"Hey, time to head to bed, Benny boy. You have school in the morning."

He started counting money but I stopped him. "Don't bother. You won. It's not even a contest." I started throwing bills in the right containers. "Liz and I will clean up."

"Ugh," he said, trudging upstairs.

I glanced over at Liz organizing money. "Since you're a free woman, should I ask Chance to take you to the movies?"

"I don't need a matchmaker."

"All work and no play makes Liz a dull girl."

"I am a dull girl."

"No. Any girl who rides horses as well as you doesn't have a dull bone in her body. Come on. You need a break from the ranch."

"The only thing I need a break from is ornery cowboys." She started to get up, but I caught her wrist.

"Movie. Saturday night. I'll find you a date."

She tugged against me. "I don't need pity dates."

"I'm not letting you go until you say yes."

"You'd better or I'll write you up to your father."

"What will you say? *Mr. Law,*" I said in a high falsetto, "*your son has been holding my hand in very inappropriate ways and performing illegal cootie checks.*"

She laughed. "Don't be stupid. I need to get to bed since I have to be up early."

"That does suck for you. Tell you what. I'll take you on a practice date to prepare you for Chance. I'll even throw in ice cream to celebrate your split from vanilla. It's the least I can do, Praline."

"I'm not Praline. I'm boring vanilla, like Mackay."

"Not even close. Macky broke up with you. That's his bad. I mean to fix his mistake and set you up with a real man, since you saved my life."

"I'm wishing I hadn't saved you."

"Come on. I won't bite. Unless you want me to." She scowled. "Come on, Lizzie. Ice cream. Movie. A handsome guy with a charming personality. What more could you ask for?"

"Peace and quiet."

I scratched my chin. "I can do that. Have you been out to the waterfall?"

She shook her head.

"Then we need to go. It'll take half an hour to drive there, and a twenty-minute hike to the falls. We should leave no later than six."

"I don't think so."

"Why not? It'll be fun."

"We work together. Besides, Mackay would be upset."

"Why should that matter? He broke up with you."

She wrinkled her nose. "It's just, I kind of promised him I wouldn't hang out with you outside of work."

My hands fisted. "Because I'm not a church man?"

"No."

"If you're not together, why are you still playing by his rules?"

Her brown eyes flashed. "I'm not."

"Prove it. Drive out to the waterfall with me Saturday night."

She smoothed her hair back. "Ugh...fine."

"You make it sound and look like I'm going to make you walk the plank into shark-infested waters."

She pursed her lips. "But it won't be a date. You'll just show me the land, as a coworker."

"As excited as you're acting, let's call it what it is—walking the plank."

A smile tugged at her lips. "Deal."

"It's a plank."

The sound of her laughter made me grin. Though it'd been like pulling teeth, I'd made headway tonight in helping Liz branch out from dating boring church fools. I vowed to add some spice to her life. After showing her how much fun a real guy could be, I'd set her up with Chance. But for now, I kind of looked forward to having her all to myself for an evening.

BENTLEY

*H*AY STUCK TO my clothes as I lifted a bale and threw it in the middle of the aisle.

"Thanks, Ben." Liz wiped sweat from her brow.

"Any time." I counted bales I'd lined up. "Need me to haul in more?"

"No. That should get me through Monday."

I brushed off my jeans as my big brother entered.

"Howdy, darling. You ready to walk the plank in a couple hours?"

I sat on a bale and gulped from my water bottle.

"About that," she said in an unpromising tone. "Mackay's dad passed away this morning. I need to cancel so I can be with him."

Rawson's jaw twitched. "I thought you broke up."

"Well, he needs me."

Rawson punched the sideboard and dropped an F-bomb.

Liz covered her ears. "You don't have to be such an…" She stopped.

"Say it," Rawson growled. He wasn't taking her news well. I didn't blame him. He'd looked forward to driving her out to the waterfall all week and had gone to a lot of effort to make the evening special. He'd driven to town to buy Japanese rolls when I'd mentioned they were her favorite, as well as a fancy-looking chocolate dessert I wanted to try. He'd also bought illegal fireworks to shoot off after dark. My brother was the king of cool.

Liz marched toward the tack room, but Rawson jogged after her and caught her by the arm.

"Say it," he said through gritted teeth. "Tell me what I am."

"Let go."

"Say what you meant. I'm such an___." He hummed the missing word.

"You're a jerk."

I wanted to pull Rawson out of there until he calmed down, but I might as well stop an erupting volcano.

"That's not it. Say the word," he spat.

There was a blur of motion, and he reeled back and let go of her. I blinked. Had Liz just slapped him?

He rubbed his cheek as she ran out the front doors.

I picked my tongue off the ground and pretended I hadn't witnessed his humiliation. My brother beat his fist against the wooden wall, agitating the horses. He turned to face me, and his eyes widened.

"Sorry, Big Ben. Didn't see you there."

Story of my life. "You feel better now?"

"Not really."

"Well, that wall ain't gonna backtalk you any time soon." He snorted. I looked up at the rafters. "A drive out to the waterfall sounds good right now. What do you say?"

He shrugged. "Why not? Bet we could have a romantic picnic. You like sushi rolls?"

I pointed both thumbs down. "Nasty."

"Well, grab some of whatever Susa's cooking and I'll finish off those rolls myself. I'm nice like that. We'll share that sky-high chocolate trifle and set off fireworks."

I chewed my lip. "You sure you don't want to save those for when you take her out another time?"

He scowled. "She made her choice. I'm making mine. I'll have lots more fun with you than with that fickle woman."

"Don't be mad at Liz. She's just trying to support Mackay in his time of loss. She's nice like that."

"She's too nice." He kicked the stall. "I thought I'd show her how fun other guys could be, but I don't think she'll ever climb out of her rut of dating lame guys who need her."

"Maybe you should start needing her...and work on being boring."

"And go to church every week in a starched collar shirt. Don't forget that." He kicked up dust from the floor.

"What do you have against church? I think the people there are pretty nice."

"Don't talk to me about *nice* right now, kid."

"Fine. Let's clean up so we can go hike and eat our picnic. I promise to be a big jerk."

Rawson made smooching sounds as I hobbled over to grab the broom.

"In your dreams, lover boy," I said.

He snickered. "You sound exactly like Lizzie."

LIZ

*G*RAVEYARDS RESURRECTED painful memories. I'd talked to Mackay every night this week as he'd vented grief. Last night, he'd picked me up and had arranged for me to spend the night at his sister's house in town so I wouldn't have to drive in early this morning for the funeral.

I'd felt bad asking Chance to cover for me, but I hadn't dared speak to Rawson. He'd seemed genuinely upset when I'd canceled our silly plank. But that was stupid. He wasn't interested in me, so why did he care if I helped out a friend? I was sick of his attitude.

Family and friends scattered to their cars as Mackay led me to his father's grave. He hadn't let go of my hand all day. I felt awful for wishing he'd give me a five minute reprieve to air out my fingers.

We gazed down at the freshly turned earth and temporary headstone. Mackay released my hand and draped a comforting arm around me. I leaned my head into him.

Why did life have to be so hard?

We said our farewells and began the long drive back to the ranch. I found it difficult to keep my eyes open. Funerals drained my very soul. Mackay pulled over on the side of the road, and I almost cried. This had already been the second longest day of my life, and he wanted to prolong it?

But when he turned to me with tears in his eyes, I smothered my selfish desire to get home and reached for his hand. He needed a friend.

"I don't know how you survived after your fiancé died." He sniffed as I squirmed uncomfortably. "I've known for months this day was coming, yet it's still so difficult. I miss him so much."

"So do I." I pulled him close and let him cry on my shoulder.

He began to reminisce, and I let him purge the tender memories. Mackay painted a vivid picture of his sweet dad and told me how much his dad had loved me. And then, he ruined everything by leaning over to kiss me.

Honestly, when he'd broken up with me, I'd been more relieved than upset. When he'd needed a friend, I'd been glad to step into that role. But our time apart had made me realize the truth.

I pulled away. "Um…" I bit my lip.

"I know what you're going to say."

"I really like you, but I'm not up to being your girlfriend. Sorry."

"Don't be. I shouldn't have done that. I mean, I'm the one who wanted us to take a break so you could figure out your feelings. But with losing Dad, I guess I got scared and didn't want to lose you, too."

"Oh, Mackay." I placed my hand on his. "I'll always be your friend."

A ghost of a smile surfaced. "Thanks for being here today. I don't know what I would've done without you."

He kissed my cheek and pulled back onto the road. At the ranch, he parked and helped me out, walking me to the porch.

He drew me close. "Sorry for being so needy."

"I'm glad I could help fill a void."

"You definitely did that. You've filled my whole world since I met you." He tipped my chin. "Can I give you a goodbye kiss?"

I squirmed. "I guess."

He leaned down and pressed his lips to mine. I'd never enjoyed kissing Mackay, but this was about friendship, not passion. The moment was actually tender and sweet. Until the front door opened and a deep voice startled us.

"Whoa."

We both jumped, and Mackay stiffened.

"You've come a long way, Macky," Rawson taunted. "I don't think a girl even looked at you in high school. Now, you're trying to get some sugar from Miss Ruthersford."

Mackay turned scarlet, which ticked me off.

"He's not trying to get sugar, Mr. Law. He's absolutely getting some. Now if you'll excuse us." I turned my back to him and reached my arms around Mackay. He about choked as I claimed his lips but recovered swiftly. Thank goodness. I'd never received more than a few pecks from him, so forcing the moment to extend felt awkward. But Rawson hadn't moved, and I wanted poor Mackay to feel like a dang man.

138

I pulled away a little breathlessly and gazed into Mackay's wide eyes, praying he wouldn't read more into that kiss than I'd meant.

Rawson clapped. "Encore! That was better than watching the *Bachelorette*." He raised an eyebrow. "I think Macky's going to die from a sugar rush though, Miss Ruthersford. Didn't you know he's diabetic?"

I ignored the rude man and took Mackay by the hand, tugging him to his car. "Don't let Rawson Law make you feel inferior," I whispered. "You're the most wonderful man I know."

Mackay let out a shaky breath. "That kiss was amazing. Thank you."

I rolled my eyes.

He glanced over at Rawson. "I know I don't have the right to tell you what to do, but please stay away from that jerk. I don't trust him."

"That makes two of us."

He squeezed my fingers. "Take care, Liz."

It was strange, but as I watched him drive away, a lump formed in my throat. I missed him. Curse my flighty female genes.

His taillights faded into the night, and I turned to find Rawson still watching me from the porch.

"Why are you still out here?" I snapped. "Don't you have a speck of decency?"

"It's a free country. Besides, I needed some fresh air."

I stormed up the steps and pushed past him. "I hope you choke on it." I slammed the door.

39

RAWSON

*D*RIZZLING RAIN SOURED my mood. It didn't improve when Lizzie climbed into my truck next to Benny and refused to look at me.

"You spruced up nice this morning." I tried to soften her up by teasing.

"Ben," she said, "will you tell your brother I'm not talking to him?"

My brother glanced between us as I pulled out of the driveway.

"Kid, can you tell that woman next to you that green looks amazing on her?" It did. I'd thought her blue dress had been divine a few weeks ago, but the light green blouse she wore today complemented her skin to perfection.

"Um, you do look really nice, Liz." He didn't sound thrilled to be our go-between.

"Thank you, Ben."

"Vanilla won't be able to keep his hands off pralines and cream today."

"Don't call him that," Liz growled.

I leaned over the steering wheel. "I thought you weren't talking to me."

"I'm not." Her nose wrinkled.

I focused on the road through the windshield wipers. She failed miserably when she tried to appear mean. She only looked like an adorable, tantrum-throwing pixie.

"I didn't know you were out on the porch when I came out last night." Maybe honesty would break down barriers.

"Ben, tell your brother to stop using up all the oxygen in the truck?"

"Tell her I'm making precious oxygen, not using it up. Every word I speak is helping her live longer."

"Tell him he's crazy…and a bully. He should've gone back in the house when he saw us."

Ben threw his hands in the air. "If I close my eyes and pretend to sleep, will you two leave me out of your battle?"

Silence fell upon us like a load of bricks, making me want to itch my skin. "That was quite the kiss Vanilla boy gave you last night. Did it make you snap, crackle, and pop?"

"Shut up." She definitely snapped right then. "Mackay is the nicest man I know. I hate you for taunting him. You were so out of line and still are. Can you only feel good about yourself by demeaning others?"

The sensation to scratch my dermal layer off increased. Part of me wanted to apologize. Another part wondered why she couldn't take a joke. I hadn't done anything but razz her a little. I pulled at my collar, wishing to yank my tie off and toss it out the window.

By the time we pulled into the church parking lot, Liz still hadn't spoken to me. The thought of seeing her with Bozo Benson made me want to punch something, so I parked in a handicapped stall and let the truck idle.

Benny scowled. "Why did you park here?" He sounded upset, and I realized he thought I was catering to his handicap. Nothing irritated him more than being treated like an invalid.

"I'm dropping you off. I'll be back to pick you up in a couple hours."

"Why aren't you coming?"

I glanced at Liz, who'd already stepped out into the rain and struggled with an umbrella. "That's why."

He gave me a sympathetic nod. "What are you going to do?"

"Go play a round of poker with the guys." Anything sounded better than starching it up in church with a woman who despised me.

His brows furrowed. "I meant, what are you going to do to make things right with Lizzie? You shouldn't hang out in bars. There's alcohol."

There was a whole lot more than booze. He'd understand someday. I needed a woman who wasn't as prickly as Pralines to soothe my overactive conscience.

I tousled his hair, eliciting a grunt.

"Stop it."

"Go soak in goodness for me, bro. When I pick you up, I'll wring you out and drizzle some on me."

He scooted out and left with Liz. They disappeared inside the white church, making me frown. For some illogical reason, I felt excluded.

40

LIZ

*S*LEEP WOULDN'T COME, despite how hammered I felt. Rawson kept hiccupping in my mind, making me wonder if he was Satan incarnate. Only someone as charming as he was could've persuaded Eve to partake of the forbidden fruit, and probably giggle as she did so. Stupid man. I wanted to be angry at him for being a jerk to Mackay, but he'd sounded so contrite yesterday after church when he'd apologized.

My phone buzzed. I reached for it and stared at a text from the very stupid man I'd been thinking about. Why was he contacting me so late?

Rawson: Did I call it or what?

:What are you jawing about?

Rawson: I heard it from the horse's mouth that Rocky Road asked you to the movies.

I grimaced. How had he found out already?

:LOL. All I could picture was you doing your impression. You were almost dead-on.

Rawson: Almost? I pegged that kid perfectly. I predict

snap, crackle, pop!

:Wrong. ☺

Rawson: *Will you pull a Stockholm if he tries to kiss you?*

:You're the only one dumb enough to pull that stunt.

My phone vibrated and Rawson's handsome face filled the screen. "Hello?"

"You really are clueless, girl. I'm definitely not the only one dumb enough to kiss you. And FYI, I was pretending to be Chance, so Chance was the idiot, not me. He likes you. That's why he's taking you to the movies to see if there's snap, crackle, pop."

"You have a cereal fetish."

He laughed, and I hugged the phone to my ear.

"And ice cream," he said.

"You need therapy, Bubble Gum."

"Keep being cheeky and I'll change your flavor to Tutti Fruity."

"You wouldn't dare."

"Don't ever issue me a challenge, Tutti."

I groaned. "Boo. That's a terrible name."

"I kind of like it."

"You would. I told you before, I'm pure vanilla."

His voice lowered. "You're pure all right, Tutti."

"I'm outlawing that name. It sounds too much like booty."

Laughter erupted on his end. "Then send the sheriff after me, because I'm breaking the law, Tutti Booty."

"You're impossible."

"So tell me how Rocky Road asked you. I thought he'd never work up the nerve and wondered if you'd give him a chance when he did."

"Well, his name is Chance, so I kind of had to give him one."

Rawson chuckled. "Will you dazzle him with a hot fudge sundae make-out session at the end of the date?"

"Absolutely not! What kind of question is that? And it's not a date. We're just going out as friends."

"Oh, come on, Lizzie. No guy wants to be friends. At least, give him a vanilla peck on the cheek."

"Fine. Maybe I'll give him one of those." I wasn't a prude as he insinuated.

"That's my girl."

"I think it's time to hang up and go to bed."

"Ummm-umm. I love when you talk dirty to me, baby."

My skin scorched like an iron resting on silk. "Uh, Goodnight," I said breathlessly.

His laughter echoed in my ears and warmed me long after I hung up on the infuriating man.

41

BENTLEY

*E*NTERING THE ARENA, I set my backpack down and called out. "Hey, Liz." She glanced up from where she and Chance were bent over Blue Boy's hooves. Chance looked like he was squeezing in on her space.

"You back from school already?" she asked.

"Yep. What do you need me to do?" Besides get Chance away from her.

"Want to clean saddles?"

"Sure." I gave Chance a chin tilt.

He threw me a toothy grin. "What's up, Benny?"

"The sky." I headed to the tack room, irritated at how much he monopolized Lizzie's time lately.

I hauled a sawhorse into the aisle and began working on Lizzie's saddle. I unfastened buckles, removed the fitting, and wiped the leather down with a moist towel to remove built-up gunk.

Chance touched shoulders with Liz across the way. "I think Blue's ready to graduate up to Seth, don't you?"

She moved away and patted Blue's flank. "Not quite. His contact and connection needs improvement. His response to the reins is too rough as well."

I grabbed a damp sponge and worked soap into a lather.

Chance closed the distance between them again. "You're the boss."

Kiss-up.

"You up for a drive after supper? There's a full moon tonight."

"What are you? A werewolf?" I muttered.

Chance heard and burst out laughing, thinking I was joking.

Liz frowned. "I have a bunch of things to do, but thanks for asking."

I scrubbed her saddle, wishing she'd be more decisive. A guy like Chance needed a good set-down. A firm "No way in hell, buddy."

"Well, if you change your mind, text me."

"I'll keep that in mind."

"Like a warning," I muttered.

Chance grinned like I was his best bud.

Rawson beat the front door like a drum as he entered. "Here's Johnny."

I hobbled over to see him, but Chance beat me.

"Hey, Rawson. I didn't know you were back. How did the auction go?"

"Great." He raised a brow. "Did I interrupt anything between you two?" His tone and raised eyebrows gave the impression that he expected them to be kissing or something.

Lizzie threw him a murderous glare. "Chance helped with the horses, but now that you're back, he can return to his regular duties." She smiled at Chance. "Thanks again."

"Anytime, Liz. Maybe tomorrow we can take that drive."

"I don't think—"

"I'll cover for Liz," Rawson said, "so she can go with you tonight."

Chance practically hugged him. "Really, man? You'd do that for us?"

"It'd be my pleasure."

"No. I can't leave all the work to you," Liz protested.

My brother gave her a teasing grin. "I insist. You work too hard and need time to play." He turned to Chance. "I expect you to wow her, dude."

She fidgeted. So did I. Rawson was ruining everything. He needed to ask Lizzie out, not push her off on Chance.

"Chance, can you take Blue Boy to his stall and find my training notebook?" Liz asked. "I think I left it in the office."

"Sure thing." He hurried away to fulfill his damsel's request.

Rawson tousled my hair. "You grow a few inches each time I see you."

"I'm 5'10". Mom had me stand against the wall last night."

"You're going to catch up to me at this rate." He turned to Liz. "That was pretty slick how you got rid of Rocky Road."

"Why did you butt in? Now I'll hurt his feelings when I say I can't go."

I hobbled back to the sawhorse, glad that Lizzie was thinking straight. I picked up a clean towel to remove excess soap residue and kept listening.

Rawson leaned against the stall in a cool pose he'd probably learned modeling. I made note to try it out later in front of a mirror. "You *can* go. I'm making it possible. Don't break Rocky Road's heart."

Lizzie pouted, which made Rawson laugh.

"You'll thank me when this is all over and you see how well the two of you combine. It'll be ice cream sundae making time."

She punched his arm. "That's never going to happen."

"Not if you keep fighting so hard," he said as she left the tack room.

What was my stupid brother thinking?

RAWSON

A DILUTED SWEAR WORD slipped from Lizzie's lips—the third since I'd shown up late and had started working. "Freaking-A," she muttered under her breath. "Why won't this work?" She had her head down, working on something I couldn't see.

"Saying the real words makes you feel better."

Her head jerked up. "Don't scare me like that."

"What's eating at you, Grumpy?"

She looked at the halter in her hands. "Nothing."

I sank onto a bale of hay and patted the spot next to me. "Sit. Something's gnawing on your britches."

She surprised me by slumping down next to me.

"How did your date with Chance go?"

She frowned. "Thanks to you, he thinks we're a couple and tried to kiss me."

I chuckled. "*Tried* being the key word."

"Seriously," she huffed, "this is all your fault."

"Don't blame me. You're the one who can't stop being so dam-nang sweet." I barely caught myself.

She pouted. If she knew how adorable I found that expression, she'd never do it again. I looked up at the rafters, something I found myself doing a lot around her lately.

"What do you mean I'm too sweet?"

"You're a total pushover with guys. Take Mackay, for example. You didn't like him, but still went out with him for months. If Chance doesn't do it for you, tell him. Don't string him along and whine about it."

She gave me the evil eye. "I tried to, but you forced me to go with him."

I stuck a piece of hay in my mouth. "No sparks?"

"No!"

"You probably need to kiss him to know for certain."

She folded her arms. "He tried kissing me in his truck, and all I felt was angry."

"You pulled a Stockholm on him?"

"It obviously didn't deter him. He's still pestering me about going on another drive."

I grinned. Chance had been slow to take the reins but was galloping fast in this relationship now. Liz couldn't keep her foot off the brakes though.

"Why are you so scared to have fun?"

She faced me, and my heart stuttered. Even with her curls contained in a boring bun, I found her captivating. The graceful tilt of her neck seemed to be made specifically with me in mind. The perfect length to bury my head in and get lost in desire.

"I'm not scared. I just don't feel anything for Chance. It's like Mackay on repeat."

I shook off my unprofessional thoughts. "That's too bad. I know he really likes you."

"What should I do?"

"Let him down easy, I guess. Here. Let's practice. I'll be Chance." I slicked back my hair and wrapped an arm around her. In an instant, chemistry sparked. I focused on acting. "Hey, baby." I leaned closer. "You up for a drive tonight?"

"Uh, Chance..." She could hardly breathe as I traced circles into her upper arm. "I really like you."

I made a buzzer sound. "Stop. That'll just make him do this." I brushed my lips across her cheek, making her flinch. "You have to be more direct or he'll think you're into him." I pulled her legs up over mine.

Her eyes widened. "I don't think Chance would do that."

"Don't be so sure."

She breathed so hard I would've thought she'd just ran a 5K if I hadn't known better. My gaze dropped to her chest. No wonder Chance acted all randy. I sort of felt the same.

"That's enough." She swung her legs off mine and tried to squirm out of my embrace.

"You can't just strong arm your way out of this." I held her tighter. "You need to use the right words. Try again." I gave her a full-teeth Chance-y grin that made her laugh.

"Chance, you're a great friend and all—"

"Perfect. The word *friend* always kills the mood. Guys hate that word."

She looked down as I caressed her free hand. "But I don't feel anything more."

"You haven't really tried, darling." I zeroed in on her neck, laying a couple feather kisses down it.

She abruptly stood, making me teeter before I regained balance. By the time I caught up to her, she was in Blue Boy's stall.

"Just be firm with Chance," I said. "No soft and sweet Praline."

She scowled. "Go away."

"Not until I help you find a man who makes you snap, crackle, and pop."

"I don't need your help."

"Describe your perfect man."

She slipped the bridle onto Blue Boy. "What are you? A dating site?"

"Hmm? That's not a bad idea." I walked over to pat Blue Boy's flanks. "Maybe I'll call my site *Lucky in Love: Ice Cream and Cereal Specialist.*"

She shook her head. "You're a nut."

"Then why did you make me bubble gum flavor? You should think up a nutty ice cream for me to be."

She placed a finger on her chin. "Pistachio. That's nutty, and green reminds me of the Kermit the Frog shirt you wore to church that one Sunday."

I laughed. "Now you're talking. I'm totally Pistachio. You can call me Stash for short."

"How about Kermie?"

I snapped my fingers. "Back on topic. Perfect man."

"Maybe Captain America?" Blue nuzzled her cheek, making me jealous.

"Qualities, Lizzie. Not superheroes."

She pursed her lips and started scratching Blue's ears. "Well, he'd have to be a man of faith."

I hissed. "Why? Vanilla was that and he did nothing for you."

"Hey, it's my perfect man. Stop leading the witness."

"Bleck. All right. Continue."

"Spiritual, sweet."

"Sounds like the Pope's puppy."

"A puppy might be better than a man. Can I describe the perfect puppy?"

"No."

She tilted her head as Blue Boy nudged her hand. He was an attention hog. "I think you have a thing for the Pope. You always use him in your similes."

I shook my head. "Perfect man."

She sighed. "He'd be strong and tall. At least six feet."

"Now we're getting somewhere," I said, standing taller. "What else?"

"He'd like horses, but he wouldn't be a crass cowboy who thinks he's God's gift to women and walks all bow-legged and swears all the time."

"Hey, I resemble that."

One of her deep barking laughs escaped, making me grin.

"Okay, so your perfect man is churchy, tall and muscular, likes puppies and horses, and doesn't walk bow-legged or spit or curse."

"I think you just described Captain America."

"Iron Man's better." Blue Boy nickered, reminding us that we'd both forgot him.

"Ew. I'd never marry a man like him," she said, clamping a leader to the bridle.

"Why not? He's rich, smart, smooth, and charming."

"Notice I didn't put any of those on my list. I will put honest and trustworthy though. Iron Man's a womanizer." She led Blue out of his stall.

I followed, thinking she had a point as my cheating ex flitted through my mind.

"What about you?" she asked. "Describe your dream girl."

I stared up at the rafters, trying to keep from ogling her backside. "That's easy. She'd be beautiful, but not high-maintenance. I've been there, done that. Sucked the soul right out of me. She'd be easy to talk to and make me laugh. Her chest would be perky." Liz huffed, making me grin. "She'd love horses and not be afraid to get her hands dirty. She wouldn't nag me about my *Star Wars* obsession and she'd bake me cinnamon rolls at least once a week. She'd be passionate and want to make love every day, and she wouldn't have wandering eyes. She'd think I was God's greatest gift to her. And she'd be at least 5'8" because I don't want to throw out my back when I lean down to kiss her, and believe me, I'd be kissing her a lot."

"Hmmm. Sounds like that Kelsey woman from Kentucky." She stopped at the tack room.

"She'd be the exact opposite of that woman. Save me Obi-Wan-KeTutti. You're my only hope."

She giggled. "Grab me a saddle, will you?"

I did as she asked. "If you bring up that blond nightmare again, don't be surprised if you receive a stinky gift from me."

"Oh, poor Kermie," she taunted. "Life is hard with so many gorgeous women throwing themselves at you."

"It's Stash," I said, throwing the saddle onto Blue. "And yes, it is excruciating, so show some respect. Maybe send me a picture of you to laugh at tonight, and I won't surprise you with a stink bomb." I yawned. A week of no sleep was catching up to me.

"Deal, my dear Kermie," she said in a pretty good Miss Piggy voice.

"You're hilarious."

"I am, aren't I?" She mounted the horse and shooed me away. "Now get to work."

When I crawled into bed that night, my phone chimed. I burst out laughing as I studied a picture and text from Liz. In the photo, she'd pushed her nose up like a pig and had her hair all loose and curling around her face.

Tutti: Miss Piggy Beauty tip #1.
Never braid your eyelashes.

The picture was silly, but my pulse increased as I stared at her mass of blond curls all wild and free. The girl was breathtaking when she let loose. I recalled the description of my perfect woman—beautiful, but not high maintenance, funny, perky chest, horse lover, unafraid of hard work, easy to talk to, passionate and true. Lizzie checked out on every single item, even her height.

"I am such an idiot," I muttered as I gazed at her silly selfie again.

My dream girl had been staring me in the face for over two months, and what had I done but try to pass her off onto some other guy. Now, I was grateful she hadn't clicked with Chance. I didn't want her to click with him or anyone else, because we already did. Searching for Kermit quotes on Google, I typed madly.

:It's not easy being green.
Sweet dreams. I think UR
the perfect girl for me.

Tutti: Hi-ya! I just busted you
in the chops for speaking to
MOI like that. Go find a lily pad.

:Time's fun when you're
having flies. Ribbet.

Tutti: Groan

I hated to end our battle of wits, but she had to be up in less than five hours to muck stalls. Kissing her adorable Miss Piggy face on the screen, I flipped off the lamp and sent her a smiley face emoji to close out this round.

"Until tomorrow, my lady," I whispered.

Now that I'd pulled my head out of the sand, she would discover what snap, crackle, and pop was all about.

BENTLEY

*R*AWSON APPROACHED the wash bay where Liz groomed Friday Night Gin. "That was a great picture you sent me last night."

I ducked, pretending I wasn't eavesdropping as I oiled Lizzie's saddle.

"Ha ha," she said.

"No joke. I loved your hair all down like that."

Lizzie blushed at my brother's teasing.

"Want to grab dinner in town with me tonight? I can hook up the trailer and pick up that load of hay you need while we're out."

I perked up, unable to contain a huge smile.

"Tempting," she murmured. "But I already told some friends I'd play volleyball with them."

"Oh." He frowned. "Any chance I can change your mind?"

She scoffed. "No. I don't go back on my word. But you could come with me if you want."

Rawson smiled. "I want."

A noise made us all jump. Chance had dropped Lizzie's binder, scattering papers. He bungled about to retrieve them, and Liz said, "Would you like to join us, Chance?"

I blew out a long breath as she once again acted kinder than she should. Rawson seemed to agree, judging by his disgruntled expression. I applied a non-detergent leather conditioner to the saddle and watched the drama play out.

"Sure. Thanks." Chance handed her the messed-up binder with a goofy grin.

"We'll need to leave around six. Which one of you wants to drive?"

"I will," they both said.

She headed to her office. "You can fight over the honor."

Rawson clapped a hand on Chance's shoulder after Lizzie disappeared. "What are you doing? I'm paying you to stay out at the homestead with Damon in the evenings."

Still pissed me off that his friend was out there.

"He'll be all right for a couple hours," Chance said. "I really want to hang out with Liz."

"Chance, man, you know I appreciate all you've done to help me out, but I'm asking you as a friend to back off. Liz asked me first. If you come along, you'll be a third wheel. Catch my drift?"

A light finally went on in Chance's thick skull. "Oh? Ohhh! You... ohhhh! Sorry, Roz. I didn't know you and Liz were..." He raised a brow.

"We're not yet. But I'm hoping to change that. I'd appreciate you keeping it quiet for now."

Chance hit his forehead. "No wonder she's been so stand-offish. All this time I thought I was doing something wrong, but she already liked you. Whew. Sorry, man. I didn't know I'd pushed in on your territory."

Rawson slapped his back. "No harm done but keep your distance now that you know."

"Don't worry." He chuckled as he walked away. "It makes so much sense now."

I wiped a dry cloth over the metal fittings. "When did this magic mojo happen?"

Rawson shrugged. "I don't know. But I think I like her."

"It's about freaking time."

He laughed.

44

RAWSON

SEVEN PEOPLE CROWDED onto each side of the volleyball court in the old church gym. Lizzie and I had been split up as soon as we'd arrived, which had irked me. She'd failed to mention this was a church social for singles. Dinner alone would've been way more enjoyable.

An overweight girl with straight brown hair prepared to serve. "Two to one," she shouted.

Liz faced me across the net, distracting me in her tight leggings. Other guys were scoping her out as well, watching as she bent and bounced on her feet. This game had brought out a competitive edge in her. It'd ignited a jealous streak in me.

The ball shot over the net. I dived, knowing Mandy or Sandy or whatever her name was wouldn't budge from her spot. Bumping the ball into the air, I scooted out of the way so Steve could set it to Landon, who fist-bumped the ball over the net. Liz set up, and her team sent it back. We volleyed back and forth until Steve set me up for a kill.

Anxious to display my skills, I jumped and spiked the ball with all my might. It would've been perfect if it hadn't landed right on Lizzie. The ball hit with such force that she fell to one knee. Blood spurted from her nose.

Heads turned from Liz to me as I released a curse worthy of the dumbest cow. I ignored the group of gapers and ran under the net to get to her, shoving one of her male teammates aside.

"Get your hands off her."

Liz threw her head back and squeezed the bridge of her nose.

"You okay?" I helped her to her feet and led her out of the gym.

"I'm fine."

"Liar." I guided her to a restroom. A crowd of tittering girls followed.

"I think I'll call you Smash instead of Stash," she said.

I chuckled and pushed the door open to the ladies room.

"You can't come in here." Liz planted her feet.

"You're hurt and I need to fix you." The volume of tittering rose behind us as I pushed her inside. I turned to the silly girls. "Somebody get some ice."

My command was met by huffing, but the door closed. I lifted Liz onto the sink and started wetting paper towels.

"Hold this against your nose." I dabbed at her poor cheek that already showed signs of swelling. "I'm so sorry. I can't believe I went all caveman on you. If I muck stalls for the next week, will you forgive me?"

"Maybe."

Mandy or Sandy stuck her head in and held out an icepack.

"Thanks." When she kept staring, I said, "You can go now."

She ducked out the door.

"Hold this." I placed the plastic baggie against the side of Liz's nose. "Sorry again."

"Stop apologizing. I'd be offended if you'd treated me like a wussy girl out on the court. Besides, it was a perfect spike."

I grinned. "It was, wasn't it?"

She laughed.

I studied the light sprinkling of freckles covering her nose and cheeks. Gold flecks warmed her brown eyes. Why had it taken me so long to notice her?

"Why don't we make like a tree and get out of here."

A dimple formed in her right cheek. I yearned to kiss that delectable dent and work my way over to those lips she liked to bite.

We escaped through the back door and worked our way around the building. I opened the passenger door for her.

"You were the prettiest girl here by far tonight."

She hit my arm. "Shut up."

I backed her up against the passenger door, trapping her between my arms. "Now, that's not what you say when a man pays you a compliment."

She tried to push back, but I stepped closer. "What do you say, Lizzie?"

"Trina was."

I shook my head. "Not even close. All us guys were focused on one beauty tonight. You."

"Liar."

"One thing you should know about me by now is I don't give out phony compliments. If I say you're pretty, I mean it." I moved my hands to her shoulders, causing her to draw in a sharp breath.

"Let's try again. You put every other girl here to shame with your beauty and kick-butt volleyball skills." She scoffed, but I pressed my body into hers. "What do you say?"

"Ah, uh, thank you? Although you're—"

I silenced her with a finger. "No *althoughs* or *buts*, Tutti."

A smile appeared.

"Your smile is stunning."

She rolled her eyes.

"I'm going to pretend your eye roll is sign language for *Thank you*."

The trembling in her body transferred into my limbs. Talk about snap, crackle, and pop. We had enough for a dazzling firework show. I licked my lips, feeling weak with expectation. Our noses brushed and short puffs of minty breath tickled my mouth as her chest rose and fell against mine. I could practically taste bliss as I leaned in.

"Rawson!"

Lizzie jumped, bumping into my head. "Agh!" She clutched her nose.

I pivoted to find Trina on the sidewalk. "Oh," she said in a breathy voice as she noticed Liz. "I didn't see you there. Is your nose still bleeding?"

"What is it?" I snapped.

The overly done-up girl gave me a bright smile. "I'm glad I caught you. I wanted to invite you to dinner this Sunday. I don't work and thought—"

"Sorry, Tina." I purposely mispronounced her name, hoping she'd get a clue. "Liz is my girl."

Lizzie's eyes widened as I grabbed her hand.

"Oh." The pushy broad's smile mutated into a grimace. "Your nose looks awful," she said to Liz. "It's probably going to bruise and—"

"We're going." I turned my back on Sharktopus to help Lizzie climb into my truck.

I drove away, and Liz gave me a narrow-eyed scowl.

"What?"

"I can't believe you used me again to get away from a woman."

"I wasn't using you. I staked my claim and posted my *in a relationship* status."

"In a relationship status with who?"

"You and me, sweetheart. We have that snap, crackle, and pop I've been talking about."

"We do not."

"How can you say that after what happened back there?"

"What?"

"That almost-kiss."

She folded her arms. "We did not almost kiss."

"If Tyrannosaurus Trina hadn't interrupted, we would have. And I can

158

assure you it would've set off more than snap, crackle, and pop, because we have that without even trying. It would've been sizzle, pop, kaboom!"

She laughed. "You never stop, do you, Kermie?"

The lackadaisical way she blew me off bothered me. Did she think I was joking?

I kept quiet until we reached the junction to Benny's Hollow. Veering off the gravel road, I pulled into a grove of trees and parked.

Liz opened her eyes. "What are you doing?"

"We're going to have a DTR."

"How do you even know what that is?"

"I've dated enough girls in my life to know the lingo. Defining-the-relationship is vital to you women."

"We don't have a relationship. Now go. I have to muck stalls in the morning."

"No, I have to muck stalls in the morning, remember? I owe you for slaughtering your cute, dainty nose."

She touched her face. "You don't have to do my chores."

"I want to." I scooted into the middle so our thighs touched.

"You're crowding me," she said.

"I know." I grabbed her hand.

She tried to tug away, but I squeezed her fingers.

"Yesterday, when I listed all the qualities in my dream girl, it hit me that I'd just described you."

She snorted. "I'm not your dream girl. Not even close."

"You couldn't be more perfect if you tried." I caressed her cheek. "We get along. You're beautiful, but not stuck on yourself."

"Ha!" She pushed my hand down. "You need to get your eyes checked. I'm more like Attila the Hun with these wild curls."

"I have better than 20/20 vision. Maybe you need glasses, because you're the only one not seeing clearly. Every guy on the court tonight watched you. Do you think that's because you're plain and ugly?"

"I probably looked like a dork with my bloody nose."

"They were drooling way before I busted your nose. We guys appreciate beauty and class, and you're the pinnacle of womanhood." When she snorted again, I chuckled. "Except when you snort. Seriously though, you're the whole package—funny, easy to talk to, kind, hardworking, graceful, honest." I glanced down south. "Not to mention your visible assets."

She smacked my shoulder.

"Ow, woman! Can't you take a compliment?"

"I don't want your compliments."

"Well, I'm giving them anyway."

"Move back to your seat, or I'll hit you again."

I focused on her lips. "You could just kiss me so we can figure out what we want from each other."

"I don't want anything from you. We're friends. Coworkers. That's all."

"The best relationships are based on friendship." I leaned down to brush my lips over her brow. "We also have chemistry."

She gulped. "Some chemical reactions are dangerous. Scoot over. You're making me uncomfortable."

I growled and slid behind the steering wheel.

"Thank you."

I stared at the roof of my truck. I thought after making it clear that I liked her, we'd make-out. Simple. We'd almost kissed in the church parking lot, and I wanted to strangle Trina for ruining that moment because nothing was going how I imagined now. I'd never opened up like this, and her response felt like a slap in the face.

"I'm sorry." Her soft voice caressed me in the darkness. "But it wouldn't work between us. Besides, have you forgotten how you tried to push me off on Chance for the last month?"

"I thought you were too good for me."

"Oh, and now you realize that's not true. I'm just—"

I stopped her before she could belittle herself. "No. Now I *know* you're too good for me. But I'm not content to be with the riff-raff anymore. I hope you'll take pity on me and lift me up to your level."

She gaped at me.

I clasped her hand. "What do you say?"

She pulled her hand from my grip. "I value our friendship too much to risk ruining it."

"Even for something a million times better?"

"It wouldn't be."

"How do you know?"

She shrugged. "We don't see eye to eye."

"On what?"

"God."

"I've gone to church with you."

"But do you love God?"

I smacked the steering wheel. She was pulling the church card on me, just as Sarah Benson had done in high school. "No. I don't love your God. What has He done for me, except throw mine fields in my path? I despise how people like you praise Him for all that's good but blame mankind for all that's bad. God is either responsible for all the good *and* the bad, or we are. You can't have it both ways."

Tears glistened in her eyes.

I pulled back onto the road. In the darkness, I couldn't gauge her

160

emotions, but I knew I'd hurt her. I'd walloped her nose in volleyball, and now I'd pummeled her faith. Slap a big Jerk label on my forehead.

Sleet-like rain began to fall. Typical for September. When I pulled up to the house to drop her off, the ground had puddled with mud.

Liz opened her door. I knew I should get out and be a gentleman, but my jerk persona won out. Why should I help her when she wanted nothing to do with me? She'd probably ignore my hand anyway.

I couldn't take anymore rejection.

"Sorry again about your nose," I called after her.

"It's all right." She gave me a half-smile that didn't reach her eyes. "Don't worry about mucking in the morning. I'll do it."

I opened my mouth to protest but closed it. Maybe I should leave well enough alone. Baring my heart hadn't worked out at all.

NOURISHING HOPE

Hope is the only bee that makes honey without flowers.

~ *Robert Green Ingersoll* ~

LIZ

*M*ORNINGS SUCKED. That's the thought that went through my head as my alarm buzzed. I rolled out of bed and pulled on dirty clothes, pulled my crazy curls into a ponytail, and staggered into the bathroom half-awake. With my swollen nose and cheek, I resembled the misshapen Quasimodo. Ugh.

I approached the stable, noticing light pouring from beneath the door. What the heck? I remembered distinctly turning off the lights last night. What bozo had been out here after me and left them on?

I hefted the door open and grabbed a mucking rake, but the wheelbarrow that usually sat by the door was missing.

"Dang fool, lazy, no-good cowboys," I muttered.

"Morning."

I screamed and dropped the rake.

"Hope you weren't referring to me in your early morning salutation, sweetheart." Rawson scooped horse droppings two stalls over, plopping them into the wheelbarrow I'd been searching for.

"What are you doing out here?" I touched my tender nose.

"What does it look like? I told you I'd muck."

His tight T-shirt emphasized toned muscles and his snug Wranglers hugged his backside, making it impossible for me to think. I gulped and entered the opposite stall.

"I told you I'd do it."

"I know." He smiled. "So talk to me. I'm not used to being up this early."

"Go back to bed. I can do it. I look like a train wreck."

He winked. "I could wake up to your kind of train wreck every morning."

I launched a rake full of horse pellets at him, making him duck and laugh. We cleaned several stalls, falling into an easy rhythm, until he joined me in Yoda's stall.

I concentrated on horse droppings, instead of the beautiful man in front of me.

"I'm heading to town Saturday night to watch a football game. Care to join me?"

"I'm not into football." I paid such rapt attention to the ground that I didn't realize he'd crept closer until he trapped me against the back wall. My breath caught in my throat as I faced him. "Rawson, what are you—"

"I'd like to get to know you outside of work, Lizzie."

He could have any girl he wanted. Why would he want to get to know me?

He stepped closer until our noses almost touched. "I like you."

My eyes widened. What did he mean by that?

He leaned in to rest his forehead against mine. I couldn't move. Couldn't think. My insides went bonkers with his hot, sexy body touching mine, minty breath teasing me, his cologne holding me prisoner. It should be illegal for a cowboy to smell so good.

"Let's see where this will go." He somehow moved even closer, though I didn't know how that was possible. He seemed serious. But we were coworkers. Just because he'd teased me with that kiss in his truck didn't mean he liked me. He probably kissed any hot-blooded, willing female.

"Probably not a good idea," I stammered. "If we crashed and burned, it'd make working together super awkward."

His thumb stroked my swollen cheek, making me hyperventilate. Heavens. The man made me feel things I'd never felt before. I didn't know if that was good or bad. Should I stay or run?

"That's definitely possible with all the snap, crackle, and bang we bring to the equation. But more likely, things will be amazing between us." His gaze dropped to my lips, and like a magnet, mine zeroed in on his.

He had the most luscious looking lips. And I couldn't unsee them since he'd kissed me that one night. They'd become my obsession. I focused on them when he was nearby. I dreamed about them in my sleep.

Gravity pulled him down, and I jerked to the side as I realized he planned to kiss me. I couldn't let that happen again.

His lips landed on my swollen cheek, making me wince. "Damn. I hurt you, didn't I?"

"I'm fine." I felt both relieved and guilty for dousing the chemical reaction between us with my evasive maneuver.

"You sure are."

I started raking again, trying to ignore my triple-speed pounding heart.

Rawson wrapped his arms around me from behind, making me freeze up. "Give us a chance, Lizzie. Please."

I turned in his arms, my body burning with need. He seemed sincere, and I longed to give in and accept. I wanted to kiss him, to see if it'd be as divine as I kept imagining from that short one I'd sampled. But could I trust my judgment ever again? Before I could talk myself out of being stupid, one word slipped out of my mouth.

"Okay," I whispered. My heart seemed to have shoved it out, over-riding my good sense.

"Really?" He cupped my chin. "You'll go out with me?"

Part of me screamed *No!* This wouldn't end well. Rawson couldn't be trusted. He was charming and kind and beyond sexy. But he was also unreliable as an assistant and broke his promises. Yet, stupid me. I nodded, slightly dazed from the intent look in his eyes.

He leaned down to kiss me, but I lifted my palm. A small part of my brain still worked, thank goodness.

His eyes twinkled. "As tasty as your hand is, it's kind of in my way."

I chewed my lips. "I'm not a fast mover."

He full-on smirked. "Honey, that's the understatement of the year."

"If we go out, we take things slow."

His brow furrowed. "Explain what you mean by *slow*."

"No kissing." Even as I said it, I knew it was extreme. I'd never had that rule with other guys. But Rawson frightened me. I'd never been so drawn to someone. Kissing him would make me vulnerable. I couldn't do that again. Not until I trusted him with my heart, if that was possible.

"What?" he cried.

I stepped back to put needed distance between us. "If you don't like it, I'm sure there are any number of girls who'd like to kiss you."

"Of course, there are." He scowled. "But you and I already don't kiss. How will this be any different? Shouldn't we maybe add kissing to the list of things we do if we're together?"

I studied the stable wall, finding the wood grain very intriguing. "I don't know if I'm comfortable saying we're *together*."

He looked up at the rafters, then shook his head. "I'll agree to the no kissing part—for now—but only if you agree to not date other guys. I want exclusive rights."

"What? I'm not a brood mare. Besides, I'd think you'd be glad to date other girls."

"I don't want other girls." He reached out and took my hands in his. "Riff-raff, remember? I want to step up my game."

I tried to tug away. Was that all I was to him? A game.

"Stop struggling, woman. You didn't say anything about hand holding, and I intend to hold your hand a lot since we're together now."

"We're not together. I can date other guys." I broke free and picked up the rake.

"Come on." He took off his cowboy hat to rake his hair, then put it on again. "You have to be willing to give a little."

I focused on my job. "That's just it. I don't want to give in at all." I'd done that too much in life. To Mom. To Dad. My sister. Justin. "See. This already isn't working. You should just date one of your normal girls."

"My normal girls?" He growled.

"You know?" I dumped droppings into the wheelbarrow. "Like Kelsey, only younger, or Trina at church. Beautiful, big-boobed models."

"Give me some credit, Liz. Do you really think I'm that shallow?" He pulled the rake from my hands and tilted my chin. "Give yourself more credit, too. Can you really not see what draws me to you?" He ran a hand over my ponytail. "I love your crazy curls." He ever so softly pressed his pinky to the tip of my swollen nose. "I love how after I smashed you with the volleyball, you joked about it with me. You make me laugh every time we're together."

He played with my fingers, and it was all I could do to keep my knees from buckling as I stared into his gorgeous blue-green eyes.

"I love your strength. You don't let me bully you, but stand up like a bull for what you believe in."

A giggle escaped. That'd been a good one.

He grinned. "I love your giggle, but what really gets me is your inner seal. When I make you bark, I feel as though I've won the lottery."

I shoved him. "Shut up about my dorky laugh."

"I adore your dorky laugh."

"Stop lying."

"I'm not. Your laugh is unique and refreshing. Most girls are so fake, even their laugh. Yours is genuine, from your gut. I can't ever feel sad when I hear you laugh."

I rolled my eyes to hide how his words affected me. Did he mean it, or was he just saying pretty words to charm me?

He kissed my forehead. "So, let me get this straight. You'll date me, but not exclusively. If someone else asks you out, like say Rusty"—I huffed when he purposely picked the youngest, pimply faced hand—"you're free to go out with him, too?"

"Exactly. And you can go out with other girls, like Bambi or FooFoo."

He raised one sexy eyebrow. "In my book, we'll be exclusive. I won't date anyone else, no matter how much they remind me of a Disney movie."

167

I squirmed out of his arms and started raking again. "Do whatever, but don't pull the jealous card on me." Justin had done that way too much.

Rawson leaned against the side of the stall. "Why do I get the feeling dating you will be more work than herding cattle?"

I tossed more manure into the wheelbarrow. "It'll be like herding cats."

We entered a stare-down, which I enjoyed since it gave me an excuse to look at him without blushing.

"Meow," he mewed.

I laughed, the obnoxious seal laughter he teased me about. That made him lose it. When we stopped after a few minutes, he grabbed my hand.

"So will you be my date this Friday? I know this upscale bar in Bozeman that—"

I whipped my hand away. "I'm not going to a bar." Dad had said nothing good ever happened there. "Besides, you told me you don't drink."

"I don't."

"Then why would you go to a bar?"

"There's more to do in a bar than drink. There's the whole social aspect —meeting people, dancing, watching sports."

"If we date, bars are out."

He pursed his tempting lips. "How many rules do you have in that cute head of yours?"

"Those are the main ones, I think."

"You think?" He puffed out his cheeks. "What did you do with Mackay besides being bored at movies? There's not much else to do around here."

"I don't mind movies. We can even stay home and watch them with Benny."

He squeezed his temple. "Oh yea. Maybe we can invite my parents and Addie along as well."

"We don't have to do anything. You can go to town and have fun with some Daisy Duke girl in a bar, for all I care."

"Why would I do that when I have a beautiful girl right here?"

"Oh, please. I'm not—"

"Don't say it." His lips next to mine arrested my words. "I swear I'll kiss you senseless if you say one negative thing about yourself."

I didn't dare move since his mouth hovered millimeters above mine. I had no doubt he'd make good on his threat.

"You. Are. Beautiful." His spearmint breath made me shiver.

"Uh, we should get mucking."

The irritating man grinned. "Okay. But first, let's work out our date. Are you free this Saturday to go on a hike?"

"Can Benny come?"

I expected him to say no—his enthusiasm definitely waned—but he surprised me by shrugging. "Why not? If I can't kiss you, we might as well have my brother tag along. Be ready by five. We'll drive out to the canyon and take a sunset hike."

"Awesome."

We finished mucking stalls, and I kept smiling. Rawson had agreed to let his brother come with us. Justin would've never allowed that. I was still nervous, or maybe that was still butterflies he'd caused inside me, but I was more excited. I wanted to get to know Rawson better. And this seemed safe.

46

RAWSON

*I*T'D BEEN AGES since I'd felt so alive. In fact, I doubted I'd felt so invigorated since I'd been a child running wild and free on the ranch. Benny hobbled ahead of us on the trail. I clasped Lizzie's hand and swung it back and forth like an eager schoolboy.

She giggled, and I couldn't help but grin. Why had I ever found the cold model-types so appealing in college? Those women were so self-absorbed and boring that if I compared them to ice cream, they'd be glued together plastic props used in commercials. They looked tasty on the outside but had nothing sweet or real to bite into. They'd only left me wanting.

Lizzie, by comparison, was made of the freshest cream, sugars, and ingredients known to man. No wonder Chance had mooned over her. It wasn't like she was drop-dead gorgeous or even the life-of-the-party type of girl, yet she drew people to her, especially males. Maybe it was her kindness and simple honesty. She hadn't tried to grab my attention like every other girl had done, which I found utterly refreshing.

As Benny disappeared around the bend, I stopped and gently touched her cheek. "You've healed up nice."

She blushed. "I'm not Quasimodo anymore, at least."

"You were a super adorable Quasimodo." I leaned down to touch foreheads. "You should kiss me."

"N-n-no," she stammered.

I chuckled at her reaction. "I'm just messing with you. Come on." I pulled her up the trail, trying to shake off her rejection. Again. Why wouldn't she just kiss me? I knew she wanted to.

The sun dipped close to the horizon by the time we reached the look-off, so we didn't spend much time there. We returned at Benny's pace and had to use our headlamps for the last section of the trail. Benny headed for the truck, and I pulled Liz behind a tree.

"What are you doing?"

"I need a few minutes alone with you on this date, don't you think?" I brought her hand to my mouth, kissing each knuckle. By how her chest rose and fell, I could tell she liked my attention.

"Rawson," she whispered.

"Yes?" I licked my lips, eager to hear her say the words I so desperately wanted to hear.

"Don't do that."

I deflated so fast it felt like a power vac had gotten hold of my insides on maximum suction. "As you wish." I threw out the *Princess Bride* reference to spark a smile, and miracle of miracles, it worked.

She took my hand of her own free will and pulled me back onto the trail.

I hadn't gotten a kiss out of her, but I was still holding her hand. Someday, I'd get my kiss...and more.

47

LIZ

*W*IND CHIMES TINKLED in the breeze as I followed Rawson out onto the deck. I looked up into the sky and watched a satellite creep across the vast inky space. We'd dated for three weeks, and despite the stupid rules I'd created to keep distance between us, he was growing on me. A lot. I'd never liked being with a guy as much as I liked being with Rawson. That made being with him both thrilling and terrifying.

I nestled my chin into my coat as he sank onto the log swing and gestured for me to join him.

His arm wrapped around me, and I snuggled closer for warmth. At least that's what I told myself. The other option was too scary to consider —that Rawson was Lucifer in disguise and I'd fallen headlong into his wicked trap.

I leaned into his chest. "I've never seen so many stars. It's amazing."

"You're amazing."

"Shush."

Rawson had talked the Orionids meteor shower up all week, making me eager to witness the celestial event. Growing up under the Vegas lights, I'd never seen more than a handful of stars in the sky. A meteor shot across my view, leaving a blazing trail in its wake.

Rawson squeezed my fingers. "Make a wish." He kissed the skin below my ear.

Though it was a brisk October night, my body experienced a heat wave as sinful thoughts filled my mind. I pushed them back. "No kissing."

"I'm not. My lips are nowhere near yours. I'm nibbling." He buried his head into my neck and continued his so-called nibbling.

I pushed him away again. "Stop it."

He pulled my ponytail free from its elastic.

"Why do you do that?" I gathered my hair to tie up again. Since he'd thrown my elastic out his truck window, I'd kept a spare on hand.

"Why do you do that?" He grabbed hold of my hands so I couldn't rein in my tangled curls. "I love your hair down."

"You're a dweeb."

He pecked my cheek.

I tilted my head to look into his mesmerizing eyes. "What are you thinking?" Had he been blown away by that shooting star as I had been?

"That I want to kiss you."

I scoffed. "You're always thinking that. What else?"

"That we should get more cozy." He lifted me onto his lap.

Fiery convulsions shot through me as the hard planes of his body pressed into me. My body buzzed from desire, which set off a chain reaction of shallow breathing, heated skin, pounding heart, and limited brain function.

"Stargazing's my new favorite hobby." The low rumble of his voice tickled the hair along my sensitized neck.

"You're not looking at the stars."

His lips claimed me in an even more pleasurable nibbling session, making me gasp. Maybe stargazing was my new favorite hobby as well. He supped on my neck, and my fingers curled into his shirt. My heart pounded time in agonizing pleasure as my sluggish mind wondered if I should stop him. Daddy had outlined the dangers of boys in my youth. Was Rawson trying to give me a hickey?

"Rawson," I whispered, "you won't…leave any…marks, will you?"

"No, babe." His tongue flicked out along my skin, making me shiver. "Just sweet dreams."

Stars were forgotten as he made love to my neck. The gentle rocking motion mingled with Rawson's tender ministrations rendered me blissfully numb. When I came to my senses, I was shocked to find that our bodies had entwined in a prone position on the swing. Definitely a no-no. Dad had warned me to never be caught in a horizontal position with a guy.

I pushed his face away. "We should call it a night."

"Night. I called it." He tried to claim my neck again.

"Stop." I rolled off him. "We really should get to bed."

I thought he might try to lure me back into his muscular arms, but he grinned instead. "Sweetheart, that's the best thing you've said all night."

"N-no," I sputtered, realizing where his naughty mind had gone. "Not together. I mean you should go to your bed and I should go to mine."

His rumbling chuckle made me gulp. "You are so dang sexy when you talk about bed."

"I'm really tired." Actually, I doubted I'd fall asleep for hours with how keyed up I felt. My body was buzzing in the most pleasurable ways.

"All right." He led me into the dark house and stopped at the bottom of the stairs. "I liked stargazing with you."

"You never watched the stars."

"Oh, believe me, sweetheart, I saw stars." He kissed my forehead.

My face burned. "Goodnight, Rawson. See you bright and early?" He'd shown up late for work for weeks now because of his cruddy friend.

"Maybe. Maybe not."

"Rawson." I tried to sound authoritative.

He winked. "I promise I'll stay late if I'm not there before noon. Mornings are roughest for Damon. I can't leave him."

My jaw clenched, frustration sweeping away the tingly bliss I'd been enjoying. I didn't know much about his friend, except what little Rawson had confided in me, but I hated the guy. He was bringing Rawson down and leaving me shorthanded.

"He's an adult. You need to stop coddling him."

Rawson sighed. "When he gets on top of his withdrawals, I'll stop coddling him. He needs me now."

I turned away, not wanting him to see the angry tears gathering in ranks. What about me? We were way behind with the yearlings' training. Chance had tried to pick up the slack, but he didn't know what he was doing most of the time.

"I'll do my best to get out there. Okay?"

I tossed all night, knowing he wouldn't be there in the morning.

And I was right. As the hours ticked closer to noon, I kept checking my watch, hoping to see my handsome apprentice.

I was riding Sidekick Shooter when Mr. Law enter the arena with the foreman by his side. Not good.

I dismounted and patted Shooter. "Hey, Bart. What can I do for you?"

"Where's my son?"

Why'd he have to ask that? I bit my lip, trying to think of a reason why Rawson wasn't here. One that would sound good.

"He hasn't shown up," Chance replied, limping over on his orthopedic boot. "That's why I'm helping out. He's been tied up with Damon."

By how red Bart's face turned, I knew that'd been the wrong thing to reveal. "He'll be here soon. He's been working late to make up time."

Bart's mouth pressed into a tight line. "Meet me in my office in ten minutes." He marched out the way he'd come.

My shoulders slumped as I led Shooter to his stall.

"I don't envy you," Chance said.

I didn't envy me either.

I trudged up the stairs to Bart's office, wanting to hurl. He'd been furious when he'd left the arena. Maybe he'd fire me for being an awful manager. Obviously, I had no control over his son.

"Shut the door," he said as I entered his domain.

I bit my lip and did as he asked.

"Have a seat, Liz."

I sank into the leather chair and picked at my cuticles. Would he give me two weeks' notice? I didn't know if that would be better or worse. The way I felt, I just wanted to run back home and hide.

Mr. Law leaned back in his swanky chair. "How long has my son been shirking his duties?"

"Uh...he hasn't shirked his duties." I might lose my job, but I didn't want Rawson to get in trouble. "Rawson's extremely capable with the horses and is much better at dealing with customers than I am."

"But he's showing up four hours late every day?"

"Not every day." A couple days he hadn't shown up at all.

"Abe wondered why your productivity had decreased, even as you seemed to be working more hours than ever. Now I know. My son's taking advantage of you."

"He's been trying to make up time."

Bart's expression softened. "I appreciate your loyalty, but my son doesn't deserve it. He's put you in a bad spot if you're having to rely on Chance."

It had been irritating relying on him, especially with his bum foot Shooter had stepped on. "I'll talk to Rawson about getting to work earlier."

"Don't bother. I'm transferring him out to the cattle. Until we hire a replacement, Chance can keep helping you. I'll relieve him of his other duties."

"I'm sure I can work it out with Rawson," I said. "He's much better than Chance, even working fewer hours. Sorry I let things get behind."

"You have nothing to be sorry about, Liz. My son's used you badly. He has a knack for that. But he won't use you anymore." Bart stood, bringing our meeting to a close. "If you need anything, let Abe know. We'll work with you until we find an acceptable replacement for Chance."

I gulped. I wasn't unemployed, but everything had spun out of my control. "Thank you, sir."

I trudged back to the arena, wanting to kick something. Or someone. Rawson would be a nice target. Yet, I didn't want to lose him. He really was amazing with the yearlings and we worked well together...when he bothered to show up.

Ugh. This was all such a mess.

48

BENTLEY

*L*IFE HAD SUCKED like a vacuum since Dad had discovered that Rawson had been spending time with his loser friend, leaving Liz short-handed. To punish him, he put my brother over the cattle and had only given him one hand to help him. Usually, there were three. I guess Dad didn't want Rawson having any free time to waste with Damon.

My brother's stupidity had made life difficult for everyone. Lizzie's workload had doubled, since Chance, with his gimp foot, was useless as a fork in soda. And now that Rawson only got home every week or so to restock supplies before he headed back to the herd, I only had Addie for company.

Thanksgiving had arrived. I'd hoped to fill the day with testosterone-filled fun, since Liz had flown home for the holiday. Mom had convinced Dad to give Rawson the day off, and I couldn't wait to ditch Addie to hang out with him.

But he'd texted this morning that Damon needed him and had asked me to cover for him until he could get home. Dinner had ended hours ago…and still no sign of my brother.

I was puttering around on a new drawing in the living room when I heard the back door slam. Rawson appeared. He hadn't shaved. Dark circles ringed his eyes. He looked like hell. Liz needed to return so my brother would have someone to impress.

"Roth-un!" Addie attacked him like he was the best thing since sweetened chocolate.

I concentrated on my drawing as Rawson laughed and fell to his knees. Addie smacked him over the head with an empty gift wrap roll.

"Oh, no! I'm getting attacked by a Jedi knight."

Addie whacked him again with the cardboard tube.

"Aghh, Benny. Grab me another light saber, man. Quick."

I shaded the side of Addie's neck on paper. Rawson could get his own dang weapon.

Mom left the room and returned with another tube from her craft room.

"Thanks, Queen Amidala," Rawson said.

Addie convulsed on the floor in laughter.

I rolled my eyes and shaded her nose with the side of the pencil.

Rawson held the tube in both hands, making amazing light saber sounds as he mimicked Darth Maul's moves from *Phantom Menace*. Not that I paid him any mind. He could go to hell since he'd chosen his friend over me. Thanksgiving was for family, yet he hadn't even apologized for ditching us. He'd just started playing with Addie like he hadn't screwed me over.

I flipped back a few pages to a charcoal drawing of Addie with her tongue inside her mouth. The good old days, before the accident. I compared the sketch to now, with her tongue hanging out like a slobbery dog.

Rawson rubbed his tube against hers. "Use the Force, Addie."

She gave him a wide-mouthed grin and reached up to fondle his face. Our sister sucked at Jedi games.

"I feel the Force in you, young Padawan."

"Roth-un funny!" She whacked him again.

In between laughing and ducking her hits, Rawson cried, "Join me, Addie. Together we'll rule the galaxy."

Part of me wanted to join them, but the dark side wondered why Rawson didn't demand she hold in her tongue. Addie would do it for him. But my brother cared more about his idiot friend than us. We got his leftovers. I shoved my sketchbook and pencil under the sofa and hobbled from the room.

Mom followed me into the kitchen and made a turkey sandwich roll for me to eat. She set that and a glass of chocolate milk in front of me. I dug into my snack while she ran her fingers through my hair.

"You look so much like your father." Her eyes glistened, but thankfully she didn't cry. "You're amazing, son. I wouldn't change anything about you." She tweaked my ear and left.

What the heck?

It'd almost seemed as though she'd read my ugly thoughts and knew I needed lifting. I'd thought when she'd got all teary that she might be recalling the good old days, before I'd got bent, and wishing I were whole again. But she'd sounded sincere when she'd said she wouldn't change anything about me.

Rawson peeked into the kitchen. "You up for *Empire Strikes Back*, kid?"

Mom's kind words had soothed my anger. Maybe I could forgive my brother for being a dummy. Holding a grudge hadn't made me feel any better.

"Sure." I followed him down to the basement.

Rawson put in the DVD, and I pondered Mom's mini-intervention. She had a gift for knowing when I needed her, but also knowing not to smother me. She understood Rawson, too; he never flustered her. Dad should take lessons. And with Addie, Mom was a saint, giving my sister endless devotion when I would've been tempted to swat her backside.

A lump formed in my throat as I thought of Detrick. He'd suffered from middle-child syndrome, being overshadowed by Rawson's greatness and my baby cuteness. That'd made him cling to her like a Momma's boy. But she'd loved him with all she possessed. Not many people could say they'd been on the receiving end of that kind of love. In that way, Detrick had received more than most people did who lived a lifetime. Mom had given him, and kept giving us all, the best gift she had—herself.

"Hey," Rawson nudged me. "You're in a galaxy far, far away."

I blinked. "I was just thinking of Mom. She's awesome."

"Amen."

We didn't talk anymore, but walls dropped between us. At one point, his hand came down on my leg.

"I need a favor, kid."

"Name it."

"I want to do something special for Liz for Christmas, to show her how I feel."

"How's that?"

"Like she's my whole world." He looked up at the ceiling. "I've never felt this way before. Lizzie's different from every other girl I've known. Any ideas what she'd like?"

I wanted nothing more than to help him win Lizzie's heart. She was a good influence on him. "What about the twelve days of Christmas? You could give her a gift each day."

"Brilliant." He tousled my hair, laughing when I slapped at his hand.

We put our heads together and came up with several ideas before he stood and stretched.

"That's a good start. I better go"

"You can't leave in the middle of the best movie ever created."

"I have to head back to the cattle." He pulled out his wallet and handed me a credit card. "Keep this. I'll need help purchasing items since I don't have internet at the cattle house."

"She's going to love this," I said.

"I hope so. See you in a week or so, bro." He headed upstairs.

I frowned at the TV. Guess I should go to bed, too. Watching movies alone was as fun as picking a sunburn.

49

RAWSON

$\mathcal{N}$ONE OF THE passengers filing through the double doors from whatever flight had just landed were Liz. I leaned back and stared at the bronze flying geese hanging from the wood ceiling. Maybe she'd be in the next group of arrivals.

I tried to imagine her reaction when she saw me instead of Abe. When I'd discovered that she'd asked the foreman to pick her up, I'd told him I would get her, as well as the load of straw he needed, if he'd cover for me with the cattle. Abe had been hesitant, but I'd busted my hide over the last month and he knew it. So we'd switched places.

This month apart from Liz had been pure misery. I'd missed her.

The terminal filled with the sound of rushing passengers. I straightened and scanned the crowds. Lizzie's tinkling giggle alerted me to her presence before I saw her. I adjusted my Stetson as she walked through the double doors beside a tall, lanky cowboy who paid her too much attention.

"That'd be great," she said.

He mashed up against her. "Let me get your number, darling."

"Lizzie!" I waved so she'd see me.

Her face lit up like Addie's whenever I brought jelly bellies. "Rawson!"

I nudged *Mr. Give Me Your Number* out of the way and picked her up to swing her around. It was only one revolution on the airport walkway, yet enough time to savor the smell of her shampoo and the way her breath tickled my neck. My body instantly relaxed, finding what it'd been craving.

"I missed you, sweetheart," I said loud enough for *Mr. Open Mouth Cowboy* to hear.

He tipped his hat. "Nice talking with you, Liz. You have my number."

She tried to wave, but I'd pinioned her arms, and no way would I allow her to give him more than a hard kick in the backside goodbye.

"He gave you his number?" I raised a brow. "What kind of Neanderthal is he?" She turned all rosy under my gaze. "Blushing becomes you, and you're welcome for getting rid of that loser."

"He wasn't a loser."

I tugged her toward the luggage carousel. "I beg to differ. He lost you, didn't he?"

She shook her head. "He wasn't trying to win me. We just sat together on the flight here. He's from Florida."

I spotted her southern seat-mate scoping her out by the carousel and steered her to the opposite side.

"I'm glad you picked me up, Stash," she said. "I missed you."

"Same. Texts only go so far." I wrapped my arms around her. "It's nice to hold the real deal in my arms."

Suitcases piled down the chute. Liz pushed away to point out hers. I smirked as I grabbed her bedazzled baggage.

"I never pictured you for a pink suitcase kind of gal."

"Courtesy of my mother."

Liz questioned me on the snowy drive home. "How do you like working with the cows?"

I sighed. "Cattle, Lizzie. Cows are—"

"I know. They've had babies."

"It's been hell."

She narrowed her eyes.

"I'm not cussing. That's the truth. Dad purposely left me underhanded so I don't have a second to even breathe or take a leak."

She scrunched her nose. "Gross. I hoped you at least changed before you came to get me."

I laughed so hard I had to pull over on the unplowed road. Unlatching my seatbelt, I scooted over and threw my arm over her shoulders.

"Man alive, I've missed you. I don't think I've laughed once since Dad banished me to the herd."

She frowned. "Is it really so bad?"

"Worse." I tilted my head to take advantage of her luscious neck.

Lizzie surprised me by reaching up to run her fingers through my hair. She'd never done anything so *normal* before. Her gentle touch fired me up faster than an incinerator. I clutched her tighter, sucking her neck as though it held the only sustenance left on earth. Even without touching her lips, I experienced one of the most sensual moments of my life as I made her sigh, moan, and shudder with pleasure. But when my hand slipped under her shirt, Lizzie gasped and applied brakes full force.

Ecstasy came to a crashing halt as she practically shoved me into the dashboard.

She straightened her shirt and pulled her jacket around her like a protective shield. "We shouldn't have done that."

"What? I didn't kiss you, though I should. We've been going out since the end of September."

"You can't count this month. This is the first I've seen you since you were assigned to the cattle."

"All the more reason to make up for lost time."

She folded her arms. "This is why I didn't want to go out with you."

I counted to ten. She seriously pushed me to the brink of crazy. "Don't you dare pull back and friend-zone me. Just tell me what you want." I ached to kiss the furrow lines from her brow.

"Maybe we should take a break from each other."

I scowled. "We just had a break. It's been almost four weeks, Lizzie. I have only this drive home with you before I have to get back to the herd. I moved hell and high water to get Abe to cover for me so I could pick you up today."

Her stern expression softened. "That's sweet."

"Don't call me sweet."

She laughed.

I tried to cuddle again, but she lifted my arm like it was chemical waste.

"No more. You're acting like we're together."

"Right now, we are together. In my truck. Alone."

She swallowed. "We're not really together. I can date other guys."

"Like who? Chance? You already made your feelings clear about him. Or maybe you want to make eyes at that idiot who sat by you on the plane today. The one who thinks just wearing a Stetson makes him a cowboy."

"Hush," she scolded. "He was nice. And he's looking for a job. I told him I'd put in a good word for him with your dad. I need someone with more experience than Chance, and Garret's worked with horses for years. He could be the man for the job."

"I'm the man for the job!" I pounded the steering wheel, upset that she was still talking about going out with other guys.

"You were the man for the job until you messed up and got stuck with the cattle."

"I forbid you from putting in a good word for that jerk."

"You forbid me?"

"Yes. Just put up with Chance until Dad switches me back to work with you. You've lasted this month. What can a little longer hurt? Besides, Dad won't hire anyone during the winter."

"Then why did he email me resumes to look over while I was gone?"

I threw my head against the seat and growled. What was my old man thinking? He knew I wanted to train the new blood. I took a deep breath, trying to relax my taut muscles. I couldn't change Dad's decision, but I could regain control of this conversation and steer Liz to a compromise.

"Forget Florida guy. Back to us. I won't try to kiss you, but I think it's way past time we became exclusive. I've never felt this way about anyone else. I want to be serious."

She gaped at me. I waited for her to say something. Each painful heartbeat required superhuman effort to maintain my composure.

"No," she whispered. "That wouldn't make sense right now. Maybe when you don't work with the cattle and I see you more, we'll discuss it."

I scooted back to my side and pulled back onto the road, my jaw aching from clenching it so tight. Lizzie knew how to push my buttons.

When we reached the ranch, I pulled up to the house so she wouldn't have to walk through the mud. I took her hand, not wanting to end the day on a bad note.

"I don't know when I'll be able to get away again, but will you hang out with me when I do? Maybe we could watch a movie with Benny." I knew she wouldn't turn me down if I used my brother.

She smiled, lifting a weight from my chest. She wasn't angry. "I'd love to. Text when you're on your way and I'll whip up some cinnamon rolls."

I brought her hand to my lips. "You are most definitely the perfect girl for me. I'm glad you're back, Tutti. Life has been all lima beans without you."

Her eyes crinkled. "See you, Stash. Don't freeze out with the cattle."

"I won't," I called. "Thinking of you will keep me toasty."

LIZ

GALE-FORCE WINDS whipped snow across the icy pasture, adding to the snowdrifts covering the rail-post fence. I yanked my scarf over my mouth and plowed into the elements. Nights like this made me yearn for a better coat. The threadbare one I wore, layered over several sweatshirts, had seen better days.

I grabbed the rope Abe had secured from the indoor arena to the house. When he'd first hammered and worked on the line, I hadn't thought it necessary. But I'd never experienced a whiteout like this. My eyelashes froze and my nose stung. Visibility consisted of blowing snow, which confused my internal compass. His rope had become my salvation.

I used my gloved hands to feel my way along the bristly twine until my boot hit something solid. I reached out and felt the door to the mudroom. I entered and shut the door quickly, but still a pile of snow blew in with me.

I sank onto a bench to extract my boots and peel off soggy layers. My denim jacket mocked me as I rubbed my arms. The moisture had soaked clear through to my Aggies sweatshirt.

"Hey, Liz." Benny bounded in and sat on the bench across from me.

"Hey."

"You look like a snowman."

"Feel like one, too. This storm's crazy."

"Welcome to Montana."

I hung my pathetic winter gear and headed upstairs. Benny followed.

"What did you do today?" I asked.

184

He wrinkled his nose. "Mom made me play with Addie. I wish Rawson was back so he could take a turn."

So did I. Chance, bless his heart, didn't have that Rawson equine instinct I sorely needed, and Bart still hadn't hired a replacement.

Bentley bounced on his feet. I'd hoped to be left alone so I could crash for the night, but it didn't look like that'd happen.

"Want to come in and talk?"

His grin turned mischievous, reminding me of his brother. "Yeah."

I gestured him into my room, but he shook his head.

"Ladies first."

I entered but stopped. A coat rack blocked the path next to my walk-in closet. A burgundy coat hung from a peg with a big card and bow attached to it.

"Do you know anything about this?"

He ducked his head. "Open it."

I plucked the envelope off, noticing that the rungs of the rack mimicked tree branches. A glittery pear hung from a peg. I read the card.

On the first day of Christmas,
Please accept from me
A Patagonia in a pear tree.
-Your True Love (Kermie)

I touched the soft jacket and read the tag. Patagonia ultralight down hoodie.

"Try it on," Ben said.

"This can't be for me."

"It's in your room. Come on. I want to see it on you."

I donned the sleek jacket, marveling at its light weight. What was Rawson thinking? "I don't have money to buy your brother a gift like this," I said to Ben.

He made a goofy face. "He didn't do this so you'd give him something back. He did it 'cause he likes you."

I stared into the mirror.

"He's worked his butt off so he could do something nice for you. Even Dad's been impressed. I heard him say so to Abe."

I knew that, too. A few days ago, I'd put on my big girl panties and had asked Bart to reassign Rawson back to me. I'd become alarmingly behind with only Chance to assist. He'd denied my request, saying his son was doing an excellent job with the herd, and that he'd hired the guy I'd met on my flight back at Thanksgiving to help out. Garret would start next week.

I paced in front of my bed. "I can't accept this."

185

"Rawson put a lot of thought into it. Don't throw it back in his face," Ben pleaded.

I studied the jacket's puffy texture. "Did he pick this out himself?"

"Yeah. I took screen shots of the jackets on the site and texted them to him. He doesn't have reliable internet at the cattle house. He said this one screamed your name."

"And who's the mastermind behind this? Did you come up with Patagonia in a pear tree?"

"I wish. It's clever, huh? Rawson wanted you to have a warmer coat for winter and thought Patagonia seemed more practical than a partridge." He grinned. "The coat rack's Mom's, so I'll need it back, but I found the pear in her craft room. I bet she won't mind if you keep it."

I swiped at my eyes.

"Are you mad?"

I shook my head. "This is so nice. Thanks, Ben."

"Don't thank me. Thank your true love Kermie or whatever code word you have for him."

I laughed and tousled his hair. "You're as crazy as your brother."

Ben left, and I pulled out my phone to text the man who'd made me feel more emotions in five minutes than I'd felt my whole life.

> :Patagonia in a pear tree.
> Very clever.

Rawson: Miss Piggy beauty tip #2: Never let your frog outdress you.

> :You shouldn't have
> spent so much.

Rawson: What would be the fun in that?

> :Seriously, this is way
> too expensive.

Rawson: You worry too much. Just say thank you.

> :Thank you. I really do
> love it. The coat's so soft.

Rawson: Like you. LOL.

                                        :Watch it, buster. No one
                                        calls me soft and lives
                                        to tell about it.

Rawson: ;) I'm shaking in
my boots.

I hugged the down coat to my chest. No longer would I have to wear three sweatshirts underneath my bedraggled denim jacket to stay warm. Now, I'd look better than my frog.

I snickered. For such a dumb guy, he made me laugh a lot.

BENTLEY

*L*IZZIE'S BARKING laughter filled the room. I wished Rawson could be here to enjoy it. It seemed unfair that he'd put so much of himself into each of these gifts, yet hadn't been able to see any of her reactions, besides what I could send him in a text. Liz had been blown away by each new present and sometimes disgruntled when they were pricey. But Rawson had wanted things perfect, and once he'd figured out what each gift would be, he hadn't been swayed. He'd told me to spare no expense and to pay for overnight shipping on what he had me order.

"This is incredible!" Liz studied the canvas I'd painted with cows and milkmaids. Her true love, Stash on today's card, had given her eight maids a milking. Rawson had brought a few gifts back from town, among them, eight candy Cow Tales. He'd asked me to paint a picture of the rest and attach the candy in the proper places. It'd taken me a whole night.

"This is my favorite so far."

"Stash commissioned it for you."

She laughed. "I know."

This had to be the cheapest gift yet, since Cow Tales cost a quarter and I'd refused to let Rawson pay me for my contribution.

He'd given her two turtle doves (a box of chocolate turtles and a bag of Dove dark chocolates), three authentic French pens that'd cost almost a hundred bucks, four calling cards, five gold strings (a set of gold chains from Miller's Jewelers in Bozeman that'd almost made her have a stroke. My idea had been doughnuts, but Rawson had wanted something fancy), six geese a laying (a bunch of stylish goose-down pillows for her bed) and a saltwater aquarium with seven fish a swimming (the eel was my favorite).

Yet today's two dollar gift had made her the happiest, since it was homemade.

"Glad you like it."

"I love it!" She wrapped me in a hug.

I glanced at the open suitcase on her bed. "You need help packing?" She would fly out tonight to spend Christmas with her family.

She shook her head. "I'm almost done."

"I'll miss you."

She tousled my hair, an annoying habit she'd fallen into after watching my brother do it so much. "I'll miss you, too. Too bad I can't stuff you in my luggage and take you with me. Maybe Mom would get off my back and not set me up on any blind dates."

"She makes you date blind people?"

Lizzie seal-barked, making me lose it. When we gained control of our laughing boxes, I hugged her and told her to think of me when she dated her blind men. That set us both off again, and I left her room clutching my side.

52

LIZ

CHRISTMAS EVE HAD been a festive occasion. My two darling nieces, Krista and Katie, had reenacted the Nativity while Mom had taken pictures and fussed over costumes. Holidays were grand affairs for Mom. She lived and prepped for them for months. Since that kept her from nagging me, I loved them as well.

I'd been charged with refreshments and had made homemade eclairs and a gorgeous vegetable tray in the shape of a Christmas tree. Mom had turned her nose up at it, but Benny would've loved it. Rawson, too.

Snuggling into my pillows, I thought about that clever cowboy's unique gifts that'd chipped holes in the protective walls of my heart. His witty texts had pushed the rest of the rubble out of the way. When I'd flown home to Vegas, I'd figured his gifts would end. No one could fault him for stopping at eight instead of twelve. But the gifts had kept coming.

My first night home, I'd received a delivery from a harried-looking UPS man. The card had said my true love had given me nine stars a dancing. The package contained seven seasons of Dancing with the Stars and two other videos—Dirty Dancing and Singing in the Rain. He'd signed the card from Bubble Gum. The next day's package had contained ten lords a leaping, consisting of all three Lord of the Ring movies, Lord of the Flies, and six racy romance novels with Lord in the title. He'd signed it from Lord Cootie Catcher. Yesterday's delivery had brought poppers popping— eleven bags of Pop Rocks.

His ingenious gifts had confused me. I was just plain Lizzie. He was handsome-as-heck Rawson Law. He could be on the cover of one of those bodice rippers he'd given me. So, why had he gone to all this trouble?

A ruckus outside made me roll off the bed. "What in the world?" I lifted the slats of my blinds to see flames dancing on the front lawn.

"Elizabeth!" Mom yelled from downstairs.

I hurried down and ran into Daddy.

"Come outside." He grinned. "This is amazing."

"Who's this secret admirer?" Mom asked.

"Just a friend."

She huffed, but it was true. Rawson was a friend, who apparently didn't mind spending an exorbitant amount of money on me.

My eyes adjusted to the dark. Twelve shirtless Polynesian men in grass skirts formed a half circle around us. Tiki torches illuminated their muscular frames. One of them chanted, and in unison they began beating an island Christmas rhythm on their drums. I clapped, wishing Rawson was here so I could kiss him. He'd sent twelve drummers drumming.

The Polynesian group danced and performed syncopated drum numbers as our neighbors all crept out to watch. Afterward, I deflected my parents' questions, pleading exhaustion.

I stared at myself in my full-length mirror, wondering again what Rawson saw in me. I was tall, not curvy. I wore little makeup. My clothes were usually dusty and worn. My eyes were a boring brown. My hair obnoxiously curly. There was absolutely nothing special about me. So why did he try so hard?

My phone dinged with a text. I glanced at my clock, surprised to see that it was already midnight.

*Rawson: On this real day
of Christmas, I wanted to
wish you goodnight. We all
miss you here, but me most.
Dream of Santa and pistachio
ice cream. I'll dream of
pralines and cream. -Your
true love ReBeL*

I laughed at how he worked his initials into *Rebel*. Another text chimed.

*Rawson: I know it's late, so
don't reply. But you could
send me an emoticon,
preferably the kissy face
kind since you won't give
me real ones.*

I sent him a bunch of kissy emojis that perfectly reflected my mood. If he was here right now, I'd probably give him some real ones.

RAWSON

*O*NCE MORE, I WAITED for Liz to arrive at the airport. My twelve days of Christmas gifts had gone off without a hitch, and she hadn't dated anyone else since agreeing to hang out with me on a casual basis. But with the new guy working with her now, I didn't dare leave anything to chance. I wanted commitment.

Liz walked through the double doors without a goofy cowboy escort. I grabbed her and spun her around. "Hey, gorgeous."

She laughed. "You made this the best Christmas ever. Seriously. Tongan drummers? No one's ever done anything so nice for me."

I squeezed her hand. "Then it's about time someone did."

We stopped at the luggage carousel, and she pulled out a present from her carry-on. "Sorry it's late. I feel bad I didn't do more."

"But you have. You've returned, which is the best gift of all."

She rolled her eyes. "That's not—"

"Truly, Liz." I tipped her chin. "Before I met you, I was miserable. But you've given me a reason to smile and laugh again. No gift can beat that."

She shook her head. "Open it."

I ripped off paper and chuckled at the *Star Wars* license plate frame. It said, *My other ride is the Millennium Falcon.* She'd also given me a decal for my window with Yoda's face saying, *Pass you I will.*

I chuckled. "You know me well."

"It's not much, but I—"

I pressed a finger to her lips. "It's perfect. Thank you." She was always too hard on herself.

Her gaudy pink luggage slid down the chute. I dragged it behind me and took her hand. I threw her girly gear behind the seat since it was snowing, and patted the middle spot.

"You ready to be my girl yet?"

She scooted over without a fight. "I guess."

"You guess?" I grinned. "Don't sound so excited."

She giggled and fastened her seatbelt. "Yes, I'll be your girl."

I wrapped an arm around her, liking her answer. She snuggled against me the whole way home.

The storm had turned nasty by the time we pulled into the garage. I knew it'd be dicey getting over the pass but didn't want to end our time together. I needed a few more minutes.

"Let's get you inside and warm you up with some hot chocolate. It's a chilly one tonight."

I dropped her suitcase at the bottom of the stairs and steered her into the kitchen. Before she could protest, I picked her up and set her on the counter.

"No peeking." I turned my shoulder so she couldn't see me creating the concoction Damon and I had discovered as freshmen. Pouring the frothy cocoa into mugs, I brought them over and set them on the counter. "Wrap these legs around me, baby."

I pulled her closer. Her still-red cheeks turned even brighter as she met my gaze. We sipped from our mugs, but all I could focus on was the golden flecks in her eyes.

"Oh, my. This is delicious."

I kissed her brow. "I've missed you like crazy."

"Me, too."

"It'll be pure torture being so close, yet so far away. Every time I'm on the Cat, I'll want to go AWOL from the herd and zip home to hold you."

"Your dad wouldn't be pleased."

I grunted. "He never will be."

"Not true. I begged him to reassign you to me, but he said you were doing too good a job with the herd. He won't switch you until after calving season."

I grimaced. "I'm damned if I do and damned if I don't. How's the wanna-be cowboy from Florida working out?"

"Garret's a godsend. I only had a week to train him before I went home, but he's a fast-learner. I think he'll be perfect."

"Perfect? Garret's a ferret."

She punched my arm. "Be nice. Your dad's super impressed with him."

"Are you?"

"Yeah. He knows what he's doing. He did the rodeo circuit for three years and spent the last one working on a ranch in Oklahoma. He's a hard worker."

"Just make sure he keeps his hands to himself and remembers you're the boss. I know guys, and trust me, that Florida ferret wants more from you than a job."

She snorted. "Don't be delusional."

Muscles in my jaw worked overtime. Why did she insist on being so clueless? I set my mug on the counter. "Tell me I wasn't delusional when you agreed to be my girl earlier." I leaned in to lay feather kisses down her neck.

"No. You were in your right mind," she said between breathy gasps.

I leaned her back to kiss her throat.

"Oh dear!" someone yelped behind me.

Lizzie jerked and banged her head against the cupboard. She winced as I turned to catch Mom blushing brighter than a Christmas ornament.

"Sorry. I didn't know anyone was in here." Mom turned to go, but I called after her, not wanting her to think I was messing around with Lizzie.

"Don't go." I stood beside my flustered girl. "I just made Liz some cocoa. Do you want some?"

"I don't want to intrude." Mom averted her gaze.

"You won't. In fact, I'd like to make an introduction." I grabbed Lizzie's hand. "Mom, meet my girl."

She stared at us before breaking into a huge smile. "Really?" When Liz nodded, Mom clapped. "That's wonderful. When did this happen?"

"Tonight." I took Lizzie's hand.

Mom danced over to hug her. "I'm so happy." She turned to me. "Good choice, son."

I handed her a mug of frothy chocolate. "I totally agree."

195

54

LIZ

*G*ARRET LEANED AGAINST a fence post. "You should come with me tonight, darling."

I pulled the bridle off the new bay gelding. "I don't think so."

"You'd like it. The kids are great, and it's therapeutic to help others. Your story would change lives."

Scenes from the accident flitted through my mind. Garret had started a SADD group—Students Against Destructive Decisions—soon after he'd moved to town, wanting to help teens avoid the harmful effects of drugs, alcohol, texting while driving, and guide them to more positive outlets. I liked that about him. Not only had he worked out well as an employee, but we'd connected because of similar tragedies. His aunt and niece had died in a car accident a few months ago, same as Justin.

"I can't get away tonight," I said. No doubt Rawson would be upset if I drove to town with another guy.

Garret brushed his horse. "Promise to come next time. You could be the guest presenter."

"Count me in." It was a good thing he was doing. I'd soften Rawson up to the idea by next week. If I could mold my tragedy into purpose and help others, I had to give it a shot.

"If you came tonight, you'd get a feel for the format of the meeting. Surely you can get someone to cover for you."

A new voice joined the conversation. "Cover for what?"

I whipped around to find my official boyfriend. "Rawson, you're here."

He pulled me into his arms and spun me around. "How's my girl?" He set me on my feet and claimed my hand, and for a moment, I was breathless.

"Great." I gulped and nodded to my new assistant. "Garret leads a SADD meeting for teens in town. He wants me to come."

Rawson's eyes narrowed. "Lizzie's with me." He stepped between us and turned his back to Garret. A direct cut. "I thought we could—"

I stepped around him, to be polite. "Garret, I don't believe you've met Rawson yet." Muscles worked overtime beneath my boyfriend's incredible jawline. "Rawson, this is the new hand your dad hired. Garret Tullis from Brooksville, Florida. Garret," I touched Rawson's arm, "this is Rawson Law, Bart's oldest son."

"And her boyfriend," he added.

I rolled my eyes.

"Nice to meet you." Garret, at least, had manners. He stretched out a hand to shake, but Rawson ignored it.

"What brought you out west?"

"Same thing as Liz. My aunt and niece were killed by a drunk driver not too long ago. I needed to get away."

I shook my head to silence him. Rawson had no idea about my past. But he frowned at my wordless warning.

Garret hit his forehead. "Wow. I'm sorry. Have you not told him?"

I couldn't meet Rawson's accusing gaze as I shook my head.

"I can certainly understand that, darling." I winced at the endearment Garret always called me. "There's the whole trust issue for sharing sensitive subjects like that."

I dug my boot into sawdust. That wasn't why I hadn't told Rawson. The rigid set of my boyfriend's lips and blazing eyes warned of imminent danger. I shoved the bridle and bit into his hands to keep him from punching Garret.

"I'm calling it a day," I said to Garret. "Can you put everything away?"

"Anything for you, darling." He tied the new gelding to a post. "Nice meeting you, Rawson."

Rawson didn't respond. He just took me by the arm and marched away. In the tack room, he mimicked Garret.

"Anything for you, darling. Please tell me you're not buying his pretty bullshit."

"Rawson!"

He growled. "Bullcrap. Manure. Poop. Say you're not buying it."

"He throws *darling* around like corn to chickens. It doesn't mean anything." We headed to the house.

"What a ferret," he said, as we dislodged our boots in the mudroom.

"Stop calling him that. He's a nice guy and just wants me to help at his SADD meeting."

Rawson faced me. "I'm certain he wants you to help him all right. Just not in the innocent way you're thinking."

I rolled my eyes. "Simmer down, cowboy. You have nothing to worry about." I took his hand, finding the situation laughable. Plain, awkward *moi* assuring the most handsome man on earth that he didn't need to worry about another man stealing my heart. Ludicrous.

He led me down to the basement, where we sank onto a couch. "Sorry," he said. "It's just when I realized you'd confided in him instead of me, I wanted to tear the limbs from his scrawny body."

I touched his cheek. "I've wanted to tell you, but there's never been a good time. It's sad and makes me cry, and all you've done is make me happy. Don't feel bad I told him. It doesn't mean I trust him more as he implied."

Rawson traced my cheek, causing me to heat up like molten lava. "He mentioned a drunk driver. What happened?"

The concern in his eyes unlocked all the ugly emotions I'd bottled up. "I was engaged before I came here." Rawson nestled me into his chest, allowing the comfort of his body to draw the sadness from me. "It was November, our marriage day. I waited at the church for Justin. He was late." That hadn't been unusual. Justin had never worried about time. "I called to see if he was close." I ached as I recalled our fight and the accusations I'd hurled at him through the phone, continuing our fight from the previous night. Would he still be alive if I hadn't distracted him while driving?

"While talking, I heard a terrible noise I'll never forget, and he cut out." Rawson massaged my head.

"My parents and I drove down Bonanza until traffic stopped. I jumped out and ran to the police barricade when I saw his car—what was left of it. A truck had run a red light. The stoned driver staggered around while Justin's mangled body had been trapped inside a prison of jagged metal."

I'd known then, and I knew even better now, that the accident had been my fault. I should've controlled my temper. I should've at least waited to speak to Justin in person. Fear had made me take the coward's way out. He'd been so angry the night before when I'd suggested we call off the wedding, or at least, postpone it until we were at a better place. He'd called me terrible names and had accused me of being manipulative. Maybe I had been. Mom had accused me of the same thing multiple times.

"I tried to get to him, but the police and my dad held me back."

Rawson stroked my neck. "That must've been awful."

A tear slipped out, and I blinked quickly to check my emotions. "I never got to say goodbye. His body was too..." I shuddered. The grisly image of Justin's totaled car would forever haunt me.

Rawson pulled me closer. "I'm so sorry."

His compassion surprised me...and soothed me. In sermons, I'd heard about mourning with those who mourned, but until this moment, I'd never realized the power that action unleashed.

"Thank you." I touched his face, wanting to throw my no-kissing rule out the window. But before I could act on my desire, a tromping of feet on the stairs made me sit up and swipe at my eyes.

Ben entered. "Rawson! You're home."

"Yep. Want to pick a movie, kid?"

Ben gave us a weird look since we still sat in the dark. Poor kid probably thought we'd been sharing saliva, instead of hearts.

Rawson put on a movie. I cuddled close to him, and couldn't help but compare my past relationship to what I felt now. Justin and Rawson were night and day. Justin had never wanted to just snuggle. Maybe Justin and I could've worked through my failings and been happy together. But I'd never felt this comfortable with him. I'd see-sawed back and forth between awe that he liked me and fear that I wouldn't live up to his expectations.

Rawson's lips touched my ear. "Dad's sending me on a purchasing trip."

I tilted my head. "That's good, right?"

He grinned like a boy who'd just caught his first lizard. "It's huge. He's sent me in the past, but always with Abe. But it's just me this time."

I rested my head on his shoulder. "You'll do great."

"The only negative is I'll be away from you for the next two, possibly three weeks."

That did suck, but I wouldn't make him feel bad about it. "We've had lots of practice being apart."

"I wish we didn't. I hate leaving you with that ferret."

I nudged him. "Stop calling him that. He's a nice guy." And he had nothing to worry about. Garret didn't like me that way. We were just friends.

The green in his blue eyes sparked like flames. "I don't care how nice he is as long as he stays away from you."

"Stop worrying."

"It's just that ferrets steal shiny things, and you practically glow."

I smirked. "I can't help my pasty, white skin."

He lifted me onto his lap, making my body tingle with heat. "What am I going to do about you, my deficiency-listing princess?" His lips were so close I could taste the air released with each word. He kissed the skin next to my mouth.

My eyes widened. "Ben's here," I whispered.

"Big Ben," Rawson raised his voice, "ignore us so Liz doesn't feel embarrassed by our PDA."

His brother groaned, and I jabbed Rawson's side. "Too late."

Rawson's eyes sparkled. "You're amazing."

"And you're full of crap." I tried to slide off his lap, but he pulled me against his chest.

"I'm full of nothing but honesty." His voice was firm, not playful. "Now we have to build a Love Triangle to shore up your self-esteem. I'll start." He played with a loose strand of my hair. "I love your kind heart. You always see the good in people...and ferrets."

I huffed.

"Seriously, I've never met anyone so kind. You love my brother and sister, you have a good relationship with Mom. You're nice to all the hands, even the awkward ones. You even get along with Dad, an impossible feat."

Though his kind words embarrassed me, I loved how Rawson always built me up. I knew I had more failings than most girls—Mom and Justin had tried to help me overcome them in vain—but Rawson made me feel like I was enough just as I was. I'd never felt that way before, and it was dangerously addicting.

"You were kind to me from the start, though I deserved a face smack."

I laughed. "If I remember correctly, I did smack you."

He grinned. "I think I fell in love with you that day you left me in the dust on the side of the road."

"Liar."

"It was short-lived. Then I cursed you to hell and back."

"That sounds more truthful."

His expression sobered. "I love how blind you are to your beauty."

My eyebrows dipped sharply. I wasn't beautiful.

"You're extremely beautiful," he whispered, so Benny wouldn't overhear. "And you have no idea."

Because it wasn't true. Yet, I was hooked like a druggie to his sweet lies, wanting more.

"Your beauty radiates from inside and makes you stand out from all other women. When I said you glow, I didn't mean your skin. I referred to how you light up a room with cheer and happiness. I can't help but smile when you're around."

"Not when I wear a ponytail. I know you hate those."

He nuzzled my nose. "Hate's a strong word." My core temperature rose as his oceanic eyes searched my face. "Annoyed, maybe. Your ponytail holds back all your gorgeous curls." He yanked another curl loose. "It's a credit to your beauty that you can wear one at all and still turn heads."

He had to stop. Lies were a house of cards, only a whisper away from falling to pieces. "The only heads I turn are horses, because of the bit in their mouth."

"You're blind, woman."

"You don't have to charm me, Rawson." I preferred the truth. Lies would only lead to heartache.

"You think I'm trying to charm you?" He scowled. "I'm telling you what I love about you. You might be the only woman on earth who refuses to believe anything good about herself. Now tell me three things you love."

"Good grief. You're more annoying than my ponytail."

He pursed his tempting lips. "I just hate how negative you are with yourself. You're not that way with anyone else, so why are you so mean to *Numero Uno*?"

His question made me squirm. "I'm not mean. I like who I am." I just wasn't ignorant of my faults.

"What do you like?"

Dang him. I'd stepped right into his stupid trap. I touched the gold chain he'd given me for Christmas. "I love your necklace."

He made a buzzer sound. "Not something you wear. Although it does look amazing on you."

"I guess I like my teeth. They're straight."

Rawson tilted my head. "Smile."

"No." His game was getting annoying.

"I check the horses' teeth. Let me see yours."

"I'm not a blooming horse."

His eyes lowered and raised back up again, causing my dumb heart to gallop like a wild stallion. "No. You're definitely all woman."

I folded my arms, feeling my whole body heat in an embarrassing blush. "Watch the movie."

"Don't think you're getting out of telling me two more loves. I might even make it three. You only said you *liked* your teeth. I want to know what you love."

I kept my eyes glued to the television. "I love my teeth."

"Fine."

"I love…" I drew the word out to make him laugh, "…my toes."

"Why?"

"Because they wiggle better than yours."

"Let me see."

"No."

He sighed. "Now I'm going to dream of your sexy toes all night."

I laughed. Though he was annoying, he was also hilarious. He said I made him happy, but he made me happier. When he wasn't being so dang frustrating.

The credits rolled up the screen. Ben said goodnight and trudged upstairs, leaving us alone.

I jumped to my feet. "We should go to bed, too."

He grabbed my hand. "I probably won't see you in the morning since I'm leaving at four."

"So early? Dang. If I'd known, I wouldn't have made you watch a movie with me."

He backed me up against the wall. "Made me watch a movie with you. That's a good one."

My heart thudded. What did he mean by that?

"You never told me a third love." His whisper made my knees buckle. Rawson was too sexy for my good.

"I hoped you'd forget."

"Never."

I licked my lips, unable to look away from his mouth. "I guess I love my height because I can get on a horse easier than short girls."

He moved his hands down my sleeves, making me shiver from the delicious warmth that swept through my skin and into my whole body. "I love your height, because it's perfect for this." He leaned in.

I ducked, and his lips landed on the bridge of my nose. My heart pounded as I met his heated gaze. He had every reason to be upset. I'd never been this stubborn with other guys. Even Mackay, who I hadn't liked, had kissed me many times. I wasn't one of those Puritan girls who placed such reverential value on their kisses that only a husband would receive them. And just before the movie, I'd considered letting him kiss me. So why was I still resisting?

He winked. "You can't blame a man for trying."

I caressed the sexy stubble on his jaw. "Text me when you stop along your trip so I know you're safe."

His eyes regained their sparkle. "Of course. You're my girl."

55

BENTLEY

*R*AYS OF SUN burst from billowy clouds as through a prism. It would've been a perfect winter day if I didn't have to share it with Garret. I took Lizzie's arm to walk out the door and scowled as I saw that cocky cowboy standing by his truck.

"Hey, Benny. I didn't know you were coming," he said.

I bet he didn't. The wily weasel probably had thought he'd have Liz all to himself on the long ride to town.

"Yep." We approached his navy blue Dodge Big Horn. Another reason not to like the guy.

He whistled at Lizzie. "Well, don't you look prettier than a glob of butter melting on a stack of wheat cakes."

I inwardly gagged at his stupid words, but she laughed.

He nudged me out of the way before I could climb into the middle seat. "Let me help you in, darling." He lifted her up into his inferior truck, leaving me fuming. Lizzie thanked him, and he walked to his side.

I grabbed the handle hold and muttered, "Ferret," as I pressed my top teeth into my bottom lip and made sucky noises.

Liz reached over to give me a hand. "Not you, too. Your brother must've poisoned you." Garret opened his door. "Behave," she whispered.

I made a goofy face, which made her laugh. Garret assumed she laughed at him, because his cheesy grin grew wider.

"Are you a member of Lizzie's church?" I asked.

"No, little man. But Lizzie's finer than a frog hair split four ways, so I figured it couldn't hurt to check it out."

I made a fist, wishing to let him check that out.

The drive took twice as long, because Garret wouldn't shut his trap. Unlike Liz, who gave him a sympathetic ear, I stuck out my lips and wished for a roll of duct tape to muffle him.

"So...you and Rawson?"

I perked up at the mention of my brother.

Lizzie squirmed. "Yeah."

"How long have you two been together?"

"Just recently."

"Long enough to be downright embarrassing," I said.

Her elbow jabbed into me. "Hush."

"Are you open to dating other guys?"

How dare he try to steal my brother's girl. I leaned forward to glare at the jerk. "She's Rawson's girl."

Ferret seemed to sense I meant business. He began regaling us with another tall tale. I didn't believe half of it, but Liz laughed and said "Really?" until I wanted to barf. What was wrong with her?

After Sunday School, we piled into his truck to head home. Exhausted from holding my head up so long, I nodded off when Garret's brag session continued. Rodeo circuit. Football hero in high school. Equine Science degree from University of Florida. Humanitarian. Counselor for teens in the SADD program. Bleck! He was probably making it all up to impress Lizzie.

I awoke to him talking low. "I don't know, darling. The more I find out about your boyfriend, the less I like him."

"I wish you two would try to get along," Liz said. "You have a lot in common with each other."

"The only thing we have in common is you. He uses you. I want to protect you."

Why that slimy toad! I yawned and stretched. "We almost there?"

"Hey, Ben." Liz turned to me. "Did you have a good nap?"

I leaned forward to scowl at Ferret.

He began talking about his SADD group. "You should join, Ben. The group's like a second family. If you want more friends, solid friends with strong values, it's the perfect place. You could drive in with Liz and me."

I almost agreed, just to watch over Lizzie, but I didn't want to indicate I thought he was as cool as he believed.

"No, thanks."

"If you change your mind, just say the word. I've helped kids like you for a while now. It's the most rewarding work I've ever done."

My face puckered. Was he inferring that I was at risk of drinking or doing drugs? I wanted to pop the loser in his big mouth, but made ferret sounds instead.

Lizzie's elbow jabbed into me again. She'd become darn good at that move.

56

RAWSON

*M*Y MUSCLES FLEXED as I approached the round pen and leaned over the top post to watch Liz ride Dunrun Outa Wiskee. She'd told me on the phone that she'd backed the two-year-old dun last week but still needed to get him used to the saddle. It wasn't his friend.

She noticed me and threw me a smile before circling the pen once more. Ferret stood inside the paddock with a clipboard and pen, jotting down notes. She brought Wiskee to a halt in front of me, and I felt perverse pleasure out of seeing the Ferret's expression sour.

I climbed the gate to greet her. "He's looking good."

She dismounted with the grace of Aphrodite.

"So are you." I grabbed my girl up in my arms and swung her around. When I set her on her feet, she blushed and patted the horse.

"Good job, Whiskers."

"Whiskers? That's no name for this fine beast. He's Wiskee."

Liz huffed. "He doesn't drink."

"Neither do I, but Whiskers sounds like an old man with no teeth."

She rubbed the horse's ears. "When did you get back?"

"About two minutes ago. I ran here as fast as I could to feast my eyes on beauty. They've been starving." Two weeks on the road had felt like forever.

"You're such a tease." She opened the gate to lead the horse to his stall.

"Hey, darling," Garret called. "Want to look over my notes?"

I cocked an eyebrow. "Darling?"

Lizzie shook her head. "He calls everyone that."

I snarled as the Florida ferret swaggered our direction. "Remind me to never call you *darling* again. He's ruined the word."

"Hey, Rawson. Welcome back."

I gave him a cursory chin tilt.

He sidled up to Liz with his clipboard. I slipped behind Liz and let my arms circle her waist. I blew in her ears and stuck my hands in the front pockets of her jeans. Of course, being women's jeans, my hands only fit halfway. She stiffened, but I refused to retreat. Benny had told me how the guy had badmouthed me when he'd driven Lizzie to town. Liz was my girl, and Garret was going to damn well take note.

"Mmmm, baby," I murmured, "I missed you."

She pried my hands from her pockets and whipped around to face me. I longed to explore her back pockets but figured that might freak her out.

"I missed you, too. But don't you have to get to the cows?"

I nuzzled her nose. "Cattle, Lizzie. Cows are—"

"I know. Females who've had babies."

"I don't have to be back until tomorrow."

A throat cleared behind us. "Should we finish?"

I glared at Garret as Liz pulled out of my arms. "We'll go over it later. Can you put Whiskers away and saddle up Yoda?"

He acted perturbed as he took the rope from her.

"Later, Gare." I sent him a taunting salute.

Liz gave me a scolding look. "Keep your testosterone in check."

I hugged her. "Can I kidnap you for the rest of the day? Hold you hostage somewhere nice and toasty, Stockholm?"

She blushed. "Tempting, but I need to finish up here."

"I was afraid you'd say that." I winked. "See you at supper. I'll take you snowmobiling afterward."

"Sounds fun."

Oh, it'd be more than fun. It would be thrilling.

For the rest of the afternoon, I helped Abe fix broken equipment. When I finally headed to the house for supper, my body buzzed. My Pavlov's response to Liz. With a spring in my step, I approached the back porch to wash up, but running footsteps from behind made me pause and turn.

Chance materialized from the shadows, out of breath and looking awful.

I tensed. "What's up, man?" Please don't say Damon.

"It's Damon."

I clenched my teeth, knowing my night was ruined. "What happened?"

"I did my best, Roz..."

I winced at the hated nickname. Only Damon got away with calling me that, and occasionally some chick I met while with him.

"...but he got away." He rubbed his swollen cheek.

"Where did he go?" When he didn't answer, I shook him. "Talk to me."

"I don't know. He punched me and took off with my truck."

"How did he get your keys?"

He gave me a sheepish expression.

"You left them in the ignition?"

He wrung his hands.

I kicked gravel. "I told you to keep them on you at all times."

"I know. He tricked me. Yelled that there was a fire. I ran in. How was I supposed to know he'd sucker-punch me and steal my truck?"

I started pacing. Liz expected me, but who knew what Damon would do if I didn't find him. I glared. "I'm docking you a night's pay, maybe two."

"Fine. But can you help me find my truck?"

I hissed. This was the fourth time I'd had to drop my plans to go clean up after him because Chance couldn't control my friend.

"Hey, Stash."

I swore under my breath. "Play along," I ordered as Liz skipped down the steps. "I don't want her knowing anything." I turned and held out my arms for a hug. Liz wore the burgundy coat I'd given her, looking beyond sexy in the moonlight. "Hey, sweetheart." My lips felt as though they might crack, but she didn't seem to notice in the dark.

"Hey, Chance." She smiled at him.

"Chance just informed me that Abe's in a bind. I'm afraid I'll have to skip out on dinner and snowmobiling tonight."

"Yeah, it's really bad. Abe is ticked."

I ground my teeth. Chance sounded like a damn robot.

Liz pulled back to look at me. "I could help."

I lifted my gloved hand to her cheek. She still hadn't let me kiss her but had me wrapped around her finger all the same. It killed me to lie to her.

"I'd love to take you, babe, but it'll be dirty work."

"I'm not afraid of dirt. Besides, if nothing else, I can keep you company."

Guilt gnawed at me, making it impossible to even throw out a joke. "We'll be out late. I don't want you tired for mucking in the morning." I leaned down to kiss her brow. "Let me walk you inside." I trudged slowly, bummed at missing out on our rare evening together. I squeezed her hand at the door. "Sorry." If she only knew how I longed to stay with her. The peace I felt in her presence was a big reason why I put up with her insane dating rules. No other girl would've made that torture worthwhile.

"Don't be. I think you're wonderful to help out after already working a full day." She hugged me.

"I'll make it up to you." I blew her a kiss, feeling like a snake.

Chance wore a wary look as I approached. With Liz still standing on the porch, I couldn't wring his neck as I wanted. "Let's go."

"Drive safe," Liz called.

"I will." I waved before pulling away. When the house disappeared from view, I pounded the wheel. Why couldn't life cut me a break?

LIZ

*T*HE TOUGH TEEN blushed. "Thanks for the ice cream, Liz," Chaz said. With his piercings and tattoos, the kid appeared intimidating. Yet as I'd gotten to know him during the last three SADD meetings, I'd discovered a vulnerable boy desperate for attention. Not having received any in his dysfunctional family, he'd sought it from the wrong crowd until the sheriff had busted him for theft and a judge had ordered him to attend Garret's class.

I hugged the gangly youth. "You're awesome, Chaz. Don't let anyone tell you otherwise. I expect you to ace that math test tomorrow. Text me when you find out your score."

He squeezed me. "I will."

"And if you need to talk, I always have my phone on me." I wanted to do all I could to support him since the odds were stacked against him.

Chaz gave me a crooked smile. "You're the best, Liz."

"That she is." Garret clapped Chaz's shoulder and walked him to the exit. "Now remember what we talked about in class. Start being a leader. See if you can bring a friend or two to our next meeting."

I shook my head. Garret never took off his recruiting hat.

After saying goodbye, Garret helped me into his truck. "Brrrr. It's cold enough to freeze the balls off a pool table," he said, making me laugh. He started his truck. "I have high hopes for that kid, and it's all because of you."

"You're his mentor."

"I've done my best, but guys are guys. A pretty girl always motivates more than good will. Chaz is in love and would do anything for you, darling."

"Whatever." He could be as bad as Rawson at times. What was with guys and their never-ending string of lies to charm women?

Snowflakes fell against the windshield, simulating hyperdrive on *Star Wars*, which made me think of Rawson. Six weeks had passed since I'd technically become his girl. I tingled just thinking of him.

"You're smiling like a goat in a briar patch. Please tell me you're not thinking of that no-good account that thinks he's your boyfriend."

I hugged myself. "He is my boyfriend."

"He's more slippery than snot on a glass doorknob."

I frowned. "I wish you'd try to get along. Rawson's a great guy."

"I can't tolerate how he's using you."

"He's not using me."

"He is, and all the hands know it. You're just too blinded by his pretty face to see that you're only his ranch fling."

His words unlocked a vault of doubts. I'd always felt inferior to Rawson. I'd felt the same way with Justin, and look how that'd turned out. Though Mackay had done nothing for me physically, he was more the kind of guy I deserved. Average.

"I saw him last Saturday in town," he said. "He was with that jerk friend of his. Did you know that?"

I gulped. No. Rawson had told me he was going with Chance to help Abe. I recalled how he'd rebuffed each of my attempts to join him, and realized he'd played me for the fool. I blinked hard.

"Yeah, he told me," I lied.

"And you're okay with that?"

No. But I should've expected it. I wasn't a gullible, naïve girl any longer. Justin had seen to that.

"I'm confident enough in our relationship to allow him time with the guys," I lied again.

"And does time with the guys include flirting with other women?"

He might as well have punched me in the gut. I must not have hidden my emotions as well this time, because Garret's expression turned smug.

"Be careful with your heart, darling. Guys like Rawson Law will shred it like pork at a barbecue."

BENTLEY

$\mathcal{M}$Y BOWL OF POPCORN tipped precariously on my lap as the movie played, but I didn't dare stabilize it and alert Liz that I'd awakened. Rawson's eyes were closed. He'd dozed off earlier. Didn't blame him. Working cattle sucked. His eyes fluttered open and he yawned and stretched.

"You're awake," Liz said.

"Sorry," he mumbled. "I'm exhausted."

She pursed her lips.

"What's that look for?"

"I didn't give you a look."

He reached up to caress her face, but she jerked away and eyed me.

Rawson chuckled. "The kid's out. Besides, even if he wasn't, it's not like we're making out. Although I'm totally open to changing that."

"Shush. I'm not kissing you."

I chanced a quick peek. Liz appeared upset as she stared at the television. Rawson didn't seem much happier. I shut my eyes and wondered why grown-ups made things so difficult. They should be happy as clams, but they'd acted stiff with each other during supper, and now they were with each other, but not really with each other, if that made sense.

Lizzie broke the silence. "Rawson?"

"Yeah, babe."

"Are you tired of me?"

He turned to face her. "Never."

"Even though I won't kiss you."

He sighed. "I won't lie and say that doesn't matter, because truthfully, it's all I can think about. But I'm willing to wait until you're ready. You're my world."

His words were smooth as a chocolate, but Lizzie's worried expression didn't melt into a clear smile as I expected.

"Maybe we should take a break from each other."

Rawson stiffened. "That's the stupidest idea ever."

"It's just that you're with the cows —I mean cattle—so often that being a couple seems senseless. This is only the second time we've been together in the last twenty-six days."

"Mm mm." He caressed her face. "The fact that you're counting proves you want me."

She scowled. "I know you get into town between seeing me and probably meet other girls."

My brother growled. "I thought I made it clear that I wasn't interested in dating anyone but you. Is this about you wanting to date Garret?"

"No." She frowned, then shrugged. "Maybe. I don't know."

Her expression showed clear distaste, but Rawson didn't catch that facial revelation since he scowled at the ceiling.

"What's going on, Liz?"

She chewed her lips. "Some of the hands saw you in town with another woman. They're calling me your ranch fling now."

"Who's calling you that?"

"I know I've made life difficult by not kissing you, so maybe we should break up. Then you can mess around with whoever you want and it won't matter." A tear worked its way out of her eye.

Rawson took her face in his hands. "Sweetheart, someone's twisted the truth to hurt you. I did go to town. Damon took off. Chance and I found him at a bar, making out with some chick. Her pushy friend got handsy with me before I could get him out of there. If someone saw that, they could have misconstrued the scene. I swear though, nothing happened."

More tears fell. From the tortured expression on my brother's face, those killed him. He wrapped an arm around her.

"I only like you. I think I even love you."

Her eyes widened.

So did mine. Thankfully, they were too involved in their conversation to notice.

He rubbed her nose like an Eskimo. "I do."

She pushed him away. "Let's not go there."

"If you'd let me kiss you, you'd never doubt again. You're the only girl for me."

She pushed a lock of hair off his forehead. "Can you not go to bars anymore? I don't like it."

His brow furrowed, but he shrugged. "If you kiss me, I'll promise anything."

She didn't respond

He prodded her. "What do you say?"

I didn't dare move as she glanced my way. Hopefully, shadows made it hard to discern my slivered eyes.

"I guess." She played with his hair. "But not tonight. Your dad's worked you to the bone. You need sleep."

He pulled her on top of him. "Let's sleep here."

She jumped off him like a Jack-in-the-box. "Rawson, I can't sleep with you."

My brother's deep chuckle rumbled across the room. "Not like that. I doubt I have the energy to ravish you, even if I wanted. Which I do. I just want to hold you. Jedi's honor. You're my girl."

"You can hold my hand in an upright position. Another day." She leaned down and pecked his forehead. "Goodnight."

Rawson grinned. "Can't blame a guy for trying. So are you serious? You'll kiss me if I avoid bars?"

She nodded. "I'm serious."

Lizzie left the room. Rawson yawned and walked past me, jabbing my side.

"Don't speak a word of what you just heard, kid."

I kept my eyes closed, hoping he'd think I was asleep. After several seconds, I peeked.

"Ah-hah," he crowed, towering over me. "Got ya."

"Yo dawg. Don't go all cray-cray 'cause you've lost your touch with the ladies. Ain't my fault she won't kiss you."

He laughed and tousled my hair. Maybe I should let Mom cut it so he'd stop messing it up.

"Let's hit the sack."

"You don't want to snuggle with me on the couch?"

He raised a brow. "Shut it, dude."

I made kissy noises as he headed to his bedroom. A dirty sock hit me in the back of my head before his door shut.

LIZ

$\mathcal{T}$HIS TIME AS I made my way to the arena to muck stalls at four-freaking-forty-five in the morning, I knew what the sliver of light under the door meant. Rawson was waiting. I stopped and stared at the closed doors. I'd hoped not to worry about kissing him for at least another week. I should've known better.

Pushing the door open, I entered. Rawson peeked over the first stall and smiled when he saw me. Flu-like symptoms hit me: flushed skin, skyrocketing temperature, a heartbeat resembling the fluttering of hummingbird wings.

"Good morning, beautiful."

"Why aren't you on your way out to the cattle?" Though the cogs in my brain turned sluggishly, I remembered the proper terminology.

"I will as soon as I make good on last night's agreement."

I picked up a rake. "What agreement?" I played dumb, though I knew it was futile. Rawson was very single-minded when it came to kissing.

"Nice try, babe." He propped the shovel against the door and walked over to trap me against the wall.

I gulped. "How do I know you won't just kiss me and toss me aside like a ripe banana, before going back to your stupid bars anyway?"

He grinned, and dang…just dang! That smile could melt Antarctica. It definitely melted my insides and short-circuited all rational thought.

"You're adorable when you try to stall."

"Uh, speaking of stalls, we should clean these."

He chuckled. "Lizzie, I promised not to go to bars, and I won't. And I swear on my grandma's grave that I won't kiss and toss you aside like a ripe banana. But I might devour you like a banana cream pie."

That frightened me even more.

"Ready to pay up?"

"I didn't brush my teeth." A bald-faced lie, but maybe it'd gross him out.

He tipped my chin. "How about you skedaddle then. Smear some toothpaste on your teeth for me to clean off later." He winked. "I'll finish mucking."

"I can't let you do that."

He led me to the Dutch doors. "I'm fine kissing you just how you are, nuclear breath and all. If you don't want that, I suggest you hightail it out of here and meet me for breakfast, because you look like a delectable banana cream pie right now, and I'm starving."

He leaned closer, and I practically sprinted from the stable. When he put it that way, what else could I do? The man made me feel as mushy as banana cream pie.

An hour later, when he entered the dining room, I hardly tasted Charity's award-winning sausage gravy.

Rawson grinned. "You look divine this morning, Lizzie." He took a bite. "How do you muck stalls at five A.M. and manage to look so tempting?"

I scowled, making him chuckle.

He took my hand after we'd both finished our meals. "Thanks for breakfast, Mom. I'm heading out after I drop Liz off at the stable."

Charity rushed over to kiss him. "Drive safe. Call me when you get there so I know you made it."

"Mom," he groaned.

She swatted his backside. "Don't *Mom* me. Just do it. You know how I worry about you in this weather." It'd started snowing earlier.

He helped me into his truck and drove to the stable. With the storm picking up, I knew he had to leave. But he wrapped an arm around me and tipped my chin.

It was totally one of those heart-pounding moments. Rawson's gaze flickered to my mouth, making my insides puddle in pleasure. He traced my top lip, before dropping a finger to my bottom one and smiling as goosebumps erupted along the length of my arms.

"You're so beautiful."

I ached to partake of what he dangled before me. "You are, too." My breathy words made me blush.

He leaned closer, and I knew the moment I had dreamed about for months would become reality. I'd held him off as long as possible but was helpless to stop him from taking the rest of my heart.

The minty coolness of his breath teased my lips, making them part.

Loud rapping on the window made us both jump.

"Liz." Garret opened my door. "Mr. Law needs to see you."

My whole body felt on fire, from passion and humiliation. I started to pull away, but Rawson stopped me. He narrowed his eyes at Garret.

"She'll be there in a minute. Now scram."

Garret pouted. "I'll meet you in Bart's office, darling."

"She's not your darling," Rawson shouted.

I hit his shoulder. "Knock it off."

He squeezed me. "You still owe me a kiss."

"I do, but your dad needs me. Can you take a rain-check?"

His dark brows lifted as I slipped from his grip. "With interest?"

I shrugged.

"I have to hit the road, but when I see you next, make sure you wear lots of Chapstick. I plan on putting your lips through Basic Training."

Oh my. I closed the door and patted my burning cheeks, not knowing whether he'd just promised me a great gift or threatened me.

60

RAWSON

*P*UTTING MY PHONE on speaker as I drove over the pass, I waited for Lizzie's phone to connect. It'd almost slipped my mind that today was Friday and she might head to town with Ferret. No way could that happen. After the week I'd endured, I needed to hang out with my girl.

"Hey," she answered out of breath. "What's up?"

Just hearing her voice made my aching muscles relax. "Can you ditch out on your SAPP meeting tonight? I'm on my way to see you."

"It's SADD," she corrected.

"That it is. I'll be there in half an hour. Please say you'll be there to greet me, sweetheart. You wouldn't believe the week I've had."

"I'll be here."

"Can't wait to see you, babe."

"Yeah, yeah." She hung up.

I punched the gas, anxious to spend the evening with Liz and collect on that kiss.

The sun had set when I pulled up to the stable. Liz walked out to greet me. "Hey, gorgeous." I spun her around. "Is Ferret gone?"

She gave me one of her *Watch It* looks. "Yes. Garret," she emphasized, "left ten minutes ago." She stroked my jaw. "So, rough week?"

"I'm working cattle. Need I say more?"

"Cows are cute. Don't you have some favorites you've named?"

"Nothing I can repeat."

She giggled as I leaned in to peck her cheek.

"Are you done?"

218

She pulled out of my arms. "Yep. Did you have something planned?"

Oh, did I ever. I grabbed her hand and reeled her into my embrace. "Thought we'd go for a drive."

She bit her bottom lip. I couldn't wait to take over that job for her.

"Let me run inside and change," she said.

"Climb in. I'll drive you to the house."

As I waited for her to change, Damon's ring-tone blared. "Yo," I answered.

"Roz, you got any beer?" My friend sounded twitchy.

I heaved a sigh. "What happened to the Buds Chance brought you?"

"I think he drank them all."

I rolled my eyes at the lie. But a few beers weren't the worst he could ask for. "Give me fifteen minutes. I'll drop by with a resupply."

"Thanks, man."

I hung up and groaned. Damon had the worst timing. I grabbed two cases of Budweisers from my hiding spot in the back of the garage and tossed them into the bed of my truck just as Liz walked out, looking sweet and kissable in a baby-blue blouse and jeans.

I whistled.

"Oh, hush." She climbed into the truck.

I wrapped an arm around her. Lizzie's warm body next to mine ignited so many fires it was a miracle I didn't explode. I needed to drop off the Buds to Damon quick so I could drive somewhere dark and cozy and kiss my girl senseless.

When I pulled up to the old homestead, I squeezed her shoulder. "I have to drop something off. Be right back." Without waiting for a response, I shut the door and lugged the cases of beer into the log cabin where Damon had been hiding out.

I winced as I entered. What had he been doing? The place reeked to high heaven. "Damon?" I kicked the door shut. "I bring you good tidings and a couple cases of Bud."

He staggered out of the back bedroom and burped. "Took you long enough."

"You're welcome."

His stained clothing told me he hadn't changed for days. Hadn't shaved either, though I didn't blame him the way his hands shook. Withdrawal was one son of a biscuit. I shook my head at how I couldn't even cuss without substituting Lizzie's silly vernacular into mine now. I set the Budweiser's on the coffee table.

He grabbed for the beer like it might fly away. "You're the best, Roz." His speech had the same tremor as his hands.

"You doing all right?"

He farted. "Life sucks."

"Ain't that the truth."

He looked up at me. "Take me to town, Roz. I swear I won't do no crank. I just need a woman."

That's what he always claimed. "I have to get back to the herd," I lied.

"Take me with you. I gotta get out of here."

"Sorry, man." I hated letting him down, but Liz waited in the truck. "I'll come next week and we'll hang out."

He dug into his scalp.

I headed for the door. Once the alcohol took effect, he'd be fine.

"Please, Roz," he whimpered. "Do-don't leave. I'm afraid I'll o-o-off myself."

I stopped, hand on doorknob. The couple times he'd talked about killing himself in the past, he'd made good on his words and attempted just that. Luckily, I'd been close by and had thwarted him both times.

"Okay, fine. Let me grab my bag."

I approached Liz in the truck, itching at my skin through my shirt. "Damon's not doing so hot. I better stay the night. Sorry to bail. Do you mind driving home and picking me up in the morning?"

The sparkle in her eyes dimmed. "Why do you waste time on him? He killed your brother. He damaged Benny."

I stiffened. "He's my friend."

"Your friendship is one-sided. You give and give and give, and he takes and takes and takes."

"You know what?" I tossed the keys onto her lap. "I'll get one of the other hands to pick me up in the morning. Don't put yourself out." I slammed the door and marched into the stinky cabin.

I sank into the ratty couch next to my friend. His mood visibly improved as mine plummeted when I heard my truck start up and pull away. The night nosedived from there. Damon tanked down on beers as I stewed on the words Liz had lobbed like nuclear missiles. My hands shook as I found myself coveting the beer in Damon's hands.

"Why don't you share no more?" He glared at me.

"What kind of tick's burrowed under your skull? I share. Freak. I brought you two whole cases of beer." I wasn't in the mood to coddle him.

He threw an empty can on the floor. "No. You got that hot babe at your place you keep all ta yourself."

I clenched my fists. "You don't know what you're talking about."

"I remember. She was with Benny and you took off after she left 'cause you wanted her for yerself."

"You're drunk."

"I'm not so drunk I don't know you're holding out on me." He pounded his chest. "You need to share. We're friends, right? Let me show her what a true man's like."

Alcohol once had made Damon a riot to hang with, but it didn't agree with him the same anymore. He reminded me more and more of his old man.

When he grew more graphic about what he'd do to Liz, I clutched him by his throat and shoved him into the corner of the stained couch. "Shut up!" I roared. "If you go near the ranch or even think of touching her, I'll break every bone in your body. You hear me?"

He slithered out from under my grip. "Oh yeah? Not if I stick your woman with a needle first and make her mine?"

I lost my mind at his threat.

When I found it again, Damon screamed beneath me as I punched his face. I stopped, and he scrambled on all fours into the corner and curled into a fetal position. Memories hit me like bricks as I recalled his father beating him through a window of his trailer in junior high when I'd peeked in. I hung my head. Mr. Hollis had been the scum of the earth, and I was just like him.

"You need to get help, man." I squeezed my eyes to relieve the pressure building in my head. "You're jacked up and not thinking straight. I don't know who you are anymore."

He began to weep.

I fled into the back room. Everything was my fault. I'd been the mastermind behind obtaining the fake ID's Damon and I used our junior year of high school. Who knew both of us would take to beer like bears to honey? We'd been the big men on campus, full of attitude that wouldn't allow us to admit we had a problem. We'd blamed our sucky lives on our dads until the accident revealed our dark secret. Damon had been tossed into juvie. My parents had thrown me into a posh rehab to finish out senior year. From there I'd been sent straight to Stanford.

For six years, I'd stayed sober. I owed my family that much. It'd been hard to decline at parties and bars, but I'd mastered my appetite for Benny's sake. Or I thought I had. Tonight proved I still harbored a rabid thirst for that which had almost destroyed me.

"My name is Rawson Law, and I'm an alcoholic," I muttered between my fingers.

Rehab had drilled into me the importance of acknowledging my weakness. Not until meeting Liz had my daily battle dissipated somewhat. She'd made me laugh and hope again. And I'd repaid her by sending her away in a fit of anger.

I hated her attitude toward Damon, but she had a point. I was wasting my time. He needed more than a few cases of beers. My friend needed intervention. I kneaded my forehead. How could I convince Dad to unfreeze my trust fund so I could access enough cash to admit Damon into rehab? Hiding out here at the homestead wasn't working.

Damon whimpered in the corner. He looked up at me with fear chiseled into his bloody face as I approached.

"Sorry, man." I tended his wounds and got him into a sleeping bag.

His face scrunched up. "Thanks for not giving up on me, Roz. You're the greatest friend ever."

I hurried out onto the porch.

Greatest friend. Bah! I should be shot for what I'd done. But I was the oldest son of Bartholomew Law, pillar in the community. Damon had been the son of a drunk. It'd been easier to lay the blame of the accident on him.

I must've dozed on the hard wooden bench. When I awoke, I was frozen solid and my back ached something awful. I texted Chance to see if he could swing by and pick me up. Checking Damon again to ensure he was out, I left when my ride arrived.

At home, I showered and headed down for breakfast. I gulped when I saw Liz, but pride wouldn't allow me to roll over and beg forgiveness. I sat beside her, but made small talk with Mom as she flitted in and out of the kitchen. Tension stretched between Liz and me.

I'd just filled my mouth with cranberry muffin when Lizzie's hand crept beneath the table to rest on my clenched fist. Startled, I turned to face her. The vulnerability in her golden-brown eyes worked like Kryptonite on me.

Sorry, she mouthed.

I relaxed in my chair. For the last few hours, I'd despaired at the thought of ruining what we'd had. I clutched her hand and thanked God for my sweet, forgiving angel.

I wrapped an arm around her on the way to the arena. "Sorry for last night. Let me make it up to you. I have a few hours before I have to be back to the herd. Put me to work."

"Are you sure you don't want to catch up on sleep? You look beat."

No wonder. The sleep I'd received at the homestead had been anything but restful. "I don't want to miss out on any more time together." I brought her hand to my lips. "Again, I'm sorry."

She lowered her eyes. "Me, too."

"You have nothing to be sorry for. But maybe we can slip in that kiss you owe me."

She blushed, which made her stunning in the morning light. "You have a one-track mind."

She had no idea.

Instead of a hot make-out session, she put me to work with a new gelding. I would've preferred she not have such a strong work ethic. Before I had to leave, I cornered her by the washing bay.

"I have to go."

"Thanks for helping."

"My pleasure." My gaze dropped to her lips.

Her mouth parted slightly as her breathing hitched. I dropped my hands to her waist and leaned in for much anticipated contact.

A startling crash of metal against wood made us both flinch. I turned to catch Garret looking smug as he knelt to pick up a pile of bits and bridles he'd probably purposely thrown against the wall.

Liz made to escape, but I was sick of Ferret ruining our moments.

"Oh, no you don't." I grabbed her arm and reeled her back into my embrace. Ignoring her startled-deer look, I covered her mouth with mine. She became rigid as a board, but as my lips plied hers, she relaxed.

Garret cleared his throat behind us, which made Liz freeze up again. I nibbled her bottom lip, eliciting an audible sigh from deep in her throat before I pulled away.

"That was a teaser." I relinquished my hold on her. "I'll call you tonight, babe." I headed to the door but looked over my shoulder at Ferret. "You should get your own girlfriend, instead of drooling over mine, Buckwheat."

61

LIZ

*K*ISSING HAD NOTHING on this. Rawson nibbled my neck, and I closed my eyes and sighed. I hadn't seen him since our hurried kiss two weeks ago that'd left me weak in the knees. But the way he savored my skin now made me weak all over. Benny knew the drill and pretended to ignore us as he watched the movie.

When it ended, he waved goodnight and limped upstairs. I jumped to my feet. No way would I stay cuddled on the couch alone with Rawson, his bedroom only feet away. Being alone with him was like taunting the devil with smoochie faces and thinking I wouldn't get a pitchfork in the butt.

He caught up to me at the stairs. "You in a hurry to hug your pillow?" He took my hand in the darkened stairwell.

"Four A.M. comes fast and furious," I said, trying to ignore how electricity seemed to shoot from my fingertips into my whole body as we climbed the stairs.

"That it does."

I paused at the landing. "Are you heading back to the herd tonight or in the morning?"

"Tonight."

I squeezed his fingers. "Drive safe."

"I will, Beautiful."

He tipped my chin. Before I realized what was happening, his mouth closed over mine. I expected the type of kiss he'd given me before—soft and gentle. But his lips didn't caress, they demanded in the sweetest agony I'd ever experienced. The only other time a man had kissed me passionately had been during my engagement to Justin. He'd swept my mouth with his tongue, and I'd pretended to like it, even though it'd sort of grossed me out. I'd wondered why movies, books, and friends had made such a big deal over that kind of kiss. It was slightly terrifying.

Now I knew.

Rawson's tongue didn't just sweep, his probed, tangled, and twined with mine in a passionate dance uniting us as one. And I didn't feel any fear. His hands wound up my back and into my hair, shaking my entire being. My fingers found their way into his hair, playing in it as I'd dreamed. He moaned into my mouth, awakening a ravenous hunger I hadn't known existed. I clutched him tighter and allowed my tongue to mimic his as he deepened the kiss. It felt incredible. And right.

Why had I resisted for so long?

I pulled back for air.

His sexy lips twitched. "Mmmm." The deep rumble of his voice made me tremble. "Sweet dreams, love." He brushed the lightest of kisses across my forehead. "I know I'll dream of you."

I took several deep breaths, too tongue-tied to speak. When he chuckled, I turned and raced up the stairs.

In the safety of my room, I slumped against the door. Touching my tingling lips, I banged my head against the door. What had I done? And why did I so badly want to scramble back down the stairs to do it again? What had happened to the careful girl who'd determined not to lose her heart?

I hid my face in my hands. So much for avoiding crashing on the highway of heartbreak. Instead of using caution and slowing down, I'd tripled my speed toward the cliff up ahead.

62

RAWSON

*T*IPPING MY COWBOY hat, I grinned. "You ready, Gorgeous?"

Lizzie blushed and seemed to spot something intriguing on the ground. "Yep." Even after almost a month of kissing, she still became adorably flustered in my presence. Of course, since calving season had started, I could count on one hand the number of times we'd spent together. Dad kept loading me with more responsibility than one man could handle.

I helped her into the truck, anxious for the evening ahead. I loved kissing my girl but hoped to push our relationship further tonight. Liz hugged the passenger door.

"I don't bite...hard."

"You're driving," she said. "I don't want to distract you."

"Too late. You're alive and sitting in my truck." Just her scent distracted me, let alone that clingy white blouse she wore. I patted the middle seat. "If you don't scoot your fine behind over, then I will, and I assure you that me driving from the middle seat will be a whole lot more distracting than if you sit there."

She rolled her eyes. "Oh, all right. You win this round, birthday boy."

I pressed the gas as she slid closer. Thank the good Lord for birthdays, and moms who coerced their husbands into giving their son the day off to celebrate his. Liz had still worked, but I'd helped her, and besides putting up with that Florida ferret, it'd been enjoyable. Much easier than working cattle.

I leaned over to peck her cheek.

"Keep your eyes on the road."

"Relax, babe. I could drive this in my sleep. Probably have at one point."

"Not funny."

I turned to head down the canyon. Liz wrung her slender hands like a nervous Nellie. Only when we reached the bottom of the ravine did she let out the breath she'd been holding.

"Oooo." She gazed out at the golden sky. "The sunset's breathtaking."

"So are you."

She scoffed. I considered making her do a *Love Triangle* but couldn't delay. This first part of the date would be better in the waning light. A breeze nipped my cheeks as I helped her from the truck. The April weather couldn't be more perfect. With our jackets, we'd be comfortable, and when it cooled after the sun set, snuggling would be essential.

I led her through thick pines to a clearing where I'd set up a table earlier beneath the cliff backdrop. She grinned when she noticed the white-clothed table and battery-lit candles flickering in the shadows.

"Wow. This is perfect."

"So are you." I pulled out a chair for her. Crimson marked her lovely cheeks and neck.

I lifted the lid from Mom's silver platter to reveal a decadent cheese-cake she'd graciously made for my special night. I picked up a knife to slice a piece, but Liz stopped me.

"I need to sing to you."

"You'd do that for me?"

"Of course."

She sang *Happy Birthday*, purposely slaughtering a few notes to make me laugh. She belted out "And many more...on channel twenty-four," and I clapped.

"That was awesome! Thank you."

She retrieved gifts from her satchel and pushed them across the table.

"Ah, Lizzie, you didn't have to get me anything."

"Open them."

"Bossy." I lifted the square gift and shook it. I used my pocketknife to cut through the packaging to see a personalized ceramic mug. I waggled my eyebrows. "Am I really the *Obi Wan* for you?"

She lowered her gaze. "I thought it was clever. Open the other one."

That gift held two pairs of light saber chopsticks. "Oh, I can't wait until Benny sees these. There's gonna be some dueling at the table for sure."

"They even light up."

I set her presents aside and reached for her hand. "Thank you. I love them."

"I thought they were perfect for you."

"You're perfect for me." I set a piece of cheesecake in front of her. I chiseled at my cheesecake but savored my girl.

"Stop staring," she said.

"No."

She pouted. "You can be so annoying."

"So can you."

She smirked. "I'll take that as a compliment."

"That's how I meant it." I scooted my chair closer. "I love you, Liz."

She choked and patted her neck. "Excuse me?"

Thinking fast, I said, "You heard me. And if you had your wits about you, you would've given me Han's most classic answer ever—*I know.*"

She visibly relaxed. "Very funny."

Obviously, she wasn't ready for the "L" word yet.

"I set up a spot for us to stargaze down the canyon. The Lyrid meteor shower's happening. Google said there should be ten to twenty meteors an hour." I stood. "Come on."

With a flashlight, I led her along the dry riverbed to a spot where the canyon opened up. I'd dropped off a mattress and a bunch of quilts earlier, to keep us warm and make tonight comfortable.

"Here we are." I motioned to my handiwork.

"What's this?"

I sank onto the mattress and pulled off my boots. "You don't want to be on the ground, do you? It's freezing. Kick off your boots and crawl in here with me." I rolled under the stack of blankets.

She hugged herself against the night chill.

I lifted the edge of the quilt. "Come on, woman. You're causing an earthquake with your shivering."

"You're not trying to seduce me, are you?"

That was exactly what I hoped to do, but if I admitted that, she'd turn tail and run. Liz was as skittish as a yearling. "Now that's the best idea you've had all night, but no. I just don't want you to freeze into a carbonite mold like Han Solo. You're welcome to lay on top of the blankets, but you'll be warmer beneath them."

Her brow creased but she kicked off her boots. "Fine."

I pulled the quilts over us and wrapped an arm around her. "There. Aren't you warmer?" I was. Her body next to me flooded mine with fiery heat. I'd never taken an anatomy class, but the powerful reactions sparking and bubbling within had me curious to know if this was normal. I couldn't remember ever feeling ready to explode like this before. Of course, no woman had led me along for so long without easing my pain. Liz had mastered the art of applying brakes before blast off. Maybe the mess my body was in could be attributed to that.

We stared into the starry sky and made small talk until a shooting star streaked across our view. I rolled onto an elbow and gazed down at her. Evidence of desire burned brightly in her eyes. She wanted me as much as I wanted her. Yet she kept holding me at arm's length.

Tonight, I'd change that.

"You are so beautiful." She gulped as I stroked her cheek. "Thanks for coming out here with me. You've made this the best birthday ever."

She reached up to caress my jaw, a grand gesture since she rarely initiated affection. "I'm glad. I just wish I'd thought of this so you didn't have to do all the work on your birthday."

"You're here. That's all I wanted." I brushed kisses across her forehead and rolled onto my back, not wanting to push too fast and scare her. "What's your favorite birthday memory?" My hand searched for hers.

"When I turned eleven, Dad took me to Disneyland. Just him and me. Best day of my life. I've never felt so happy and carefree."

"I've never been there."

She rolled over to stare at me. "Serious? Your parents never took you? That's just…wrong."

"What are your favorite things about Disneyland?"

She rested her head on my chest. "I love the theming and attention to detail. The pirate ride's amazing. I felt like I was in a bayou. Space Mountain's fun, too. Even the baby rides like Dumbo and Peter Pan are fantastic." She played with the hair around my ear. "You *have* to go."

"Want to fly down with me next weekend if I can convince Dad to give me a couple days off?"

She snorted and rolled onto her back.

"You could be my guide. Make sure I get the full magical experience."

"What's your favorite birthday memory?" She changed subjects.

"Tonight. By far."

She scoffed.

I faced her. "Really. I'm twenty-four years old but feel as though I've only begun to live. You make me feel the pure joy of a child." I focused on her lips. "Yet still feel the deep passion of a man."

She self-consciously licked her lips, and my restraint dissipated. Cupping the back of her neck, I brought her close enough to claim those moistened lips for my own. Kissing Lizzie could only be described as glorious. The combination of innocence and eagerness heightened the experience. I'd never been with someone so pure and untouched. All the women I'd dated had been experts in seduction and had known how to move me physically. Liz seemed to be a child in that regard. When we'd first kissed, her hesitation and lack of response had surprised me. She'd told me of a previous engagement, but her fiancé had obviously failed in the loving department. I'd done my duty that night and since to tutor her in the art of osculation.

We tangled tongues beneath the stars, and I knew I loved her. Liz brought out all my tender, protective instincts, which humbled and frightened me.

True to her nature, she cut our intense make-out session short. "That's good," she said breathlessly, pushing me away.

It'd been more than good. It had been mind-boggling. Though innocent, she'd been a quick learner under my tutelage. The passion she unleashed in unguarded moments promised a healthy sex life between us.

"Tell me about your past girlfriends. You had them, right?"

The way she phrased it as a question stung my masculine ego. "I've never wanted for female companionship." I wanted to drop the conversation there. Past entanglements, even ones that'd fizzled, were a sure way to squash the new bloom of romance.

"Have you been serious with anyone before me?" She winced. "Not that we're serious. I didn't mean to imply that you—"

I propped up on my elbow. "Oh, I'm serious. How could you think otherwise? Haven't I shown you—"

She silenced me with a finger. "You're wonderful. I just didn't want you to think I was pressuring you into more." Her big brown eyes revealed a mass of insecurities. I still couldn't understand why. She seemed so confident in everything except herself.

"I love you, Lizzie. How's that for serious?"

She chewed her tasty lips. "You don't really know me."

"That's why I haven't asked you to marry me but know that's the path I'm on—the place I want to reach with you. I know we haven't been able to see each other much, but that's about to change. Dad hired a new guy to replace me with the herd next month."

Her countenance brightened. "Really? That's great."

"It's news that saves my sanity. I despise working cattle."

She gave me a tender smile.

Her lips mere inches from mine, I closed my eyes and leaned in. Lizzie met me halfway. I pulled her on top of me and kissed her like a starving man. She opened to me and had me moaning from unfulfilled longing as she initiated tongue swirling and probing like a pro. Her fingers twisted into my hair as she pulled away to lay feather kisses along my jaw and down my neck. I flipped her over, trapping her beneath me. Her chest heaved, making me ache to take her right then.

"Stop," she panted, applying brakes full force. "You're going to leave a mark."

Too late. I rolled onto my back and trembled. "You're welcome to mark me as much as you want, sweetheart." I pulled down my collar, exposing as much skin as possible.

She tapped my bicep. "You're a goof."

The girl would seriously kill me. "But I'm your goof, right?"

"I guess."

I tilted my head. "How can you kiss me like that and only guess I'm your goof?" I pulled her closer. "Maybe we need to practice more so you *know*."

She laughed as though I teased. "I don't think that's a good idea."

Her words said no, but her eyes and body screamed yes. She bit her lip. "Tell me about your past girlfriends."

Her words dumped ice water over me. Probably how she intended them.

"No one compares to you, love." I tried to sidestep her curiosity.

"You said you want to know everything about me. I want to know everything about you, too. Tell me." Her voice sounded determined.

"Girls were fun diversions. That's all. I only got serious once in college. It turned out to be a huge mistake."

"What happened?"

I squeezed my eyes shut, wishing she'd let me leave the past where it belonged. "I met Vanessa my senior year at Stanford. I thought I loved her. Now I realize I just loved the idea of her. Long story short, I drew out a chunk of change, bought her the largest diamond I could, and went back to my place to propose. Pretty romantic, right?" My jaw clenched. "But my passionate bubble burst when I discovered her in bed with my loser roommate."

She gasped.

"I wasted eight months and an exorbitant amount of money on that cheating bi—" I caught myself, "—bitty."

Lizzie rolled her eyes.

"Vanessa only wanted me for what I could give her: backstage concert passes, jewelry, outrageously priced purses, you name it. I even took her to Maui for Christmas break, thinking that'd secure her love. In the end, she still screwed me."

My hands clenched into fists. Even now, I fought feelings of emasculation from my time with Vanessa. How foolish I'd been to think I'd been even slightly in love with such a vain, selfish woman. She'd looked like a goddess, but she'd sucked my soul dry. I didn't mourn her. I only regretted taking so long to figure out what virtues a real woman possessed. One like Liz.

63

LIZ

SHOCK WAVES ROCKED me at Rawson's revelation. He'd taken his girlfriend to Maui? And had caught her in his bedroom with a roommate? My stomach churned. If he'd taken her to Hawaii, it hadn't been just to hold hands or nibble her neck on the beach. Now that I thought about it, he'd never said he was a virgin. I'd just assumed he was because of his conservative background. Ben had told me his mom's expectations regarding girls, and I'd figured Rawson held to the same high standards.

"So, you were intimate?"

"Yeah, normal couples have sex. We don't just nibble." His scoffing tone stung.

I scrambled into a sitting position. "I'm sorry you don't think I'm normal."

"That's not what I meant." He pulled me into his arms.

I slapped at him. "Don't touch me."

"I'm not with her anymore. You asked about my past. I told you. "

"How many other girls have you, uh…slept with?" Heat crawled up my cheeks at the blunt question. It wasn't one I usually asked my dates.

He blew out a long breath. "I have no clue."

"What?"

His brow furrowed. "I've been sexually active since tenth grade. Trust me, I'm very experienced and know how to pleasure a woman."

I breathed hard. "You sound proud of that."

"Would you rather I be a bumbling virgin like Mackay? He wouldn't know the back end of a—"

232

"I'm a virgin!" I scrambled to my feet.

He grabbed my wrist, flipping me around to face him. "Liz honey."

"Leave me alone."

"No. I can tell you don't understand. I know you're a virgin. I think that's wonderful. Truly. I'm not demeaning you. That's the most beautiful gift you can give a man. But it's different for guys. You wouldn't want a partner who'd never worked an iron before to brand you, would you? It'd be a mighty unpleasant experience."

I gaped at his crude analogy. "I'm not a cow. And FYI, if I was, I'd still choose the man who didn't know how to work his iron, because he wouldn't be a cold-hearted jerk." I wriggled free of his grip and ran.

"Liz!" He caught me again.

I flailed, catching his neck with my nails.

"Damn it! Will you just listen?"

I didn't want to listen. My heart hung in tatters from what I'd already heard.

Rawson brushed his lips over my cheek. "I love you. I never cared one bit for any other girl. Shoot, I don't even remember most of their names."

"Is that supposed to make me feel better?"

A tortured expression marred his handsome face, sucking anger away but deepening my sorrow.

"Please, let me go."

He released me. "I didn't know my experience would upset you."

How could I have fallen for a player again? Did I have no sense? Yes, I did. I'd just ignored the warnings, because my body had craved Rawson Law like a drug. But I refused to be another slash on his headboard.

He tipped my chin and traced my lips. I closed my eyes, trying not to let his gentle touch sway me. But it did.

"You're mad at me."

"No." Just horrifically disappointed.

"I swear I haven't been with another woman since I started liking you."

I met his gaze. "Do you wish I would sleep with you?"

"Of course, I do. I want to share everything with you, but not until you're ready. That's why I haven't pushed you."

Having this conversation made me realize we were worlds apart, especially in how we defined love.

"And if I told you I was ready?" I asked.

The smoldering hunger animating his expression answered me. His scorching look stole my breath as he captured my waist.

"Are you?"

His sensual question made my toes curl. What would it be like to have a taste of what he offered? Could I sample without falling all the way into the flames?

"Ah, Lizzie." His fingers danced along the top of my jeans. "Are you scared because it'll be your first time?"

Words strangled in my throat as he pressed his lips to my forehead.

"I'll be gentle, love. It won't hurt. Not like you've been told. I'll make you feel incredible. Promise. I'll go slow so your first time is unforgettable."

My hands shook as I brought them to his chest. We stared at each other —him with barely concealed longing and anticipation, me with heartache and regret.

"What about afterward?"

His brow creased.

"After you've taken that which I hold most sacred. What then?"

"You'll be mine."

The lump in my throat made swallowing impossible. "Like all the other girls who are now yours?"

"No, it's not—"

"Do you know what that'd do to me if you took my innocence tonight?"

"Lizzie, I—"

"It would destroy me. You'd shatter every piece of my heart and leave me with nothing but shame and regret in the morning. I have no doubt you'd make me feel incredible, but afterward, when I was left with nothing but ruin, I'd loathe you for stealing from me."

His nostrils flared. "So you're not ready? You just played me to see what I'd admit so you could throw my words back at me and judge me a sinner?"

"I wanted to know, yes."

"And let me guess. I failed."

I bowed my head.

His hands clenched. "I failed because I'm not a halo-wearing, celibate monk like your doormat Mackay."

I marched away from him. "You don't have to be such a jerk."

He grabbed me and spun me around. "You have it bad for me and that scares you because it doesn't fit into your set little plan." He yanked me against his body.

"Rawson, please." I could feel his heartbeat pounding against me. Or mine. Who knew? His anger stirred something inside me to life, and I wanted him more than ever.

But I couldn't.

"I feel how you want me every time we're together." He brought his head down as though he meant to give me a crushing kiss, but paused, searing my lips with spearmint breath. "If you want to deny that and marry some fool like Mackay, go ahead. But you'll regret it the rest of your life because he'll bungle everything on your wedding night and leave you unfulfilled and bored stiff."

I pushed out of his arms. "At least, we'd bungle our way together, and I wouldn't wonder if he might be comparing me to all his other conquests and finding me lacking. And I promise you, even if it took fifty years, we'd figure out the mechanics and make our love life amazing—more amazing than you can imagine, because we'd have something you and I don't have. Trust. And respect."

He let go of my arm and stormed over to the truck. "No reward is worth this."

My shoulders sagged as I hefted myself onto the seat and leaned against the passenger door. The drive home was silent and terrifying. Rawson didn't speak and seemed bent on breaking some unwritten speed record. I clutched the door and prayed to get home alive.

Thankfully, we did. When he pulled into the garage, I hurried into the house. Rawson took off the other direction. I slipped upstairs and stood in front of my mirror. The red oval brands on my neck made tears well up in my eyes. They reminded me of Rawson's true intentions, and of what I'd lost of my heart tonight. I'd never get those pieces back from that wretched cowboy.

6 4

RAWSON

*A*FTER LEAVING LIZ in the garage, I stomped away to sulk in my hammock. At first, I was furious with her for ruining my evening, but soon a pang of guilt stung me as I stared into the inky expanse of heaven. Mom had taught me to treat girls like a delicate white rose, never doing anything to soil or damage them. I'd cast her teachings aside as being too old-fashioned. But I wished I'd listened now and lived up to her expectations.

"Oh, God," I groaned, "don't let me lose Liz. I know I shouldn't ask You for anything, but I need her." My voice cracked. "I love her."

In that moment, love became more than physical fulfillment. I realized love focused on what was best for the other person, and tonight, I'd wanted what was best for me. Not her. I'd gone to all that work to make the evening nice, not so I could build Liz up and help her see how incredible she was, but for the sole intent of weakening her resolve and tricking her into letting down her guard so I could steal—she'd called it as it was—that which she held most precious. Speaking smooth words of love had meant nothing to her. Actions spoke louder than words, and mine had been deplorable tonight.

I clawed at my scalp, wondering how to make amends. Or if I could. Could I regain her trust? Had I ever had it in the first place?

I swung my feet out of the hammock and looked at the house. Liz had made me believe I could be a better man.

Time to be one.

My watch showed half past midnight as I climbed the stairs. No soldier on the front lines could've felt more frightened than I did as I stood in front of her door and tapped lightly.

The door cracked, revealing Lizzie's face. She'd been crying.

"May I come in?"

She shook her head.

"Can you come out here then?"

"I think we've seen enough of each other tonight. Don't you?"

"Lizzie, please."

A tear slid down her cheek. "I can't do this, Rawson. I thought I could, but we want different things."

"Don't tell me what I want. You don't know."

She pulled down her robe to reveal several hickeys on her neck. "I think you made it very clear what you wanted tonight."

I blew out a breath. "Will you please listen to what I have to say?"

"Fine." She glared at me. "Speak."

I looked at the ground. "I haven't been able to stop thinking about what you said, and I feel awful, because you're right. I didn't respect you as I should have." I licked my lips. "I never thought of it that way. I've always equated love with sex. When I took you out to the canyon, I had every intention of pushing our relationship further, but not to hurt you. I wanted to show you how much I loved you. I thought you wanted me, too, and were just too shy to ask. I had no clue being abstinent meant so much to you. Now that I do, I promise to never take advantage of your innocence. I'll protect it with my life."

Her eyes glistened.

"Will you forgive me? Please."

A tear slipped down her cheek, right before she rushed into my embrace.

I buried my face in her loose curls. "I don't expect you to trust me yet, but I'm begging for a chance to earn that from you."

"That'll take time."

"Probably a whole heck of a lot, which I'm totally willing to give you. My mom did teach me better." I touched her neck. "No more nibbling or whatever makes you uncomfortable. We'll take things slow. Cross my heart."

"I don't know."

"Tell me you don't care for me."

"That's the problem. I care way too much."

I reached down to twine fingers. "Then stay with me, Liz. Let me earn your trust...and love. Help me become a better man."

She lowered her head. My tensed muscles started to ache.

"Okay." Her whispered reply hardly registered, but that one word seeped deep into my soul, bringing unspeakable relief and hope.

I pulled her into my arms. "Thank you, Lizzie."

LIZ

CUDDLING NEXT TO Rawson made me happy. But I wished he'd at least stroke my arm. Since his birthday fiasco last month, when I'd laid down the law, he'd become gun-shy about even holding hands. I'd given him signals that I'd welcome more. Whenever he showed up, I took his hand. I cuddled during movies. I'd even initiated a few kisses, hoping he'd kiss me like he once had.

He never did.

Tonight, he'd acted even more aloof than usual. The new guy had taken over the herd last week. Rawson had time to spend with me now, at least more than he used to when he'd worked the herd. Yet, besides sitting by me at meals and squeezing my knee occasionally, Rawson hadn't made any effort to monopolize my time. We watched movies in the basement with Ben once or twice a week, but that's all. I'd hoped he'd make me a priority and prove to everyone that I wasn't just his ranch fling.

A whiff of cologne made me yearn to pull him closer, but I didn't dare instigate a kiss that might meet with his gentle, yet clear, rebuff. A woman could only take so much rejection, and Rawson had demonstrated several times how he felt about me pressing him. He didn't welcome my advances.

I stayed still, hoping his finger massage might turn into more. A light nibbling session, perhaps. Or a kiss. I missed his amazing, world-changing kisses. Just thinking about them made me want to crawl into his lap.

"You look lovely tonight." His deep voice next to my ear sent tingles through me.

"So do you." I blushed when he chuckled. "Not lovely. You're not. I mean you are, but in a manly way. Oh, you know what I mean."

He cupped my chin. "Maybe if I kissed you, I'd understand."

"H-h-uh-yeah," I stammered.

His lips claimed mine, and I eagerly claimed his. Fair's fair, right? Orcs battled on screen, but we gave them no heed. I prayed Ben did, though. Normally, I didn't condone PDA, but it'd been so long since Rawson had kissed me that I didn't dare stop him. I needed proof he hadn't tired of me.

The gory orc battle ended as Rawson pulled away. He gave me a dreamy smile as I settled back to earth. A peek at the other couch showed a blushing Benny. Poor kid.

Rawson draped an arm over me. I rested my head on his shoulder and smiled. *Lord of the Rings* wasn't my favorite. I found the movie tedious with all the orc battles. However, tonight's kissing session had changed my mind. Maybe another fight scene would start and Rawson would minister to my mouth again.

I rested my hand on his chest and traced hearts into his shirt. He hummed, bolstering my confidence. I let my other hand drop to his leg.

He jumped up, making me fall into the cushions where he'd been sitting. "I need to use the little boy's room." He almost ran from the room.

Benny looked at me and shrugged. "When you gotta go, you gotta go."

I forced a laugh, although I failed to see the humor. Rawson had done it again. I'd tried to make him feel good, and he'd run.

He didn't return until the orcs were at it again...or maybe they were warlocks. The ugly things all looked alike to me. I wondered if Rawson might instigate another kiss, but he yawned.

"I might have to call it a night, babe. I'm beat."

There'd been a time when he wouldn't have cared what time it was or how tired he felt, he wouldn't have cut our time short. But lately, he seemed anxious to escape my company.

Before he could bolt, I leaned over to touch his arm. "Next Friday there's a dance in town. At the church." He didn't say anything, which didn't give me much hope he wanted to go, but I continued. "I'm on the committee and have to go early to set up. Could you come with me? As my date?" I held my breath.

"How early do you need to leave?"

"Around five."

"Hmmm."

I frowned.

He tipped my chin. "Of course, I'll go." He rested his lips against my forehead. "But would you mind too terribly if I left you right now so I can get some shut eye?"

"That's fine." But disappointing. "I've seen enough orcs to last me a lifetime. I'll go to bed, too."

He helped me to my feet. We waved goodnight to Ben and wandered to Rawson's bedroom. I stood on my tiptoes to peck him goodnight, but he surprised me by pulling me close and kissing me deeply. His hands spread fire through my body as he rubbed my back. Once, his hands even swept dangerously low, but he raised them and never ventured down again. Still, my mind grabbed hold of some rather wicked thoughts.

Rawson pulled back, acting as if his whole world hadn't been knocked off kilter by that kiss, as mine had. "Night, love." He gave me a sexy half-smile. "See you in the morning."

I made my way upstairs, a bit woozy. Every single one of his passionate kisses threw me off balance and made me know it could never be topped; yet he easily put it to shame the next time, before saying "Night" and moseying into his bedroom, as if nothing out of the ordinary had happened.

Well, his kisses might be par for course for him, but they rocked my world.

I climbed into bed and smiled. He'd agreed to come to the dance. A very public event. I couldn't wait to tell Garret and prove to him and every other hand on the ranch that I wasn't Rawson's temporary plaything.

I was his girl.

66

RAWSON

S weat trickled down my back in the June heat as I rode ahead of my brother.

"Hey, hold up," Benny called.

I pulled on Bayder's reins and glanced over my shoulder. Seeing him struggle to escape his light jacket, I almost spurred my horse over to help. But he wouldn't appreciate my coddling.

"Okay, I'm good." He brought Han up beside me. "So, you and Liz are going dancing tonight?"

"That's the plan. But knowing her, she'll work the kitchen all night because she can't say no." As though she'd read my thoughts, my phone rang. "It's her," I said, before answering. "Hey, beautiful."

"My cookie person just fell through, so I need to get to town earlier to stop by the store. Can you be ready to leave at four instead of five?"

I grimaced. "That'll be tricky. Abe needs me to pick up some new foals from the Johnsons' this afternoon."

"Oh."

I hated disappointing her. "Can I meet you there later?"

"Yeah, sure. If you don't want to go, you can just—"

"Hey, I want to go, but there's no way I can get away early. Jeb's leaving town. He's counting on us to watch those foals. I'll be there before the dance starts. Promise. Wear lots of Chapstick."

That made her laugh before she hung up.

I made a note to grab some flowers on the way to the dance. Lizzie had stressed over this stupid dance for weeks.

Benny and I headed back to the ranch, and I kept thinking about Liz. I loved her. Of that I had no doubt. But staying within the physical boundaries she'd set up killed me. Every time I kissed or touched her, my body went into auto-pilot, wanting to arrive at the destination. Sex. That's all I'd ever known. I'd kissed and aroused with the sole intention of getting women's clothes off and bedding them. Now that I couldn't do that, I didn't know how to act. The few times I'd kissed her as I'd wanted, my body had become so thoroughly aroused that it'd taken every ounce of willpower I possessed not to drag her into my room. In her innocence, she had no idea how completely she tempted me with her butterfly kisses or leg stroking. She might as well douse me with gasoline and tell me not to erupt in flames when she lit a match.

It made sense why so many church folk married younger than their counterparts. Not being able to have sex had me consumed with wedding vows as well. But I refused to broach the subject until I'd wiggled out from under Dad's thumb. Until then, I'd keep some distance and rely on cold showers and long, lonely rides on Bayder to contain my physical desires.

67

LIZ

$\mathscr{T}$HE EARTHY SCENT of leather wrapped around me as I pocketed my phone. Rawson's parting Chapstick comment had made my body sizzle like a sparkler.

"You look as happy as a tick on a fat dog." Garret's voice from the doorway startled me.

"Oh, you scared me."

He emptied his load onto the sawhorse. "Is everything ready for your big dance tonight?"

I wished I'd never agreed to be on the dance committee. It was stressful beyond belief. "I just found out the person over refreshments is sick, so I need to go to town early to buy cookies and drinks. But this storm has me worried. I hate driving in weather."

"Why isn't your *boyfriend* driving you?"

"Rawson can't get away early. He'll meet me there."

"That man always has some slick excuse, doesn't he?"

I hung a bridle on a peg. "He actually has a great excuse. Abe needs him to pick up two foals from the Johnson's ranch before they head out of town. You should stop thinking the worst about him."

"That man thinks the sun comes up just to hear him crow." He threw a blanket onto the rack. "If Rawson really cared, he wouldn't leave you in a bind. He knows how important this dance is to you. But he never takes you out in public. He just hides you away like you're his dirty little secret."

I clenched my teeth. "He doesn't hide me away. He's going to meet me there."

"I hope so, for your sake, darling." We worked for a few more minutes before he spoke again. "Do you want me to drive you and help set up, since your *boyfriend* is as useful as a pogo stick in quicksand?"

Fear of driving in a storm surpassed my pride. I'd be more comfortable if he drove, and I really could use help setting up since others had flaked last minute. Best of all, if Garret came, he'd see he was wrong about Rawson. I'd solve three problems at once.

"You wouldn't mind?"

"Not at all."

I grinned, hopeful that everything would work out.

For the most part, it did. I managed to get my hair to fall in perfect spirals down my back. The new coral dress I'd ordered fit to perfection. The drive to town wasn't bad either. Garret didn't harass me about Rawson. We purchased refreshments, and I shaved another twenty bucks off the budget with an Oreos two-for-one deal. The gym turned out spectacular with the gauzy tulle and twinkle lights to go with the *Happily Ever After* theme. And the guests seemed thrilled when they began to arrive.

The only piece missing from my Cinderella dream was a handsome cowboy prince to sweep me off my feet.

I balanced a plate of cookies and pushed through the door into the darkened gym, searching for Rawson. The clock showed half past nine. Where was he? I'd tried calling several times, but his phone had gone straight to voice mail.

Garret sidled up next to me. "Let me take those from you, darling." He transferred the trays to his hands and walked with me to the kitchen.

"You're a lifesaver." I hadn't stood still for hours. Neither had he.

"And you're a workhorse. Let's dance. The refreshment table will be fine for a few minutes." He tugged me into the hall.

I tried to pull away. "Don't waste your time. You have your own fan club."

"You need to have fun, too, darling."

He led me into the gym, where *Country Man* by Luke Bryan played. I noticed a group of girls glare at me when they noticed my partner. Twisting back and forth, Garret danced without releasing my hands.

"Thanks again for all your help," I said.

"My pleasure, darling."

He swung me out by one hand and tried to reel me back in, but I became twisted up in my feet and stumbled. Dancing wasn't my thing.

He pulled me against his chest. "Whoa. Can't have you falling."

The song ended, and *Home* by Blake Shelton began. "Thanks for the dance." I tried to extricate myself from his embrace, but he pulled me closer.

"One more, Liz."

I glanced around the darkened gym.

Garret pulled me close. "Maybe he's not going to show."

I frowned as he voiced my fear. "He'll get here." Rawson knew how important tonight was to me. Even if he arrived for the last dance, it'd be enough. The thought of snuggling up during a slow song as he whispered in my ear kept me going.

Garret whispered in my ear, instead. "You look ravishing tonight."

I wrinkled my nose. "I bet you say that to all the ladies."

"Just you. The others look like something the dog's kept under the porch."

I laughed. "That's awful."

"But true." He brought my hands to his neck and claimed my waist, pulling me into an intimate position.

I dropped my gaze. Surely he didn't hope to spark something between us. He knew I liked Rawson.

"Yakama Yoda's going to be something special, isn't he?"

I relaxed as he brought up horses. A safe subject. "Yeah. He has a ton of natural ability."

Blake's beautiful voice sang the last word and I pulled away. "I need to get back to the kitchen." I didn't give him a chance to protest, I just high-tailed it out of the gym. There was a punch spill to clean up and trays to refill. The next chance I had to breathe, the clock showed quarter to eleven.

I slumped against the fridge. Time to face the truth. My handsome prince wasn't coming.

"Come on out and dance with me again, darling."

I looked up to see Garret standing in the doorway. How long had he been watching me? I shook my head. "Go ahead. I'm not feeling well."

He marched across the linoleum and took my hand. "All the more reason for you to get out there and have some fun. You've been busier than a one-legged man in a butt-kicking contest."

His words surprised a barking laugh from me, the kind Rawson swore he adored. But my laugh was obnoxious. Mom had always said so.

"There's that smile I've been missing." He pulled me out the door.

I allowed him to lead me to the middle of the gym. He held my hands through another fast song and then shifted them to his neck for *I Still Miss You* by Keith Anderson. I opened my mouth to tell him I didn't feel comfortable dancing so close, but he put his lips next to my ear and said, "That song was faster than green grass through a goose."

I laughed. His outrageous sayings always caught me off guard.

His gaze swept the room. He grinned and leaned in to touch foreheads. "You're incredible, Liz."

I squirmed. "Uh, Garr—"

That's as far as I got before his lips claimed mine.

68

RAWSON

*O*RRENTIAL RAIN AND sporadic bursts of hail made it difficult to see, but I was determined to reach the dance. My girl was counting on me. I checked the dashboard clock, calculating arrival at just after ten. That'd give us fifty minutes together. Not perfect, but it'd have to do.

Murphy's Law had caught me this afternoon and held me hostage. Everything that could've gone wrong had done so. By the time I'd left the Johnson's, the sun had set. I'd grabbed a quick shower, before heading to Bozeman. But at the pass, a freak hailstorm had hit, making visibility practically zero.

An explosion from a tire made my truck spin out. I hit the anti-lock brakes and struggled with the steering column to regain control. My Ford limped to a stop, and I pounded the steering wheel and unleashed an arsenal of swear words.

I marched through marble-sized hail to see that the rear tire had blown. I kicked it and called it a few more names that would've burned Lizzie's sensitive ears, before grabbing the jack, gloves, and a tool kit from the back seat. I threw my cowboy hat on to protect myself from the elements and began loosening lug nuts. The rain and hail didn't improve my mood or tire-changing efficiency.

With the spare on, I hopped inside the warm cab and wished I could text Liz. But along with everything else, I'd dropped my phone while helping Jeb and had busted the damn thing. Hopefully, she had a sense of humor when I told her about my boxing match with Murphy's Law tonight.

I peeled out. There was still time, if I hurried. Liz would understand and be glad to see me, even if I was a sopping mess.

The church appeared. I parked and ran inside, savoring the warmth. Loud music came from up the hall. I jogged toward it, peeking into the kitchen first to check for Liz. Empty. I marched into the gym and stopped to let my eyes adjust. This was tamer than the dances at nightclubs. People milled around the edges of the gym as a few brave couples danced all prim and proper in the center to country music. A slow Keith Anderson ballad played as I sauntered around the periphery, studying each blond-haired woman I could see. It didn't take long to realize Lizzie didn't hold up the walls.

I folded my arms over my damp shirt, and checked out the couples on the dance floor. My eyes zeroed in on Lizzie right away, her curly hair an angelic halo around her head. She was dancing with Ferret. Ugh. And they appeared way too cozy. She laughed at something he said, and my fingers clenched. The ferret whispered in her ear, the one I liked to kiss. For a moment, I thought our gazes connected, before the jerk leaned down and mashed his lips into hers.

A growl escaped as I watched him kiss my girl and waited for her to knock him out of his heady orbit. When she didn't, the cold found me with a fury and I shivered violently.

I stormed out of the gym and headed to my truck. I beat the steering wheel and cursed Lizzie to hell and back.

She'd lied!

How long had those two been in cahoots? I'd thought Liz was different than my cheating ex. But no. She was worse.

69

LIZ

𝒰SUALLY, BRAIN FREEZES occurred when I drank a Sonic slush too fast or when superheroes were frozen into carbonite molds, like Han Solo in *Empire Strikes Back*. Han's shocking ending had always appalled me, though it sent Benny into fits of laughter. Seeing Han's twisted grimace frozen for all time had made me shiver and wonder if he'd been conscious under that frozen mask. I now knew he'd experienced every second of horror, helpless to change his fate, because that's how I felt as Garret kissed me.

His lips claimed mine as though he had a right to them, and though it felt terribly wrong, I couldn't move to stop him. Shock bound me. If his mouth hadn't been all over mine, I'm sure my expression would've mirrored Han's agony. I blinked frantically as his tongue probed.

"Garret," I managed to say from my iced-over throat. "You—"

"Rawson's one fry short of a Happy Meal to have stood you up tonight, darling. You know that, right?" He pecked my lips. "I know for a fact he could've been here. Chance texted when he left the ranch a couple hours ago. Rawson didn't choose you, Liz."

I shoved him away. "Don't ever kiss me again!"

I heard him call after me as I fled out of the gym. I locked myself in a stall in the restroom and tormented my eyes with tissue until they stung. When the area crowded with giggling girls, I knew the dance had ended. I stayed put until the squealing receptacles of joy vacated the premises.

I really was Cinderella, forsaken by her prince.

Eventually, I exited. Garret paced the hallway. His anxious expression transformed into relief when he saw me.

"Liz, I'm sorry. I shouldn't have—"

"Are you ready to go?" I didn't want to have this conversation.

He looked at the ground. "Yes, darling."

"Before we go, I have some things to say."

"I'm listening."

"First, I'm not your darling. So don't call me that."

His Adam's apple bobbed. "Yes, ma'am."

"Second, if you kiss me again without my permission, I'll haul off and knock you to the other side of the state. Do I make myself clear?"

He wrinkled his nose. "Sorry."

Dang his humility. It made it difficult for me to stay mad.

"And third, don't stir up gossip about my boyfriend."

"I just care about you and don't want you to—"

"Do you understand?"

His jaw clenched. "Yes, dar—I mean, ma'am."

Ma'am conjured up images of a stern matronly woman who would paddle your backside with a frying pan if you stepped out of line, but maybe that image would keep Garret from acting out again.

I followed him to his truck, hugging the passenger door as he started the engine. He opened his mouth to speak, but I held up a hand.

"Just drive. I don't feel like talking."

Rain fell as we pulled out of the parking lot. Maybe Rawson had been caught in the storm. Maybe he'd slid off the road and was hurt. We'd almost reached the old highway when Garret pulled to the side of the road.

I lifted my head. "Why are you stopping?"

He pointed out the window. My gaze followed his finger, and I inhaled sharply when I made out Rawson's truck parked in front of a bar across the street. A bar he'd promised never to patronize to get his dang kisses. Hope I'd clung to evaporated in steamy disappointment that left tears streaming down my cheeks.

Garret sighed. "I'm sorry."

My lips quivered as my fairy tale bubble popped. Mackay and Garret had been right. I hadn't meant anything to Rawson. Only, he'd recently convinced me that I'd meant everything to him.

"You might not believe me, but I wish he'd deserved you. But I'm not sorry your eyes are open now."

I sniffed. "Can you just take me h-home?" I didn't want to talk. I just wanted to lock myself in my bedroom and have a good cry.

EMPOWERING HOPE

Forgiveness is about empowering yourself, rather than empowering your past.

~ T. D. Jakes ~

RAWSON

SWERVING OVER TO the side of the road, I slid out of my seat and bent over to toss my cookies. A vice seemed to squeeze my head. Nausea engulfed not only my stomach, but my heart. Over the last twelve hours, my actions had been pathetic. I knew right where they'd lead. After six years of sobriety, I couldn't allow a woman to throw me off course like this.

I wiped vomit from my lips. Not even finding Vanessa with my roommate last year had hurt this bad. I crawled into my truck and grabbed the cheap pay-by-call phone I'd picked up at a gas station. I dialed Mom and waited.

"Hello?" she answered.

"It's me."

"Rawson? Where are you? Your dad—"

"I know. He's probably on the warpath." I kneaded my pounding head.

"What's wrong?"

Her concern made me want to weep. The liquor I'd ingested had turned me into a sniveling fool. "I'm on my way to his office. Can you meet me there in five minutes to talk to him?"

"Of course."

I ended the call and concentrated on getting home. The temptation to drive off the road and end my misery consumed me.

Mom waited for me outside the stable when I pulled up. She opened my door and noted my condition. Her eyes glistened but she still opened her arms.

I fell into them. "I'm sorry," I choked.

She didn't accuse or chastise. Mom just held me, and at that moment, that was exactly what I needed.

Arm in arm, we tread up the stairs to Dad's office. Mom must've warned him of my arrival because he didn't act surprised when we walked in together. He gazed into my bloodshot eyes though and erupted like Mount Vesuvius.

"Where have you been?"

I hung my head. "With Damon."

He banged his desk and swore, making pain explode in my cranium.

"Can we discuss this without profanity?" Mom's voice silenced him. She rubbed my back. "What did you need to talk to us about, son?"

I lifted my head and met Dad's furious gaze. "Can I go back to the rehab you sent me to after the accident?"

He pursed his lips.

"I need to get out of here. Clear my head."

"Rehab costs an exorbitant amount of money."

I stood. "If you're not willing to help, I need to leave. I don't care where. I just can't stay here."

"Sit down."

Too hammered to defy him, I sunk into the cushion next to Mom. My drinking binge had resurrected the past, and I wasn't strong enough to fight that. I teetered on a tightrope, one drink away from losing everything I'd fought so hard to regain.

Dad flipped through his contacts. "If I do this, you need to promise you won't contact Damon ever again."

I grimaced. "He has no one else."

"And look where he's brought you. Is this what you want?"

Mom threw her arms around me. "I admire your loyalty, son. But this is about helping you, and sadly, your friend has never had your best interests at heart."

"Fine. I won't see him." I'd say whatever they wanted.

Mom held me as Dad called the center. It was beyond humiliating. I'd sworn I would never fall this low again, but here I was, back in the same pathetic, wasted position I'd been my senior year of high school.

Dad hung up. "They'll have a spot for you next week. Will you be all right until then?"

I glanced at Mom.

"I'll watch over him until he leaves."

Tears filled my eyes as I met her sober gaze. "Don't tell Benny."

She brushed a lock of hair from my eyes. "If anyone asks, we'll say you went away to that training school in Portugal we've talked about."

I squeezed my pounding head. "I'm sorry. I didn't—"

"You're our son, Rawson. We just want you whole and happy."

I buried my head in my hands. There was no chance of that, but maybe the strict regimen of the detox center would bump me out of despair. More importantly, it'd get me away from Liz.

Mom walked me to my bedroom. "Pack a bag. I assume you don't want to see your brother or a certain young lady. We'll drive over to Susa's and stay there until you leave."

I shoved every clean shirt I owned and other necessities into a suitcase. We drove several minutes down the road to our housekeeper's abode. The perfect hideaway—close enough so Mom could pop in to check on me but secluded enough to give me needed exile until I could escape.

I entered. Mom followed and pulled out a chair from the kitchen table. "Have a seat, son."

Since I'd had two mugs of coffee, I felt somewhat better. I leaned forward with my elbows on my knees. "You don't have to stay. I'll be fine."

"This is a great time for me to stay. The kids are in school and I haven't had a heart-to-heart with you in ages."

"Like never. Guys don't have heart-to-hearts."

"Ah, they're not so bad. Humor me."

I glared at the floor.

She fished in my murky waters. "What happened between you and Liz? I know she's involved."

"I caught her cheating."

Her eyes widened. "Did you confront her?"

"No, though that might've been better. Maybe then I wouldn't have screwed up with Damon."

She took my hand.

"I can't tell you how liberating it felt to drink again. No yelling Dad, no cheating girlfriend, no accident." I gave her a sheepish look. "Felt like hell this morning though."

She tousled my hair. "I bet you did." She opened the fridge. "Susa said there was bacon and eggs. I know it's after noon, but do you want breakfast?"

My stomach growled, making us both laugh.

"I guess that's a yes." She pulled out a frying pan.

Soon the smell of sizzling bacon permeated the air. Coffee, too. My headache dulled to a minor throb as I related the incident at the dance to her.

"From what you've said," Mom said, "Liz is unaware that you caught her kissing the other hand, correct?"

Just the memory of her on the dance floor with Garret made me want to binge drink all over again. "Yeah."

She poured eggs into another pan. "I've never known you to run from a challenge."

"I didn't. I ran from a disaster."

"No, you ran to a disaster."

"Mom, I don't want to talk about her."

No more was said until she set a plate of bacon and eggs in front of me. "It might help to know Lizzie's side of the story."

I threw her a glare.

"Don't scowl at your mama. I brought you up better than that."

"Can you just drop it?"

"You need closure."

I filled my mouth with eggs.

"A wise man always listens to his mother. That's all I'm saying."

LIZ

$\mathcal{T}$ONIGHT MARKED THREE days since the dance. I stared at my phone and mourned what could've been. What almost was. Rawson had been eerily silent since Friday. At first, I'd wanted him to call so I could tell him off. But as time had passed without even an electronic word to soften his rejection, anger had given way to grief. I'd hoped he thought enough of me to at least send teasing texts. He didn't know I knew the truth.

I chided myself. What had I expected? Did I really believe a guy like him could ever truly care for a nobody like me?

A knock on the door made me flinch. Silly hope sparked as I crossed the room to open the door. It extinguished when I saw Mrs. Law.

"Hi, Liz. I hope I'm not disturbing you. I wondered if we might talk."

I gave her a weak smile and stepped aside. "Sure."

She gazed around my room. "I haven't been up here since I painted. I'd forgotten how charming it turned out."

"It's beautiful. Thanks for making me feel welcome."

She pulled out a wicker chair from the desk. "I feel like you're part of the family, especially since you're dating my son."

"Oh." My mood plummeted. "I, um…don't think we are anymore."

"Why ever not? You two are perfect together."

I squeezed my hands. "My guess is he grew bored. He was supposed to meet me at a dance Friday, but never showed."

Her concerned expression brought tears to my eyes. Charity lived up to her name. "Maybe he got tied up helping Abe."

"Maybe."

"You don't sound like you believe that."

"I don't know what to believe. Apparently, I'm clueless when it comes to guys. Your son isn't talking to me. And Garret's talking too much."

She laughed—a pure, tinkling sound I envied. Why couldn't I laugh like her instead of a seal?

"Oh, honey. You aren't clueless."

"Oh, yeah? The one man I wanted to come to the dance didn't show and the other guy I thought was my friend kissed me, and like a lame-o, I let him."

Charity groaned. "This is Garret you're talking about?"

I nodded. "When he offered to drive, I thought he was being kind. I never imagined he'd pull a fast one." I looked up at her. "I feel so stupid. My brain literally froze."

"Sounds like he used your emotions against you."

"Well, he knows not to try again. I told him if he ever kissed me again, I'd smack him to the other end of the state."

Charity laughed. "I wish I could've witnessed that. You're a gem."

At least, someone thought so.

She gave me a sweet smile. "Have you tried calling my son?"

I frowned. "On the way home, I saw his truck at a bar. He did show up, just not to the dance as he promised. And since he hasn't called or texted, I assume he's done with me."

"Oh, Liz."

"I knew this would happen. I mean, your son is gorgeous, and I'm just"—I waved a hand in front of me—"well, you have eyes."

Charity opened her arms for a hug.

I walked into her embrace, savoring her acceptance. She really was a sweetheart.

"You're the most beautiful girl I know, inside and out. Don't give up, my dear. Law men can be foolish. I know since I've been married to one for twenty-five years. But their love can't be matched. Rawson's like his dad. He's dated numerous women, but you're the first to capture his heart. And once a Law man loses his heart, they'll live and breathe for only you."

I didn't believe her, but her caring sentiments soothed me.

When I crawled into bed after she left, I made two vows. First, I would try to emulate Charity in thought and deed. She really was the kindest woman I'd ever met. Second, I'd avoid men like the plague. They only brought misery and heartache.

72

RAWSON

*M*OM CLIMBED INTO the driver's seat as I threw my duffel into the back of her Tahoe. "What are you doing?" I raised a brow.

"Oh, get in." She waved for me to go to the other side. "I'm just driving to the house. I forgot my purse. Surely you can handle being a passenger for a minute."

I didn't move. "If you don't have your purse, you don't have a license. Scoot over."

"Heavens. You're acting like a Law man."

I cracked a smile. "Punny."

Mom slid over, and I climbed into the captain's seat. I don't know why she always messed with me. She never won. No one had except for Liz. I winced as she hijacked my thoughts.

"I'm really not a bad driver. You should let me show you sometime," Mom teased.

"Maybe." Not.

Like my weird sensitivity to cloth, my driving fetish was ingrained in me. The loss of control I felt when others drove made me mental. As a child, I'd dug my nails into my arms until they'd bled whenever we'd taken trips to town. So why hadn't I minded when Liz had driven? It hadn't hit me until now that I'd made a huge jump into the realm of impossibility by letting her sit behind the wheel. Sure, I'd nagged her and riled her to the point she'd gotten out to hoof it home, but when I'd apologized and she'd insisted on driving again, I'd acquiesced. Why?

"You going to sit there all day and daydream, big man?" Mom grinned at me.

"No, ma'am." I turned the key and pulled away from Susa's place. As we neared the ranch house, my muscles tensed. I lifted my foot from the gas and coasted to a stop. "I don't think—"

"Hop in the back and lay down so no one sees you. We're almost there. You can handle ten seconds of me driving."

The thought of running into Liz, Garret, or my little brother made me comply. Mom switched spots and pulled back onto the road. I dug my nails into the soft skin at my wrist until I felt pain. Maybe after six weeks in detox, I'd be stronger.

Mom parked and hopped out. I relaxed. A few minutes passed before she returned.

"Hey." She peeked over the seat. "Addie has a fever. I don't dare leave her. I asked Liz to drive you to the airport since everyone else is busy. Don't get up. You need to rest after what your dad put you through. Have fun in Portugal," she called as she backed out of view. "Thanks, Liz. I owe you."

I scrambled into a sitting position as Liz climbed into the driver's seat. Just the sight of her packed a punch that sucked the air right out of me. Her soulful brown eyes met mine, long enough for me to notice they didn't hold their usual sparkle. I turned to see Mom blow a kiss from the porch. Traitor.

"Hey," Liz said as she caught my eye in the rear view mirror.

I checked my watch. "We better go, if I'm going to make my flight."

She pulled away, and I realized that once again I'd relinquished control to her without thinking. That had to end.

"Pull over," I snapped. "We'll never get there at your turtle pace."

She braked hard, launching me into the back of her seat.

"Oh, I'm sorry," she gushed. "Maybe you should check to make sure you're wearing a seatbelt before you order the driver to stop."

I threw open my door and jumped out. Liz pulled forward.

Out of sorts already from being blindsided by Mom, I stewed in helpless rage as she drove up the road about fifty feet, before stopping and leaning out her window.

"Gotcha."

My jaw ached from clenching it so tight.

"Show some respect. I'm missing out on Yoda's training to drive you."

"I'm driving," I growled.

"Whatever."

I jogged to the Tahoe and climbed in while she scooted over to hug the other door. The SUV fishtailed in the loose gravel when I punched the gas.

Her hands splayed out, searching for something to grab onto for support. For the next ten miles, I fed off her fear. I took turns practically on two wheels and caught air on every hill.

Just as I tipped the speedometer over seventy, a deer bolted out of the scrub oak. I slammed on the brakes and swerved to avoid hitting it and plowed into a tangled mess of willow bushes on the other side of the road.

The past rammed into my conscience with the same force as the SUV broke through the bushes. I wheezed, trying to rid my brain of the image of that deer jumping in front of Damon and me years ago, exactly like the one today. I peeled my fingers off the steering wheel. No matter what Liz had done or how I felt about her, that didn't justify showing such blatant disregard for her life. I could've killed her just now, like I had Detrick six years ago. Or I might have maimed her, like Bentley.

Liz struggled to undo her seatbelt. "Why do you hate me so much?" she cried. "I knew you'd eventually tire of me, but I thought we'd stay friends. I didn't think you'd try to kill me."

The sight of her swollen red eyes made me feel like a louse. "Sorry."

"Keep your sorrys to yourself." She ran a jerky finger beneath her eyes and tried to open her door. The willow bush outside trapped her.

"I thought we had something special."

She turned to meet my gaze, and I realized I'd spoken aloud. She slumped against her seat. "We did."

"Then why, Lizzie? Why did you kiss him?"

Her delicate brows pulled together. "Kiss who?"

"You damn well know who! That Florida ferret!"

"You came?"

"Yes, unfortunately. I saw every nauseating second of you trading slobber with your new boyfriend."

She lowered her head. "You came?" She looked back up at me. "He surprised me and—"

"Save your breath." My side wasn't covered by bushes. I jumped out and slammed the door. Marching around the Tahoe, I surveyed the damage. Nothing major, but the windshield was cracked, the fender buckled, and the body scratched and dented everywhere. I dug my hands into my coat pockets, aching for another beer. How could Mom have tricked me? The last thing I needed was to be near Liz.

I took a few deep breaths before climbing back into the Tahoe. I only had to endure her poisonous presence until we reached the airport. Then I'd wash my hands of the traitorous woman forever.

Gunning the engine, I rocked the SUV back and forth until I broke out of the thatch of willow. I turned back onto the road, noting that Mom's vehicle didn't drive any worse for the beating, but it'd need tons of body work. I'd donned a fresh shirt before leaving, but the stress of sitting so close to Liz had me digging my nails into my sleeves. At the airport, I'd need to change. This shirt was now tainted from her close proximity.

Liz didn't say a word until we pulled into town. Then she surprised me. "I'll tell your parents I lost control of the car."

"Why would you do that?"

"I don't want your dad to kill you. This way you can enjoy Portugal without having to deal with his anger."

Her kindness made no sense, especially after what I'd done. I pulled into an empty parking lot and cut the engine.

"Tell me why you did it? I moved earth and hell that night to get to the dance. Things took longer at the Johnsons' than I expected. I broke my phone. My tire blew, and I..." I paused when I noticed tears cascading down her cheeks.

"I'm sorry," she cried. "All night I watched for you. Garret kept telling me you weren't coming, that you didn't care. He dragged me onto the dance floor, said I had to have some fun. When he kissed me, I froze." She threw her hands over her eyes. "I know that's no excuse, but I didn't know what to do."

My stone-cold heart began to thaw. The poor girl seemed miserable, and I realized she'd been played. That sneaky ferret had looked up and seen me while they'd danced. I knew it. That's why he'd kissed her. I should've stayed. Confronted them. Liz would've told the truth, and maybe I could've flattened the ferret and saved us all this pain. Instead, I'd fled the scene like a sniveling coward and had escaped into booze.

I pulled her into my arms. "I'm such a fool."

"Me, too. Garret drove me home and pulled over by a bar to point out your truck. I thought you chose to go there instead of coming to me."

I ground my teeth, hating Garret more with each second. Lousy, sneaky vermin.

73

LIZ

*R*AWSON SCOWLED, AND his fists clenched tighter. "I should've flattened that guy."

"It's over," I said, glad to have the misunderstanding between us cleared up. "When you get back from Portugal, we'll start fresh."

He frowned. "Lizzie, I'm not going to Portugal."

"But your mom said—"

"I know what she said. But I want you to know the truth."

"O-kay."

He looked down at his hands, brow furrowing. "I got drunk that night with Damon after seeing you kiss Garret."

Oh, no. Rawson had gone so long without drinking. Ben had told me he'd sworn to stay sober after the accident.

"I'm sorry," he said. "I know I promised to stay away from bars."

"I understand." If only I'd pulled away sooner. Part of me felt responsible for his relapse.

He nudged my chin up, and his lips settled on mine. The walls I'd thrown up to protect myself fell, like the ones in that Bible story Daddy had told me about as a little girl. Joshua's army had brought down the walls of Jericho with the sound of trumpets. Rawson's kiss did the same to me. No walls. No rules. No inhibitions as we kissed like crazy in the front seat of his mom's beat-up Tahoe. Our explorations became almost desperate in our desire to make up for lost time. He loved me. I loved him. His hands became too friendly, but my walls were down. I dared not raise them, not after driving him to the brink. In penance for doing nothing when Garret had kissed me, I allowed Rawson to claim me now. It wasn't as if he could go too far in a public parking lot in the middle of the afternoon. Right?

He pulled away, and I licked my lips. There was one thing I needed to say before we began kissing again and the last bricks crumbled.

"You need to cut things off with Damon."

His eyes narrowed, but Garret was right.

"You haven't taken a sip of alcohol in six years, and then you ruin it with him. Can you honestly say that would've happened had he not been there to goad you?"

"It wasn't his fault."

"Rawson, I know you want to help him, but he's pulling you down. Can't you see that? Besides, he killed your brother and hurt Benny."

He squeezed his brow. "Have you ever wondered what Damon feels, knowing he took Detrick's life? Knowing he ruined Bentley's? Don't you think that tortures him every single day, especially when he sees Bentley walking with his gimp leg and crooked neck?"

Thinking of his sleazy friend made the past burn hot in my mind. I recalled how the stoned driver who'd killed Justin had laughed as the police had led him away in handcuffs. He'd felt no remorse.

"That monster feels nothing. He lost nothing in the accident." I hid my face as memories washed over me with the force of a tidal wave.

"You're wrong." His voice cracked. "I think Damon suffers more than anyone."

"You can't know that. He's nothing like you."

He hung his head. "He is me, Liz."

I stared at him, trying to figure out why he looked so tortured.

"I drove the night of the accident. Not Damon." He patted his massive chest. "Me."

"That's not true." I'd heard Ben and Charity both talk about the accident. Damon had been driving.

"It is true!" he roared, making me flinch. "Do you honestly think I would've let Damon drive my Explorer? You know how possessive I am with my vehicles and horses. Damon's the last person I would've trusted behind the wheel. But no one questioned that, not even my parents. I was unconscious after the accident. Damon switched places so when the police arrived, he was in the driver's seat. When I awoke in the hospital, the story was in place. Damon took the fall and went to juvie for me."

No. My eyes stung. That couldn't be.

"Not a day goes by that I don't wish I'd been the one to die. I killed Detrick. I've known all this time that I ruined Benny's future. And my cowardice allowed my best friend's reputation to be destroyed by a lie. I've suffered like you can't even begin to imagine."

I covered my mouth.

263

"I cleaned up my act in rehab and busted my butt in college to succeed so I could run the ranch and give Benny anything he wanted to make up for what I took from him. I've tried to help Damon, too, since no one else would give him a chance. He gave up everything for me." His jaw clenched. "I owe him."

Even after he stopped speaking, his words pummeled my mind.

"Say something, please."

I blinked, trying to stem the tide. "You were in rehab?" It was a lame question to ask after everything he'd just revealed, but I was in shock.

"Yeah. Drinking had been a problem for over a year before the accident. Rehab helped me regain control. Until last week. I'm catching a flight to Salt Lake to enter a program again." He bit his quivering lip. "I need help."

I faced forward, my whole body trembling. He'd killed his brother. Maimed Bentley. I shuddered to think I'd fallen in love with an addict, like the one who'd killed Justin.

"We'd better go so you don't miss your flight." My voice sounded calm, though my insides felt as jittery as a crowd held hostage by a gunman.

We drove to the airport without speaking. He pulled into the Departures lane and parked. I climbed out to switch places. Rawson caught hold of my arm.

"Lizzie."

My body betrayed me by softening under his hypnotic bass voice. I peeked up at him, wishing I could wake up from this nightmare.

"Please say you'll be here to pick me up when I return. I need you."

Emotions raged under my surface calm.

"Lizzie?"

I pushed his hand off my arm. "Go." A guttural sob revealed how close I was to an imminent breakdown. "Go!" I slapped at him. I couldn't believe he'd lied about something so terrible. I hopped into the driver's seat and slammed the door.

"Lizzie!" His muffled voice came through the closed window.

I swiped at my eyes. The fool still stood outside my door. "Get your luggage."

He walked zombie-like around the car and opened the back door. "Liz, honey?"

I wiped a string of snot onto my sleeve. I'd always been an ugly crier.

"I'm sorry, love. Let me—"

"Get your suitcase." I hyperventilated as I recalled the carnage at the scene of Justin's crash, caused by a thoughtless impaired driver. Like Rawson!

He hefted his bag out. "You can't drive all upset like this. Pull up to the end. We'll talk."

"Shut the door."

The door shut. Rawson reached for the passenger door, but I peeled out.

No more lies.

I heard him scream my name as I viewed the world through tears and maneuvered out of the terminal. At the first gas station, I pulled over and succumbed to wracking sobs.

After emptying the first round of grief, I sat up and wiped my face with a towel I found behind the seat. My stomach cramped. My throat burned. Pressing Dad's face on my phone, I waited for him to answer and save me from my nightmare.

"Hey, baby doll."

Tears gushed out again as the magnitude of my loss pounded me squarely in my broken heart. "Daddy," I whimpered, "can you come get me?"

Without me having to say another word, he made arrangements to be in Montana by the next morning. "Get some sleep, baby girl. I'll be there soon."

That's all I needed to hear.

74

RAWSON

*M*OM'S PHONE WENT to voice mail. I sank onto a concrete bench, stifling the urge to scream. Liz was in no state to drive. I shouldn't have let her go. My phone vibrated. I answered breathlessly. "Mom?"

"Son, what's the matter? Did you make it to the airport?"

"I'm here, but Liz just left and she's..." I closed my eyes against the throbbing pain in my head. "I broke her heart," I whispered.

"What?"

"You need to send someone to find her. She was crying so hard I don't know how she'll manage to drive. I keep calling, but she won't answer. I'm scared she'll have an accident."

"Son, what happened?"

"Just call Liz. Maybe she'll answer you."

"Rawson." The disappointment in her tone made tears sting my eyes. "Just send someone. Please. And let me know when you talk to her."

"Son, you need to get on your flight."

I paced the length of the bench. "I can't. I have to talk to her."

"Get on the plane." Her firm command stopped my ranting. "Your father will be livid if you don't make your flight. I'll send someone after Liz, but you get to your gate. You can't help anyone else if you don't help yourself."

I gazed in the direction that Lizzie had disappeared. All I wanted was to jump in a taxi and find her, but Mom was right. I'd be no help to anyone right now. Especially Liz.

"Okay. I'm going. But promise you'll find her."

"I promise."

I headed into the terminal and tried to cast Lizzie's gut-wrenching sobs from my mind. Mom would make things right. She always did.

I made my way through security and barely made it to my gate on time. Finding a seat, I turned to the window to avoid conversing with my seatmate. I checked my phone for texts. Why had I thought Liz would accept my horrible secret? She'd lost her fiancé to a drunk driver. I checked my phone again.

"Sir, you need to switch your phone to flight mode."

I glanced up at an attendant and nodded. Mom still hadn't texted.

My hands began to shake. The skin on my chest prickled. I threw my head against the seat and clenched my eyes. The nonstop flight would only take one hour and twenty minutes, but that might as well be forever.

I wanted to order a beer. The stewardesses wouldn't blink an eye. I'd already blown it. So what would it matter? I had a problem, but my problem actually helped me cope.

But no. I stared out at the runway. Liz deserved a strong man. A good man. I wasn't either, but I wanted to be.

I bowed my head and begged God to help me until I made it to Salt Lake City, where a counselor would meet me. And I begged Him to keep Lizzie safe, wherever she was. I'd become strong. I'd become good. I'd become whatever it took to return the sparkle to her eyes that I'd stolen. I wanted the chance to make her happy again.

75

LIZ

*R*HYTHMIC RAPPING on the door made me bolt up in bed. Who was knocking? I'd thought everyone had gone to bed. *Please don't let it be Mom.* I paused my movie.

"Are you decent?" Dad called.

I swiped my eyes and breathed in relief when Dad cracked the door. "Hey, Daddy."

His expression oozed fatherly concern, making me feel bad for creating so much drama. As if it wasn't bad enough that I'd called in the middle of the week to beg him to drive up to Montana a month ago to get me, now I couldn't stop moping around, feeling sorry for myself.

"You up for a blizzard at Dairy Queen, baby doll?"

My heart had been shattered into a million pieces. No amount of distance, ice cream, or fatherly love would fix it. Besides, I was in my pajamas.

"Can I take a rain check? I'm in the middle of a movie."

He glanced at the screen. "*Star Wars* again, huh? I didn't know you liked sci-fi movies."

It was *Empire Strikes Back*, and I hadn't liked them until Benny and Rawson turned me onto the space saga. I meant Benny. No one else had anything to do with my obsession, especially not that handsome, lying, deceitful piece of work Rawson Law...who I missed with all my heart.

I shook my head at the moronic addendum my conscience slipped into my thinking thread. How could I miss that horrible man with all my heart when I had no heart left? He'd taken care of that.

"Sweetie?"

"Yeah. I love them." I chewed my lip. "I've been thinking about that charity gig Dalton's doing in El Salvador. I think I should go. I already applied for a passport."

Worry lines furrowed his brow. "Honey, that's a terrible idea."

"Why? You've always taught me to reach out and help others. Dalton's orphanage project is the perfect opportunity to do that."

"It would be if you weren't using it to escape again."

I stared at the carpet. "I'm not escaping."

He took my hand and waited until I met his gaze. "I'm worried about you, baby doll. You've never been the same since the accident. Have you ever gone and seen the driver who ran into Justin?"

I whipped my hand away. "You mean the man who killed him?"

"Oh, my sweet girl, you know he didn't wake up that day with the intention to kill anyone. It was a tragic accident. For Justin, for you, and for him. Probably more so for him. Can you imagine how that one moment changed his life? He lost more than anyone that day."

His words sounded like Rawson's justification for his horrible actions. "More than Justin? And more than me? I lost my chance at having a husband and family that day."

He cracked his neck. "You didn't lose those opportunities. They just got delayed. And Justin's death was tragic, but that driver lost his freedom, peace, maybe even his will to live that day. Surely with the passing of time, you can feel some compassion for him. Some forgiveness."

Why was he making me talk about this? It was so cruel. "That druggie stole everything from me. Do you honestly believe he deserves anything good?"

"I don't know what he deserves," Dad said. "But I know you don't deserve the pain you hold onto so tight. Forgiveness isn't for him, Lizzie Belle. It's for you."

I grimaced as he used my hated middle name. "I'm fine, Dad."

"Then why do you cry so much, baby doll?"

"Because I'm a hormonal girl." When he opened his mouth to say more, I cut him off. "I really don't want to talk about this. I have a headache."

His slumping shoulders stacked more guilt onto my own. "I love you, Daddy, but don't worry. I'll be fine once I get to El Salvador. You always taught me that our sorrows fade in service to others. I have faith that this trip will heal me and make you proud."

He pulled me into a tight hug. "I'm already proud of you, baby girl."

That made one of us. I burrowed my face into his burly chest and inhaled the scent of sawdust. My dad was the greatest, but he was wrong. I wasn't running from the past. I was running to a future.

76

RAWSON

*M*Y LIPS QUIVERED as I rounded the corner and saw Mom standing in the lobby. The smile on her face as she ran across the room to hug me made me tear up. "Stop it," I muttered. "You're making me act like a boob."

She laughed. "Oh, it's so good to see you, son. I've missed you more than chocolate."

I grabbed my suitcase. Forty-five days in residential rehab had crawled by. I knew life wouldn't be easy from here on out, but my counselors had motivated, inspired, and cheered me on while I'd been quarantined from the world. I now felt strong enough for battle. I was a new man, not the messed up, confused eighteen-year-old boy I'd been the first time I'd left this place and had been ushered onto a plane heading to Palo Alto.

Mom walked to the driver's side as if she would drive back to Montana.

I rolled my eyes. "Scoot over."

"Don't talk to your mama like that."

"Sorry. I meant, Scoot over, ma'am, so I can be a gentleman and drive you home."

She laughed. "You're full of pickle juice."

I settled behind the wheel and pulled onto I-15, relief seeping into every muscle of my body. "How is everyone?"

Her brow furrowed. "A lot has happened."

"Like what?"

"Addie's been really sick."

"What's wrong?"

"I don't know. We're hoping to learn more next week when Dr. Patterson gets the results back from her last test."

That wasn't what I wanted to hear. "How about Benny?"

"Junior high's rough. He came home with a swollen lip and black eye on Friday but won't say who did it."

I gripped the wheel tighter. "He'll tell me."

"Probably not. He won't even let me take it to the principal, although I did talk to Mr. Daggerty on the phone before I left and asked him to alert his teachers to the possibility of Benny being bullied."

"Damn."

She hit my leg. "I hope you can spin a believable tale about your time in Portugal because he's been extremely inquisitive."

I blew out a long breath. "I'm going to tell him the truth." My heart pounded as I met her worried gaze. "You, too."

"Is this the same thing that sent Liz running?"

"Yeah." I wanted to ask how Liz was doing, but in a few more hours, I'd see for myself.

"Enlighten me."

I clenched the wheel so tight my knuckles turned white. I wanted to put this off but had resolved in rehab to expose the truth. No longer would I hide behind the lies Damon and I had fed everyone. My friend needed to be set free.

"The night of the accident," I chewed my lip, "I drove. Not Damon." I kept my eyes on the freeway. When she didn't say anything, words tumbled out between heavy breaths. "I was out, so I don't remember anything, but Damon must've moved me from my seat and buckled me into his. I never let him drive my Explorer. Ever. But I allowed you to believe he did that night because I couldn't deal with what I'd done." A vice seemed to tighten around my chest.

We were somewhere between Malad and Pocatello when Mom reached over and patted my shoulder. "Why don't you pull over, son?"

Exhausted from holding back Mount Vesuvius of emotions, I obeyed. I parked on the side of the freeway, and she undid her seatbelt and pulled me into her arms.

"This makes no difference to me, son. I love you. It was an accident. An accident," she repeated.

A sob tore out of my throat. "But don't you see? It was me who killed Detrick. Not Damon. Everyone's hated Damon for years, when it was me they should've despised. Benny's messed up and getting bullied because of me." I swiped at tears. "Dad will disown me."

"He never hated your friend because of the accident. He hated him because of how he pulled you down, even before that terrible night. The accident just brought everything to an ugly head."

I shook my head. "I should've taken the heat and gone to juvie. Damon's life is messed up because of me. I have to tell the sheriff. Get Damon's juvenile record expunged. Show the town he's not the bad guy they've made him out to be. That I've made him out to be because I was too cowardly to own up to the truth."

She touched my cheek. "Oh, son, nothing you say will matter now. Damon might've got a bad rap back then, but he's earned it now. A few weeks ago he was arrested for possession of a controlled substance. He resisted arrest and was sentenced to two years in prison."

"No." The strong walls I'd built to support me began to crumble.

"I'm sorry. I know you've tried your best to save him, but sometimes people don't want to be saved."

"I'm sure Dad was happy about that. Liz, too."

"Rawson?"

I shuddered as I looked up to meet her sorrowful gaze.

"You knew Lizzie left, didn't you? I thought when you called from the airport all upset..."

I didn't hear anything else. My heart began sinking to the bottom of the Marianas Trench, going numb as emotions iced over in despair.

LIZ

*S*EEING MY DAD'S Chevy pull up and park in front of the office made me smile. Just the man I wanted to see. My passport had arrived. I'd called Dalton to let him know I was ready to go. Now to break the news to Daddy.

My lips did a quick downturn when the passenger door opened and Daddy's drywall contractor stepped out. Dad stayed in the driver's seat, talking on his phone. Mason—the man I definitely didn't want to see—approached the front door. I yanked a file drawer open as the front bells jingled.

"Good afternoon, Liz."

"Hey, Mason." I concentrated on the orderly files I'd redone three times already out of boredom.

"How's your day going?"

I lifted files and dropped them willy-nilly into the drawer. "Pretty busy. What can I get you?"

"Uh, I thought maybe, um…well, your dad said you…" He paused, and I wondered why I drew out such awkwardness in men.

"Have Cokes in the back fridge?" I finished for him. "Yes, we do. You must be thirsty working in this heat. Let me grab you one." I ducked around the corner and hid in the backroom until I heard the bells again.

I grabbed two Cokes and walked out into the hall, but ran smack dab into Mason. He grabbed hold of my arms to steady me.

"Sorry about that."

I looked up into big brown, teddy bear eyes. Mason wasn't bad looking, if you overlooked his slightly crooked teeth and the hairy mole on his cheek. But I didn't want a man in my life, no matter how good my parents thought it'd be for me.

"No problem." I held out a can.

He looked at me like I was a cold Slushee on a hot summer day. "I wondered if you'd like to go out with me tomorrow night."

"I don't—"

"Your dad said I shouldn't take no for an answer."

I clenched my teeth. "Sorry, Mason, but Dad doesn't know what the hell he's talking about."

I quick-stepped around the corner and found Dad sitting in my secretarial chair, looking sheepish. "Here's your Coke," I muttered as I entered his office.

He followed and shut the door behind him.

I turned and glared. "How could you sic your contractor on me like that? Have you been taking lessons from Mom?"

"Oh, now, don't get huffy, baby girl. Mason's a great guy."

"I don't care if he's freaking Clark Kent. I've told you and Mom I don't want to date. Period!"

"Lizzie Belle, you need to get out and socialize. You've been a hermit all summer. I promised your mother you'd get out this weekend."

"So you're siding with her now?"

"I'm not siding with anyone. You need to put Justin and that guy from Montana out of your head. Live again."

"Don't you dare lump Rawson Law and Justin together. They're nothing alike. Justin was perfect."

Dad sank into his chair. "Justin was a jerk. You were just too blind to see it, and you've immortalized him in death."

Tears stung the back of my eyes. I knew he wasn't perfect. He'd been very, very imperfect, but that made the guilt for his death even worse. I'd wished him dead the night before his accident. I'd wished him dead to God in my prayers.

He pursed his lips. "I kept my mouth shut back then because of your mom, but I shouldn't have."

I wiped my eye against my sleeve. "You never gave him a chance." Maybe Justin had acted the way he had with me because Daddy had never liked him.

"Believe me, I wanted him to be good enough for my princess, but the only person he cared about was himself."

"That's not true."

"You gave up everything for him, Lizzie, and he just kept on taking. He made you change how you dressed. How you talked. How you acted. I doubt he ever would've been satisfied until he took every part of you."

I dug my hands into my scalp. "He wasn't like that."

"What about the horses? He said he was allergic and you gave them up."

"I loved him, Daddy. What would you do if Mom was allergic to sawdust? Wouldn't you pick another profession?"

"So why haven't you gone to Viktorya's since you got home? Are you still trying to please a dead man?"

"It has nothing to do with Justin."

"That's your passion. Your life. Yet whenever Viktorya calls, you give me some lame excuse to tell her that neither of us buys. Is it because of the other guy, Mr. Montana Cowboy?"

I glared at him. "I'm not hanging out with the horses because it's one hundred and ten freaking degrees outside." I walked out and slammed the door behind me.

He marched out after me and cornered me at my desk. "Don't walk out on me, young lady. I'm your boss as well as your father, and I'm not done talking."

"Well, I'm through listening." I grabbed my satchel from the bottom drawer. "You can throw away the boss card, because I quit."

"You can't quit."

My gaze flicked to the side, where a slack-jawed Mason watched our standoff from the couch. Just jolly great.

"I'm not only quitting but leaving the country. I'm going to El Salvador next week, so eat that in your Wheaties." I pushed past him and headed out the door to my silver Fiat.

Dad called after me. "Wait, Lizzie. Don't—"

I slammed the door as he ran after me. He pounded on my window, but I backed out without looking at him. Tears formed as memories bombarded me. I couldn't stay. The tiny piece of my heart I still possessed had splintered into painful pieces from Dad's attack.

I had to get out of here before the dam burst.

BENTLEY

OLDING MY ARMS, I sulked against the passenger side window. "Leaving church early to drive to the prison seems wrong on so many levels."

Rawson didn't take his eyes off the road. "At least you got to go for some of it."

"Yeah. Thanks," I muttered.

Since my brother had returned from Portugal, I had a ride to church again. Still, I wished he would've let me stay for Sunday School so I could've seen Alice, instead of driving hours out of the way to visit hell. That's what the Montana State Prison in Deer Lodge felt like. We'd gone there for the first time last week so Rawson could visit his friend. I'd left with a bad taste in my throat. Prison sucked, but I despised Damon even more.

"I saw you talking to that Alice girl at church," Rawson said. "Are you sweet on her?"

"What if I am?"

"She talks too much for my taste."

"Well, good, because I don't want to share."

He snort-laughed.

"How long do you think before the doctor knows anything?" I asked. Our sister had been diagnosed with kidney failure right after Rawson had returned. She'd gone onto dialysis until she could get a kidney transplant.

"There's a bunch more tests to run to see if any of us can be a live-donor. Doc said it could be months before we know more."

I folded my arms. "That stinks."

"Sure does."

We reached Deer Lodge, and Rawson hopped out of the truck. "Let's go, bro."

I shook my head. "I'll stay here."

His brows drew together. "We're the only visitors Damon gets. Come on. I'll buy you a soda from the vending machine."

"I'm not going in again. That place gives me the creeps."

"I can't leave you out here alone."

"I'll be way more comfortable out here than locked in with that jerk who caused the accident."

His lips tightened.

"When you gonna give up on him, Rawson? He doesn't want to change." It irritated me how he wasted hours driving out here just so his friend could blame him for being there. "You're not making a difference."

"Makes one to me." He walked away.

I frowned. I loved my brother, but I couldn't face Damon again. He'd ruined everything. I sketched in my notebook for a while but must've dozed. The door opened and something poked my leg.

"Wake up, kid."

I shook myself awake.

Rawson looked down at me. "You okay?"

"Yep." I stretched.

He clapped a hand on my shoulder. "Sorry I took so long."

I didn't reply.

Rawson was silent as we put Deer Lodge behind us. No surprise there. Damon upset everyone. My thoughts turned to the accident as I watched trees whiz past.

After our car had run off the road and rolled six years ago, eerie silence had fallen over our mangled vehicle. I'd tried to move, but a burning sensation had seized my whole body, making me puke and pass out. When I'd awakened, Damon had patted my brother's shoulder.

"Roz?" My brother hadn't answered.

I hadn't been able to see Detrick anywhere. The whole left side of my body had been crushed into the door. Remembering the overwhelming pain that'd rippled through me the last time I'd moved, I hadn't dared even twitch to search for my brother.

Damon had started dragging my unconscious brother into the passenger seat, which had given me hope. Maybe he would look for Detrick. He didn't seem hurt, like the rest of us. But he'd pulled the seat belt over Rawson and had wedged himself into the crumpled driver's side and harnessed himself. When he'd glanced into the rear view mirror and had caught me staring, he'd scowled.

"I drove. Got it, Upchuck?"

Being only eight years old, I hadn't cared who drove. I just wanted someone to find Detrick and help me escape the jagged metal digging into my leg and spine.

"You don't want yer big brother to get in trouble, do ya?"

I'd shaken my head.

"That's what I thought. Keep yer mouth shut when the pigs get here or they'll haul yer bro off to jail."

Those words had struck home. I hadn't wanted Rawson to go to jail, so I'd sputtered out that I wouldn't say a word, and I'd guarded my secret ever since.

Rawson nudged me, snapping me into the present. "I need to tell you something, Ben."

"What?"

He bit his lips. "I, um...wasn't in Portugal all summer."

I studied his profile. "I didn't think so. You never sent a postcard. Where were you?"

He focused on the road. "I, um...had to go to, uh...rehab." The last word came out a strangled whisper.

I gaped at him, totally blindsided. "Is that why Lizzie left without saying goodbye?" I'd always wondered why she'd left like she had.

He looked pained at the mention of her name. "Yeah. I told her the truth about the accident. She wasn't happy." He merged onto the highway. "Now I need to tell you."

"I already know."

I recalled the hours of fear and pain I'd endured before the sheriff and fire truck had arrived to cut me out of the wreckage. Though I'd been barely lucid, I remembered clear as day watching as they'd pulled Rawson out onto a stretcher. I'd thought he was dead. The sheriff had made Damon breathe into a cup. When the paramedics had placed me on a stretcher and given me a shot in my arm, the last thing I'd seen was Damon being handcuffed.

"It was my fault," Rawson said. "I drove. Not Damon. He switched places after we crashed."

"You think I don't know that?" Every muscle in my body clenched. "I watched the fool move you when you were unconscious."

"Then you know he took the fall for me."

"As he should have! He pushed your hands off the steering wheel and caused us to roll. Detrick's dead and I'm bent because of Damon's stupidity! Not yours."

"Don't hate him, kid. Hate me. I should've taken you home when Detrick told me to. If I'd listened, he wouldn't have died. You wouldn't have been crushed into the door." His hands tightened on the steering wheel. "Instead, I knocked him around like a bowling pin on his last day on earth."

I rubbed my eyes, thinking of that last fight. Detrick had taken a cheap shot at the back of Rawson's head while he'd been driving. Rawson had pulled over to teach him a lesson.

"In your defense, Detrick egged you on."

Rawson chuckled. "Detrick always had more brawn than brains."

I stared at the distant mountains. "I miss him."

"Me, too. We'd probably still fight like wildcats, but I'd take his surly attitude in a heartbeat over not having him here at all."

I didn't speak until we reached the turnoff. "Do you think he was scared?"

Rawson picked right up on my thought thread. "Detrick wasn't scared of anything."

"But he was all alone after he was thrown from the Explorer. In the dark. At least I had you in the car with me, even if I thought you were dead. Detrick had no one."

Rawson squeezed my shoulder. "He wasn't alone, kid. You heard the sermon today, how angels watch over us. I'm certain angels kept our brother company until they led him to the other side."

"Do you think?"

"I know."

I leaned back and closed my eyes. "Good. I hated thinking of him being all by himself." I sighed. "I'm glad I still have you."

"Even though I'm a major screw-up?"

"Especially because of that. It'd suck only having a sister."

He laughed and we drove the rest of the way in comfortable silence.

For six years, I'd waited for Rawson to open up about the accident, but he'd shut me out and had dragged an impossible load of guilt around instead. We could've helped each other through the pain and eased one another's burdens. Instead, we'd suffered alone. For years.

But now we were talking, and it felt darn good to set the truth free.

79

LIZ

𝒯HE CLOCK ON the wall ticked loudly as Mom and I had a stare-down. Her baby-blue eyes bore into my rock-hard brown ones, willing me to blink. *Rock crushes baby,* I chanted in my mind. She wouldn't win this contest of wills.

"You will go, young lady."

"No, I won't." I didn't even live with her anymore, yet she tried to control my life.

Neither of us blinked.

"I'm glad your father's not around to see what an ungrateful brat you've become."

My eyelids slammed shut, making me lose...just as I'd lost my dad a month ago after spewing hate. My last words to him still haunted me. An hour after I'd yelled at him and stormed out of his office, he'd driven back to a work site and died in a freak construction accident. The next time I'd seen him, he'd been stiff and cold in a casket.

My lips quivered as I turned away from Mom.

Her voice crescendoed. "I went to a lot of trouble to set you two up when I ran into him at the grocery store. You can't break his heart by calling and saying you're not going to meet him."

"You're right. I'm not calling him. You made the date. You break it."

"Elizabeth, what am I going to do with you? You're so selfish. Life isn't all about you."

No. It was about her. I could see that clearly now. She wanted me to find a man because she wanted a man in her life, to fill the void Dad had left behind.

Throat-clearing behind me made me spin around. My brother-in-law, Cam, and my sister, Esther, had arrived. Thank goodness. I threw my arms around Cam.

"How are you, Liz?"

I blinked back tears. "Hanging in there."

Esther hugged Mom. "Don't you look beautiful, Mama." That's why she was the favorite daughter. "I'm going to take Liz off your hands. Can you keep Cam company?"

"Certainly, but Elizabeth has a date with that luscious Dallon."

I shook my head when Esther glanced at me.

"I'll call and postpone, Ilene," Cam offered. "Liz and Esther need some sister time, don't you think?"

She pursed her lips. "I guess."

Cam pulled Mom into the kitchen, and Esther whispered, "Let's get out of here."

She didn't need to tell me twice. We booked it out of the house and into her posh Range Rover.

"I wish you wouldn't rile Mom every time you come over," she said as we pulled out of the driveway.

"I don't mean to. It's just I don't want to date every guy she tries to hook me up with." I leaned my head against the window.

"She has your best interests at heart. So do I."

That's what they kept saying.

She pulled into a Baskin Robbins, and I perked up. My emotions were at an all-time low. Cream and sugar could only help.

I ordered a pistachio cone, and Esther and I sat at a table. I sank into my rich, nutty ice cream and groaned.

"You look like you're in love," Esther said.

I licked the melting green goodness. "I could marry a tub of pistachio ice cream and enjoy happily-ever-after." A frown formed as I realized I'd ruined all chances with the real Pistachio. Dad had told me I was running away, and he'd been right. How I wished I'd listened to him, instead of arguing. Maybe he'd still be alive today if I had.

"You look like you just found a fly in your ice cream," my sister said.

A fly in my brain, more like. "I'm just thinking. Do you want to go visit Daddy's grave? I didn't get over there to put new flowers on this week and—"

"I don't have time." She bit into her raspberry sorbet. "I brought you here to discuss Mom."

I winced. That wasn't my favorite subject.

"Two days ago, I dropped by to check on her and found her comatose and unresponsive on the couch."

"What!"

"I rushed her to the emergency room and they discovered that she'd overdosed on Seroquel."

"Why didn't you tell me? What's Zerowell?"

"Seroquel. It's bipolar medicine."

My mouth hung open. Mom had bipolar disorder? I'd always figured she was a narcissist. Maybe she was both. It'd explain a lot.

"The doctor said she ingested a week's worth of her prescription in one sitting. He believed it was a suicide attempt."

I squeezed my eyes, wondering if Dad had known about her mental illness. Maybe that's why he'd always seemed drained. I'd assumed his job wore him out. But maybe manual labor had been his release from dealing with Mom.

"Mom needs help. Cam and I have discussed this and think the best solution would be for you to move in with her, to be her caregiver."

"What?" She couldn't be serious.

"You'll need to be discreet since her pride runs deep. But I don't trust her, sis. All it'd take is one dark thought, and she might try to end her life again."

My throat stung. "Why can't she live with you?" Esther and Cam had a posh house in Seven Hills.

Esther glared. "I should've known you'd only think of yourself. It's what you do best. Is it not enough that we've lost Dad? Do you want to lose Mom, too?"

Her words made me feel small. "I didn't say no. I just wondered if you'd considered having—"

"Cam and I have a life, Elizabeth. You don't." I opened my mouth to protest, but she plunged her knife in deeper and twisted. "You live in that ghetto basement by yourself. With Dad gone, you have no job or any prospects. You need a place to live, so this makes sense for both of you. If you don't do this and Mom tries to overdose again, it'll be on your head."

That was harsh.

"I know you and Mom don't have the best relationship."

That was an understatement.

"But this could give you a chance to build one. Maybe if you showed an interest in her, instead of always pounding out your own way, you might see you have more in common than you think."

"Maybe." Although I wouldn't hold my breath. At least, in the big house we wouldn't cross paths too often.

My sister reached across the table. "Thank you." She finished the last bite of her cone. "Oh, and one more thing. Dad's finances weren't in order. The company assets didn't cover his debts. Mom's going to lose the house. It'll go into foreclosure tomorrow."

I dropped my spoon.

"First item of business will be finding a suitable place to rent until the life insurance comes in. Cam's made a list of places for you to call. If you run into any problems, we could put Mom up in our guest room and throw you on a cot in the playroom, but I'm sure you'll find something."

I walked out of Baskin Robbins in a daze. Esther chatted the whole way home, but I didn't hear a word. The weight of responsibility rested heavily on my shoulders. I loved my mother, but being her caregiver seemed beyond my capabilities. She didn't like me. And she would lose her home —the one Daddy had built with his own two hands. I didn't doubt she'd find a way to blame me for that.

Esther dropped me off at Mom's. I told Mom goodnight and drove back to my basement apartment to watch *Phantom Menace* again. Every scene had memories attached to it—snuggling with Rawson during certain scenes, listening to him and Benny throw out one-liners. Not a day passed that I didn't think of them and wish I'd stayed at the ranch. I regretted how I'd handled everything with Rawson at the end. He hadn't been lying to me as Justin had done. Even when I'd confronted Justin with proof of his betrayal and we'd fought, he'd made me feel like the bad guy. The nagging, non-trusting, headcase fiancée. He'd never owned up to his mistakes. Rawson had been trying to confess the truth, and I'd punished him for it.

I missed him. I missed the horses. I missed Benny and Addie and my tastefully decorated room at their house. I missed the mountains and the smell of manure and hay mingling in the breeze. I missed Susa's cooking and Charity's kindness. Most of all, I missed the sense of belonging I'd felt at the ranch.

I stared at my popcorn ceiling. Dad had somehow known the truth, though I'd denied it for years. Bitterness for the man who'd killed Justin had crippled me and made me turn my back on the man I'd grown to love when he'd needed me most. I'd failed Rawson, as I'd failed everyone else.

I pulled out Rawson's Tagheur watch from a side drawer. Why hadn't I listened to him? He'd cried out for help, for understanding, for mercy. I'd swung the ax of justice down, instead.

The man who sat in prison for killing Justin didn't have a clue I'd loathed him all these years. My festering hate had only hurt me. Forgiveness had been the key Daddy had wanted me to reach out and take. He'd wanted me to work through my hate so I could be happy again. Instead, I'd told him I never wanted to see him again and had walked away.

And I never did see him again.

RAWSON

S UNDAYS HAD BECOME a day of rest, not because of church, although I didn't mind sitting through the service as much as I once had. I liked the day because I got a break from Garret, my new boss. Dad had put me on probation to see how I'd adjust after rehab. Might as well be in prison with Damon as to put up with the arrogant ferret.

But today, I refused to give him a second thought. Life had set up a pitching machine on full throttle since I'd returned, but today I'd hit a home run. The doctor had called an hour ago to inform me that I was a match for Addie. Mom and I had cried together on the couch afterward. It was a miracle. I could give my sick sister one of my kidneys and save her life. No more dialysis. It didn't make up for Detrick dying, but it meant the world to me.

"Mom," I called as I headed out the door, "Benny and I are heading to town. After church, I'm driving to the prison to see Damon. I'll be back late."

"Drive carefully." Tears glistened in her eyes as she waved from the porch.

"When the doctor calls back, schedule surgery as soon as possible. Nothing comes over Addie."

"Will do. Love you, son."

"Love you, too."

Benny climbed into the truck and we pulled away to go pick up one of my old friends from high school. When I pulled up to his curb and honked, Mace came barreling out of his door like an angry bull.

"Hey, Mace," I said as he opened the door. "This here's my little brother, Benny."

He reached out to shake hands. "Nice to meet you, kid. You have one hell of a brother."

Benny looked like a frog catching a fly as Mace belted out a staccato laugh and pounded my back.

"How's it going, you ornery son of a—"

"Great," I interjected. "Thanks for doing this."

"*No problemo.* Glad to help a friend out." Mace had diarrhea of the mouth and proceeded to spew out stories on the drive across town.

I chuckled when I caught Benny's wide-eyed stare as Mace wheezed in between bursts of laughter. "Anyways, your brother has always been the king of cool. Even in tenth-freaking-grade, he was taller and stronger than most of us seniors. The ladies loved him." He whistled. "I was two years older and jealous because he had senior chicks throwing themselves at him. A freaking sophomore."

I cleared my throat. "You up for the drive to Deer Lodge after the service?"

He belted out a round of laughter bullets. "You trying to change the subject, Roz?"

Yes, I was.

We made it to church and listened to an uplifting sermon on God's grace. I was seriously grateful for that as I pondered the last two months. Since I'd come clean and had taken the blame for the accident, many people in town had shunned me. I didn't blame them. But it made me more grateful God was my Judge. I felt certain I'd receive a more merciful judgment from Him than some of my fellowmen.

The meeting ended, and Mace and I drove to the prison. Benny stayed behind with Alice. Her parents had invited him over for Sunday dinner.

We made it through security, and Damon smirked at my white shirt and slacks, as he always did.

"I can't believe you, of all people, are going to church."

I pulled out a deck of cards, trying to ignore my itching collar. Damon grabbed the cards from my fumbling hands and shuffled.

"Mace, I didn't know you went to church," he said.

"I didn't until today. I've been on an eight year sabbatical." He peppered the room with laughter bullets, riddling us with good moods. "Rawson made me return."

Damon dealt. "Roz has been cramming his religion down all our throats. He thinks I should attend service here each Sunday." He snorted. "Can you imagine that?"

"If I can, you can," Mace drawled.

We played Five Card Draw and near the end, Mace left so I could speak to my friend alone.

"Damon, Addie's real sick and needs a kidney. I'm giving her one of mine, but that means I won't be able to come see you for a while." I pursed my lips. "Mace will visit while I'm laid up. He's a good guy."

Damon hung his head. "So are you, Roz. I'm sorry for letting you down." I almost didn't recognize him without his mocking mask. "It was me who messed up and killed Detrick. Not you. I wish you hadn't been noble and took the blame like you did."

A lump formed in my throat. "I should've told the truth right away. Maybe then you wouldn't be here."

"Nah, I would've ended up here eventually. I know it. I also know I pushed your hands off the wheel and rolled us down that hill. That's why I traded places."

"We both screwed up. We never should've gotten drunk when I had my little brothers with me. But it's in the past. Forgive yourself. I want you to get out of here and live the life you always dreamed—become a welder, get married, be a good dad and break your old man's cycle. That's how we repay our debt, by making something of ourselves."

Damon blinked as the warden called time.

I clapped his burly shoulder. "I'll see you as soon as the doctor clears me to drive. Start becoming a better man."

"You make me believe it's possible."

I followed the warden out and said over my shoulder, "It is."

81

BENTLEY

*H*OLY THERMAL detonators! I wished life would stop scaring the crud out of me. I shuffled out of the cramped hospital waiting room my parents and I had called home for the last three days. Right step. Left-swing-shuffle-step. Right step. Left-swing-shuffle-step.

I focused on speed and fluidity as I made my way to the cafeteria. Mom had kicked me out of the waiting room and had said not to return until my belly was full. I picked up a basket of chicken fingers, a burrito, a slice of pizza, and a berry parfait to balance it out. After paying, I found a corner table and slumped down to eat.

I recalled the day of the surgery. Rawson had been stoked to give Addie his kidney. He'd been all smiles before they'd taken him and our extremely sick little sister back for the procedure. But the routine surgery and recovery hadn't gone as expected.

Refried beans spilled into my lap. I wiped my jeans and shoved the rest of the dried-out burrito into my mouth. My sister and brother had developed complications and were in the ICU, where I couldn't see them. Mom had tried to get me to go home with Susa, but I'd dug in my heels until she'd let me stay. All I could think about was what would happen if one of them died. No way could I bear it.

I bit into my pizza. The doctor had said something about acute kidney failure. I didn't have a clue what that meant, but the word failure never sounded good. I bowed my head, asking God to heal my brother and sister. To fix what was broken. Tears stung my eyes. I wasn't normally so weepy but being tired and run-down had turned me into a wimp. I shoveled yogurt and berries into my mouth and disposed of my garbage.

When I returned to the waiting area and saw Dad holding Mom, my stomach clenched. "Is Rawson all right? Or is it Addie?"

Mom looked up with red-rimmed eyes as Dad answered. "They're still fighting, son. Your mama's just tired. We received one piece of good news though. Addie's finally responding to the medication."

I sagged into a chair and bowed my head to thank the good Lord.

Hours later, we moved to a private space off of the ICU where we could see Addie through a window. I stared at her, thinking she looked angelic in sleep. Why had I wasted so many years wishing she looked different? I missed her tongue hanging out of her mouth and would celebrate if I could see it now.

We returned to the waiting area and I dozed. Mom shook me awake sometime later.

"Benny, she's awake. The doctor said we can visit for a minute."

In the ICU, Addie's slanted blue eyes focused on us. "Roth-un loves Addie mostest," she said in her low, growly voice. It was the clearest I'd ever heard her speak.

Mom cried while Dad held her. "Yes, he does, honey."

Addie grinned with all her mouth. A full-out miracle.

Though her brain worked slower than most, my sister seemed to sense things intuitively. She knew Rawson loved her, and I had to agree. He'd just given her one of his kidneys and now fought for his life in another area of the hospital.

Tears streamed down Dad's face as he hugged Mom. Made me feel better that I wasn't the only crybaby. I pushed a sweaty lock of hair off my sister's pudgy face and grinned at her thick tongue lolling out of her mouth.

It was the most beautiful sight I'd ever seen.

82

LIZ

S TUDYING THE VARIOUS visitors made me gulp. The rougher elements of society surrounded me. In the corner, a black man with tattoos on his bulging arms wore a menacing scowl. On the bench across from me, a middle-aged woman who reeked of nicotine fidgeted. A young girl with pink hair and multiple piercings smirked from her seat next to a scary-looking biker. A beat-down looking couple in their fifties stared somberly at the walls.

The prison's waiting area hadn't been designed to inspire cheer. Drab gray walls and faded blue tiles made my soul shrink. I'd already walked through metal detectors, had my purse X-rayed, and had endured a humiliating pat-down by a female officer. I must see this through to the end.

I considered the last few months since I'd moved in with Mom. Life had become a war zone again, as it'd been in high school. Except now, instead of intermittent gunfire aimed at my fragile self-esteem, Mom directed intense bombing missions with the intent to obliterate. Daddy no longer was around to shield me from her attacks, and Esther believed I goaded her into attacking me. With the life insurance Mom had received, we'd paid off her debt and had bought a two-bedroom attached house in old Henderson. Not the greatest neighborhood, especially after the quiet, gated community we'd lived in before in Vegas, but Mom owned it outright and we couldn't be evicted.

A buzzer sounded. I waited for my name to be called before walking past a stone-faced guard and entering a secure room divided by a wall and security glass. Another intimidating officer led me to a cubicle and motioned for me to sit.

I gave him a perfunctory thank you and stared through the smudgy glass into the lock-down area on the other side. I repeated a quote by Lily Tomlin in my head. "

Forgiveness means giving up all hope for a better past."

Those words had hit me hard, as did the quote by T. D. Jakes.

"Forgiveness is about empowering yourself, rather than empowering your past."

For years, I'd bemoaned my fate and had empowered my past, just like Daddy had said. Because I'd kept hope alive that things could've turned out differently, I'd never been content in the present. I'd never been able to forgive the man who'd made all my dreams impossible.

This was the man I'd come to see today, to let him know I'd given up hope. In a good way.

A prisoner with shoulder-length black hair entered, followed by a muscular guard. Spiky symbols and tattooed demon heads littered his left arm. He slumped into the seat and picked up the phone.

In a voice as harsh as his appearance, he said, "Who are you?"

I gazed through the smeared glass at the man who'd killed Justin. Part of me cheered to see him locked away. I'd spent the past few months trying to come to terms with his part in what had happened, to do as Daddy had asked and forgive him. But as I stared, bitterness flooded my soul once more. He'd killed Justin and had ruined everything! I'd never received closure, which had haunted me.

I reminded myself to give up false hope in the past. Justin and I had been on shaky ground. The accident had kept us from marrying, and that was tragic, but it'd still been an accident. This man hadn't purposely set out to take Justin's life that day.

"Uh, I'm Elizabeth Ruthersford."

"Am I supposed to care?"

His rudeness flustered me. "I guess not. But, uh…I care about you."

His eyebrows shot up, making me feel foolish. But then a thought floated through my head.

I do care about him.

It made me pause and take a closer look. His hair, tattoos, and attitude were frightening, but as I looked past his tough-guy exterior, a miracle happened. Love that wasn't mine settled on my heart and I knew without doubt that God did love this man.

"Are you another lawyer?"

"No." I pushed a curly strand of hair behind my ear. "I was affected by the accident that put you here."

His brown eyes widened. "Was he your brother?" I must've looked confused. He repeated the question. "The man I killed when I ran the red light. Was he your brother?"

Suddenly, I felt sorry for this man on the other side of the filthy partition. With shocking clarity, I understood how selfish I'd been, only thinking of *my* pain, *my* grief, *my* loss. This man had been hurt, too. Daddy had been right.

"No. He wasn't my brother. Justin was my fiancé." Now, I was grateful I'd made the effort to come here, to give up hope so this man could gain some.

"I'm so sorry." He looked up at me with glistening eyes. "I've tortured myself, wondering about the man I killed. Wondering who he was, if he had a wife and kids, whose son he was." He grimaced. "I've wanted to tell someone who knew him how sorry I was for what happened. You must hate me."

I blinked back tears. "I did, but I came here to tell you I don't anymore. I forgive you."

His mouth hung open.

"When you get released, I hope you'll make a good life for yourself and not let the past define you. It was a horrible mistake."

I sensed the presence of a stone-faced guard behind me. My time was up. I placed the phone on the receiver as the tattooed man stared at me.

When I reached the door, I turned to view him one last time. Anthony Dulles stood, watching me through the streaked glass. I lifted my hand in farewell, and the barest hint of a smile played across his lips. He raised his hand and mouthed *Thank you* before the guard guided me out the door.

As I exited the prison, I threw back my head and savored the winter sun. I felt happy but had no reason to feel that way. I still would drive home to a mom who seemed to hate me. I still nursed a broken heart from walking away from the best relationship of my life. I still worked at a dead-end job. Yet none of that could douse my joy. I felt freedom not only from physical bars, but from bitterness that'd bound my soul for years. I'd finally given up hope, a false hope that things could be different. Nothing would ever change the past—not even hope—and I realized as I opened my car door that I didn't want the past to be different. I'd learned and grown so much from what I'd suffered.

Why would I want to throw all those lessons away?

83

RAWSON

CHRISTMAS HAD BEGUN with Benny parading into my room with a fake beard and wearing red long johns, bellowing, "Ho, ho, ho." And the day had wrapped up with him tucked into a chair next to me, reading *Twilight*. When you're bored and reliant on others, you can't be picky about your entertainment. His friend, Alice, had given him the book for Christmas. He wanted to impress her when he returned to school by being able to discuss it with her. I had to admit, though the story reeked of sap, I enjoyed hearing Benny read the different voices, especially Bella's. Her character sort of reminded me of Lizzie.

Nine months had passed since I'd shattered her heart. That's how I measured time now. As Benny continued to read, I closed my eyes and wondered what Liz might be doing. Had she gone home? Returned to school? Taken a job with another equine business? Part of me wanted to get in the truck as soon as the doctor cleared me for driving and head to Vegas to search for her. But the smarter side knew that'd be a fool's errand. Liz knew her own mind. Leaving like she'd done had sent a clear message that she didn't want anything to do with my sorry hide.

Truth be told, she was better off without me.

The same wasn't true for me, though.

Benny yawned and stuck a *Star Wars* bookmark between the pages. "It's good so far, isn't it?" He didn't wait for an answer. "Alice said this series is her favorite ever."

"Well, that's saying something since she's probably been reading books for nigh on a year now."

He shot me a scowl.

"Just kidding. It's not as bad as I expected."

He grinned. My baby brother had grown three inches since summer, surpassing me in height. He was still all legs and arms, but what fifteen-year-old boy wasn't? The most impressive change I'd noticed was in his gait. When I'd returned from Europe, his left leg from the knee down still jerked out awkwardly. But with the help of his therapist and lots of hard work, his spastic swing had become less pronounced. It looked more like a bad limp now.

"Did you have an awesome Christmas?" he asked.

If I hadn't, it was no fault of his. He'd gone beyond the call of duty to entertain my bedridden self. I reached out to rub his head, but he ducked back a few steps and smirked.

"Sure did, bro. Thanks for keeping me company."

"You're welcome."

"How are things between you and chatterbox Alice?"

He blushed. "We're just friends."

"Have you tried to kiss her?"

"Nah." He squirmed. "I don't think she likes me that way."

"Why not? You're a handsome kid, and she seems to go out of her way at church to talk to you."

"Why don't you try to find Liz?" he retorted.

"Maybe I'm just waiting to get my strength back so I can."

He bounced up and down. "Really? You're gonna look for her?"

I rolled my eyes, not wanting to talk about the woman who'd stolen my heart. "Why not? Grab my laptop." I'd humor him.

He crowded onto the bed with me as I typed *Elizabeth Ruthersford* into the search bar. I'd dialed her number several times after I'd gotten out of rehab, but she must've changed numbers. Still, Benny was right. I needed to try again. If the girl was going to burrow in my head, I had the right to talk to her in person and receive closure.

"There's a match." My brother pointed at the screen.

"That Elizabeth lives in West Virginia."

Google didn't bring up any other promising morsels. I scanned news sites in Vegas, and discovered that a construction worker named Bradley Ruthersford had died in October when a CAT had knocked him over and snapped his neck. I had no clue what the name of Lizzie's father was, but I did recall her saying he'd owned a construction company. Could this guy be her dad?

I read the clipping and realized it wasn't. The only survivors were a wife named Ilene and two daughters, Esther and Belle. I wrote down their names to contact later. Maybe they were relations.

"Wait," Benny said. "Liz worked for a lady in Vegas who Dad knows, right? What was her name?"

I hit my head. Why hadn't I thought of that? Typing in *Viktorya Lohman*, I found the number of her dressage facility. Surely, she'd know Lizzie's whereabouts. Calling the number, I waited and hoped.

"Hello?" The thick Russian accent made me smile.

"Hey, Viktorya. Rawson Law here."

"Rawson! How's my favorite Montana cowboy?"

"Doing good. And you?"

"Can't complain. Business is decent."

"Great. I hope you had a merry Christmas."

"We sure did. How about you?"

"It was perfect." I cleared my throat. "I called to ask a favor. That girl you sent up to us two years ago—Liz Ruthersford—do you have her contact information? Ours is outdated."

"Lizzie? I haven't heard from her since she left to work for your dad. I heard she was home last summer and tried to call her, but her mother said she was moving to El Salvador."

She gave me the address and phone number she had on file, but it matched our outdated ones. That house had been foreclosed on a few months ago.

Sensing my disappointment, Viktorya said, "Sorry I can't be of more help. If you have any luck finding her, tell her to give her Russian friend a call, no? I miss that girl."

I promised I would and ended the call. "Damn it!" I pounded my blanket.

"What?" Bennie cried.

"Lizzie moved to South America." How in the blazes would I ever find her now?

84

LIZ

*P*USHING THE HEAVY drape aside, I peeked out the window. The frantic beating of moth wings against a hot light chased away the graceful butterflies I should be hosting in my stomach as I waited for my date to arrive.

"Are you expecting someone?"

The curtain fell as I whipped around to face Mom. I'd hoped to sneak out without her noticing. Three weeks ago, when Gary had shown up to take me on our first date, Mom had drooled all over the man during introductions. She'd definitely approved. A little too much.

"Umm, yeah." No sense lying. She possessed a sixth sense when it came to sniffing out my lies. "Gary flew into town again. He's taking me out tonight."

Her smile surprised me. I couldn't remember the last time I'd seen her happy. "That's wonderful, dear. You must not have made too bad of an impression on him last time."

I ignored her subtle jab. "Guess not."

Gary had been Justin's best friend in college. Justin and I had double-dated a few times with Gary and Diane and had become engaged the same month. When Justin had died, I'd lost contact with them. All I knew was that Gary and Diane had ended up getting married and Justin and I hadn't.

Last month, I'd opened Facebook to find a message from Gary. He'd written that he remembered me fondly from college and wondered how I was doing. I'd replied that I was fine and had asked about him and Diane.

He'd answered that they'd recently divorced. Not knowing what to say, I'd sent a crying-face emoticon to end the conversation. Dealing with Mom was difficult enough. I didn't need anyone else's problems.

A week later, my phone had rung. Not recognizing the number, I'd hesitantly answered.

"Hey, Liz," an exuberant voice had boomed.

"Who is this?"

"It's Gary. I messaged you on Facebook, but I guess you didn't check."

"Uh, yeah. I don't get on very often."

"Smart girl. Facebook is the biggest time waster on the planet."

I'd gnawed at a hangnail.

"If you'd checked, I told you I'd be in Vegas for a convention tomorrow and thought it might be fun to reconnect."

"How did you get this number?"

He'd hem-hawed, and I'd realized I was being catty, as Mom always accused. Who cared how he'd gotten my number. He was a friend—one of Justin's, at least. I owed him civility, not an interrogation.

"Never mind. So, you'll be in town?"

"Yeah. Would you like to get together?"

I'd had a mountain of assignments to complete for my online college course, and had told him so, but he'd convinced me to spare him an hour.

He'd picked me up the next night, and I'd been startled by how much more handsome he was than I'd remembered. Of course, in college, I'd only had eyes for Justin. He'd been the jealous type. I hadn't dared look at other guys. When Mom had gushed and thrown herself at Gary, I'd figured it'd be a one-date wonder. No man would be coming back for more crazy.

But I'd been wrong.

Gary had taken me to an over-the-top restaurant in the Monte Carlo Resort, with chandeliers and tablecloths, crystal goblets, and fine china. He'd told me about his successful law career in Los Angeles and how he competed in surf contests on the weekends. I'd felt his eyes on me the whole night—and it'd ended up being much longer than an hour. Gary had brought me home way after midnight and had gently brushed his lips across my cheek at the door.

"You know, even back when I dated Diane, I was jealous of Justin." I shook my head at his charm. He'd leaned down to kiss me, and I'd thought, *Maybe, just maybe I can do this again.*

"Well, make sure you don't scare him off." Mom's abrasive voice interrupted my reflection. She pushed a stray curl from my face. "You should have taken time to straighten your mop. I'll never understand why you insist on this wild Merida style. She's the only Disney princess who didn't get a man."

I silently built a Rawson-inspired Love Triangle. *I love my thick, curly hair. I love the freckles on my nose. I love my sense of style.* His insistence that I tell him three things I loved had rankled when I'd lived at the ranch, but it'd become a life preserver in the stormy waves of Mom's disparaging remarks.

Rhythmic rapping on the screen door saved me from Mom's assault. I wanted to leave, but she had other ideas.

"Invite him to come in, Elizabeth. Don't be rude."

I gestured Gary inside, hoping for the best.

Mom pranced across the room and grabbed him by his tie. "Ooo-la-la, don't you look scrumptious, Gare-bear."

I wanted to crawl behind the couch as I watched the woman who'd brought me into this world flirt with my date as she apologized for my appearance.

"I tried to get her to straighten that rat's nest, but Elizabeth has never had any sense of fashion. I mean, look at that dress." She didn't finish her statement, but her look conveyed disgust.

He chuckled. "Ellie's a handful, Ilene. That's for sure. How about I take her off your hands for the evening?"

I whipped my hand away from him. He hadn't outright mocked me, but close enough. Whose side was he on anyway? And when had he become so chummy with Mom that he knew her first name?

By the time Gary extracted us from Mom's claustrophobic grip and led me to his red sports car, I was ticked. It irked me that he'd kissed up to Mom, chuckling at her put-downs and acting as if he was doing her a favor by getting me out of the house, like I was a child who needed tending.

Cool air blowing from the vents caused goosebumps to form. I folded my arms across my dress and chalked up another point against Gary.

"Why so quiet, Elle?"

That was another thing. Where did he get off creating nicknames for me? I'd cringed when he'd started calling me Elle as we'd Skyped. Mom had told him my middle name, and he'd thought he was clever combining both.

"I'm cold. Could you turn off the A/C?"

"Sure, baby."

Since when had I become his baby?

"I've missed you, Elle."

I didn't respond. He was losing points fast.

He pulled onto the side of Boulder Highway. I stared at him as he undid his seatbelt. What was he doing?

He pulled me into his arms. "I haven't been able to stop thinking about you, baby." He pressed demanding lips to mine.

"Gary," I pushed against him.

He retreated, leaving me breathless and befuddled. What in the heck? We were on the side of a busy road.

"I've dreamed about kissing you since I last saw you. Skyping each night's only made me want you more."

I still smarted from his interactions with Mom. It wasn't what he'd said necessarily, but what he hadn't. Did he agree with her that I looked crummy? Were my curls too crazy? Rawson had loved them.

Clenching my teeth, I reached for Gary's hand and pasted on a smile. No thinking of Rawson Law tonight. The past was behind me.

Gary reached behind his seat and retrieved a silver package. "For you."

I opened the gift and covered my mouth. "No way."

He removed the diamond necklace and swept curls back to clasp it around my neck. "They're real."

My eyes widened. The white gold chain with eleven diamonds forming an elegant V must've cost a fortune. "This is too nice."

He winked. "I'm sure you'll think of a way to repay me." His lips claimed mine again, more insistent.

I experienced another brain and body freeze as my insides looped into painful knots. When he pulled back, every muscle clenched, on edge. I'd never been so indebted to a man.

"Let's start this date, shall we?"

And off we went in his sleek Series 4 car that could go light speed. He told me how many miles it could go in 5.5 seconds, but my mind spaced off during his car talk. His plundering kiss had disturbed me. Why? Gary was the real deal. Okay, he was a fast mover, but we'd talked for almost a month online. I needed to stop thinking of this as a second date. We were farther along than that.

He took me to an expensive dinner at the Bellagio hotel and to a show called O. Dumb name, but the production was spectacular, with acrobats diving into water to the beat of exotic music and contorting their bodies in unimaginable ways. Though annoyed by his earlier interactions, I shoved off my reservations as he wrapped an arm around me. Gary had it all. I should be grateful for his attention.

But when he pulled into my driveway to drop me off, I had to psych myself up for his possessive kiss.

"I love you so much, Elle." His hand moved under my dress to stroke my thigh.

That stupid nickname and his invading hands made me shove him away. "I'm not a make-out-on-the-second-date type of girl."

He scoffed. "I'm not a make-out-on-the-second-date kind of guy, but I can't help myself around you, Elle. Your mouth says no, but your eyes say go, go, go."

He pulled me closer and began what Rawson had called nibbling. Only, Gary's mouth didn't tantalize. He conquered.

"Ow!" What was he doing? Sucking snake venom from me? I squirmed out of his arms and opened my door. "Gotta go." I walked to the porch

Gary rolled down his window. "I'll be over tomorrow night at six. Wear something nice, and don't be afraid to show off those sexy legs."

I gaped at him. He hadn't mentioned going out again, and now he just assumed I was his for however long he stayed in town? "I don't think—"

He backed out of the driveway. "I'll dream of you, Elle," he shouted.

I made my way to my room and locked the door. "Moron," I muttered as I ripped off my stupid dress. I don't know if I referred to Gary or myself. Unclasping the diamond necklace, I threw it on the carpet and sank onto my bed.

I don't know how long I sobbed or why I even cried, but my eyes began to sting and my chest ached. Daddy had been right. Gary was Justin all over again, except the first time around, I'd been too blind to realize how much Justin had walked all over me. He'd never listened to me, because it was all about him and what he'd wanted. Being a silly, naive girl, I'd handed over my dreams in exchange for holding onto his coattails. For all the good it'd done me. He'd never respected me as a person. I'd only been a trophy to him.

I pushed a DVD into the player, though it was almost one in the morning. As I watched *Phantom Menace*, Yoda's wisdom slapped at my heart.

"Fear is the path to the dark side...fear leads to anger...anger leads to hate... hate leads to suffering."

"Believe me, I know," I said to the twenty-eight-inch screen on the wall. I'd learned firsthand how those emotions made one suffer. My irrational anger had made me push away the one man who'd truly loved me, and now I was stuck with a jerk who looked good on the outside, but did nothing but make me feel weak, vulnerable, and worthless.

"No more," I growled. I refused to lick up scraps guys like Gary threw at me. Time to take charge of my life. Do what was best for me, not bow to others' wishes in order to keep the peace.

The next day, I clocked out of work and drove my Fiat hatchback across town. Time for step one in Project Lizzie. My chest tightened as I neared Gary's hotel. In the parking garage, I texted him that I was there. Seconds later, he sent me a winky face emoji with his reply.

Gary: Come on up, baby.
I'll show you my room.

:Can't. Meet me in the lobby.

299

It took the vain man ten minutes to appear. I smirked at his horrified expression when he spotted me in all my *Hot Dog on a Stick* glory. My colorful striped uniform would never win a prize in a cool contest.

"Elle!" He clamped onto my arm and dragged me into an adjoining hallway void of spectators. "What are you doing here in that...monstrosity?"

I'd purposely not changed out of my gaudy uniform to gauge his reaction. Would he be as controlling as Justin? "I just came from work. Sorry. I probably smell like mustard."

He winced and let go of me. "You didn't tell me you worked fast food."

"Yeah, it's great," I lied. "I make nine bucks an hour and get Sundays off."

His sneer revealed his thoughts.

"I wanted to give this back." I pulled the diamond necklace from my purse. "I think we shouldn't see each other anymore."

"Yeah." He slipped the expensive gift into his pocket. "That's probably best." His judgmental gaze dismissed me. "Long-distance relationships rarely work."

Thank goodness for that, and thank goodness for my striped uniform that'd definitely made this whole breakup easier.

I stopped to use a restroom on the way out, changing into jeans and an old T-shirt. Then I drove to the edge of town and hopped out of my car.

The smell of freshly turned hay, manure, and dust made me sigh. I threw my hands out to the side, wondering why I'd avoided this place for so long. I walked through the gate, following the rhythmic sound of hoofs. In the arena, I saw my dear mentor, Viktorya, putting a stunning Paint through his paces.

I leaned over the railing and became lost in the beauty of horse and rider becoming one. When she noticed me, she trotted the Paint over and dismounted. Pulling off her helmet, she shook out her dyed red hair.

"Liz? Is that you?"

I felt self-conscious standing before her in my beggar shoes. "It's me."

She tethered her horse. "How many years has it been?"

"Two."

She surprised me by pulling me into a hug. "I've worried so much about you since I read that your father died. I tried calling, but you must've changed numbers. I haven't known how to reach you." She released me only to cradle my cheeks in her calloused hands. "How are you?"

Her concern was my undoing. I lowered my head and began to bawl as the heartache of the past year rushed out. Why had I cut this dear woman out of my life? She'd been like a mother to me—at least, one who'd cared.

When I reined in the waterfest, I sniffed. "Sorry."

"Don't be. You're my daughter, no? If you feel like crying, you cry." She gestured to the house. "Should we go in and feed you? You look hungry?"

I shook my head. Vikky had always thought I looked underfed. "I came to hang out with the horses. Can I feed them or exercise them for you?"

Her brown eyes glistened in the harsh sun. "Have you been with horses at all since you left Montana?"

I shook my head.

"I'm glad you came."

I was too. "I've been living with Mom since October."

She pulled me into her arms. "You poor girl."

"It's been difficult. Since Dad died, she's become unbalanced."

She muttered something not very kind in Russian.

"I'm burnt-out." I bit my lip. "That's why I'm here. I need horses. They understand me, and I get them."

"And it gives you a break from that witchy woman, no?"

I laughed. It might've been the first time I'd laughed in months.

Vikky patted my cheeks. "I'd love to have you around again." She stepped back and eyed me. "Womanhood agrees with you. You are *krasavitsa*. Beautiful, no?"

Was it any wonder I loved this woman?

We led the Paint to the stable as Vikky pried information from me. "Tell me about your love life. Is there a special man?"

"Thank goodness, no."

"What? No hunky hero to sweep you off your feet? How's that possible?"

"I was seeing a guy, but he was part of the problem." I grimaced. "I broke up with him on the way here. I don't care how many dinners or necklaces a man buys me, he doesn't own me."

"Amen, sistah."

I giggled. Whenever Vikky tried to sound hip, she came off sounding stiff and superior.

"Your hero will come along someday."

I inhaled the scent of the stable, already feeling better. "I don't need a man to make me happy. Just getting away from Mommy Dearest does that."

We both laughed. It was cleansing. I meant no disrespect. It was simply the truth. Mom seemed to hate me. I knew her mental disorder was partly, or even mostly, to blame, but it still hurt being on the receiving end of her spite.

Time passed like a snap of my fingers as I helped Viktorya and reintroduced myself to her horses.

After the sun set, I wrapped her in another hug. "Thank you for today."

"Come back as often as you like."

"I will." My sanity depended on it.

85

RAWSON

*V*EGAS SPRAWLED OUT before me as I crested the rise. I couldn't help but think of Lizzie. This had been her home. Did she still have family somewhere in this vast desert metropolis? I hoped so. Even after searching the internet and calling Viktorya, I'd gotten nowhere. But Vikky needed new stock, so I'd offered to drive down to bring her some horses once spring cleared the roads. I hoped to find more leads in my quest to find Lizzie as well.

When Dad had discovered I was going, he'd booked visits to Temecula and Phoenix as well to sell some quarter horses and buy foals from a champion breeder. After eight days on the road, I'd made it to my final destination. Almost. I still needed to maneuver my truck and trailer down I-15 in rush-hour traffic. In this city, rush hour seemed to last twenty-four hours. Made me grateful to live in Montana.

I merged onto I-95 North and relaxed my grip on the wheel. Exiting the freeway on the outskirts of town by Lone Mountain, I worked my way to the Lohman's neighborhood and parked on the side closest to the stables.

"Hold onto your saddles," I said to the horses eyeing me out their windows. "I'll get you out in a few minutes."

I entered through the back gate and headed to the ranch-style house. Viktorya's husband answered when I knocked.

"Hey, Rawson." Mr. Lohman patted my shoulder. "It was good of you to make this trip. I'm much obliged."

"No problem." I glanced around at the southwest decor. "Your wife around?"

"She had to run to the feed store for some grain. She'll be back any minute."

I checked my watch. "Sorry I'm late. I got caught in traffic. Do you mind if I start unloading?"

"Go ahead."

I left him to throw down the ramp and lead horses into empty pens. Viktorya pulled up behind me as I led the second to last horse down the ramp.

"Is that one of mine?" she called as she stepped out of her Dodge truck. We'd never seen eye to eye on vehicles.

"Yep. Isn't he a beaut?"

"I'll say." She took the rope from me and patted the gray. "Do you think he'll go white or flea-bitten?"

"Both parents are pure white."

She led him to a stall. "Good."

Anticipating her next question, I said, "He turned two and is saddle broke. Figured you'd want 'em young enough to train to walk like ballerinas." She knew my feelings on English style. I was a Western man.

"You figured right."

I returned to my truck, Viktorya close on my heels. But a sweet voice from the past made me go rigid.

"Hey, Vikky."

I looked past Viktorya and glimpsed a willowy form coming from the arena. She waved and disappeared into the stable. Wide-eyed, I turned to stare at Viktorya.

"You told me you didn't know where she was."

She smirked. "I didn't. Liz showed up four days ago, begging to help in her free time. The poor girl's been stuck with her wicked witch mother since her dad died." She laughed when I just gaped at her. "I'd say this is good timing, cowboy."

My heart thudded against my chest. I wanted to run into the stable and scream Lizzie's name, but dust coated my jeans and I'd spilled Pepsi down my shirt when someone had cut me off coming up Cajon Pass.

"I have to see her, but I'm a mess."

"Calm down, Cassanova." She squeezed my arm. "Grab a change of clothes and clean up in the guest bathroom next to the kitchen."

I retrieved my duffel bag from my truck. "Don't let her leave. I have to talk to her."

"Lizzie's here 'til dark, cowboy. Now shoo. I'll keep her in the stable so you can make a grand entrance, no?"

I scrambled around the gate and into the house, baffled at how fate had brought us together. Almost. I needed to clean up first so I didn't send her running.

I changed and splashed cologne on, then headed to the stable. Should I strut in all cowboy and act as though I hadn't seen her? Or should I yell her name and run to her as I wanted? Would that appear too desperate?

Catching a glimpse of Liz at the end of the aisle with Viktorya, I had to make an effort to breathe. She was so beautiful with her curly hair pulled back in a ponytail. I'd always teased her about those, but seeing her poofy ponytail made me smile.

My foot hit something with substance—something that moved and yelped. I lost my balance and planted face first into sawdust as a mutt dog streaked past my head. I spit out muck and looked up at the woman I'd never stopped loving.

Lizzie's mouth hung open. "Rawson Law?"

I scrambled to my feet and brushed sawdust from my clothes. "The one and only." I felt like the biggest idiot to walk the earth.

A high-pitched squeal split the air as she ran over to hug me. Caught off guard, I pulled a Mackay and let my arms dangle at my side. Never had I imagined a positive reaction from her.

She pulled away and blushed. "Sorry."

"Don't be."

Viktorya elbowed me. "I'm going in. You two feel free to ride horses, or go somewhere dark and private, no?" She winked.

Liz squirmed, clearly uncomfortable.

"Do you want to see my new foals?" I asked to break the awkwardness Viktorya had left in her wake.

"I'd love to."

I gestured for her to follow me to the pasture, where Viktorya had let me turn the two foals I'd purchased out to graze. Entering the paddock, I swallowed hard to moisten my throat.

"I bought him in Temecula. His pedigree's faultless."

Liz put her hand on the young bay's neck. The foal nibbled at her shirt as she rubbed him. "He's beautiful."

"Yeah." She was.

"Do you want to ride?"

"Yeah." Call me the king of one-word responses. Nerves had me tongue-tied.

She led me to the tack room, where I saddled a large black. "That's Bo Jangles," she said as she led a bay roan out and started loving on him. "And this is Strawberry Patches."

She walked away without saddling her horse. In the arena, she grabbed hold of the mane and swung herself onto Patches' back. I'd seen her do it before but had never gotten over the surprise. Liz was so delicate. The horses massive. Yet she'd jump, pull, and swing in one fluid motion and be on the back of the mighty creature as I sat gaping, wondering how she'd done it.

Liz sank onto the gelding's back, her head cradled into its neck. Her boot dug into his side, and Patches took off. She clung to his mane as she guided him around the arena with her fingers along his ears, a trick of hers I'd never been able to duplicate.

I climbed onto Bo Jangles and trotted after her. "You sure you don't want a saddle?"

"I haven't been on a horse since I left Montana. I'm enjoying riding bareback."

I had to admit, she looked breathtaking all molded into the roan's body. After several laps around the arena, we walked our mounts.

"Could I take you to dinner?"

Her expressive brown eyes widened. "Do you want to?"

"I've never wanted anything more in my life."

"You must really be hungry."

I stifled a grin. "You could say that."

We looked at each other, trying to read almost a year's worth of emotion in each other's eyes. Patches bit Bo's neck, breaking the spell. I slid off my horse and led him to his stall. We untacked and brushed our mounts, and Liz headed to a Fiat that'd seen better days.

"I'll drive so we don't have to unhitch your trailer."

She drove to a Wendy's. Trying to earn my man card back, I touched her hand as she ejected her keys.

"Let me get your door." I stepped out and jogged to her side. Opening her door, I reached for her hand. "My lady."

She grinned at my Prince William impression and placed her dainty hand in mine. I wanted to pull her into a hug and never let go. But we walked inside and stood in line to order.

I shook my head when she dug into her purse for her wallet. "Are you trying to de-man me? I asked you to dinner. I'll pay." I handed my credit card to the pimply-faced teen.

"I don't want to feel obligated—"

I placed a finger over her lips. "You're under no obligation to sit and talk. I hope you will. I came all this way hoping to find you, but if you still don't want anything to do with me, you can leave. I'll walk back to Viktorya's."

The cashier returned my card.

Liz grabbed my hand and yanked me to a corner booth. I willingly became her victim. She pushed me onto the bench, before scooting across from me.

"You came here to find me?" I'd never noticed how cute the stress lines between her eyebrows were.

"Yeah. I've been looking for you online for months. Viktorya said you'd gone to South America on some adventure. I know I hurt you, Liz, and I'm sorry, but—"

"No. I'm sorry." She reached for my hands. "I shouldn't have run. I was just so shocked and angry still with things in my past. When you told me about the accident, I took out my anger on you. It wasn't fair—"

I stood and growled. "Scoot over."

Sliding onto the opposite bench, I threw my arm around her. Liz laid her head on my shoulder and the long miserable months apart fell away as my senses received sweet overload.

I traced hearts into her upper arm. "Can we start over?"

She sniff-laughed. "Please. I've learned a lot and hope I'm better now."

I caressed her face. "You've always been perfect."

"Sixteen!" A worker yelled.

I rested my forehead against hers. "Don't move a muscle."

"I'll be here."

I retrieved our food and gave her a silly grin as I divvied up our chow. "You know, when I asked you to dinner, I was thinking more along the lines of fancy and quiet, but fast and easy is so much better."

Her laugh came out a sharp bark, and her elbow jabbed me.

"Oww. What was that for?" I bit into my hamburger. "You trying to get fresh with me, woman?"

She laughed in the middle of sipping Coke. I patted her back as she held a hand to her mouth until she could swallow. "Stop making me laugh."

"Stop making it so fun to watch you laugh."

We stared into each other's eyes.

"I'm so glad you found me," she said.

"Me, too."

For the next hour, we took turns talking the other's ears off. But when a group of rowdy teens took over the booth behind us, I decided to leave. We walked out to her Fiat and I opened her door.

"I like these." I brushed long bangs to the side of her head. "You don't look like a strict librarian anymore."

"You're obnoxious."

My cheeks hurt from grinning. "And you're more beautiful than I remember." I blew her a kiss as I walked around the car to claim the passenger seat. We returned to Viktorya's, but when she parked behind my trailer, neither of us opened our doors to get out.

"I'm sorry about your dad."

Her eyes glistened. "I miss him."

"Viktorya said you moved in with your mom."

She nodded. "She overdosed on pills after the funeral."

I closed my eyes. "That sucks."

"I won't lie. It's been hard."

I touched her chin. "I love how loyal you are."

"Your *Love Triangle* game saved me. Remember how you used to make me do that?"

"You hated it."

"I've learned its value. After Dad died, I discovered that Mom had bipolar disorder. I seem to trigger her nasty side, so I've become a pro at building triangles to survive her verbal attacks."

The thought of anyone belittling Lizzie angered me. For it to be her own mother made me absolutely livid. I took a long, cleansing breath to keep from ranting.

"Can you give me a demonstration? All I recall is how much you sucked at the game. You came up with the lamest loves, like your toes or your beating heart." I gasped. "Not that you suck or are lame. Gosh, that sounded terrible."

She laughed. "No, you're right. I sucked. It was impossible to see anything good in myself when Mom had told me for so long everything that was wrong."

"There's nothing wrong with you. Nothing!"

"Oh, I wouldn't go that far." She smiled. "I definitely have my share of faults, but the past few months have forced me to dig deep in order to find my strengths."

"I love your smile."

She gifted me with another one. "I love my smile, too."

"What else do you love?"

"My hair, especially in a stern librarian ponytail." Her lips twitched as I reached to pull the elastic from her hair. Curls fell around her face and over her shoulder. "I also love my hair curling wildly around me." She closed her eyes as I ran my fingers through her vibrant curls. "And I adore my hair when your fingers get all tangled in it."

"My, my." I leaned closer. "You have become a master triangle architect. What else?"

"My neck." I watched her gulp and peek up at me.

"What about it?"

Her minty breath brushed my forehead as I leaned in to plant my lips on the graceful tilt of her throat.

"I love how sensitive it is to your lips."

The emergency brake dug into my side as I leaned over to properly nibble. She'd given me all the permission I needed with those words.

"Oh, Rawson, I've missed you."

I trailed kisses down her neck and worked my way back up to her chin. "Not a day's gone by that I haven't missed you, too, sweetheart." I flicked my tongue out and heard an accompanying moan. The way her throat vibrated aroused me like gas on a flame. I forced myself to pull back so my brain could function.

Her eyes glistened with tears. "I can't believe you want anything to do with me after I ran away when you needed me."

I pressed a finger to her freckled nose. "What can I say? I'm a sucker for girls named Lizzie."

She frowned. "Are you okay now? Did rehab help?"

"I'm much better, especially now that I'm with you." I took her hand in mine. "Life's thrown me some hard knocks. When I returned home to find you gone and Damon in prison, I became super depressed. I tried to stay busy, volunteering in Benny's Scout troop, putting in extra time at the ranch, but nothing helped. Then Addie got sick and needed a kidney. I was a match, so I gave her mine in November. There were complications and I only started getting up and about two months ago. But saving my sister's life turned my own around. I know it doesn't make up for what I did to my brothers, but it meant everything to me. I'm at peace now about the accident. My life doesn't consist of that one moment."

"I knew there was a reason I loved you."

I raised an eyebrow. "You love me?"

"Yes, Stash." Though quiet, her answer echoed in my heart.

"That's good, Praline, because I felt complete those months we were together, and have had a huge chunk missing from my heart since you left." I couldn't look away from her misty brown eyes. "I know I'm not perfect. Heck, I'm as imperfect as they come, but I don't have any secrets anymore, and I know that no man can love you as much as I do. My love is real. It's true. And it's all yours if you'll just say you'll marry me."

Her mouth fell open. "What?"

I couldn't believe I'd just said those words either, but the sentiment was true and had burned a hole through my lips to release its message. I wouldn't take it back.

"Marry me, Lizzie. I don't want to live without you anymore."

Her eyes sparkled in the darkness of the cramped Fiat as she wrapped her arms around me. "Yes. A million times yes!"

I kissed her, and we didn't stop for a long time. We had lots of time to make up for, and we made up for it pretty good, if I must say so myself.

LIZ

$\mathcal{M}$OM PUSHED HER plate away and scowled. "What is this garbage?"

I closed my eyes and counted to ten. I only made it to six before she banged her fist on the table.

"You don't expect me to eat this, do you? No wonder you can't find a man, Elizabeth. You're a terrible cook."

At least, I cooked. If Mom had to fend for herself, she'd live off pita chips and hummus. It didn't matter how healthy those might be, that alone did not a balanced diet make. I grinned, thinking I sounded Yoda-ish.

"Wipe that smirk off your face and sit up straight."

A weary sigh escaped. I wished Rawson had been able to come this weekend. Since we'd reunited, he'd flown down the last two weekends to spoil me rotten. Last night on the phone, he'd suggested eloping to a wedding chapel on the Strip, instead of waiting to marry in the small church I attended. I hadn't told Mom. She'd only spoil my happiness. Esther knew, because she'd be moving Mom in with her after the marriage. Rawson hadn't told his family either, wanting to surprise them when he brought me back to the ranch.

"Should we say a prayer?" I suggested as Mom picked up her fork.

She humphed. "You think I'm a sinner since I don't bless my food?"

"Not at all, but you raised me to always say grace."

"Well," she huffed, "this garbage needs all the help it can get."

In the middle of my prayer, the doorbell rang. Mom didn't wait for an Amen. She scraped her chair against linoleum and raced to the door. I took advantage of her absence to dish up a huge serving of Shepherd's pie and take a bite without her judging my etiquette.

"Well, come on in, cowboy. Aren't you the most ruggedly handsome creature I've ever seen?"

My loaded fork froze in front of my mouth. *No!* My heart began to pound. He wouldn't have come without warning me, would he?

"I'm here to see Liz. I'm Rawson Law. And you must be...?"

I covered my mouth. Crap! I'd been so careful the last two weekends to keep him busy so he didn't have time to meet my crazy mom. The back door tempted me to run, but as I eyed that means of escape, Mom entered with my incredible fiancé in tow.

"Elizabeth, you never told me you had a date with a hot cowboy. How rude."

"That's my fault, Mrs. Ruthersford. Lizzie didn't know I was coming." He walked over and pecked my cheek.

"Why are you here?" I whispered.

His loving gaze made a lump form in my throat. "I wanted to surprise you."

Well, he'd done that. And as soon as Mom humiliated me, Rawson would either join her in laughing at me, like my other dates had, or he'd pity me. Either option was unacceptable.

"Join us, handsome. We were just about to eat."

Rawson took a seat beside me.

Mom snapped her fingers. "Elizabeth, don't zone off. Make yourself useful and get a plate for your guest."

I crossed to the cupboard and heard her whisper loud enough for me to hear, "I apologize for her lack of manners. Elizabeth can be extraordinarily obtuse."

I rolled my eyes as I turned with plate in hand.

"Your daughter is the most amazing woman I've ever met. I won't allow you to belittle her that way."

I froze. No one had ever stood up for me against Mom. Not even Dad. He'd thrown support beams up to fortify my crumbling self-esteem behind closed doors, but he'd never outright opposed her tactics.

"Well, I never." Mom huffed.

Rawson turned to me as if he hadn't just fought a battle on my behalf. "Thank you." He grabbed my wrist as I set down his plate. "You look more beautiful every time I see you."

Mom snorted. "Love is blind."

My hero's eyes narrowed into slits. "I've never seen more clearly in my life, Mrs. Ruthersford."

Not wanting them to come to blows, I placed a hand on his shoulder. "Let's eat."

He took a bite. "This is delicious."

Mom's lips puckered. "It's one of Elizabeth's crazy concoctions."

He turned to me and grinned. "You'll have to teach my mom how to make this. I hate her Shepherd's pie. I always slip it into a napkin to toss."

I laughed, which caused Mom to glare.

"Forgive Elizabeth's unladylike laughter."

Rawson's hands clenched.

I rested my hand on his leg and mouthed, *I'm okay.*

He relaxed but addressed Mom. "Mrs. Ruthersford, there's a game I like to play where you say three things you love about yourself. I'll start. I love my hands because they're strong. I love my brain because it's pretty quick on the draw. And I love my mouth, because it's excellent at kissing." He winked at me.

Looking down, I bit back a smile. I definitely agreed.

"Your turn. What are three things you love about yourself?"

Flattered by his attention, Mom batted her fake lashes. "I love my eyes. They're my greatest asset."

"They are stunning. You passed them onto your daughter, you know? Lizzie's are your same unique shape, only brown."

Mom stared at me across the table and shrugged. "I love my firm body. I've kept it in good shape as I've matured." She didn't condone the word *old.*

"You do take good care of yourself. I'll be proud to have you as my mother-in-law."

I kicked him beneath the table as Mom started choking on her food.

"Yes," he said with a cocky grin. "I've asked your daughter to marry me, and she said yes."

"Elizabeth?"

"Yeah. Lizzie." He wrapped an arm around me.

I frowned.

"Elizabeth Belle," Mom snapped, "sit up straight and wipe that scowl off your face. This handsome cowboy wants to marry you. Don't make him run away."

"Oh, I'm not running, Mrs. Ruthersford. If anyone should run, it's Liz. And as for her scowl, she just wishes I'd stop talking and start kissing her. She gets grumpy when her lips are missing mine."

I bowed my head and tamped my amusement into a twitching smile as Mom stared at me as if I'd grown horns.

"What's the third thing, Mrs. Ruthersford?"

"Oh," she gave him a coy smile. "I love my hair. It's tame and manageable, unlike Elizabeth's chaotic mane."

"One of the things I love best about Liz is her curly hair." He pulled out my ponytail and let my curls fall about my face. "You created the perfect woman for me, Mrs. Ruthersford. I'll always be grateful to you for that."

He grabbed my hand under the table as Mom studied him through goopy eyelashes.

"I'm glad you approve."

So was I. When he'd first arrived, I'd been sure Mom would cast doubt onto our relationship. That's all she'd ever done when I'd introduced her to men. But Rawson had handled her like a pro, leaving no doubt in my mind how he felt about me.

He led me out to his rental car, and I gave into my desire to make love to his mouth. "You're incredible," I murmured into his demanding lips. "But why didn't you tell me you were coming?"

He gathered me in by the waist. "I knew you wouldn't let me meet your mom if I did."

"You were amazing with her."

"I wanted to wash her mouth out with soap."

"Thanks for standing up for me."

He tipped my chin. "Thanks for loving me."

"That's extremely easy to do."

"It hasn't always been."

I pulled his head down to meet mine. "Kiss me, Lord Cootie Catcher. My lips are missing yours."

Rawson graciously gave into my request. "Okay, Stockholm. Don't want you getting grumpy."

87

BENTLEY

RUSHING HAN'S COAT, I chewed on my bottom lip. Since Rawson had gone off on that purchasing trip, he'd acted super distracted. For the last three weekends, he'd taken off to who knows where, making me worry he might be sliding back into destructive habits. I stabled Han and walked to the house, wondering what to do. I didn't want to tell Dad my concerns, unless I had some facts to back them up.

I extracted my boots and headed to the kitchen to grab a snack. The phone rang in the other room. I stopped in the hallway as I heard Dad pick up.

"Are you sure?" he asked, before swearing a doozy. "All right. Thanks for calling."

"What's wrong?" Mom asked as he slammed the phone down.

"That was Dave at the airport in Bozeman," he muttered. "I asked him to check into whether Rawson was flying out of there."

"Has he?" Mom asked.

I tensed, curious about my brother's secret trips.

"He said Rawson chartered a flight out of there this afternoon to Vegas. Dave checked the logs and discovered he's booked the same flight each of the previous three weekends as well."

"I'm sure he has a good reason."

"Reason be damned, Charity. The boy's probably chasing after skirts or gambling away the inheritance I just released into his name. He's definitely not thinking with his brain. And just when I thought I could trust him again." He swore, but Mom didn't get after him.

I couldn't move.

Rawson wouldn't do those things, would he? Yet, when I'd caught him before he'd driven off last night, he'd had a suitcase in hand and had smelled of cologne. When I'd asked where he was going, he'd patted my shoulder and had shot off some lame answer I hadn't bought. Come to think of it, he'd acted suspicious for weeks, whistling for no reason, staring off into space as he worked, smiling constantly. If I didn't know better, I'd think he was in love.

That idea settled on me like a cockroach in mashed potatoes.

I hobbled up to my bedroom and turned on my laptop. Typing in *Elizabeth Ruthersford*, I began searching for clues to her whereabouts. Rawson hadn't had any luck finding her, but Liz might be back from South America. She was the only hope my lonely brother had of not losing his head to some money-grubbing bimbo. If I could locate her, maybe I could stop Rawson from doing something he'd regret for the rest of his life.

At least, I hoped so.

88

RAWSON

*N*EVER HAD I FELT so enamored by a woman. I touched Lizzie's sleeping face, tracing her delicate cheekbones and pixie nose. Though the clock showed it was the middle of the night, I couldn't sleep. I caressed her jawline and circled her perfect lips, before letting my fingers meander down her neck and continue beneath the sheets.

A faint hum alerted me that she'd awakened. Long lashes fluttered as she smiled in the darkness and lifted her graceful hand to rest against my chest.

"I didn't mean to wake you," I fibbed. Actually, I'd been anxious for her to awake once my eyes had opened and I'd found her cuddled next to me.

Her adorable dimple dented her cheek. "I love you."

"I love you more, Mrs. Law." I rolled over to give her my full attention.

We'd married last night—eight hours ago to be precise—in a simple ceremony in front of Lizzie's minister and a few witnesses, including Viktorya. Seeing how anxious Liz had become, thinking of planning a wedding that aligned with her mother's exacting standards, had made me nix that idea. I'd called her ecclesiastical leader when I'd arrived and had asked him to marry us that night. Neither of us cared about pomp and ceremony. We'd just wanted to be legally bound together as husband and wife.

She was my girl now. In every possible way. Thinking about it gave me a case of goosebumps.

Liz hummed and closed her eyes as I stroked and kissed her body beneath the silken sheets, playing the part of a newlywed quite well.

"I think I'm smitten with an acute case of love and there's no cure," I murmured as I clasped her thighs.

"It must be contagious." She nipped my ear. "I caught it, too."

"We'll have to quarantine ourselves and never leave this bed, to save the world."

She moaned into my mouth as our passion crescendoed. "My hero," she managed to get out before we tangled beneath the sheets.

Liz and I were more than compatible. We were complete. As we became lost in each other for a second time that night, the *Star Wars* theme began to play at full volume on my phone.

I rolled onto my back and brought my phone to my ear. "Hey, bro, this better be good," I snapped. It was almost three, and he'd blown the mood with his obnoxious ring tone.

"Rawson, where are you?" He sounded anxious. "Dad's ticked."

I rolled my eyes as I looked at my wife. "I left a note telling him I was taking the week off. What's his problem? I'm a grown man and not under his curfew."

Liz smirked. I nibbled her neck, making her giggle.

"Who're you with? It's the middle of the night."

"You're right. It is the middle of the freaking night. And I'm with this amazing woman I've fallen for big time." Lizzie's eyes teased me, so I kissed her.

"Are you kidding me? Dad figured you'd fallen for some skirt with fake boobs who batted her eyelashes, but I thought you were smarter than that."

I grimaced. "What do you want, Ben?"

"I found an address for Liz. I've searched all night. It's her mom's place in Henderson, Nevada. It's right by Las Vegas. Want me to give it to you?"

Though touched by his efforts, I refused to spoil my surprise.

"It's too late. Lizzie hated me anyway." My wife huffed as I winked. "I'll be home in three days," I said, before dropping the bomb I knew would keep my brother awake for nights. "Let me enjoy my honeymoon, kid. You'll understand someday and not want people calling when you're in bed with your brand new wife."

Lizzie punched me as I grinned and caressed her tantalizing body.

Benny sputtered on the other end. "W-what? You went and got yourself hitched to the floozy?"

"For your information, I happen to love this floozy."

Liz shook her head. She thought I was being mean. If it'd been up to her, she would've let my family in on our plans. But what's the point of eloping if you can't shock anyone?

"You've only been seeing her for a month. You don't know her at all," he shouted.

"Well, I have the rest of my life to get to know her now." I moaned as Liz started kissing the sensitive spot behind my ear.

"But what about Lizzie?"

Good old Benny. Loyal to the end.

"Well now, Liz was an amazing woman." I sighed as she nibbled my neck. "But it's too late. I flew to Vegas and married my floozy. And just so you know, her boobs are real. Now let me enjoy my wife before we have to fly back to Montana."

She gave me a look of playful disgust as Benny went silent on his end.

"Don't be mad, kid. I promise you'll love your new sister-in-law." When he didn't respond, I said goodbye and hung up.

My utterly adorable wife gave me a feisty look as I threw my phone onto the nightstand. "Did you seriously tell him my boobs were real?"

"They are."

She giggled as I tickled her.

Could I just say how much I loved being married? I'd been hitched for less than a day, but already knew forever would not be long enough.

"I don't know why you insist on torturing poor Ben," she chided as my tickling turned into tantalizing caresses.

"Trust me, love. The look on his face when he sees you and realizes the truth will be priceless. Let him stew on this for a few days. It'll make the surprise so much more fun."

BENTLEY

UMBLING WITH THE phone, I nestled it to my ear to listen to Alice.

"Ben, you need to get over your anger. Be happy for your brother."

I knew she was right, but that was easier said than done. Since I'd talked to Rawson on the phone, I'd wanted to punch something. Never had I imagined he'd go and do such an idiotic thing as a Vegas shotgun wedding.

"I'll try, Al, but the fact that he sneaked off to get hitched to a complete stranger without even telling me bites."

"She might be sweet. Give her a chance. You sound like you hate her already."

I did. It killed me that I'd found Lizzie a day too late. Maybe if I'd searched earlier, I might've saved my brother from his stupidity. When I'd told Dad that Rawson had married a strange girl in Vegas, he'd sworn a long line of stinkers and had kicked a hole in his office wall.

"I don't hate her. I just don't like her. She stole my brother from me."

"They're coming back to the ranch. That doesn't sound like she's stolen him from you."

"Whose side are you on anyway?"

Alice giggled, and I couldn't help but smile. She'd become my best friend.

A fly tapped its face against my window. I swatted at the pest and noticed a trail of dust zooming toward the house.

"Hey, I'll call you later, Al. I think my bonehead brother's here."

"Be nice."

"Yeah, yeah."

I hung up and closed my eyes, praying for patience. And kindness. Rawson had sounded happy on the phone, and he'd definitely acted livelier this past month. Who was I to shoot him off his cloud, even if he was bound to fall back to earth eventually?

His black truck pulled into the driveway. The rear window had *Just Married* painted on it. I let my head slump to my shoulder.

It was true then. My brother hadn't been messing with me.

Rawson jumped out with a huge grin, holding a woman in jeans and a turquoise blouse. A silly veil hid her face. Maybe she was ugly. I grunted. That'd be the day. My brother had too good of taste in women to settle for a chick who needed to wear a bag over her head.

He carried his marital baggage to the porch.

I swallowed a lump in my throat, knowing I should go meet them. But I doubted I could fake a smile. That woman had ruined everything.

I turned from the window as I heard Rawson tramping up the stairs. Dang. He was bringing her to me. I slumped into a chair to hide my disability. I didn't want the strange woman to pity me first thing.

Rawson made it to the landing and cried out, "Ben, I thought you'd come out to meet us."

I blinked back threatening tears.

He crossed the room and sat on my bed, cuddling his plaything. "Big Ben, I'd like you to meet my wife." He lifted her veil.

I sat there transfixed, unable to speak as the clock ticked on the wall. Lizzie's beautiful face beamed at me from beneath the shimmery material.

Bolting to my feet, I threw myself into them, making us all topple onto the mattress. "You tricked me!" I punched my brother's arm. "Big jerk!"

They laughed as I grinned at Liz. It'd been almost a year since she'd left. Stupid tears rained down my face, but Liz gathered me in her arms so my brother wouldn't see.

Mom came up to see what all the ruckus was about, and she squealed when she saw Lizzie and hugged her for dear life. She called Dad and told him to come to the house to meet Rawson's wife. She didn't want to spoil the surprise.

When Dad marched in with a surly look on his face, he stopped abruptly when he saw Liz standing beside my brother. Not until he glanced down at their clasped hands did a huge grin transform his face. He crossed the room to kiss Liz on her forehead and pulled Rawson into a bear hug.

"Well done, son. Well done."

This day will go on record as the happiest ever, at least until I get married someday and blow the record off the charts.

EPILOGUE

*H*APPINESS. JOY! THE past year had dumped a mother lode of both in my life, but this moment topped them all. My husband couldn't hold still as he held my hand and studied the ultrasound screen as the technician moved her wand over my stomach.

"Can you tell if it's a boy or girl?" he asked.

"Yep."

He still didn't know the doctor's suspicion that I carried twins. When the technician didn't expound, my impatient husband prodded her. "So?"

"There's one of each." The Asian nurse looked up and grinned. "You have a healthy set of fraternal twins."

Rawson whooped and pulled me into a bear hug.

I cleaned up and stopped at the front desk while my husband swaggered into the waiting area with a silly grin.

"My wife's having twins," he announced to everyone in the room. "A boy...and a girl."

"That's one proud papa." The receptionist giggled as she took my Visa.

She had no idea. Ever since I'd surprised him a couple months ago with the news that I was expecting, he'd been as giddy as a kid with cotton candy.

He climbed into the truck and pressed his hands against my stomach. "I can't wait to announce the news to everyone," he said between kisses.

Rawson drove straight to Roy's welding shop and hollered to his friend in the back. Damon had been released on parole last month. Rawson had instantly taken his friend under his wing and had worked out an apprenticeship with Roy Montagne at his welding shop.

Damon took his safety goggles off and stormed out from the back. "Hold your horses, homey. Some people have to actually work for a living."

Rawson grinned and pointed to my stomach. "Twins," he announced, like I'd won a prize.

Damon's eyebrows shot up and his lips twisted into a grin beneath his mustache. "You don't say." He slapped Rawson's shoulder. "That calls for a celebration, dawg." He ran into Roy's office and passed on our news to his boss, who offered up congratulations. Damon opened the mini fridge and pulled out a Coke and threw it to Rawson. "You want one, Liz?"

"No, thanks."

Rawson sat in a chair and pulled me onto his lap. "Why don't you keep a few Pepsi's around? You know I hate this shi—"

I elbowed him.

He kissed me behind my ear. "Sorry, babe. I mean crap."

"Buy your own Pepsi's if you want 'em, Roz. I like Coke."

Rawson took a long sip and smacked his lips. "You know they clean toilets and car engines with this *crap*, right?"

I kissed him for remembering not to swear.

"That's why I get 'em. Cleans me out, too." Damon opened his soda and guzzled. "Congratulations, Liz. That's awesome news."

After we left Roy's, we headed down the main drag and stopped at Freda's so Rawson could grab some of the greasy chicken he loved.

"Yo!" he shouted after he'd ordered. Diners turned to gawk at us. "We just found out we're having twins. A boy and a girl. Everyone's meals are on us." He left several hundred dollar bills with Freda's teenage daughter and took me around the room to shake hands and be congratulated.

We finally made it out of town and onto the lonely backstretch of road heading to the ranch. A light dusting of snow started to fall. Rawson veered off the road and parked. He wrapped his arms around me and kissed me like a man possessed. I thoroughly loved being possessed by him. Seatbelts were cast off as he pushed me into a prone position. I loved bench seats, too.

"I'm so happy, Lizzie." He kissed the V of my T-shirt, before pausing to gaze at me. "Do I make you happy, love? I know I still slip and swear and leave the toilet seat up and pull the covers off you sometimes when I'm sleeping rough."

I framed his cheeks between my hands. "Don't forget how you annoy me to Canada and back when you yank my ponytail out."

"You love when I do that." He gave me a roguish grin, his atom bomb when it came to my defenses.

"In your dreams, cowboy."

He took that as his cue to render me breathless again. The man had a definite gift when it came to kissing. We didn't talk anymore, at least with words. My husband talked plenty with his hands and lips as we steamed up the truck windows.

A rapping on the glass made me open my eyes. "Someone's outside."

Rawson pulled me up as he rolled down the window and let freezing air envelop us. "Evening, Sheriff."

"Rawson Law," he said with a deadpan expression as he pulled out his citation pad. "Don't you know it's against the law to pull off the side of the road and assault innocent young women?"

"Disturbing the peace is also a misdemeanor, last I heard, and it was pretty peaceful in here until you whacked on my window. Besides, Sheriff, this woman is anything but innocent."

I smacked his shoulder.

"She's not! She's carrying not one, but *two* babies in her belly." Rawson patted my slightly protruding stomach proudly.

"Is that right?" The sheriff chuckled. "You're probably the SOB who put them there."

"Yes, sir, I am." He draped an arm around me.

Sheriff Jenks leaned in to smile at me. "Would you like me to take this hooligan in, Mrs. Law?"

I grinned. "I'm willing to grant him leniency for good behavior."

"All right. I'll let you off with a warning, but if I catch you out here canoodling with your wife again, I'll have to book you. Your warning is: get up with the babies when they fuss at night. If you don't, these steamy windows won't be happening ever again."

Rawson reached out to shake his hand. "Warning noted."

"Congratulations, you two. That's great news."

The sheriff pulled away, and Rawson waggled his brows. "Where were we, my overachieving wife?" I giggled as he once more pushed me down onto the seat to kiss me senseless. Not even two minutes later, another tap on the window interrupted us.

Rawson growled. "You'd think I pulled over on the I-5, not the I-don't-know-where-the-heck-I-am."

He lowered his window to find Ben staring at us. The kid had been driving for the past two months. He still couldn't get his driver's license because of his physical limitations, but Bart let him drive around the ranch as long as he didn't go too far. This probably straddled the *too far* mark, especially with the sheriff about. His confidence had soared with the freedom to get around on his own.

"What are you two doing out here? Did your truck stall or run out of gas?"

Rawson grinned as I finger-combed my curls into a semblance of respectability. "I was running low on kisses, bro. Lizzie's refueling me. But I think I got her pregnant."

I elbowed him. My husband thrived on shock value.

"And get this, Ben. I'm so good at this whole marriage thing, I knocked Lizzie up with not just one kid, but two. Efficient, am I not?" He turned to wink at me. "You can thank me later, honey."

Ben made a face. "You two are gross. Are you really having twins?"

A girly squeal escaped me. "I am. Isn't that exciting?"

"It's awesome! Have you told Mom and Dad?"

"We will soon." Rawson started closing his window. "As soon as I finish kissing my wife. We keep getting interrupted."

Ben grimaced. "Well, if you're not stranded, I'm leaving you losers."

My husband made good on his promise to finish kissing me. I could hardly think after he pulled back and gave me a smug grin.

"I'm more in love with you than ever, Lizzie." He started the truck as I fastened my seatbelt. Pulling me close, he steered onto the road and hit the gas.

I snuggled closer and closed my eyes. "I love you more, too, Lead Foot."

Driving with my husband made me *analogize*, if that was a word. Life could go by real fast—like his truck down the highway—but if we concentrated on those we loved and hoped for the best, we'd eventually get to our destination safely. That's at least what had happened to me. Halfway between hope and the highway, I'd lost my heart to Rawson Law, and thankfully, I don't think he'll ever give it back.

I'm okay with that.

TO MY READERS

Thanks for reading *Between Hope & the Highway*. If you enjoyed the story, please consider leaving a review on Amazon or another site to help spread the word. It doesn't have to be long or fancy. Just write your honest opinion (no one grades you, I promise).

Visit www.CharissaStastny.com to sign up for my monthly *Stuck on Love* newsletter. You can also join the *Stuck on Love Facebook Page,* where we have weekly giveaways, birthday drawings, and more.

ACKNOWLEDGMENTS

Oodles of thanks go to my beta-readers: Summer Bell, Larry Skelton, Taylor Dean, and Jennifer Peel (especially since some of them read it twice. Sorry). Your honesty, friendship, and support mean the world to me. I owe a debt of gratitude to Maria Hoagland, my editor, for making this story shine and building me up when doubts arose. My talented sister, Tiffany, took beautiful photographs for my cover, and my incredible daughter, Christina, used her crazy-mad design skills to create the gorgeous cover. I'd be remiss if I didn't tell my family how much their support and love carries me through each day. Without them, I would write tragic tales of woe. Because of them, my stories end happily ever after.

BOOK GROUP QUESTIONS

1. Liz's mother's mental disorder and perfectionism cause her to lash out at her youngest daughter, using her as a scapegoat for all she finds wrong in the world. How has this affected Lizzie's sense of self-worth? How has it affected her relationships with men?
2. Rawson has carried a terrible secret for years. How does the truth free him to be a better man? Why does guilt have such confining control on people?
3. Bentley wants so much to be normal that he is blind to his *amazingness*. Why do we do this? How can we overcome the tendency to only focus on the negative in ourselves?
4. I purposely didn't delve into details of Liz's past relationship with Justin, but I dropped hints into the story to give readers a foundation to imagine their own scenario about why she carried guilt and anger inside her from his death. What do you think they fought about the night before their wedding and his accident? What kind of relationship do you think she had with Justin? How did this affect her relationship with Rawson?
5. Lizzie goes to the prison to forgive the man who ran into Justin and killed him. Do you believe forgiveness has healing powers? Why?
6. Do you believe that letting go of hope that the past could be different can help one move forward in the present?
7. Several readers have asked for Bentley's story going forward. Ideas are marinating in my mind, but what challenges and

heart-tugging adventures would you imagine for him as he becomes a man?

8. Rawson's friend, Damon, has lived a rough life. He's brought Rawson down in the past, which has been the reason the Laws have despised him. At the end, I show him back in the picture. Do you see this as a positive or a negative for Rawson? Why?

OTHER BOOKS BY CHARISSA STASTNY

BENDING WILLOW TRILOGY

  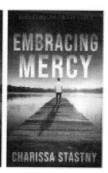

Threads of love, loss, and forgiveness weave an emotional tapestry through this gripping journey that both inspires and captivates.

Finding Light – *Finding love can be a dark journey.*

Guarding Secrets – *Time reveals all secrets.*

Embracing Mercy – *True love must sacrifice.*

What do you do when forever unravels?

"An epic romance that will leave you rooting for true love to triumph. You will love this story about rising up, changing, and discovering worth." - **Taylor Dean, author**

RULED OUT ROMANCES

In this stand-alone series, star-crossed lovers meet, but rule each other out. Yet life, with its quirky twists and tangled turns, brings each of the unlikely duos together to find their unique happily-ever-after.

Game Changer – 1 – *Can he catch here with charm?*

Package Deal – 2 – *Angels come in different packages.*

Collateral Hearts – 3 – *Can a bet lead to love?*

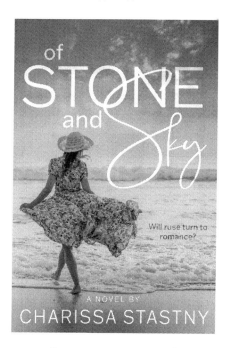

Can ruse turn to romance?

"Take a chance on this one-of-a-kind romance novel!" - **Taylor Dean, author**

ABOUT THE AUTHOR

Charissa Stastny is married to her high school sweetheart and has four children who are the light of her life. She's an avid reader, happy writer, BYU graduate, and lover of irises, clouds, chocolate, and sushi (but not together). Though born and raised in Las Vegas, Nevada, she has never pulled a handle of a slot machine and can't shuffle cards to save her life. She shuffles bills, laundry, and church responsibilities rather well though. She currently lives in central Utah with her growing family, where shuffling cards isn't required. Whew.

f facebook.com/c.stastny.author

instagram.com/c.stastny.books

BB bookbub.com/authors/charissa-stastny

Printed in Great Britain
by Amazon